THE IMMORALIST

A serial killer who makes murder personal

NATHAN SENTHIL

THE BOOK FOLKS

Published by The Book Folks

London, 2020

ISBN 978-1-913516-71-0

www.thebookfolks.com

I dedicate this book to the victims of violent crimes and their families, and to the cops who bring them justice, or at least try their damnedest to do so. Sometimes, justice is easier to obtain in fiction than in real life.

Prologue

I exhale and warm breath permeates my mask. It puffs up and then deflates as I take in air that carries with it vapors of a cheap lemon-scented car freshener.

A leafless tree stands on the curb some five yards in front of the vehicle I have stolen, its skeletal limbs moving gracefully in the cold night breeze. In the dimly lit street, they look like the scorched fingers of a stealthy demon breaking through the ground from the fiery pits of hell and reaching for the sky to grab one of the angels. Two raindrops splash on the windshield, as if the all-knowing owner of the heavens sees the future but is unable to intervene.

A fleeting movement at the corner of my eye snatches my attention.

I raise my head and peek at the window in the house neighboring Rita's, my eleventh victim. The drapes hang inert, and the flickering in a slit between them attests to the presence of an idiot box melting someone's brain. I take a quick meticulous look around. Nothing seems out of place, so I lower myself and lie back on the seat again.

Tonight I'm *almost* skittish, because I've prepared for this event for more than seven thousand days. Though I spent most of the nineteen-odd years reading books and teaching myself the art of serial killing, I also used it to weave a special sheepskin that cloaks the primal evil within me. And of course, it gives me the ability to walk among the oblivious herd, unnoticed. Duh!

A penetrating glare lightens the dark interior of the car. Two bright headlamps have turned onto the street and drive onwards. I know this car—a black and white BMW i3 that eco-conscious Rita drives.

It's amusing what people say about Karma. How can they explain this? A person who curtails her carbon emissions and does her bit healing the world will be killed tonight for reasons normies can't grasp.

I had imagined I'd feel some sort of fear or anxiety, as Rita is one of the five *casualties* that will actually matter in my mega plot. But I don't. My calm is a reward for all the hours of meditation and breathing exercises, as well as the torture and killing I've been practicing.

As the car passes me, I scrunch lower into the seat and turn my head the other way. Her right blinker reflects in my rearview mirror, and the BMW pulls in behind my car. It should be four to five yards between her trunk and mine.

A slim woman in a navy-blue cotton shirt and white pants gets out and makes her way to the trunk, where her groceries will be. I know her schedule like the back of my gloved hand. Friday night shopping for an elegant dinner, though I'm not sure why, given her husband is in Illinois. An affair? I haven't noticed anything to back up that possibility. Perhaps she's just treating herself. Is she going to invite Mrs. Young, her next-door not-so-young neighbor who made my recon a nightmare with her constantly parting drapes?

Now Rita is taking the groceries out. The BMW's trunk lid hides her from the front, and my car covers her from the back.

It's time!

I reach for the backpack resting in the passenger seat, pinch the zipper and drag it open, and slide my hand in. My warm sheathed fingers wrap around a cold piece of plastic—a stun gun with enough juice to bring down a hungry bear.

I nudge the door open without a sound and sneak out. The air is crispy with a hint of petrichor. I love the rain—it washes away evidence. Not that I'll leave any. But still.

I crouch and slither along the tarmac to the back of my SUV. I take a look at the ever-vigilant windows. The excrement-colored drapes are at rest. The street is quiet except for the faint sound of gunfire emanating from Mrs. Young's house. So, her jobless grandson is home, watching an action movie or playing a videogame or something? That could explain the inactive drapes. She must be making something for the slacker to eat, meaning the bored old cow won't need to look through the window anytime soon.

Perfect.

I creep up behind Rita. The same cold breeze that's been rustling the tree now carries a whiff of her perfume. Taking a deep breath, I clear my thoughts.

Then I charge.

As comforting as it is to believe that humans can sense danger, it is *so* not true. Rita never hears the ungodly crackle of electric current before I press the device to the side of her neck. I pull her head back and secure it with my left forearm, hand and bicep, and dump fifty million volts through her nervous system. And no, I don't get zapped while I'm electrocuting her—the fundamental properties of electricity ensure my safety.

She gasps for a fraction of a second before her body jolts. The shock works her muscles, a rapid exercise converting her blood sugar into lactic acid, draining all her energy in a flash. After four seconds, a second longer than necessary, I release her.

She falls sideways and I catch her in time, holding her waist with my forearm as her back arches. The scene would have been romantic if not for her grimace of pain, the shiny drool under her chin, and the crossed irises.

Wasting no time, I open the tailgate and toss her into the roomy cargo space I've made by folding down the seats. Then I climb into the SUV, pull the door shut, step over the convulsing body and get into the driver's seat.

One down. Three to go.

Chapter 1

March 15, 2019. 11:47 P.M.

The unwelcome claws of consciousness yanked Harry out of his painless stupor. He gasped and jolted awake, but didn't dare open his eyes. Every inch of his upper body resumed aching—his head throbbed, neck and wrists burned, and his right nostril wouldn't draw air. Dried mucus? Or... blood?

His voice quivered as his chapped lips muttered, "The Lord is with me. I will not be afraid…"

But the taut gag distorted the words before they escaped his parched mouth—the words he directed at the Almighty, imploring him to let him out of this looping nightmare. And fast.

It must be a nightmare, right? Why else would his motorized wheelchair, with him tied to it, rest on an industrial-sized ice block? Oh God, and why else would he have a noose around his neck? Like a laid-back but determined anaconda, the rope squeezed his airway a millimeter tighter in its deathly embrace as each second passed, as his landing melted away one drop at a time.

After what seemed like an eternity, he controlled his trembling and found the courage to *just do it*. His wet eyes fluttered open, hoping to see the familiar ceiling of his bedroom.

But his heart sank. Again. His devoted prayers had changed nothing. He still sat on his old wheelchair, still stuck in this senseless—senseless... *reality?*

No, no, no!

An anguished howl roared from the pit of his stomach and rushed past the esophagus, but the gag muffled it down into nothing more than a throaty grunt. Tears, sudden and warm, cascaded down, and the rim of the cloth tied across his cheeks absorbed them just as quickly.

Hours ago, when Harry unlocked his front door and rolled into his house, he got the shock of his life. He found an intruder in a pink tracksuit slouching on his sofa, who, upon seeing Harry, lazily pointed a gun at him. He wore a green surgical mask, a hairnet, a pair of reflective sunglasses, and blue gloves. Half an inch of folded cloth, or a sponge of some kind, covered his shoes. The last thing Harry remembered was the intruder approaching him with a stun gun, its tips buzzing and sparkling blue flashes between the prongs.

Harry was in this strange place when he came to. Why would anyone want to do this to him?

As he sniffled and lifted his chin, he spotted something near the wall in front of him, probably some fifteen feet away. He squeezed his eyelids, jerked his head and blinked away the tears. When his watery vision unblurred, the objects slowly manifested. They were heaters.

What?

Though March wasn't exactly freezing in NYC, many people preferred it warmer. However, one heater was fine. Two's okay. But seven was definitely overdoing it. What's the need for so much heat?

Then the answer dawned on him, and when it did, a sharp chill spread over his skin. His eyelids drooped and the all-consuming darkness engulfed his world.

* * *

Something—a dull noise, he'd guessed—dragged Harry out from under the safety of oblivion. He pried his heavy eyelids open and a kaleidoscope of shapes danced in front of his eyes.

Though he sat above the melting ice, not a hint of cold vapor brushed against his sweaty skin. On the contrary, the air around him hung humid and sticky, like in a sauna, but no mystery there.

He frowned when he heard again what had woken him up—the sound of distorted sobs. It came from his left, and he turned. A gym buff stood on top of another ice block with a noose around his neck. Gagged like Harry, his wrists were bound behind his back. He wore red shorts and a gray T-shirt, exposing muscles that reminded Harry of a young Arnold Schwarzenegger.

A piercing scream froze the blood in his veins and stopped the teardrops on the brink of his now wide-open eyes from spilling over.

He slowly turned right, towards the source of the gut-wrenching shrill. A battered lady perched atop a different ice block. Another mortal rope coiled around her slender neck, reddening it while she thrashed about like a fish pulled out of water. A thick bruise, cementing her eyelids shut, stretched from her left jaw to her temple. She yelled what Harry guessed were curses into the gag and desperately tried to distance herself from something on her right-hand side, but the rope didn't let her.

Seeing the hysterical woman amplified what Harry had been feeling inside—unadulterated terror. Shaking with fear, he bent forward, craned his neck, and looked further down the right, past the woman. What he saw there arrested his one-nostril breathing.

An old lady's limp body hung from another noose. It swiveled around, slowly exposing her ruffled white hair, bulged red-rimmed eyeballs, and the most disturbing of all, a thick tongue. It was grayish violet, contrasting her wrinkled pale skin. It didn't loll out loosely, but just poked out of the contorted mouth.

Unable to watch the ghostly woman's face anymore, Harry looked down at her ashen feet. No ice block under them, but a large puddle flowed from there and merged with the water from the ice blocks of the living trio. Harry should feel sorry for the poor granny, feel angry at the cold-blooded animal who did this to her, but he could only feel his ticker banging against his ribcage, as if it wanted out as much as he did.

God, please let this be a nightmare.

But other people, strangers whom you'd never met, didn't share your nightmare, did they? It was all real.

Sick to his stomach, Harry turned away. No use in flooding his mouth with puke and risk suffocation. Now that his mind finally accepted the situation to be real and bloodcurdling, it freaked out in full force.

Taking quick and shallow breaths, he scanned the room to find something that might aid his escape, though the back of his mind whispered it to be futile. The abductor—no, the *murderer*—didn't make mistakes. This whole setting gave out a vibe that he'd been planning this for a long time.

Still, Harry looked around, hyperventilating. What else could he do?

The spacious but narrow room would be empty if not for the heaters, the death apparatus, and its occupants. Overhead fluorescent bulbs cast a harsh light that brightened the white walls. Harry's eyes rested on a door to his left. It seemed robust and had some kind of insulation in its frame. He rotated his head further to the left, as much as he could without cramping his neck. A blue curtain hung behind them, covering the entire background. He turned the other side and encountered the same blue cloth. No windows he could detect from his limited visual arc.

Wait... what's that—

He jerked when he heard a sound—a clunk followed by a metallic grating. The door opened, bringing in a cool breeze. The fresh air carried the smell of damp earth. But before it ventilated this sweltering dungeon, the door closed.

The murderer, still wearing the same stupid attire, lugged a tripod in one hand and a professional video camera in the other.

The duo flanking Harry bawled, probably begging for release, but their gags transformed their pleading into loud incoherent babble. Harry joined them and cried for a chance to explain. It must be a grave misunderstanding. He hadn't harmed a soul in his life. And if it's not a misunderstanding and it's all about money, Harry would pay millions to be released. He wanted to live, and he would do anything for it.

But the bastard carried on with his work as if the four people he'd abducted weren't even there. He fixed the camera on the tripod which he had installed in front of them and did something behind it. Moments later, an LED light beside the camera's lens lit up.

The murderer straightened and walked towards the door. He tugged it open, letting in another whiff of that heavenly scent of rain, but paused on the threshold as if he'd forgotten something.

He turned back slowly and addressed them. "You have no inkling as to what your sacrifices mean to the world. But know that they mean the world to me. For that, I will forever be grateful."

Then he slammed the door shut.

Chapter 2

March 15, 2019. 11:47 P.M.

Gabriel picked at a scab on his knuckle, staring at his elongated face on a metal water jug above the table. Seeing his reflection, he couldn't help but think he looked like someone who should be outside pushing a cart full of all his worldly belongings around.

So, by rights, he shouldn't have been let into the Chinese restaurant, but a kind waiter had allowed it since he was the only one on duty. The waiter, an Asian kid, had put him in a shadowy corner, just in case more customers came in, which was fine by Gabriel, considering his purpose of being there.

At present, only one other person occupied the restaurant, and he sat five tables in front of Gabriel's. His name: Don Miller. Height: 6'2". Weight: 220 pounds. Age: forty-three. Profession: making the world a little worse.

The waiter glanced at Don, then at a digital clock mounted on the wall beside his chair. He kept his distance, warily eyeing Don's tattoos—flaming skulls on his shoulders, roses and wire mesh covering the forearms, and a dragon on his neck. Its head peeked out from underneath the shirt and spewed fire onto the back of his bald head. But the most prominent were the word *SON* tattooed on each of his cheeks.

Don pointed at the waiter, with a fork. "Come here."

The waiter obeyed, clutching a piece of paper.

"That a check?" Don asked.

"Yes, sir."

"You decided when I should stop eating just because you own this stinky diner?" Don gripped the fork.

"I don't own this… uh… I just work here part-time—"

"The check, boy. Why'd you bring it?" The weapon now pointed at the waiter's stomach.

"Because… it… it's late and I have college in the morning… uh…" The waiter couldn't finish his sentence.

"Uh…uh…" Don imitated the waiter, but in a low-pitched voice. "Uh what? Speak up, chicken!" His balled-up hands thumped on the table with a boom, making the waiter nearly jump out of his skin.

Gabriel quit scraping dried mud off his pants, but he didn't want to intervene. Not yet.

"Nothing, sir. What else would you like to have?" the waiter said when he could speak again.

"Fried chicken wings and onion rings, a whole lot of them. And that sauce. You know, the hot kind?"

"Chiu-chow chili."

"Let's call it Chinese hot sauce."

"I'm sorry, sir, it's all served. I could suggest an altern—"

"Come close," Don said.

The waiter hesitated but moved forward, his hands held together in front of his crotch.

"Where's the cook? Bring him here."

"I'm the cook, sir. The waiter's gone home, so I waited your table." He looked down at the linoleum floor.

"You the cook? That's dandy."

"Yes, sir. I am the—"

Don grabbed the collar of the cook's white uniform and pulled him closer. "Tell me, what do cooks do?"

Gabriel methodically rolled up his rumpled sleeves. He suspected he wouldn't be able to wait until Don's dinner date made an appearance.

The cook's gaze met Don's, but he averted it after a few seconds.

"They… they cook."

"And do I look like a man that takes no for an answer?"

The cook shook his head.

"Then go make my food if you ain't got none. Or do you want me to take you back there and help you?" Don winked and grinned menacingly.

"I… I will go and prepare the order. Please let go of me."

"Now there's a good bitch." Don shoved him away.

The cook stumbled and lost his grip on the check. Don laughed as the cook wiped his leaking forehead on his sleeve and hurried back to the kitchen.

"You better not be bringing me any dog meat, boy!" Don shouted after him and laughed again.

It was Don's belief, as he'd made clear in certain circles, that everyone involved in the underworld—cops, robbers, and gangsters—was softer in New York City compared to Don's hometown, St. Louis.

Part of Gabriel's job required him to learn about guys like Don before moving in on them, and Don was certainly no boy scout.

By the time Don turned eighteen, he'd already stolen twenty cars, robbed thirteen grocery stores, and killed a kid for selling dope on his turf. But the case didn't stick, partially because the kid was an illegal, and partially because of a botched investigation.

Don did his serious time at the age of twenty-two, for attempted murder. He'd splashed a shot glass full of sulfuric acid at his girlfriend's face. The poor girl, rather than go through life with a disfigured face, threw herself off of her twelfth-floor balcony, but since Don had pled guilty earlier, they hadn't charged him with murder.

Don joined a white supremacist gang called Soul of Nation while inside the Western Missouri Correctional Center. He grew a thick goatee, shaved his head, and as final proof of his allegiance to the *brotherhood*, he got tattoos of the gang's symbol on his cheeks.

According to the jailer's report, Don had harassed black and Hispanic inmates numerous times, and it often got out of hand and became full-blown assault.

The head honchos did not ignore Don's penchant for violence. So, when the system released the forty-two-year-old animal back into society, Don's leaders told him to get in touch with their outside contact, George. Don did, and George invited him to Queens, NYC.

George used to sell drugs, but quit after the guys at 107th precinct booked him in for dealing. Since the drug business was a serious no-no for George, he and Don took up another line of work—robbery. They robbed supermarkets, liquor stores, and sometimes, houses.

The previous month, on the evening of Valentine's Day, they'd broken into the house of one Francis Cooper from Bay Terrace, Staten Island. In his statement, Francis said that he tried to protect his home, but he couldn't fight off two stocky guys operating on meth. They broke his arms in three places, dislocated his shoulder, and tied him up.

Even though Francis revealed the locations of the valuables in the house, they turned their attention to the wife, Loretta. They pushed her down and took turns raping her and recording the horror with a cellphone, traumatizing Francis for the lifetime.

Loretta died in the hospital a week later, succumbing to the extensive internal injuries she had suffered. They'd gotten married only the previous month.

George burrowed himself away because he was known to the local cops. Gabriel was in the restaurant because he'd gotten a tip that George was meeting Don here.

The cook returned with Don's food. "Your order, sir." His hands shook as he transferred the contents to the table.

"About time. I almost decided to come in there after you," Don said. He picked up the knife and stood. "All right. Let's go see today's collection."

"Wh-what?"

Don grabbed the kid's arm and dragged him to the counter.

"Open it up, boy. You know the drill. I want all bills, no coins, you hear?"

Ugh. It would be wrong to let the prick have his way any longer. Gabriel shoved himself to his feet. His shoes scuffed, making Don turn around with the cook's arm still in his grip. He became cautious as Gabriel approached from the dark corner table. Don's hand inched towards his back, where a gun would be, but when he took a long look at the harmless, if not straight up pathetic, man approaching him, he relaxed.

Gabriel glanced at a reflective window on the kitchen. His five-inch uncombed hair flew out like Einstein's, and his two-inch beard was untrimmed. He wore a mud-stained black turtleneck and a long beige coat, torn at chest and elbows, over it. He swayed along the path between the tables, talking to himself.

"Hey, you! Get out!" Don shouted.

Gabriel let out a wheezing drunken laugh and walked straight towards Don.

"You better skedaddle, or else I'm gonna rip your throat off, you hobo filth."

Good. He bought it.

"Be cool, man. I'm a cop—" Gabriel hiccupped. "Sorry about that."

Don jumped at the word *cop* and let go of the cook, his hand instinctively reaching into his back. But he did not pull the gun out. Instead, he took a second good look at Gabriel, who kept his eyes half-closed and hung his head like it was too heavy for his neck.

Don scoffed and shook his head. "Funny guy, huh? You a cop? You think I'm stupid?" He grabbed Gabriel's shirt, and decided he didn't need a gun to beat up a homeless man. "You asked for it, bastard," Don said as he swung his right arm.

Gabriel shrunk his eyes, dropped the act, and became super aware. His left forearm blocked Don's punch almost effortlessly. At the same time, his right fist shot up into the pit of Don's stomach. The rapist's pupils narrowed and his knees buckled.

He lay in a fetal position at Gabriel's feet, no doubt wondering what was happening. Apparently, Don had never lost a fight. Not on the streets. Not in prison. Now to be defeated by a drunk—no, no—by a drunk *hobo filth*, should be humiliating beyond imagination, which brought Gabriel a sliver of glee.

Don tried to get up, but a sharp kick to his right temple prevented him from doing that. The next kick landed on his mouth. Two teeth came loose, along with a thick slime of blood. Gabriel swung his foot at the same spot. Two more teeth gushed out, this time with *Chinese hot sauce* and chicken wings.

"Four blows and you puked? Some tough guy," Gabriel said, but the only response he got was a grunt.

As he turned Don and made him lie on his stomach, the stupid maggot tried to get his gun. Gabriel, with the tip of his boot, moved the hand away. He lifted the tank shirt and removed the weapon from the waistband.

Then he cuffed him. "I Mirandized you, didn't I?"

Don mumbled something like, "Stupid pig."

Gabriel, thanking Don for giving him a reason, lifted his leg and stomped him on the shoulder, squeezing out a cry that reverberated throughout the small restaurant.

"Do I look like a man that takes no for an answer? I said, I read you your rights, didn't I?"

All Don could manage was a lousy, "Yes."

"Excuse me, sir," Gabriel said to the cook, who had his clasped hands on his chest. "I'm Detective Gabriel Chase from 122nd Precinct, Staten Island. You remember seeing this man resist arrest and try to attack me after I announced myself as a cop?" He tilted his head down and lifted his eyebrows.

The cook, though dumbstruck, had the timid mind to play along.

"Oh yes, sir, I remember."

"Thank you, sir. Have a good night. Sorry about the muck. I'm cleaning it away now." Gabriel bent down, pulled Don up by his beard and pushed him toward the exit.

As he dragged him to an unmarked police car parked a few yards from the diner, the images of Loretta's autopsy flashed before Gabriel's eyes. Gang raping a newlywed into murder demanded harsher things than merely five hits. So, when he pushed Don into the backseat, he scanned the area for cameras or witnesses. Having found nothing, he grabbed hold of Don's bald head and banged it against the side of the roof.

"Sorry, my bad," he heard himself mutter.

However, he let the *accident* happen three more times. Or seven. Gabriel couldn't be sure, because he lost count, along with a reason, after the third.

Nature vs. Nurture

3/15/19. Somewhere around 7:00 p.m.

Who is a serial killer? For all intents and purposes, I'm one, aren't I?

Something churns in my stomach and a vibration, like static, goes through my body. My face feels odd as my cheeks stretch in an awkward angle, so I pull off the mask and look in the rearview mirror. The man staring back has a peculiarity plastered over his face. It's something different. Something alien.

A real fucking smile.

Could it be? Is this what people call *happiness*?

How ecstatic!

But why do I feel so happy to, um… feel happy?

To answer that, I need to revisit the original question. Who exactly is a serial killer?

Personally, I believe humans are pathogens, a sickening malady to the planet, and us serial killers are the covert squadron of Mother Gaia's immune system. Even gods, purported to be omnipotent and omniscient, are members of our esoteric clique, what with them turning a blind eye to the bombing of children's hospitals and letting humanity eradicate itself.

But I couldn't give two shits about the Earth or terrorists. Aside from my preposterous, albeit philosophical, take on the subject, who is generally considered to be a serial killer? And what drives him?

Is he someone who is compelled by the desire to kill humans, so as to achieve the feeling of power and control he wished he'd had when his childhood was traumatized by someone stronger than he was?

Is he someone who cannot experience sexual gratification by typical means, which are deviant enough as they are?

Or does a sense of failure and underachievement, fueled by poverty, coalesce with his grandiose self-perception and force him to act out his murderous fantasies in which he isn't just someone that matters, he is also infamous?

Or is he simply an unhinged schizophrenic?

Aforementioned theories pertain to various emotions, and if an emotional trauma of a person's deleterious past and present is what begets a serial killer, then I'm not among them.

My conventional years of childhood are attributable to my parents, who gave me everything that would constitute a non-traumatized, if not happy, person. I never felt compelled to kill, even though I've killed ten people to date. I didn't get an erection, or even a decent adrenaline rush, when I saw their eyes drain of life, and my mouth didn't froth in excitement due to the release of pent-up rage—if there was any to begin with.

Then what about bad neighborhoods? I didn't grow up in one. I'm from an upscale part of the city. Even if I'd grown up in a ghetto, it wouldn't have made a difference, since meaningless conflict—or meaningful ones, for that matter—isn't in me, and I seldom instigate any altercations. Last, no sinister voices whisper in my head, coercing me to murder the heathens, gays, prostitutes, or homeless.

Something bumps against the back of my seat. I turn and spot a disoriented Rita trying to find her bearings. My heart misses its rhythm. Nothing untoward should happen this evening. I'm at last on the homestretch of the crimson trail that leads to my destiny.

Scanning the surroundings, I pull the car over in a dark and quiet street. I retrieve a pair of zip ties from the bag, slip through between the front seats and bind the still-dazed woman. For good measure, I gag her, too. She is not moving any longer, but I need extra security. So, I take the stun gun, kneel on her back, and press it in the same place I did earlier. This time, however, I zap her for at least twelve seconds. When I let up, the smell of burnt meat replaces the scent of her perfume. Feeling more secure, I get back to driving, and to my reverie.

So… although I fit the technical definition of a serial killer, since it's a work *I had to do* to reach my goal, I'm not actually one. Then what am I?

Supposedly, when I was a child I cried only when needing food, or if an ant locked its little stingers somewhere on my body. I neither smiled nor cried as I grew up. Worried, my parents took me to a psychiatrist.

I was diagnosed with alexithymia, a condition that renders me unable to understand what they call *emotions*. Doctors didn't know if it was inherent or if I hit my head and damaged a vital section in the right hemisphere of my brain where emotions originate. They only knew it was incurable. Plainly put, I am a born psychopath.

Alexithymia exempted me from not just empathy, but all the entries in Mr. Plutchik's wheel of emotions. I feel nothing except boredom and fear, which some say is an emotion, while others dissent. I don't care. If fear is an emotion, then it's the only one I feel, and I've always tried to avoid it.

When I was a child, growing up was nothing short of grueling. I remember not wanting toys or bicycles, baseball gloves or footballs, Game Boys or puppies. I never enjoyed playing with kids my age. No, scratch that. I never enjoyed playing, period. I just didn't comprehend what *fun* was. As a result, I was always bored. It's the only thing anyone will feel if they can't feel anything else. And boredom isn't the most sublime of feelings. To this day, I consider it to be my worst enemy.

My father had warned me that if I didn't mingle with others, I might become a *weirdo*. No sooner had my father revealed his reasonable concerns—not very eloquently, I might add—than I recognized people might distinguish me as *that quiet kid*. The realization scared me, kicking in a primeval survival mechanism. It told me that uniqueness was dangerous. It's safe to blend in, fake laughs, love, and friendship. Better to prevent remembrance by leaving character evidence.

I started being *friends* with children of my age. Solitude doesn't matter if your ambitions don't have murder in them. But if yours is similar to mine, you must stitch a perfect *mask of sanity*, as psychiatrists like to call the social camouflage of deranged killers. But I'm sane. What I've stitched is more like a mask of emotions.

And the million-dollar question—why does my ambition have murder in it? What does the screwed-up wiring in my brain have anything to do with me having a tied-up woman in the back? Not every psychopath becomes a murderer. Even I never thought I'd be a serial killer, back then.

A thud breaks my flashback. Anxious as ever, I turn and check on Rita. She's still gnashing her teeth in agony from the long shock, and one of her legs thumps on the car's interior panel—inadvertently, I hope.

Either way, I couldn't help chuckling.

Chapter 3

March 16, 2019. 06:11 A.M.

He knew this place. He hated this place. The mother sat on the bathroom floor with her arms hugging her knees, rocking to and fro as she murmured to herself. He peered into the tub. A baby's bloated body floated on the surface of the stinky water, its skin white and sodden. When he reached in to lift it, the baby rolled its bulging dead eyes and stared at him. It caught his forearm with its tiny hands and pulled him forward. His head plunged inside the water in a second. The mother, who was now standing, pushed him in from behind, laughing maniacally. He started to choke. The baby grasped his hair and rammed its forehead against his. Each ram exploded into a boom, and his lungs begged for air.

Gabriel awoke with a start. The chair fell back and his thighs bumped the table as he shot to his feet. His hands searched his right hip in a hurry. No holster. He skipped a heartbeat.

After solving the confusion about his whereabouts, he heard the thumping on the door again.

He breathed a sigh of relief.

Gabriel's iPhone XS, his father's Christmas gift from last year, rested on the table. He retrieved it and pressed the home button. 6:13 a.m.

The pounding on the door grew wilder.

He skirted the table on which a 21-inch Dell monitor somehow still stood upright. He took a Vicks VapoInhaler from his front pocket, twisted it open and inhaled. Not a deep breath, but not a shallow one either. He remembered doing this from high school, knew he was addicted to it because he sure as hell wasn't using it for a stuffy nose.

He stifled a yawn with the back of his hand and opened the door, revealing a rugged-looking woman.

She was 5'10" and leaned toward the heavy side. Not that she didn't work out. On the contrary, she worked out a bit too much. Her blonde hair was styled in a so-called pixie cut, the sides and back faded. She held a Styrofoam cup in her left hand, while the right balled into a tight fist. To knock out the door? Most likely to knock out the doorman.

Detective Emma Stein had been with the Auto Crime Division before the captain transferred her to the homicide and robbery squad. That was three years ago, and Gabriel had yet to regret the bureaucratic decision.

"Why'd you pull that Dirty Harry shit last night?" she said. "Are you trying to kill yourself?"

Gabriel and Emma had begun searching for Don and George when the DNA results from Loretta Cooper's case came back. It was easy to find George's place, as he had a record in New York City. Emma and Gabriel had been watching George's apartment for well over a week now, but they didn't make a move because George never showed up. Only Don frequented the house, most times drunk or high, always with a working girl.

The plan was to wait for George to let down his guard, underestimate the police and reappear. Last night, Gabriel's informant called and said that George was going to meet Don in ChickHun, a Chinese diner located in

Pomonok, Queens, and Gabriel had gone there. Maybe if he had waited for longer, he might have caught George, too.

Not anymore.

George escaped, true, but letting Don rob the poor kid insulted everything Gabriel had ever believed in. Don had been stewing in the holding cell for a while, and with a little temptation of a deal, he would puke his partner's hiding location in no time.

With her upper lip forming an inverted tick mark, Emma gave Gabriel a look, bottom to top, before her gaze settled on his.

"You intentionally dressed up as a bum, or you've become one? I swear to God, I can't tell the difference anymore." Without waiting for an answer, she barreled through him into the office.

"It's a costume. Convicts have got an eye for cops. And I was beat last night. I couldn't find the energy to change, not after writing a really tricky report." He followed her into the room. "Imagine you didn't know me, and I introduce myself as a detective. Would you believe that?"

"I wouldn't." She gave him that look again, bottom to top. "I'd mace you, though."

"Neither did Don, which was what I'd counted on."

She slumped onto a metal chair across from his usual place at the table.

"You waited until I left and went on your own."

"Last night was Kate's birthday, right? I didn't want to spoil the romance for the sake of some Nazi from the Midwest. Hey, about that, you said you wanted to get her a puppy or a kitten. Have you?" he asked.

Emma stared at him with her piercing blues, and he felt a dreadful déjà vu. He couldn't figure out its source, but he thought it might have something to do with his childhood days when the principal summoned him to her office. In fact, Ms. Sullivan questioning him about just why the hell he would not quit pulling on pigtails and stop making little girls cry, was one of his earliest memories. Standing didn't help the dread, so he went around the table, lifted the fallen chair and sat on it.

"No, I didn't," Emma finally said. "Kate wants to adopt, not buy. We're going to an animal shelter later this week." The features on her rough face softened. "You should have taken someone with you." Then she sniffed the coffee in her hand and took a long sip.

"No one was around at the time," he said.

He was lying, and he knew that she knew he was lying but wouldn't know why. The truth—he went alone to beat up Don and George without having someone around to pull him off.

"No one was around?" Her tone rose. "That bigot destroyed so many lives. You know Francis put his house up for sale and left New York?" She pointed toward the holding cells. "Don doesn't deserve to sit there, all cozy in a blanket. I wish you'd taken me last night. I could've beaten the shit out of that mother—"

"I know." Gabriel took his phone from the table.

"What? I was saying something. You can't—"

He raised his hand, cutting her off again. That made her furious. She started to give him a piece of her mind, but he put his phone's display in front of her face.

When she saw the photo, her jaw loosened and the pulsating blue vein in her neck sank back in. It showed Don propped up in a hospital bed with a big bandage wrapped around his head. His eyelids were swollen black, and four of his teeth were missing. Gabriel had made him smile for the camera.

He moved the phone away. "With a rap like that, he should've known not to take a swing at a cop."

Emma nodded.

"You're good now?" he asked.

"Yeah, Gabe. I'm good." She smiled for the first time since she'd come in. "Isn't he going to press charges?"

"I got a witness," he muttered and deleted a notification on his phone that said *Casey's Anniversary*. "Are you going to tell me why you woke me up?"

"Oh, shit. I almost forgot." She had no urgency in her tone, which one would expect from someone who just realized they'd forgotten something. "Bulldog said you'd be here."

"Smart man."

"He told you to ungag your phone."

Gabriel pressed the sides of his phone. "Done. Anything else?"

"Meet him and the commissioner at the Plaza. Nine, sharp."

"Both at once?"

"Yes." She took another sip.

"Perhaps you'd like to start with that the next time? Priorities, Emma. Know how they work?"

"Then be available when people try to call you. Or how about leaving the door open when you nap in here the next time?"

"He told you why?"

"Nope. Oh, and he sounded…"

"Pissed? What's new?"

"No. He sounded sad."

"That's weird. I'll check it out."

"And…" She hesitated.

"Yeah?"

"Um… get eye drops from a drugstore. You know, your eyes are bloodshot. Bulldog will get crazy if he thinks you're at it again," she said.

Gabriel's puzzled expression transformed into a poker face when he understood what she meant. Everyone in the precinct knew Gabriel's climb out of the bottle had been a tough one, and if he slipped, he would become miserable again.

Not that he wasn't miserable now, as his appearance publicized. What with the combination of long unruly hair and a thick beard with a few premature grays showering them, and coming to work in same-colored clothes—most days in the same clothes—the homeless costume couldn't have suited anyone better. But it was still a better misery than the one that would descend on him if he reacquainted with Mr. Smirnoff.

"You're going to drink that?" he asked.

She slid the cup across the table and got up. "Nine o'clock."

"Yeah, yeah, I got it."

He sipped the coffee—which was sugary. He liked days that started sweet.

Chapter 4

March 16, 2019. 08:41 A.M.

Gabriel hailed a cab in Hylan Boulevard, gave his destination to the driver, and slept in the backseat. The driver woke him up an hour later, after parking the cab on Centre Street, in front of David N. Dinkins Manhattan Municipal Building. Wiping the drool off his cheek, Gabriel paid with cash and gave a good tip.

Lack of sleep the previous night wouldn't have improved his reflexes much, so he had resisted the temptation to twist his motorcycle's throttle that morning. One more layer of a day's dust would settle on his green Kawasaki Z1000.

He walked under the colossal archway, starting his five-minute stroll to the meeting.

This one-mile radius comprised almost all of his life—friends from One Police Plaza, City Hall, the Supreme Court, One Hogan Place, and other smaller courts, and his haters from the Metropolitan Correctional facility. Most criminals from his borough ended up there because Richmond County, where Staten Island was located, didn't have a prison for major detention. Not after the one in Arthur Kill was closed back in 2011.

He passed Tony Rosenthal's *5 in 1*, a CorTen steel sculpture, on his left as he ambled along the narrow Police Plaza Path. The sculpture had five large red discs which were welded together at various angles. They symbolized the five boroughs, and the interconnection represented the smooth relationship between them. But the Islanders had always carped that compared to the other four, the government neglected them. Hence the nickname *The Forgotten Borough*.

Into his view came the 1PP, with its brutalist architecture that looked more like a lunatic asylum than the police headquarters it actually was. He jogged up the small series of steps, entered the building and crossed an echoing hall. He walked to an elevator at the corner and rode it alone to his destination.

Ding.

He got out on the fourteenth floor. Staring at his reflection in the elevator's shiny doors, he found himself thinking about Emma's comment that he was becoming a bum. Emma and everyone in the precinct were accustomed to seeing him in his usual choice of attire, which he wore to the plaza that morning—a white shirt, a brown jacket, and jeans. It wasn't hard to misinterpret his indifference toward the deficiencies in his wardrobe as poverty and lack of personal hygiene. But there was a method to his sartorial madness—this uniform was his armor.

The commissioner's assistant sat in her usual post, behind a work desk that carried stacks of files, a PC, a telephone, and a penholder.

"Good morning, Margret. I have an appoint—"

"I know. Go right in, Gabriel. Mr. Hughes told me to send you in soon as you've arrived."

"Okay, thank you." He smiled.

A burp vibrated in his throat and reminded him of the spartan breakfast he'd eaten. He knocked on the door and opened it without waiting for an answer.

The NYPD's commissioner, Raymond Hughes, sat behind a huge mahogany desk. Raymond was a tall man with big arms, barrel chest, and a slight paunch. He sported a white mustache that matched his hair.

Gabriel had known Raymond for a long time. He and Gabriel's father, Joshua Chase, were good friends even before Gabriel was born.

Victor Ivansky, Gabriel's captain, sat across the desk in one of the two chairs there. He was bald, with a short neck and the thick body of a dock worker. His clean-shaven, round face gave him a strong resemblance to Winston Churchill.

Gabriel wanted to smile, but his superiors' grim faces told him something was very wrong.

"Good morning, sirs."

"Come and sit, Gabriel." Victor pointed his chin at the empty chair beside him.

Wisecracking and borderline racist jokes were atypically absent in him. Strange.

Gabriel sat with an unreturned smile directed at Raymond. Now that he was closer, he noticed things that didn't make sense. The cufflinks of Raymond's uniform had smudges of wetness, his cheeks and eyes red, and he was having a hard time breathing.

"I received a video clip to my email this morning," Raymond said, his voice deep, but unusually low and quivery. "What I'm about to show you is one of the most heinous things you're ever going to see, Gabe. I wish I could tell you what this is, but I… I just can't." His voice failed him.

He typed something on his laptop, and when he turned it in Gabriel's direction, its rubber feet squeaked on the smooth wood.

Victor stood. "I'm sorry, boss. I don't wanna see it again." He walked over to the window overlooking the park.

Disconcerted, Gabriel returned his gaze to the laptop.

Raymond had backed the video all the way to 00:00. Gabriel dragged his finger on the touchpad and clicked the small white triangle in the center. The video was high-quality and the audio crisp—he could hear a clear whirring sound.

The first thing that caught Gabriel's attention was the hanging old woman on the far left. She wore a long skirt and a cardigan, her body slowly swiveling on the rope. It looked unreal. Some kind of sick prank?

Not counting the hanging body, three other people had nooses around their necks, and one of them sat in a wheelchair. They were positioned on three huge ice blocks, which appeared to be close to two-feet tall. A thick blue curtain covered the entire background, and the ceiling was not visible.

Gabriel moved his focus right, to the next person. She wore a dark blue top and white pants. The shirt clung to her body as if someone had poured a pitcher of water over her. Sweat? Large bruises covered her face. He took a closer look because he'd seen her before.

And then his world crashed around him. In an instant, his mouth dried up and his tongue stuck to the palate. Breathing became labored as he made a conscious effort to fill his lungs. His heart began racing and fear seeped through his pores.

The woman was Rita Hughes, the commissioner's wife. Gabriel's godmother.

He looked up at the police commissioner, who had his eyes buried in the heels of his hands, weeping silently. Gabriel's own prickled, too.

Gabriel's mother had left when he was just two years old. He'd been led to believe Rita was his real mother, until he was ten. It didn't make any difference, even after they broke the news to him.

Seeing her now, beaten up, crying and squirming, didn't make any sense at all.

He hit the spacebar, pausing the video. "What is this?" he asked.

No one spoke.

"What the fuck is this!"

Raymond didn't move, but Victor returned to his seat, sat down and sighed. Then, he put a trembling hand on Gabriel's shoulder.

No… it didn't feel right.

It's *him* who trembled.

"I'm sorry, Gabe," Victor said. "We don't know anything. That's why we've called you."

"But why are you calling me just *now*? Why didn't you inform me sooner?"

"Because we had to make sure it was real." Victor gave a soft tap before letting go. "And we did."

Gabriel forced himself to look back at the screen, at the people frozen in it. Perhaps if he didn't resume playing the video, they would live forever, albeit very uncomfortably. With extreme reluctance, he clicked the spacebar again. Honed detective instincts warned him what was about to happen. His mind searched for ways to narrow down suspects, and his heart jumped to his throat.

The living three were gagged, the nooses squeezing their necks, but without doing real damage, at least for now.

The person next to Rita was Harry Moore, a famous paraplegic stand-up comedian. Gabriel didn't watch TV but read the news. Harry was a *comedic genius,* according to one article. Well-known for his philanthropy, he donated 95 percent of his paychecks to various disabled communities across the globe, mostly to children.

Harry had his head angled towards the person on his left. The kid looked like he was in his twenties. He wore red shorts and a dark gray T-shirt, which, like Rita's clothes, were drenched and stuck to his body. The muscles on his shoulders, chest, arms, and gigantic but ripped thighs suggested that he could be a professional bodybuilder.

Gabriel didn't know who the people on the far sides were, but he'd known Rita for thirty years. He remembered the smell of her waffles and cookies, the sound of her heartfelt laughter, and most of all, the pivotal role she'd played in curing his alcoholism. Now he watched her die one breath at a time as she cried and moaned into the gag. Gabriel guessed she was begging to the camera, hoping that whoever put it there was watching it and would be kind enough to let her go. Raymond's posture inferred that was not the case here.

One day, I will break you.

Their wet hair stuck to their foreheads and the sides of their oily faces. They were scared, but their perspiration was abnormal. Though March wasn't exactly freezing, the average temperature in the city hung around fifty degrees. People weren't supposed to even sweat, least of all as much as they were doing in the video. Had they been taken somewhere else?

In the midst of tears and unheard deals with the Almighty, Harry began to choke. He bit the gag so hard that the cloth in his mouth became invisible, his face so red that a pinprick might have caused it to explode. As his body convulsed, his right arm tore free and pushed the wheelchair's control knob. Rita and the kid watched in horror as the machine lurched forward.

The wheels did not touch the floor—the rope made sure of it—but they weren't on the ice block either. His chair fell off the edge and the wheels spun above the ice, spritzing water. Harry's contorting face told agonizing stories of death that no one would ever understand.

Minutes later, Harry stopped moving. But his wheelchair didn't, as if it could still save its master from his bind if it ran faster.

The video was on its twenty-fourth minute, and Rita struggled to keep her feet above the ice, which was fatally smaller now. Her efforts to hold on to her life with the help of her tiptoes failed. She made dry choking noises as she suffocated, and her legs kicked around. Eventually she stopped thrashing about. Her eyes rolled into her skull and her body stiffened.

Gabriel shut his eyes and covered his ears. He started to count in his mind. No one could watch their mother's suffering, even if that person spent his life witnessing the dark side of humanity and solved murders for a living.

When he reached one hundred, he opened his wet eyes. Rita's desperate feet and toes had given up the fight and protested in silence. She must be just unconscious, but she would die very soon. Feeling utterly helpless, Gabriel fought the urge to grab the laptop and smash it on the wall.

One fine day, I will obliterate you.

Now the kid—as tall and strong as he was, it didn't help him in the slightest when the noose did what had been done to the other victims. He looked defeated even before his windpipe constricted. His hope of living died long ago. If God didn't save a senior citizen, a disabled person, and a battered woman, why would he bother to come down and save him?

Two bloodcurdling minutes later, the kid stopped brisk walking in the air.

The ice blocks shrank on themselves like they couldn't face what they had helped a madman do. They were so small that they couldn't shoulder anyone anymore, except Harry.

His wheelchair, which still ran on the edge of the ice block, moved at an awkward angle. The right wheel slipped back when it lost contact with the ice, and the wheelchair turned in Rita's direction. Then the left wheel, as it was still whirling at its best speed, climbed the edge and propelled the wheelchair forward. It crashed onto Rita. She swung to her right and almost touched the old woman, then came back with a vengeance and transferred the momentum back to Harry.

It was like watching an inverse Newton's cradle—the extremes were at rest, and the two in the center played tag. After seven seconds, the small series of unforeseen events Harry's desperate hand had set in motion came to rest.

Thirty-seven minutes and four dead people later, Gabriel wondered if it was all just a nightmare. The scene was surreal—four hanging people, one sitting in a wheelchair. All of them had different life stories, but cruel, lazy fate had spliced their last chapters.

The nooses, ice blocks, and even the camera—they were all guilty of abetting a psychopath in murdering these people. People who were loved, who were going to be missed.

Gabriel heard a sound from the laptop—shoes on a tile. Clack… clack… clack…

He wrung a teardrop and opened his eyes.

A man entered the frame from the right side of the video, ignoring the hanging bodies. He was around six-feet tall and had an average physique. He wore a black suit, shirt, gloves, and a gold tie bar clipped a red silk tie to his shirt. All this didn't creep Gabriel out, but the man's head did.

He wore a white rabbit mask. It was flat instead of conical, and it had sky blue eyes with black pupils. Two ears stood atop—one ear erect, while the other folded down on its middle. Beneath the cheap plastic mask, he wore a black ski mask so his hair and skin color weren't visible.

He approached the camera and brought his hands forward, showing an A4 paper. Three words in block letters ran across its center.

YOUR MOVE, BLOODHOUNDS.

Serendipity

3/15/19. After grabbing Rita.

I exited Rita's neighborhood a while ago, and I'm now negotiating my way through Brooklyn-Queens Expressway. As I expected, it overflows with traffic, fumes, and murderous rage. Listening to angry horns is boring, but I don't turn on the radio. Who needs it when you have a wild imagination? And why resort to wild imagination when your past is wilder?

Where was I before? Flashback, I know, but where?

Where? Where? Where?

Ah, yes! I have it. I was thinking about how fate made me a serial killer. In retrospect, the inciting incident seems like a marvelous gift of chance, but I didn't recognize it as such when it occurred.

After my father told me I behaved like a *weirdo*, I began spending a considerable amount of time with children my age. One thing I learned from those intellectual dwarfs was mischief, a product of curiosity. I deigned to act interested in things my peers found curious and experimented on. One day, copying cartoons, an acquaintance of mine wanted to try something—to burst a firecracker in the mouth of a garden lizard.

Pop went the lizard!

When the detonation of blood and guts ended, he cried and ran home. Maybe the ephemeral show of horror didn't match what he'd seen on TV.

But I was entertained for the first time in my life!

Remember how I said boredom was one of my greatest nemeses? For a person who's as bored as I was, entertainment was like water to a parched throat in the middle of a desert. So, I continued to dispatch any living thing that wasn't able to fight back and hurt me. Experimenting with them became my hobby. When dying, these animals communicated with me through the only emotion I feel. Fear.

Though I hadn't murdered people yet, I did understand that killing frogs or dogs wasn't unlike killing a person. My mind saw the difference only in penalties—from a stern *no* from a parent to an electric chair. For me, it was only ever a short time-kill, like how you pop bubble wrap.

But how long could you pop them? Like all good things, my hobby eventually became mundane, and murder began to lack its savor.

As I grew older, I wanted to euthanize myself. The boredom pained me to such an extent that it might as well have been a physical injury. The feeling was similar to not being able to differentiate the tastes of Coke and water. Not understanding emotions. White torture.

So, my choice became, suicide or kill boredom by living for something. I began searching for a purpose. But where do I fit in? A man of science, arts, or business? Don't CEOs possess the same level of empathy as I do and show psychopathic traits?

And then I happened upon my destiny.

On a cold Bostonian morning, I met a professional criminal by pure coincidence. It's as if I was foreordained to meet him. Conservative religious fanatics would have called him an incarnation of Beelzebub. He was superior to me in every sense of wickedness. His dead eyes saw through mine and understood me for what I was. He made me feel what I made my little animal friends feel. But I didn't show fear in his presence—if being afraid made you weak, showing it made you weaker. Maybe for this reason—fear—or maybe because he was the only human I've ever related to, that day I acquired the first part of an answer to my quest.

I wanted to either become a master criminal like him, or a competent policeman who could fight men like him. I flipped a coin, and it said police. I flipped again to get the same outcome. I was uneasy with the result, so I didn't follow through.

Police or criminal?

The business of both is crime. Unlike other jobs, these could protect me from fear, because each business deals with violence, and violence is real power. Men of violence always look out for themselves. No matter how rich you are or what kind of political power you wield, if a man who is not a stranger to violence decides to kill you, you die.

Police or criminal?

Both have riveting days that other prosaic jobs couldn't offer. Both could destroy the boredom that's been seeking to kill me for a long time. But which one should I choose? Where can I be in the top of the hierarchy? Love and hate. Happy and sad. Justice and injustice. They all mean the same to me.

I've always wanted to excel at what I do. If I'm to become a cop, I need to understand what justice is to excel at that work. Police are so infatuated with justice that they are even willing to die for it.

But what is justice? Simply, it is compensation for being wronged. It comes from anger and revenge when our rights are stolen. The government has orders, sets of rules, punishments, and penalties called the law, and by enforcing this law, they protect justice and establish it.

I know all that from sociology textbooks, but haven't experienced any of it. I've never felt angry or wanted to take revenge when something of mine was stolen. If I don't understand what justice is, then how can I become its lackey, let alone be the best lackey?

I got my answer. Crime it is.

Two crucial parts of crime, violence and planning, have the potential to destroy my two greatest enemies—fear and boredom. Since I always wanted to excel at what I do, I aimed to be the best among criminals. Like how children dream of becoming a fireman, a teacher, or a wrestler, I dreamed of being a criminal legend.

But isn't becoming a criminal complex, like wanting to become a doctor and deciding which branch to pursue? There are many specialties to choose from. So, I researched. And after reading statistics about unsolved crimes across the nation, I decided to become a serial killer.

Aren't serial killers the worst nightmare for the police? Their toughest enemies? Ask any veteran detective if he wants to investigate a case relating to a seven-foot cop-killing drug dealer, or a diminutive serial killer. He would choose the cop-killer any day. The reason is simply that catching a serial killer means he has to be identified first. And identifying the serial killer, who camouflages as an average person and hides among the population of millions, is what daunts the authorities. Not to mention the political outrage and bad PR if the cops fail to catch him.

I consumed books on forensic science, police procedurals, novels, and everything related to crime that I could acquire by fair means or foul. I took notes, memorized dos and don'ts.

Four years into being a teenager, when most of the adolescents I grew up with were drooling over images of naked women, I committed two of the greatest crimes of that time—murder and bank robbery. Not just to prove to myself that the knowledge I was acquiring from books could protect me, but also because I needed to commit them.

Much later, after my first murder, I introduced an addendum into my original ambition. When I graduated, the things I learned about justice and injustice, and the control they had on people started festering in me. I was, and still am, proud that I chose injustice, but everyone else picked justice. Or they acted like it.

I mean, why wouldn't you steal a candy bar from a baby that can't defend its food or hurt you back? Why should you offer your seat to a pregnant woman or a senior citizen when riding subways?

I acted like I cared. I acted like I had morals, whatever they are, but I just don't comprehend them. I know my condition prevents me from understanding emotions from which morality sprouts, but it doesn't make existence easy. If this is how nature made me, and if this is how I'm going to live for the rest of my life, then I must advocate immorality.

Justice, an abstract concept based on every emotion I don't feel, became something I wished to see die. I wanted to prove to the world that it is not real. That's how I established my second goal. Why couldn't I merge my new goal with my old one? To become a criminal legend *and* to prove that justice doesn't exist? It would require lots of practice and meticulous planning of events. Constructing ambitious plans was one of the activities that killed boredom. And for a person like me, a psychopath, killing boredom always takes precedence over killing anything or anyone.

Chapter 5

March 16, 2019. 11:32 A.M.

Back in 1PP, Raymond contacted the Special Agent in Charge of New York's FBI field office and requested him to coordinate with the NYPD's Major Case Squad. However, he also ordered Victor to form a separate team and to choose detectives from the precincts where the victims had died. After Victor handpicked the candidates, Raymond would talk to the Chief of Detectives and free them from their current assignments.

Gabriel was to spearhead the investigation. Raymond gave him this responsibility, though technically he shouldn't have, as one of the victims was closely related to him. Gabriel would solve it the fastest, because he had the second-highest clearance rate among all the homicide detectives of the NYPD.

Riding back to the precinct in Victor's car was bleak for Gabriel, but also educational. As they crossed the Brooklyn Bridge in morning traffic, Victor started with what he knew. Excluding Raymond, the video had been emailed to two other persons who were related to other victims. Rita's laptop, phone, and email ID were used to send them.

The old woman in the video was Martha Nelson, wife of Samuel Nelson, who owned the Daily Herald, one of the biggest news networks in New York. Samuel's PA reported Martha missing the previous night. She had filed a missing persons report in the 84th precinct after she went to Samuel's home in Brooklyn Heights and found it open without Martha in it.

Samuel stayed awake the whole night, trying Martha's unreachable phone. As soon as he received the video, he called Raymond's personal phone. Gabriel interrupted

Victor to ask how they knew each other. Victor said they became friends at the police fundraiser held that January.

The kid on the far right was Doug Bastian, age twenty-one and the son of New York City's DA, Steve Bastian. Gabriel's best friend, an assistant DA, shared a lot of good things about Steve. After including Steve in the equation, they got hundreds of revenge stories as possible motives. But having numerous leads deluging the investigation was the same as having none at all.

Like Samuel, Steve Bastian called the commissioner, but around 8:00 a.m., after he woke up and checked his email over morning coffee. Doug wasn't reported missing. Apparently, Steve trusted Doug with his independence and unanswered calls weren't unusual between them.

The Computer Crime Unit tried to triangulate the victims' phones, but they could locate only Doug's, which was in his house. The others' phones had vanished without a trace. They weren't just switched off—if they were, cellphone towers would have registered them. This meant that the killer had removed the batteries to prevent the detectives from tracking the phones.

These were all the salient facts Victor learned from Raymond before Gabriel had arrived at the meeting. As they crossed Fort Hamilton, Victor began making calls to put together the special task force that Raymond wanted.

* * *

Muscles on Emma's jaw flexed, and the throbbing blue veins on the sides of her neck resurfaced. She was watching the shocking video on her phone.

Gabriel sat on his chair with his back hunched, elbows and forearms resting on the table. If he cried, he wouldn't be able to stop the stammer that had humiliated him too many times in the past. So, he elected to battle his loss in silence.

"What the hell is this? It doesn't make any sense." Emma seethed when the video stopped at the rabbit's face.

Gabriel moved the inhaler away from his nose. "It doesn't, but I don't care. I just wanna get him."

"When we get him, I'm gonna shoot him in that overbite."

"Let's not make it too easy. So, what do you think?"

"The DA's got enemies. Gangs here could be learning new tricks from Isis or cartels?"

"That doesn't explain the other three."

"Yeah," she said. "What about Samuel Nelson?"

"The captain told me that his news channel doesn't pick sides, push any hot buttons, or give attention to the atrocities in other countries. The Daily Herald covers local crimes, celebrity news, pollution, things like that. I don't see Samuel having many enemies, like our commissioner and the DA."

"Listen to me," Emma said. "Last night, the Daily Herald broadcasted a video of a bank robbery. The gang killed a security guard. The Daily Herald reported that the infamous Lolly was back in the game after a ten-year hiatus. Could it be him?"

"Robbery could be Lolly, but not this." Gabriel inhaled again. "He doesn't kill for anything except dollar stacks. Plus, if he wanted to kill them, he would have gunned them down so fast they wouldn't have known what hit them. He's a one-hit murderer. Not a tormentor."

"I agree, but he—"

"You're missing a huge thing, Emma. How could Lolly have had the time to plan all this? The Daily Herald showed the robbery just last evening!"

"What if the robbers knew it before? Maybe they somehow got access to inside information?" she asked, her voice weak.

She was aware her theory was shaky. But sometimes she played devil's advocate so they could be sure they didn't miss anything.

"Really? Fine, my original question stands. What about the remaining three? I can't vouch for the others, but I know Rita. She is a saint. We all—" He swallowed.

His eyes became distant for a second and his mind traveled to another dimension.

Then he clenched his teeth. "I knew Rita. She was a saint. I guarantee that."

"I agree, Gabriel." Emma's voice turned soft. "But maybe to get back at the commissioner?"

"So, we're looking for people who are getting back at the commissioner. They planned to get their revenge, and when Samuel broadcasted the robbery, they added his wife to the list. What are the odds?"

"When you put it that way, it doesn't make a whole lot of sense."

"And they just decided to kill Harry and Doug for shits and giggles?"

"Okay. That doesn't make any sense at all."

"It's all right," Gabriel said, embarrassed. "You're at least trying. I'm not coming up with anything."

They countered each other's ideas and threw darts through the holes in their theories. Whenever they were assigned a difficult case, they played this game to find the most foolproof approach to work on. However, when the captain knocked on the door and called them for their team meeting, they started toward the conference room in mutual defeat. No one had won.

"You know, we're going to catch him, right?" Gabriel said, as they walked. "The whole department will work for free to find someone who hurt one of our own."

"Not just the police," she said, her voice optimistic again. "People loved Harry, and they'll help, too. We got media on our side—it's personal for Samuel."

"And when we get him, Steve will not rest until the DA's office makes sure that the killer is locked away in the deepest pit of our system." Gabriel stopped walking and thought about what they'd just said.

A perfect team. So perfect, it made Gabriel question the coincidence.

"What's up?" Emma slowed down.

"Nothing," he muttered and resumed walking.

Chapter 6

March 16, 2019. 12:47 P.M.

As Emma and Gabriel neared the conference room, the commotion from inside swallowed the sound of their shoes. Their entry caused no discernible disruption in the babble.

A whiteboard hung at the back of the room, and an oval table dominated its center. It could accommodate fifteen people, but held only eight that day. Victor sat at the head of the table, and when Gabriel caught his gaze, he beckoned him over. Gabriel greeted two familiar faces with nods as he squeezed past the revolving chairs.

"Captain," he said, taking a seat beside him.

He grabbed sheets of paper from Victor's outstretched arm and thumbed through them. They were the profiles of the detectives selected for their team.

"I didn't get anyone from the 68th and 78th," Victor said. "Too many cooks and all that."

He was referring to the precincts that had jurisdictions over Bay Ridge and Park Slope, where Rita and Harry had lived. Cases like this called for veteran detectives. When a bunch of them were put in the same pitch, methods differed, disputes arose, and in rare instances, fists flew.

"That's reasonable, Captain."

"Is this guy for real, Gabriel?" The color in Victor's skin deepened. "He doesn't know what he's brought on himself!"

"I guess he does."

"What?" Victor scrunched his brow.

"You saw the message he held up at the end of the video? Like it's some sort of game?"

"Maybe he—"

"And why go through all that trouble of abducting the victims? Why use ice blocks and ropes? The biggest question—why videotape it and send it to the families?"

"To scare them?"

"He could have shot them on their streets, called the families and told them about their dead son or wives. It's much easier and less risky."

"Where are you going with this?" Victor frowned.

"I don't think this is personal."

Victor's disbelieving stare partnered with his loss of words.

Seconds later, he said, "I understand if you say that the victims aren't the real targets and the people who received the video are. A blind man can see that. But don't say it's not personal. He might have sent the video to make them suffer, like revenge. Who knows, maybe even to warn the DA or the commissioner in some way?"

"When you warn a person by killing someone close to that person, what does it mean, Captain?"

"That he has someone else to lose?"

"Yes. But the three who received the video didn't have anyone to lose except the ones who were murdered. This isn't a warning. Could be revenge. But seeing that he killed four people at the same time, I don't buy into that angle."

"And I'm guessing you have a theory?"

"Random killer. Did it occur to you that he's mentally unstable—"

Victor fake sighed. "Nah. Don't go there, Gabriel."

"I go where the possibilities take me."

"It's too soon to use your gut. Let's do it how we're taught to do it. Study the victims, their past, use forensics." Victor looked at the time on his phone—1:01 p.m.

His aversion to Gabriel's suspicion was well-founded. Most murderers were someone from the victim's past. Since the victim almost always knew the killer, the cases themselves weren't mysteries, not in the real sense. For this reason, random killings proved harder to solve. The chance that the murderer might escape increased as each hour passed. What Gabriel had suggested to Victor would mean a tedious and complicated line of investigation. Hoping he was wrong, he looked at his new team.

Detective Nash Parker and Gabriel had attended The Academy together. Nash served in the Narcotics Bureau, and then on the Gang Squad, both in the bad parts of the South Bronx. Four years ago, he was moved to the Homicide Unit in a better precinct. It covered docile neighborhoods, one of which was where Doug Bastian resided.

Among the other three detectives, two men and one woman, Gabriel didn't know who was handling Martha's case. The male and the female in the last seats were new recruits, according to the papers, so the man sitting across from Nash should be it. He had a pair of sunglasses hooked on the middle of his shirt.

The only person in an NYPD uniform was also the only person who chose to stand.

Wild Bill.

He was from 122nd and had a rep as a hard worker, but also as a hothead too fond of experimenting with batons and pimp-slapping suspects. His nickname wasn't terribly creative.

Victor pushed back his chair and stood. "Let's start."

The chatter died down, and Victor opened the discussion.

"This is Detective Nash Parker from the 76th Precinct. He's investigating Doug Bastian's murder. Doug lived with his father in Columbia Waterfront, Brooklyn, and it comes under Nash's precinct."

Detective Nash Parker's unusual six-feet-five-inches was backed with 280 pounds. With his blond ponytail and broad forehead that sported quite a few scars, he looked more like an '80s biker than a cop.

Victor turned left and addressed Sunshades. "This is Detective David Gustavo from 84th, Brooklyn Heights, where Martha Nelson lived." He paused. "This is a joint operation, and we're all going to play along without stepping on each other's toes. Both Nash and Gabriel are first-graders, but Gabriel's got more years in Homicide, so you all report to him." He tapped Gabriel's back.

"Oh! He's a detective?" David said. "I thought he made a mistake, thinking this was a soup kitchen or Salvation Army, and walked in." He snickered.

"Hmm. Now that we've solved the mystery of who the group's tool is, let's get down to the other." Victor signaled to Wild Bill.

He picked a stack of files from the table and distributed one to each person, before returning to his place.

Victor opened his copy. "These are the preliminary details, like where the victims went to school and college, where they lived, worked, and shopped, their phone numbers, their friends. Bill called the families and got them."

Bill gave an uncomfortable smile as everyone looked at him for a moment, before turning back to the captain.

"As for any evidence to make headway, it's zilch. We don't even know how the victims were abducted. At 7:00 p.m., Rita Hughes spoke on the phone with our commissioner, who at that time was in Chicago, at a meeting with his counterpart. Around 9:00 p.m., he called the landline because her phone was unreachable. No one picked up and he thought she'd gone to sleep. The next morning, Samuel Nelson woke him up and told him about the video. The commissioner found out that he'd also received one, and caught the next flight home." Victor looked up from the pages. "I got some new information a while back. The internet connection that the computer used to upload the video and email it to everyone? It came from Rita's phone. With that, the CCU found the location from where the emails were sent. It was an exit on I-95, from East Brunswick, New Jersey. I've dispatched SWAT there."

Gabriel reckoned that Highways weren't popular for their signal strength. Because of its quality, the massive video must have taken quite a while to upload. The murderer could have used one of the many free high-speed Wi-Fi hotspots in the city, but he chose a desolate area with poor network strength. It meant he knew the cops would find the spot where he'd uploaded it. And the inner city that provided good signal also had a lot of cameras and people to avoid. Highways didn't.

Taking all this into account, Gabriel decided they weren't dealing with a run-of-the-mill criminal, after all.

"SWAT is there now, searching the nearby buildings. But they were certain when they said there are no cameras at the exit or anywhere near it. Lucky, huh?"

Gabriel didn't believe it was luck, and he didn't think Victor did either. Their killer clearly possessed a certain amount of knowledge about criminal investigations. Cops all over the world hated the so-called CSI effect, where a criminal learned police methodologies to escape them.

"We'll operate with flexibility. There's no definite division of labor. We all do what we can to catch the killer. But we'd be fools if we didn't use our unique skills and experience." Victor looked at David. "Anything related to technology and CCTV must go through Detective Gustavo. He's got experience with them from when he did a stint in Computer Crimes. Detective Nash and Emma are in charge of canvassing and interviewing. And Bill?" Victor motioned toward the uniform. "You'll act as a link to our precinct and other departments. You are going to be the desk jockey in this."

Bill nodded solemnly.

"As soon as we find what kind of car the murderer used, we'll issue a BOLO. Until we get the bodies, until we get something to work on—and do pray we get something—it's going to be stabs in the dark."

Victor dismissed Bill to call the encircling counties and raise requests to notify them if they found four bodies with ligature marks.

When the door closed behind him, Victor said, "The reason I didn't even allow Peter inside the room is that he's not up to it. He's already undergone two bypasses."

Detective Lieutenant Peter Lamb had the highest clearance rate in the NYPD, pushing Gabriel to second place. Peter would turn sixty-three this week, the mandatory age for retirement. The younger Lamb inside the man, who'd worked in Robbery, Gang, Special Victims, and Homicide, still went around and pried information from detectives, after which he built his theories on them.

"He'll be mighty pissed," Emma said.

"He retires next week," Victor replied. "God forbid, but if we fail in this, we don't want him to feel responsible."

"That's right, Em. Let him have a few good days," Gabriel said, looking at the papers in his hands.

It was his idea to leave Peter out. Senior cops thought that if the juniors failed in their presence, then they were responsible for their failure. Questing for justice, standing up for little men, and protecting the city from its own grime wasn't Peter's cross to bear anymore.

"A little too sensitive, aren't you, Captain Ivansky?" David smirked.

Detective David Gustavo was a medium-sized Hispanic man with short curly hair and an attractive pear-shaped face. The sunglasses, Ray-Ban Aviators, were now in his hands.

According to the file, if it wasn't for David's sharp detective work in cases involving electronic evidence, he would have received the boot a long time ago.

"We're like that at the Rock, thank you," Victor said. "You're a second-grader, I hear?"

"Sharp hearing." David was still smirking.

"You ever wanna become a first-grader, David? My report in this investigation will go a long way in that. I can screw it up," Victor snapped his fingers, "like that. You're here because you are one of the best our city has to offer. So, act like it."

David's smile faded and he looked down.

"Mark and Laura," Victor called to the rookies in the back. "Detective Parker insisted you two come along for this. That's why you're here." Both looked at Nash, who winked at them.

So he had persuaded Victor to let him include his underlings, like how Gabriel had made him include Emma.

Gabriel looked at the team once again. He got Nash and Emma—a big bully and a small bully. Then David—the undisputed king of the not-very-magical Douche Land. Mark and Laura—a pair of inquisitive, squirrel-eyed probationers still battling pimples. Some team.

Victor's ringtone interrupted the discussion. He held a finger up and took the blaring device from his pocket. As he looked at the screen, he stiffened.

"Yes, boss," he answered. "No way… thirty minutes, tops." He hung up. "Commissioner's got another email."

"From the killer?" Nash said.

"Yes, but this time it's not just the commissioner." Victor spoke into his white knuckles, looking down. "Every major news network in New York got the same email."

"What does it say?" Gabriel asked.

"It's a list." Victor looked up at them, his face colorless. "A list of people he's killed so far."

Knight in Shining Armor

3/16/19. Mid-morning.

Years of hard work, discipline, and patience have served me the confection I'd been waiting so long for. Now that I'm just a few steps from my goal, let's hark back and marvel at my journey.

But the telephone on my desk intrudes.

I lift the receiver indolently with my thumb and forefinger until the ringing stops, and then drop it again—not this morning. I call my maladroit secretary and remind her about my *migraine*, ordering her not to route calls to me.

When I began my spree last year, I didn't *want* to leave any pattern for the police to discern a serial killer. If I did, I would've been forced to deal with the complete arsenal at their disposal, and I wasn't ready back then.

First, I needed training. I knew I couldn't just make up rules and regulations from books and imagination. I had to test them in the real world. I needed exercises in trapping, stunning, incapacitating, and killing people. I required practice at controlling my breath, heartbeat, and perspiration—all of them the side-effects of fear. Only then could I remove myself from the equation. After all, this killing business is merely a process, a means to my end. Once I'd ascended to this higher plane, I could concentrate on my actual goals and the opponents—police and justice.

I experimented, fixing errors and plugging holes in my observations, and gained an understanding of police investigations and human physiology. I acclimated to the sights, screams, and the stench.

Before Rita's group, the individuals who comprised my heterogeneous quarry were all unproductive members of society. They rejoiced in destroying the very fabric of their community's good image, so slaughtering these bipedal vermin didn't instigate clamant investigations.

Let's time travel to the beginning and reminisce about Léonie Böhm aka Cherry, my third victim, a sixteen-year-old pallid prostitute. Ah, Cherry. You're special to me because you were the first person I killed after so many years. A long pilgrimage into bookishness ended when you became my third step in the fifteen stepping-stones that will lead to my uncontested throne.

After dickering in half-murdered English and settling for five hundred dollars, you entered the car to spend the night with me. I know five hundred is a lot, but it isn't like I was actually gonna pay you or anything. My dear Cherry, you didn't talk much, did you? I don't remember hearing much of your throaty voice on our ride back to my place. When we arrived, you excused yourself for a moment to tinkle.

We sat down to dine, and then came the non-stop chatter. I really didn't need to know how your grandparents escaped the *oppressors* and left East Germany forever, as refugees, carrying only the family name with them. Whereas you tried to embrace a belief in their tragic heroism, all I saw were the urine trails of displaced weaklings who ran away from their problems with their tails tucked between their legs.

You told me about your family's desperate life in Eastern Europe, moving from hovel to hovel, surviving hunger, cold, and what have you, and how you were abducted. You weren't this loquacious during our car ride.

I went to the bathroom, and as I suspected, a tin foil powdered with fetid white dust glinted in the bathroom wastebasket. Drugs made you remember and tell the best parts of your life, didn't they? I wondered, if gypsy life was the best part, what would be the opposite? So I asked you, letting you live for another five minutes. You told me your story.

Your abductors forced you into addiction at the age of twelve, and then sold you into prostitution. Fat madams held you in diseased, drugged, and toxic-fume haunted brothels where Joe Six-Packs took away what little innocence you had left. Though by this time, you neither cared nor cried. You got used to living in that shithole of a country.

New York provided you with an oasis when a charterer bought your carcass and shipped it westward. Customers here were relatively clement, as you were just fifteen. At an age when most of our girls gossip about boys, eat burgers, and experience their most feathery first kiss, you were already chewed, digested, and defecated out of a devil's system.

Prostitutes aren't known for their veracity, but I believed your story. Your eyes inferred that even though your metabolism was barely functioning, you died a long time ago in a faraway land. If there is one thing I know, it's the dead's eyes.

Anyone else in my place would have teared up and given you a better chance at life, or at least more money than you wanted. In a philosophical way, I did give you more than you bargained for. By bashing in your head with a pipe wrench, I actually did you a favor. I saved you from your past horrors and pain, and a future full of more of the same. I became your knight in shining armor.

You fell forward, pulling the plate and half-eaten steak along on your way down. I either underestimated my strength or overestimated the endurance of your collagen and calcium, because in that one swing, half your skull caved in. Your exposed pinkish brain, which started oozing blackish red blood, didn't repulse me even though my heartbeat skyrocketed. I controlled it, telling myself this anxiety and fear were the real enemies that would make me slip, and practicing was the only way to destroy them, or at least bring them down to an imperceptible level.

I removed your clothes and washed your body cap-a-pie several times. I didn't want any fibers or specks of dust from my place on you. I might have even left my fingerprints on your skin. Then I cleaned your body with a sponge immersed in a special homemade chemical. I never bother to clip any of my victims' nails because I never gave them a chance to fight back. I'm the stealthiest predator on Earth.

I covered the car trunk with trashcan liners and threw you in. Drove you to the same spot I picked you up from, and took the same route that had the least CCTV cameras. Backed into an alley and jettisoned your body.

I drove back, your cell phone and its battery jittering on the dashboard. I didn't touch mine for hours—it was back home. I never take my phone whenever I'm doing something crime related. Cell phone masts are helping police track and catch criminals more often than bloodhounds these days.

I picked my next two victims from The City of Brotherly Love and Miami, and instead of a pipe wrench, I used a machete and a hammer.

I didn't stick to one particular modus operandi and signature. My knowledge of crime saved me, and my fear control worked like a charm. At my fifth victim in Florida, a gay illegal immigrant, I felt no fear.

Next practice was torture.

But why? A man strong enough to lift one hundred kilos could lift ten kilos with ease. Likewise, if a man could maintain a calm heartbeat when torturing people and taking apart human bodies, he could easily stay calm when merely killing without any blood or screams. When I finished this part of my training, I could bid farewell to anxiety and hurried heartbeats.

Now I know I didn't torture Rita's bunch *too* much—that would have had an opposite effect. It wouldn't have motivated anyone, but made them crazy with uncontrollable anger.

Then why did I practice torture?

Why do millionaires hoard more money than they'll ever need? Because pursuing money is what makes them go on. This purpose I've chosen means everything to me, and without it I would have died a long time ago. It stands on two legs—brains and cruelty. I've already siphoned everything there is to gain from books. Knowledge-wise, I'm at the top. But violence-wise, I am but a novice. I may not use my cruelty to its full extent, like how a billionaire wouldn't spend all his money, but still, it's essential for me to have it.

For my first practice in torture, I chose Atlanta and a Jamaican gang member called Froggy, who was indicted on several counts of murder. I tied him to a chair as he made angry promises, the most memorable being, "A lotta hurt comin' ya way, mon." I didn't think the half-wit could understand or appreciate the irony that was about to befall him. So, I smiled and patted him on his mohawk, then plugged the handheld sander into an outlet—

I'm yanked out from the nostalgic trance when my cell phone chimes. I look at it. Annie Jones has messaged, *Having lunch in our fav place. Come soon. I miss u. Eu amo você.*

I put the phone on silent mode and close my eyes, immersing myself back into the remembrance.

Where was I? Yes! A particular tenement in Atlanta that smelled of cannabis. Froggy's threats became driveling beggary, and then hoarse solicitations for a quicker death. The three hours of knowledge I gained from sanding him was quite stimulating. It smelled and tasted metallic.

I will admit that this lesson almost gave me a heart attack.

He wouldn't have resembled anything human if not for his skeleton. When police came around for his missing court hearings, they identified it only by DNA. And the case went nowhere. I *knew* the cops didn't want to bother, because to them it was all a *scum-killing-scum* scenario.

I hid my victims behind a plenitude of other crimes—gang violence, kinky violence, and redneck violence. My plan went like clockwork. The police, the FBI, even the ViCAP, which the BAU created for the exclusive purpose of stopping people like me—serial killers—didn't have an inkling I existed. To defeat it, I changed my modus operandi eight different times. As far as the police in different states and counties are concerned, there are eight different murderers at large, among a thousand others.

I completed the course last December. To control my fear when killing people, it took just three kills. But to control my fear in torturing them, it took five. Raspy cries, macabre scenes, or blood squirting on my face from snipped carotids no longer perturbed me.

The hard part was over. All I had left to do was find my last set of victims, for whom I've prepared myself all these years. Victims whose deaths will help me de-sanctify the hypocrisy known as *justice*. As per my plan, I need to kill people close to the commissioner, the DA, a prominent media person, and the common people. These four elements are the most critical components to solve any case and deliver justice. I should motivate them, unite them against me in their misery, and create the most proactive team.

And defeat it.

But I didn't know who those four victims would be. I searched the internet and found them in a night. Then I followed them around, learning their routines… you know, the typical reconnaissance. It took me three months. And at last, I made my move yesterday. The past is over. Now, for the future.

My other phone vibrated. Rosa had messaged, *Got the 2K. Muito obrigado!*

Should I ignore her as I had Annie? I type, *não há de que*, and hit send. I will need her if things, shall we say, as the uncouth and the unread so colorfully put it, *go south*. There are still things to do, such as delivering four foul-smelling piggies to the people of NYC.

Now that I've prospered from all my practice and achieved 90 percent of my goal, it's time to let the police and the world know about me.

When the largest police force in the United States gets all the help it needs and still fails to find me, I will have achieved my first goal of becoming a criminal legend. I will achieve my second goal when the world witnesses their defeat and learns that justice is a mirage. A sanctimonious lie. A felonious fallacy.

I take a bag that contains Rita's laptop, cell phone, and a brand-new black hoodie. I rise, open the door, and step outside.

It's time for the New Yorkers to meet their scariest denizen.

Chapter 7

March 16, 2019. 02:45 P.M.

Victor was wrong, but Gabriel didn't feel good about being right. In fact, he never wanted to be as wrong about something as he wanted to be about his suspicion that the murders might not be personal.

The second email the commissioner received contained a list of six people that the sender claimed he'd killed. Following this, Raymond said they should meet the mayor, and he ordered Victor and Gabriel to join him for the meeting.

Raymond arrived before them—City Hall was just a short walk from 1PP, five minutes tops. He was holding a booklet containing the information they had thrown together about the six murders, when Victor and Gabriel got there. Victor relieved him of it and delved into it, clearly hoping to find anything that might help them.

The mayor made them wait after they went inside, and informed his secretary about their appointment. Ten minutes of continuous silence in the reception shattered when Raymond's phone rang.

He listened to the caller and stared at Gabriel; his jaw pulsating and nostrils flared. Then he hung up.

"It's… it's the tech team," he said in disbelief. "The second email he sent us? He sent it from my building."

That was ballsy, but also stupid. The commissioner's office was one of the most surveyed places in the city. Anti-vandal CCTVs covered the structure on all four sides.

Meeting with the mayor could wait.

* * *

Victor was the only one catching his breath when they got to 1PP's security room. An old uniformed man who watched the video feeds—*Carlos*, his nametag read—came to their aid. With the time Raymond had received the video as a reference point, they divided and searched the two rows of big TVs.

The search didn't take long.

A thin man in a black hoodie entered the display of the last screen in the mid-column. He was carrying a silver laptop on his side. The hoodie, which looked new compared to the jeans that hung low on his boney hips, covered the better part of his head. He stopped some ten feet from the camera and unfolded the laptop. He balanced it on his left forearm while supporting the screen with his palm. He pressed the spacebar with his right thumb, and the display woke up. As he rubbed his fingers over the touchpad, the shapes of the contents inside the display changed.

Once he was done, he snapped the laptop shut, turned and walked out the same way he'd come in. Besides his pale face and week-old dirty blond beard, Gabriel could see brown stains on his jeans. They were the kind of stains someone got if they slept on park benches or in subway stations and bus depots. Gabriel had firsthand experience with them.

The man was a street dweller.

Carlos confirmed what Gabriel had feared. The hoodie was called Bones, and he was indeed a local homeless man. No other name. Even Bones couldn't remember his real name, thanks to all the years of crack and meth.

Carlos picked up the receiver of a landline telephone and dialed an extension.

Gabriel and Carlos went outside and waited. Twenty minutes later, a uniform dragged Bones along by one of his thin arms. He carried a laptop in the other.

"He lives around here?" Gabriel asked.

"You could say that. Bones used to be a meth head. Miranda and I—she's the night shift woman in the kiosk, by the way—we let him sleep in the park. He's pinky promised he won't use again. Isn't that right, Bones?" The officer winked at Gabriel and turned his attention to the stickman, who was concentrating on the ground. "You took something that don't belong to you?" His grip on Bones's arm stiffened. Bones shook his head, although Gabriel didn't know which question he was answering.

Carlos took Bones to the security room.

"Is he the only person who sleeps here?" Gabriel asked.

"One of a few," the officer replied. "It's not exactly legal, but I don't mind letting them in as long as they sleep without causing any trouble."

"You noticed anyone watching them? Following Bones?"

"Following a homeless junkie?" The officer made a face as if Gabriel's question didn't make any sense at all.

"Never mind." Gabriel excused himself and went back in.

Everyone in the security room was waiting for him. He signaled Victor to begin as he closed the door behind him.

Bones sat on a metal chair, while the others stood. It's an old police technique to constrict the suspect's personal space and induce a false sense of danger to make them more forthcoming.

Victor asked Bones how he came to possess the laptop.

"A Mister came to me at the other spot where I sleep and shook me up. Then—"

"You remember his face?" Victor said.

"Yes. Viking beard and cool glasses."

When they eventually get the guy, Bones's eyewitness statement wouldn't hold water in court, not an addict's, but they could still find the man. But Gabriel didn't invest much hope in Bones. It would be a miracle if the druggie, whose fried brain didn't even remember its own name, saw the same person that day and identified him.

"What happened then?" Victor asked.

"Mister gave me a hundred and told me I gotta go to this building." Bones pointed the floor. "Go near the left side wall and—"

"He said left, *specifically*?" Gabriel said.

"Yes." Bones's head bobbled.

"But you went right," Victor said.

"No, man. See that's left, and I went there," Bones pointed to the right.

"That's because now you're facing the—" Victor let out a huge breath. "Forget it. What else did he say?"

"To open the gadget and click the green button on the screen that said *Send*. If I do, I'll be eligible for two more hundreds."

"You didn't ask him what happens if you press the button?" Victor said. "Thought about something going boom?"

"Nah, man. I ain't no stupid. The gadget can't hold no bomb. Too thin. Plus, Mister was white. So don't worry about no *booms*." Bones used air quotes with his fingers and seemed proud of his answer.

No one volunteered to correct his racial stereotyping or misconception about bombs.

"He came in a car?" Victor asked.

"No. One of them tourist types, I guess."

"And why do you guess that?"

"It's not very cold out, right? But Mister's wearing gloves. So I figured he's not from around here."

"Then what did you do?" Victor massaged his temples.

"I went back, but Mister wasn't there no more. I gotta sell that gadget, man."

"We're taking it."

"How much?"

"How about not locking you up?"

"Man! This is brutality. I have rights. That's my property."

"No, it's not. He gave it to you, asshole. Don't you remember?" Victor spewed. Most cops hated druggies more than they hated murderers.

"Let's not forget about the phone, Mr. Bones," Gabriel said.

"How did you—what phone? I don't know about no phone," Bones's dry mouth said, but his fidgety feet told a contradictory tale.

"We don't have time for this." Gabriel rubbed his eyes with his knuckles. "The internet you used to send out that email came from a phone. A phone your Mister must have given you, along with the… gadget."

"No, man… you are wrong. I don't—"

"I'm going to frisk you, and if I find it on you, I'll lock you up. How does a week without your poison sound?"

Bones thought things through, apparently, and inserted his right hand into his front jeans pocket. He took out a blue Motorola and placed it on the table.

Raymond's face betrayed desolation when Gabriel looked at him. Rita's phone.

Gabriel turned to Bones. "That hoodie looks new. Where'd you get it?"

Meth heads were real pieces of work. Bones hopped up, the metal chair screeching on the floor. Carlos threw his right hand to his holster. With angry fingers, Bones dug into the bottom of the hoodie and pulled it up. He fought out of it and threw it on the floor. He seemed thinner with just a dirty orange T-shirt that read *Shame on you girls. I'm still single.*

"Fine. Take it, too!" Bones spat.

"What the hell!" Carlos said.

"You want everything Mister gave me, right? You thieves!" Bones tried to storm out, but Carlos blocked him with ease.

"Why would he give you a hoodie?" Gabriel said.

"To keep me warm at nights. Mister told me he can't stand human suffering. He's not like you lot. Good man. God bless him."

Since nothing was left in it to be contaminated, Gabriel took the now-inside-out hoodie from the floor. He dropped it on the table and spread it out. There was something on its back.

A thick white vertical line had been drawn in the middle, flanked by two pairs of fat dots.

It vaguely resembled a middle finger.

Chapter 8

March 16, 2019. 03:54 P.M.

When he won the election in 2014, Taylor Roth was the youngest person ever to be elected mayor. According to The Economist, 2015 saw the lowest number of homicides since 1940, making New York the tenth safest major city in the world. That was a big deal, considering the rise of population in the last seventy-five years.

Due to his political acumen and the results of his policies, which the city wore like badges, the people re-elected him in November 2017. Gabriel remembered seeing Taylor's lively face on posters, flyers, and TV shows.

But now he looked helpless. Who was Gabriel kidding? He felt helpless, too. It wasn't like he was Superman. Even if he were, it wouldn't do much good in catching this murderer. Superheroes might save the world from alien invaders or impish gods, but when it came to battling serial killers, they couldn't do a whole lot. The responsibility to catch them fell on good ol' cops.

After offering condolences, Taylor broached the topic that he'd set up the meeting to address. Raymond updated him on everything that had taken place so far, including the latest drama with Bones.

"Is the list real, Mr. Hughes? Not a wild loony trying to grab his fifteen minutes?"

"It checks out. The victims' names, the places where their bodies were found, and the dates… they all match." It'd been only ten hours since Raymond had received that video, but his face looked like he hadn't slept for a week.

"You must take a few days off, Mr. Hughes. You know you don't feel well." It was as if Taylor had read Gabriel's thoughts.

"I'm fine, thank you. I'll grieve when I'm done putting this feral dog down." While Raymond's tone conveyed a warning, his eyes revealed an expression similar to a hurt animal licking a fresh wound.

"I'm sorry. I'm just trying to help you," Taylor said. "Now about the other problem. People who were wrongly accused and convicted for this man's crimes. Where do we stand on that?"

"A little silver lining here," Victor said. "According to the list, nobody was arrested in our state. But he murdered only one in New York before yesterday. A prostitute who went by the name of Cherry. But the states of Pennsylvania and Florida aren't so lucky. Pennsylvania convicted one Martin Brown for the murder of Alisha Webb, and Florida convicted a Tony Freeman for the murder of Luis Garcia." He looked up from the booklet, and after getting no questions from anyone, he continued. "Our killer's operational area stretches from New York to Florida, and then from there to Ohio, and from Ohio back to New York. The problem is that there's no pattern here. It's not like he traveled in one big tour."

"Then his profession must have taken him to these places," Taylor said. "Can't we use that to find him?"

"Unfortunately, no," Victor said. "Many jobs require people to travel—bus drivers, pilots, musical bands, train conductors, to name a few. We can't use that to find him, but only to be positive of his guilt when we have him in custody."

"I see."

"Rest assured, he's all over the eastern side of our country, and in a random way, either by purpose or by blind luck."

"I don't think he's leaving anything to luck or chance," Gabriel said. "Before yesterday, he murdered six people in less than four months. That's one every"—he shut his eyes for a few seconds, before opening them—"twenty days. But we didn't even know he existed until he told us himself. This person… he's planned everything and doesn't count on luck."

"Planned everything?" Victor said. "Where do you get ideas like this?"

"It's not crazy, Captain. You can't believe it's pure luck that he got away this many times from different states. He may or may not be from New York, but he must have grown up in some place. And if he's confident enough to leave this place, go out of the town—or the city he's used to—and kill someone without getting caught, then he's planned his actions and knows what he's doing."

"Yeah, I agree," Taylor said. "He doesn't seem to have what you call a *comfort zone*. So maybe he is a long hauler? A trucker serial killer wouldn't be new."

"He isn't a serial killer," Gabriel muttered.

"What?!" Victor said. "At our morning meeting, you said it's not personal and hinted that we may have a psychopath on our hands, didn't you?"

"Psychopathic killer? No question. A serial killer? Yes, he fits the definition. But if you ask me if he is one… I don't know, Captain. I have my doubts."

"What doubts?"

"Why'd he murder six people in such a short span? Most infamous serial killers weren't this fast when they were active. It's not like they couldn't murder more. Stacking numbers isn't their goal. They take their time to enjoy it. They store the moment in their disturbed brain, savor it. And only when they can't use that worn-out memory anymore, they stalk their next victim. It's usually months between each murder. But this person struck every three weeks, like an exercise."

"What if he needs it sooner?" Taylor said. "He could be a crazy guy with uncontrollable urges."

"If that's the case, he'd be the type of man who struggles to keep his emotions in check. It's tough, if not impossible, for him to be in control of his actions. So he wouldn't have been cautious, which our guy's proved that he's nothing but. Twice. I'd even say he's meticulous."

"Maybe he's following some screwed-up ritual," Taylor said, "and it makes him kill people at regular intervals?"

"I'd agree, if there was one. I haven't gone through the list yet, but the captain made a start on it." Gabriel turned to Victor. "Did you find a similarity between any of them?"

"No, I didn't."

"That's what I thought. If there was a ritual, then these six murders would've been highlighted by ViCAP. The feds would've come into play a long time ago, as soon as he murdered his third victim."

"Yes, boss," Victor said. "He's got a point. The Violent Criminal Apprehension Program is a federal database that—"

"—searches for patterns in violent murders and sexual crimes across the nation," Taylor said. "I know what it is, thank you. And I prefer Mr. Mayor or Mr. Roth."

Paying no attention to the rebuke, Gabriel resumed. "As ViCAP didn't raise any red flags, it makes me think that those six murders may have different MOs and different signatures. That's not what happens when someone is killing people for some sick ritual, as you said. It's another reason to entertain the possibility that he may not be a serial killer."

"How are we going to proceed if we don't even know what we're dealing with?" Taylor asked, irritation creeping into his voice.

"Honestly, we have no idea," Gabriel replied. "We've got the victimology—that's where we usually start. If what we think is true, that these are random killings, I don't think that line of investigation will produce results." He turned to Victor.

"This guy doesn't give out much hope, does he?" He smiled.

Victor gave an equally fake smile. "No. But he is the best you're gonna get in New York. Plus, he's the only person in this room with an actual degree in criminal psychology, unlike those of us who play Criminal Minds. So, there's that."

Sometimes Gabriel wanted to grab that shiny head of Victor's and kiss it.

"Are you going to skip the usual procedures?" Taylor said, between his teeth.

"Hell no," Victor replied. "We've scheduled interviews. We're looking into CCTVs, trying to find what car the murderer used to abduct them."

"Forensics?"

"There isn't much they can do now, not without the bodies of the last four. We're taking measures to find them. In the meantime, we've requested forensics to search the houses of the victims. And the computer nerds aren't much help, because this guy used Mrs. Hughes's phone and laptop to contact us and the news."

"Any other way?"

"This list," Gabriel said.

"What about it?"

"It may prove to be his downfall."

"I'm sorry to be skeptical, but with what you've just told me, this guy appears to be smart. Could he have left any evidence?"

"Oh, he is smart," Gabriel said, "but no one is born smart. Learning from mistakes makes people smart, doesn't it?"

"I don't follow."

"It's possible that he's not giving the names of all his victims."

"What? Why?" Taylor seemed worried, but for the wrong reasons.

He just wanted to save his own skin.

"Because doing something serious and getting away clean is hard," Victor said. "We can't always get a conviction, but we usually find out who did it."

Taylor looked like he was beginning to grasp the point.

"Killing someone without leaving evidence is almost impossible," Gabriel said. "When you do that many times over, you're bound to slip at least once."

"But how can we find where he slipped? If he's smart, then he'd know where he's made a mistake. He wouldn't have included that name on the list, just like you said. How are you going to find that victim?"

"Not sure, sir," Gabriel said, "but he's slipped somewhere. That's where we'll find a trail. In the past. I don't have a plan now, but I'll work on it."

Taylor turned to Victor. "Is that doable? You told me he's all over the map. I won't be surprised if he's murdered someone in Hawaii or Alaska. It could be the place where he left the evidence. But it's impossible to find that victim, isn't it?"

That was stretching it a bit. So far, the killer had stuck to the East Coast.

"And you, Detective...?" Taylor looked at Gabriel.

"Gabriel Chase, sir."

"You told me he has six different MOs, and he also kills people in short intervals. So he's more like an invisible serial killer on steroids. How do we know he's stopped now and not going to send us a new email next week? For all we know, he could be killing someone right now, and we'd be none the wiser." Taylor turned to Raymond. "You informed the FBI, Mr. Hughes?"

"I've ordered the Major Case Squad to call the FBI's field head, Conor Lyons, and coordinate with him. They are officially in charge of the case, and they'll be handling the chaos with the press, too. But like I told you over the phone, I'm using one more team to investigate."

"That's good. And I'm not going to question your methods. But don't get in each other's way."

What the mayor meant was Raymond's team shouldn't get in Conor's way.

They all stood up and shook hands.

Chapter 9

March 16, 2019. 04:32 P.M.

Raymond looked lost as he made his way back to his fort. Once he was out of sight, Victor and Gabriel opened the booklet and skimmed through the six murders. They couldn't find a pattern. More detailed reports and case histories would be needed, and Victor said he would arrange them.

Gabriel declined the lift back to the precinct, saying he was going to talk to Noah Smith, his assistant district attorney friend, and try to learn about Steve or Doug Bastian. But that wasn't the only reason he was meeting him.

Even if his phone's notification hadn't reminded him that morning that it was his friend Casey's anniversary, Gabriel wouldn't have forgotten it. And he would never miss his routine on this day, no matter what, because Gabriel blamed himself for Casey's untimely death. Shame and guilt had kept him from visiting Casey in his final resting place. So, he made excuses to see Noah on that day every year, because Noah was Casey's brother, and they looked alike. It was Gabriel's way of apologizing to Casey.

Gabriel headed toward the DA's office, cutting through Foley Square.

* * *

When he saw the Triumph of the Human Spirit sculpture, it brought a pang of heartache, and memories of Elizabeth, his ex-wife—also his only true love—flooded his mind. It was a black granite statue shaped like antlers, the plinth referencing the Middle Passage during the era of the Atlantic slave trade.

Foley Square was cultural. It exhibited things that reminded humanity of its past mistakes, the horrors they'd brought, and the human perseverance that survived them. Walking through that place, Gabriel couldn't help but remember his tarnished former self.

A month after graduation, he applied for the police job he'd been dreaming of since childhood because of his father. He should have stayed a beat officer, serving people. But a year later, he'd taken the exams and gotten promoted to detective on the Homicide and Robbery Squad.

Then his life took a turn for the worse. In his second week, when he visited his first crime scene, he was introduced to the works of real monsters.

A middle-aged woman and her seventeen-year-old daughter lay face down in a pool of gelatinous blood. Their heads had tiny bullet holes, but the small caliber rounds didn't kill them. It just rendered them unconscious. To prevent the wastage of lead, the robber had taken a kitchen knife to finish the job. And to be sure that he did it right this time, he hacked at their necks until he almost decapitated them. Gabriel was sick throughout that day and the next. Weak stomach. Weaker heart.

It angered him. Saddened him. As the truth about the dark side of people sank in, he grew restless. Unlike crimes of passion, such criminals calculated the loss of human lives, in premeditated murders. Gabriel vowed to fight these deviants and bring each and every one of them to their knees.

But reality brought *him* to his knees. Though he was a boxing champion in college, he was no match for the sucker punches the job threw at him. Regardless of his dedicated pledge, not every murder could be solved.

Unsolved cases piled up and reached double figures. To drown the images of dead people and their voices crying for justice, he experimented with the same self-medicating quackery cops all over the world have subscribed to since the policing profession first began—the bottle.

Since he had to reheat the cases that grew cold, he spent more time in his office and less time at home. He didn't give himself time to even shave or bathe. Instead of spending the time on what he'd started to call *vanity*, he spent it on trying to find justice for a child who'd lost her father to someone else's greed.

During these times, Gabriel looked through Liz, the high school sweetheart he'd married a year ago. He never heard her pleas. She stopped existing altogether. A few months after living in this craziness, Liz packed her bags one day and left him. She was an iron-willed, no-bullshit kind of woman. Gabriel begged her to come home by promising he wouldn't drink again. She believed him and returned.

But the lack of sleep caused by cold cases, and the alcohol proved stronger than the promise. He could have chosen to leave the job, but he didn't. The police department hadn't stepped in, because he never drank during the 18-20 hours he spent in the office.

When Liz left him for the eighth time, she left for good. That she came back the first seven times said how much she loved him. She never responded to his messages or calls, but her lawyer sent him the papers. Without rebelling, he signed them while his tears fell.

Times got worse. No matter how hard he tried, he couldn't get all the murderers, and more predators roamed free. Since he had no one back home, he took to sleeping on sidewalks, stone benches, and overpasses when he couldn't drag his inebriated body home. The blackouts got worse, too. Sometimes he'd wake up in a place he didn't recognize or remember visiting. Places he wished he could forget. Every week, he reached new lows.

One morning, he woke up in a hospital bed, and he had no idea how he got there. The doctor said a woman dialed 911 when she saw Gabriel passed out beside a dumpster, shivering under a newspaper blanket. Fearing that he was dying, she'd made the call.

He did almost die from alcohol poisoning.

While lying in the hospital bed, Rita slapped him. When he looked at her, she slapped again. Then the crying began. Noah hugged Rita and consoled her. He looked angry, his eyes watery. Gabriel's other best friends, Stanley and Liam, were also there. Stanley was a forensic scientist, and Liam was SWAT.

Rita wiped her eyes and sat on a chair beside the bed. She took out a photo album from her bag, opened it and placed it on the comforter above Gabriel. She turned the pages and showed him the pictures of his childhood and teenage years. Most were taken with Liz in his arms—at pool parties, barbecues, carnivals, Coney Island, and such.

Rita said, "You remember this?" as she turned the pages.

He beamed with happiness in every photo. Innocent and hopeful.

When the album ended, she returned it to the bag. Then she retrieved a small mirror from it and held it in front of Gabriel, her hands trembling.

He hadn't looked in a mirror for months, so the creature he saw shocked him. Its head was a big mess of chaotic hair. The eyes didn't look innocent anymore, not with the dark circles under them. Its face was bloated and sported a few light scars. There was something grave and sad about the shaggy creature. A disowned beggar couldn't have looked more pitiful.

"Can you do me a favor, sweetie?" Rita caressed the cheek she'd slapped.

Gabriel couldn't talk, so he nodded.

"Please, just kill yourself. I'll get you a straight razor or a rope. Or maybe mix poison in your favorite pasta and feed you. I'll even steal Ray's gun, shoot you and go to jail if you are too scared to do it yourself. Anything is better than seeing my boy ruined like this." She gripped him with all her strength and wept.

The sound of a mother's cry is insufferable, even for homicide cops. Gabriel closed his eyes. Rita's white sweater absorbed a few teardrops that escaped his untrimmed thicket of a beard.

* * *

"The dead never leave you alone, Gabriel," said his father, Joshua, once he took Gabriel to his house.

Not Gabriel's abandoned den, but an actual home.

"There's no way out?" Gabriel said.

"It's an occupational hazard for detectives who have a heart. A disadvantage in this work, but what can you do? It's congenital."

"Just tell me how to stop them, Dad." Gabriel grabbed the hair above his temples. "When I close my eyes, I see dead bodies, maggots, flies, white eyes. I'm scared that I'm going crazy."

"This fear of losing your mind is not you. It's the alcohol speaking. Don't worry. Your body will cleanse itself, and this panic you feel now will pass. But the ghosts won't." Joshua took out a can of Skoal Bandits Mint.

He had been dipping tobacco as long as Gabriel could remember.

"You know what makes us good at this job?"

Gabriel didn't answer because he didn't feel like he was good.

"Murder brings out primal pain. Unlike robberies or assaults, the agony brought to the families of the victims is final. There is no recovery from it. And us Chases, we are idiosyncratic in our deep empathy. Most cops—the smarter ones, that is—leave the cold cases after a certain period.

But to us, it's never numeric, not just another unsolved murder tossed onto the pile of unsolvable cases." Joshua cleared his throat. "We understand that mothers hug their daughters' teddy bears, waiting for us. Fathers cry themselves to sleep with the taste of cold gun oil in their mouths, waiting for us. So many indirect victims, people—shells, really—clinging to life, waiting for us to bring them justice. It's a huge responsibility. But what can we do?" He scoffed. "We couldn't move the case forward. The trail's gone cold. The resulting frustration, after corrupting our cognition, seeps into the subconscious and manifests as petrifying nightmares."

Joshua was one hundred percent on the mark.

Gabriel's eyes welled. "You mean, if I don't leave my job, I'm doomed forever?"

"Can I tell you a secret, boy? I never slept peacefully since the day I came to know about Lolly. I chose the same poison you chose, and I lost important things in life, as you did. Your mother left me, like how Ms. Elizabeth left you. It's like they say, isn't it? Like father, like son?" Joshua gave a dry chuckle with no humor, took two pouches from the Skoal tin and buried them between his gums and cheeks. "Anyways, I couldn't concentrate on my job. I was too focused on that godless robbing bastard. Before Lolly, I had the highest clearance rate in the city. You know what happened then?"

Gabriel did.

"My score dropped. What does that mean?"

"More murderers escaped."

"And the reason for that was my inability to turn away from Lolly. I couldn't let go, so I quit my job because I'd become inept. Your mother left me and I had to stop drinking to take care of you. In a way, you saved me." He paused and smiled at Gabriel. "Whatever I did, I didn't stop chasing Lolly."

"I know, Dad." Gabriel let go of his hair and rested his elbows on his thighs. "You're hurt, too."

"Doesn't matter. I'm still chasing Lolly, even though no one's heard from him for years. I'd continue to do so, come hell or high water. Even if I die chasing him, I'll die fulfilled."

"What's the point in all this if we're failing?"

"To be a martyr, Gabriel. And as cops, our religion is goodness. The point is to accept and live a life of suffering to ease others' pain. To bring as much justice and comfort as we can into the lives of people who were wronged. But you're no martyr. You're trying to escape pain instead of accepting it."

"Wh-wha-what do you want me to do?" Gabriel shouted and punched the armrest as hard as he could, tears falling without his consent. "You think I-I-I like dr-drinking? I-I…" He clenched his teeth and swallowed, giving up.

His speech impediment showed up only when a storm brewed inside him. Sometimes, he wished he didn't feel any emotions. His empathy for the murdered, lack of sleep, even his choppy articulation all stemmed from his inability to stop being oversensitive.

"That's real simple, son." Joshua spat brown liquid into a coffee cup. "Either you leave the booze, face the ghosts, and accept pain… or leave the job because you're incapable of doing it. You'll do more harm staying on the job with your alcoholic brain than leaving it."

Gabriel felt his old man's unwavering eyes on his down-bent head.

"What we do, it's not something you do for money. It's a cause. Can you handle it, son? I mean handle this unappreciated job that gives you nightmares? Handle it without booze? For the sake of justice and goodness?"

Gabriel didn't answer. He avoided eye contact.

"Yeah, I didn't think so. Deep down, you're a chicken. A kid cowering inside a blanket to keep the ghosts away. But the ghosts always stay near the edge of the bed, questioning you with their dead eyes. Except your ghosts are real, and your blanket is Smirnoff." Joshua spat again into the coffee cup. "Cowardly boozer."

This time, Gabriel's tears didn't fall. His eyes burned, but they were dry when he finally met his father's eyes.

"One day." He dug his nails into the armrest. "Mark my words. One day, I'll quit drinking."

And Gabriel did. Starting from that day, that moment, he began to create himself anew. With plenty of help along the way.

Rita made him promise to attend meetings, and she supervised the schedules. Every night, she called to check up on him. The two times he relapsed, she came to his apartment and sobered him up. She knew he was drinking to get some sleep, and she destroyed that sleep with a bucket of cold water whenever he got it with alcohol.

On some particularly dark days, he'd stand embarrassed at the counter of a liquor shop. His head would hang from the weight of disappointment. But he knew what he had to do. Just a second of rash action would save him. As soon as he opened his apartment door, he'd run to the kitchen and empty the bottle into the sink. He did it more than a dozen times, and every time he wasted the booze, he felt a little stronger.

With the support he got from his father, godmother, and his group, he achieved temperance. His body became healthy, thanks to the boxing he'd picked up again, and his bloated face started to look fresh. He kept his beard and outer appearance as a reminder of what he would become if he ever touched alcohol again. That was the reality of addiction. There was no permanent cure for it. All it took was just one moment of weakness, and bam! You were at the bottom of society again. For this reason, he wore the same-colored clothes he'd had on when he almost died in the cold street.

He finally learned to suffer the pain and to keep the ghosts at bay without any medicine. More than anything, he learned about the dynamic nature of his cause—justice.

He couldn't enforce it every time some poor person was wronged. Life was unfair like that.

* * *

His mind boomeranged to the present as he climbed the steps of One Hogan Place, the DA's office. Gabriel paced along the broad corridor and stopped in front of an open door. He knocked and entered his friend's office.

Noah, distinguished by three-day stubble, bitten-off nails, and ruffled blond hair, wore a wrinkled suit. He belonged to that category of hyperactive caffeine lovers who looked perpetually stoked and untidy. To those who knew he preferred coffee over food, his slim physique didn't come as a surprise.

"I called you as soon as I saw the news." Noah rose and hugged Gabriel.

After a hard clasp, he let go and sniffled. A glassy layer of water filmed the blue of his irises.

"I am sorry, man. I know how close you and Rita were."

"Let's not talk about that, Noah. Not now."

"I-I don't… fine…" Noah looked at the floor and nodded. "I guess you're here to ask about the DA?"

"We want to question him, but he isn't reachable." Gabriel perched on Noah's table. "His wife said that we could meet him this evening." He puffed from his inhaler.

"Are you ever going to stop doing that?"

Gabriel shrugged.

"She's not with him anymore." Noah sat in his chair.

"So I've heard. But she said she'll make Steve see us."

"That's what she said? *Make* him?" Noah's face became stiff.

Loyalty to his mentor went up a notch and triggered a defensive response where none was needed. Anger had always been Noah's Achilles' heel, but it revealed itself only after Casey's death. So Gabriel blamed himself for Noah's anger issues, too.

"No, man, it's not like that. She said she'll somehow do it. She's sad as well. Doug was her kid, too."

"Oh… that's right…" Noah's voice dropped, and his features softened.

"Enemies?" Gabriel asked.

"You're joking."

"Enemies resourceful enough to pull something like this?"

Noah thought for a moment, and then gave him a name that every cop in the NYPD had heard of.

Terry Carvalho, street name Hercules, had begun his act as a run-of-the-mill gangster. Then he became one of the most dangerous criminals in New York. Steve Bastian, back then, an administrative assistant, beat Terry with RICO and helped the city banish its most notorious menace. There were rumors of Terry living like a king inside Attica—a supermax correctional facility where the system locked up the worst of the worst, including Son of Sam.

Noah said Terry had appeared before the parole board the week before. But the motion was denied with a lot of *not-very-official* persuasion from Steve. That might have opened the old wounds and encouraged a final shot at revenge.

Gabriel bought into it with a half-hearted, "Yeah."

"You don't think it's him?" Noah lifted an eyebrow.

"I can't say that. I'll look into it."

"But?"

"Doug was killed to hurt Steve. That much is clear. But what about the other nine?"

"Don't tell me! We're dealing with a serial killer?" Noah asked. "Man, do we still have those?"

"We do. Long Island Killer, Daytona Beach Killer, and hundreds of unsolved highway murders. It seems like we'll always have those." Gabriel hesitated. "I have an idea. You shouldn't think I'm crazy."

"Sorry, pal, too late for that."

"The six people he killed before these four were social rejects. Victor and I, we were reading their profiles—"

"Victor?"

"Yeah, my captain. So anyway, these people are what we call *high-risk victims*, the kind of people who don't get attention from the cops. Those who aren't missed and are easily accessible. You get the idea. But from the seventh, that changes. Rita, the police commissioner's wife. Martha, the wife of a media giant. Harry, a celebrity. And Steve was the most powerful of them all. Can you see the pattern?"

"The killer shifted from killing nobodies?" Noah said, more to himself than to Gabriel.

"And?"

"He killed people who are—I'm sorry—who were related to important people."

"I guess he was warming up to these four victims all along."

"I can see that, but I can't believe it. Why would he want to bring that kind of attention to himself?"

"I don't know."

"So, what you gonna do now?"

"The usual. We're following our routine, looking for evidence. Let's see where it takes us. While on the subject, could you give me a list of criminals Steve Bastian pissed off? Recent prosecutions, motions filed against parole applicants, and their criminal status in the city?"

"Yeah, yeah, sure." Noah switched on his PC. Ten minutes later, he said, "Done."

The printer was smooth and soundless. The papers warm in Gabriel's hand.

"Thanks a lot, Noah."

"*Thanks?* Are you kidding me? You and Steve, you two are like..." Noah's eyes became glassy again.

Gabriel understood his pain, because Steve was to Noah what Raymond was to Gabriel.

"How is Mr. Smith?" Gabriel asked.

"You know, doing as good as a man with one kidney in an old people's home can do," Noah said, in a low voice. "Leave that. Have you eaten?"

"Not yet."

"I understand that hunger is the last thing on your mind right now, but you're going to eat first thing when you leave here." Noah looked at his watch. "It's almost five. You can't function on an empty stomach."

Gabriel got up from the table.

"And, Gabe?"

Gabriel stopped at the doorway. He didn't turn around because he knew what Noah was going to say. He heard it every year.

"It's not your fault."

Gabriel left the building. He walked to Foley Square again and sat on a park bench sprinkled with wet, yellow leaves. The seat offered him an unhampered view of the Triumph of the Human Spirit. He called Detective Nash Parker and told him to meet him in the park. They had a meeting scheduled with Samuel and his secretary who'd reported Martha missing.

After he hung up, he rested his head back, closed his eyes, and thought about the case. Emma said it could be Lolly. Could it really be him? It was the first time Lolly had ever been shown on TV. No news channel had access to Lolly's crimes—the FBI made sure of that—so how did Samuel get it? Did Samuel bring this upon himself? Like most detectives, he found himself wishing for a time machine. He needed the answer to one simple question—what exactly happened the previous day?

Chapter 10

March 15, 2019. 11:32 A.M.

Ashley was lying on the mesh backrest of her office chair, beside Samuel. His laptop sat on the table, playing the preview she had put together for the seven o'clock news. Every time she examined the horrible murder clip, her repulsion intensified. Black bile bloomed in her stomach and tendrils of melancholy climbed up to her throat.

But her seventy-year-old boss, a long-sufferer of cardiovascular problems, watched the heart-stopping footage with ease. In fact, he was ecstatic, and although she had worked with the Daily Herald for fourteen years, she could recall only a handful of instances where she had seen him the way he was that afternoon.

The reason for his happiness was the same as the one that made her sick. The fat old Santa had finally done it. He'd gone after and procured what was claimed to be unattainable—the CCTV recording of a bank robbery perpetrated in Bristol, Connecticut, which left one dead and one gravely injured. The bloodbath morphed into a national sensation because it marked the re-entry of the most notorious bank robber in the history of super-violent bank robbers—the man the media had called Lolly.

Like other news networks, the Daily Herald had tapes of interviews with the victims and their families, but not any exclusive content. This video could be called exclusive because even though the FBI credited Lolly with more than thirty robberies, no ordinary person had ever seen an actual recording of any of his crimes.

The video was five minutes long. The robbers, wearing Halloween masks, starred in it for just two minutes and seventeen seconds. For Ashley, who battled perpetual bouts of anxiety, which sometimes brought along its dreadful minion of panic attack, that two minutes and seventeen seconds was pure hell.

"It's simply unbelievable," Samuel said, when the video ended. "Let's watch it once more." He clicked play again.

If there was one thing that hurt Ashley more than anxiety, it was her stubbornness. So unsurprisingly, she chose to watch the video. Anyways, Samuel was too invested in the short horror flick to notice her labored breathing, tight jaws, and closed fists under the table. Still she inched back in the chair, as if the further away from the video she was, the better her chances of unseeing it.

The three robbers entered the bank, which was almost empty, given the early hour. They wore black T-shirts, black bomber jackets, and camo pants. Two of them ran in different directions just as soon as the swing doors closed behind their backs. The remaining one, a stocky blue-masked demon, locked the only entrance to the bank with a device that looked like a thin wheel clamp. Then he grabbed an assault rifle strapped on his back and manned the door.

Lolly wore his famed pale green zombie mask. In his right hand, he carried a shiny silver-plated pistol with a longish barrel. Samuel paused the video many times throughout its length to point at a white lollipop stick poking out from the zombie's mouth hole.

"See! Right there," he would say with the excitement of a kid who had been taken to a toy shop for the first time. "It's been his trademark for more than thirty years."

Lolly cannonballed toward the space between the cashier's table and a confused-looking security guard. When he was close to him, he shot the guard in his face. This was when Ashley felt the kick in the gut. She gripped the armrests as her body stiffened and heart redlined.

Lolly, however, didn't give a shit that he had just killed someone. He didn't even slow his sprint, but angled himself toward the cashier's table and slid over the marble floor. Without waiting to check if the preemptive strike had made a kill, Lolly leaped over the counter.

His movements were precise, aggressive, and slick, like a quarterback with a football in his hands. In just four seconds, even before the blue demon locked the entrance, Lolly killed a man, made a sharp turn, and jumped over a tall table.

Lolly pulled one of the dumbstruck cashiers up as if he were a ragdoll, and held the gun to his temple. The hostage repeated a set of instructions whispered into his ear. Linda, the second cashier, put her hands up. Another dumbstruck but unharmed security guard and every one of the bank's five morning customers lay on their stomachs and placed their interlaced fingers at the back of their heads.

A red demon, which dashed in a different direction when the front door closed, went out of the camera's focus, to the right. A few seconds later, he reemerged with a black pistol in his hand.

From the victims' accounts, the red demon had barged into the bank manager's office and buried two bullets between his ribs. The cops said it was a brutal but effective tactic. The manager was the only one who wasn't in the lobby, and he could have called for help when the robbers were busy.

The red demon jogged toward the sleeping security guy and took the machine gun he'd kept over his head. Then he headed toward Lolly. When he reached the counter, he unstrapped the bags from his body and threw them at Linda. The bags hit her chest and fell at her feet.

Linda put her hands down, doubled over, and brought up the bags. She started filling them, wiping her cheeks at irregular intervals. Ashley wanted to cry, too. She wanted to hug the poor Linda and console—

No! She would shake Linda and scream at her to not cry. *Don't give the robbing motherfucker the satisfaction.*

When Linda finished filling the bag and handed it over, Lolly kicked his hostage's right buttock hard. Linda's frantic attempt to catch her colleague from hitting the floor would have been comical if it weren't for the blood spreading under the head of the dead security guard.

Then they beelined towards the entrance and all three disappeared, making the video finally come to a stop. Ashley let out an enormous sigh inside.

When something outrageous like this happened, the cops released the crime video to appeal for the public's help. But this was the FBI's case and they weren't famous for candor.

Samuel said he had bought the video from a kid who'd replaced the dead security guard. He invited the kid to New York and took him for a ride around Manhattan in his Rolls Royce, explaining to him why people needed to see the video, about the necessity for the truth to prevail and other similar baloney. He also paid a lot for it.

Smiling, Samuel turned to Ashley. "Know what?"

"What?" Ashley asked, praying he didn't want to play the video again.

She would definitely throw up over the keyboard if he did.

"Being happy makes me think of dinner. Also, today's Friday, my treat day." He put the landline on speaker, dialed a number and let it ring.

Good for him. She couldn't eat anything that day. Diet pills had nothing on a good dose of anxiety and murder videos. It wouldn't be the first time she was denying her body its sustenance. For someone who had been jumping from one foster home to another, going hungry and sleepless wasn't new. The only thing that mattered to her was coming up in life, and she would sacrifice anything for it, including her body or mind.

"Darling?" Martha answered.

"Surprise me with dinner. But for dessert, I want a big bowl of my favorite ice cream."

"Already on the shopping list. So, tell me the reason for your good mood."

In spite of feeling sorry for the human condition, especially her own, Ashley smiled. How well Martha knew him. You couldn't have everything, some said. Bullshit, because Samuel had it all. He said that on Sundays he thanked Jesus for bringing Martha into his life. He prided himself for still remembering every little thing about the day he fell in love with his wife, forty-four years ago—the white shirt, a polka-dot skirt, and the glossy red hair.

"What are you talking about?" he replied. "I'm always in a good mood. Ashley is here. Say hi."

"Hello, sweetie. How are you?"

"I'm great, Martha. You?"

"Same, sweetie. Always the same. Okay, dear. I need to go tend to my flowers in the garden."

"All right, Martha. Bye." Ashley disconnected the call, thankful that she had not only a job she loved, but also such kind people as bosses.

Ashley Stuart had started as a reporter at the Daily Herald and worked her way through different postings before Samuel appointed her as his assistant, the second most powerful position in the operations part of the company. Samuel had remarked that apart from her sharp intellect, there was a kind quality to her voice and gestures, like she really cared. *Sweet.* That was the word. A young Martha. For this reason, Samuel considered her to be a daughter they never could have.

Samuel closed the laptop. "It's wonderful."

"Yeah, well, it's not exactly doing wonders for my stomach." She felt distaste blanketing her face.

"You are not responsible for what those men did."

"But I am for broadcasting it! Should we really do this, Sam?"

"Quite sure."

"Won't the FBI be pissed?"

"They will be. Our lawyer tells me they will even threaten to sue us. But they won't. They know they can't win. We got this pesky thing called the First Amendment on our side."

"Can't I make you reconsider?"

"That you can't, dear."

"Okay." She got up to leave.

"You did a good job editing. It's one of the most tantalizing previews I've ever seen. It's going to make people crazy to wait until seven to see the full video."

"Thank you," Ashley said to the floor, not caring about the praise.

"Look at me. The Daily Herald shows its viewers the world as it is. Mostly it's beautiful, but sometimes it's the ugliest."

"But that's not like the Daily H..." Ashley's gaze skipped past Samuel's head.

There, hanging on a wall behind his chair, was a painting of Martha. He'd had an artist from Italy paint a portrait of his wife at her current age, seventy-one.

"I know it's not like the Daily Herald, Ash. We don't make people edgy by constantly bombarding them with sensationalist crap and flashing headlines, like something serious is happening and they're missing out. You know what I always say about criminals, right?"

"That they amount only to a small proportion of the world?"

"*But?*"

"But they're still out there."

"And we have to show the world what these men are capable of. We'll fail in our duties as journalists if we don't."

* * *

As predicted, the seven o'clock news made history. The ratings would have been higher if Joshua Chase, an ex-detective who'd quit his job to go after Lolly, had agreed to do a guest appearance. But his decision was set in stone when he said he was not interested.

Ashley espied Samuel excuse himself from the celebration and retreat to his office. He closed the door, but she doubted the teak wood would stop the sound of party blowers from penetrating it.

She followed him, just in time to see him circle the table and plunk himself into his chair.

"What's wrong, Sam?" Ashley spotted the worry on his face.

"Nothing… it's just that I've been trying to reach Martha for about"—he looked at his Rolex—"about twenty minutes now, but she isn't answering. She goes out to buy groceries on Fridays. She's too stubborn to get a driver, but her eyes don't work like they used to."

"Could she be cooking?"

"Yeah. But…"

"But?"

"You know, her heart doesn't work the same way it used to, either. Doctors said that as long as she takes her meds, there's nothing to concern ourselves with. But I'm worried. If not for this meeting with my board of mud monkeys—"

"My work's done. I could take a detour on my way home."

"That'd be lovely. Thank you. You have something… right there…" He tapped his neck with his forefinger.

Ashley frowned and searched her neck, finding a piece of mylar confetti.

"Fucking Greg."

"Mind the French, dear. Call me when you get there."

Ashley looked at her phone, and then at Samuel with a sheepish smile. He got the point.

"What percentage?" he said.

She scratched the back of her neck. "Two."

"It's surprising, really. Girls your age never let their phones die. Learn from that gum-chewing intern of yours."

"Sam, I'm not a girl. I'm thirty-five. I don't have any use for my phone. I practically live here. And learn from Emily? Whoa, no thank you." Ashley bowed.

Samuel laughed his big, Santa Claus laughter. "Charge it in your car. When you get there, tell Martha you're dining with us. If it's not your date night, that is."

* * *

Ashley got in the elevator. *Date night?* When was the last time she had gone home to a man to drink wine and watch movies? Though she couldn't remember it, she didn't miss it either. By herself, she could watch one while pigging out on chocolate. On second thought, it's a lot better than being with an unmotivated jerk who thought he had the right to interrogate her, asking why she came home late at night.

She located her car and got in, pushing aside all thoughts of her ex. Some people weren't worth the expense of brain cells.

After shrugging out of her suit jacket, she threw it on the passenger seat. She hunched low and took a cable that was connected to a USB port in the dashboard and plugged the other end into her phone. A lightning bolt appeared above the battery indicator for a second, and then it was gone. The display dimmed once again and popped a message that the phone would be switching off now.

She yanked the cable from its port, the metallic end whipping her on the shoulder. She threw it down and stomped on it a few times. She had meant to buy a new one, for almost a month now, but oh God, only if she could find the time.

Calm yourself...

She breathed in and breathed out. Ten times.

What was up with the mood swings? Sleeping only four hours a night, eating junk food, and the stress she'd been subjecting herself to in the office couldn't be the only reason. A visit to her doctor was in order.

She tapped on a playlist she listened to every evening on the way home. Blasting heavy metal, shaking her head like she was having a violent seizure, and letting the noise silence her mind always alleviated her mood.

The first song—Animal Alpha's *Bundy*.

She eased her yellow Mustang out of the parking lot and merged with the Friday night traffic. Headed southeast on West 23rd Street and turned onto 7th Avenue. It was a good mile with no traffic. But then on Varick Street, she got stuck in a jam in front of Citibank. Eons later, she joined West Broadway, which led to Brooklyn Heights.

As the tenth song, Slipknot's *Psychosocial* ended, Ashley took a right into a quiet lane and parked the Mustang in front of an intimidating steel gate. She looked in the rearview mirror, tied her hair back, and stepped out. She strode to a small touchscreen security box protruding from a wall beside the gates and keyed in the pin code. The gates parted, opening into a long driveway. She could use some exercise.

Her armpits were sticky with sweat when she had almost reached the house. The front door was ajar and Martha's car was parked a few meters from it. It wasn't like Martha to leave the door open.

Ashley skirted the gray Bentley. The sensation of hot vapors from the hood and the ticking sound of the engine suggested that Martha had just parked her car. Maybe she'd carried things in both hands and would come back for the door any minute now. That idea relaxed Ashley.

She went straight to the kitchen. There was a grocery bag on the island and a sweet smell of butterscotch wafted from it. She peeked inside and found yellow goo floating above eggs and celery. After seeing the abandoned bag, she *knew* something was wrong. She searched the house, calling Martha's name.

On their bedroom floor, she found Martha's Prada, its contents scattered about. Martha's prescription specs were also on the floor. She didn't go anywhere without them. Ashley sat on her haunches and retrieved the eyewear. There was something on it.

She held it up by the frame and spotted drops of blackish water. It had crisscrossed on the surface of the glass and rested in the grooves, where the water was darker.

Her heartbeat rose and her stomach knotted as raw fear climbed up her spine. Every woman in the world who had dated a douchebag one time or the other knew what that water was—eyeliner mixed with tears.

She sprinted out, not bothering to close the door, and piled into the Mustang. The muscle car took off like a rocket when she stood on its accelerator. Precious time was being lost and she had to do something to make use of it.

Charger cable!

She scrunched her tall frame, lowered her left hand down in the footwell and felt the mat down there. *Please just work this one time.* But her hand or eyes couldn't locate the thin plastic-sheathed wire. Cursing, she straightened and looked at the road. Her eyes widened.

Her car was about to climb the back of a red SUV!

She made a hard left. To avoid slipping from the tarmac, she veered right, the Mustang's rear side almost swiping the front of the SUV.

She had a brief urge to stop and apologize, but there was no time. She angled the rearview mirror. The red SUV, after struggling to gain composure, found its balance. Then it honked. She scolded herself and raced to the nearest police station.

Hamstrung Aegis

3/15/19. Past 8:00 p.m.

For a wealthy man, I found Samuel's protection against home invasions rather dismal. A protean lock-pick set, an expensive drone, and an even more expensive RF jammer broke the defense provided by a high-ticket security firm.

Modern home safety equipment uses wireless technology. When the property is breached, the sensor fires radio signals in a unique frequency and alerts the central unit, which has a router connected to it. If the pin code is not entered within the preset time, or if a wrong one is entered, it will alert the world.

Enter the frequency jammer, a device that makes strong radio signals which disrupt and overlap the frequency emitted from the sensors. It's illegal in our country, but I'd had someone smuggle it in from South America.

I'd parked the vehicle fifty meters down from Samuel's bungalow, six weeks ago. I flew my drone some twenty feet over his head. On top of providing me with much-needed stealth, the black drone also had the best nocturnal camera on the market. It transmitted everything it spied in HD, to my handheld controller, and it took me three tries to get the pin code for certain. Not to say the time spent with my toy during the two failed attempts is useless. I learned a lot of things about the Nelson family from my one-eyed infiltrator. This new information altered, and ultimately, made the plan of abducting Martha a lot simpler.

I learned that whenever Martha drove back home from the grocers, she'd use the front door. If she didn't go shopping, she'd use the door inside the garage. She does this because, I surmise, her kitchen is on the left side of their colossal living room, and the garage door would lead her to the right side of the bungalow. It's easier for the old woman to park her car at the doorstep, go left, and put the groceries in the kitchen. She'd then come out and back the Continental GT into the garage.

Martha will be in for a surprise if she strays from her routine and decides to park her car in the garage tonight. My car, which carries one tied-up-Rita in its cargo space, is occupying it now.

I turn off the engine, reach under the passenger seat, switch the jammer on, and get out. With my slim, surgical-like tools, I work on the keyhole. I crack the lock in under a minute and slip in.

As I expected, there is a panel beside the door. I should either deactivate the alarm in sixty seconds, or keep the jammer on as long as I stay here. That's risky. When I leave, the alarm will blare.

I hold my breath and enter the same code I've used on the front gate. The little blue screen displays *Welcome!*

I disable the jammer, take two cell phones from a bag and go in again. I know I said no cell phones, but this pair isn't mine.

The ceiling is high, and it's painted white. There are no floors above. The Nelsons are humble with their decor. I keep close to the right side wall and open the first door I come across. It's the bedroom. There's a king-sized bed on the left and mirrors run the length of the wall on the right. There's a door beside it. I nudge it open with my Nike sneaker. Bathroom. It smells like fresh fruit. I close it again.

There's a big closet at the end of the room. It looks like it's made from precious wood. It's reddish-brown with shiny brass handles. I open it. The right side doesn't have any shelves, just clothing on wooden hangers. The left side has three drawers. The first one contains watches, diamond necklaces, and other meaningless valuables. Meh.

I take a soft handkerchief from the second drawer and pocket it. Before proceeding any further, I need to locate an important thing to break the last line of defense in Samuel's home security.

I search two other rooms on this side of the bungalow—a small movie theater with four comfortable seats, and a smaller room that has tools and chemicals for a greenhouse Martha maintains in her backyard. But I don't spot what I set out to find.

I half-cross the living room and stop at the fireplace. It's as tall as I am, and beautiful columns shaped like Roman pillars support its slick ledge. I place one cell phone on it, between a china plate and a vase. I cross the other half and go to the left side of the bungalow.

I search, and yes, my assumption is correct—there is a kitchen here. At the second door, I arrive at Samuel's office room. It has millions of pictures of him and Martha, popular news the Daily Herald has published over the years, Pulitzers, and other boring memorabilia. However, I also find what I'm looking for here. It's connected to the back of the CPU under Samuel's table, and I decide to come back for it later.

I'm waiting in the kitchen, standing still. The silence is beating against my eardrums. My nemesis, boredom, creeps in and a yawn breaks out. That's not good.

A flash image of the closet crosses my mind. Hmm. That could work. And it would be mischievous of me. Do I risk leaving evidence? No, I don't risk anything if I change the plan to decrease the boredom.

I walk to their bedroom, open the closet, step inside, and close the door. Can't wait to see the dramatic effect it will have on Martha when I come out. The bogeyman inside a closet—something we all feared once.

I look at the cell phone I'm holding in my left hand. Nothing. I video called the first phone from the second. I kept one above the fireplace and trained its camera on the front door. This way, I can prepare myself if Martha decides to bring home a guest.

I'm wearing a new Puma tracksuit. It's pink. Why pink? I'm in this closet for almost ten minutes. My clothing would have undoubtedly left fibers around me and on Martha's dresses. It's like how lint and dead skin cells collect in the navel. Not only here, but wherever I've gone earlier tonight or have yet to go, this physical evidence will vouch for the presence of a man in pink.

The scene of crime officers will collect these pink fibers and pat themselves on their backs, and possibly laugh at the choice of my color. Joke's on them, though. If they ever catch me, they can't prove my presence anywhere with the help of fibers, because no clothing in my house is pink, so they will get nothing to compare with what they'll recover here.

I used cheap gel to cement my hair to my scalp. When—not if—a hair breaks apart, it won't detach from the cluster. I'm also wearing a hair net, because I'm deliberately overcautious.

I've covered my face with a green surgical mask, like the ones used in operating theaters, to stop spittle from shooting out when I talk to my chosen ones. This can prevent my DNA from showering on the crime scenes. It's a long shot—a practical impossibility—for a forensic detective to find evaporated spittle, but there is still a theoretical possibility. Overcautious.

I didn't touch anything that didn't need to be touched. I'm wearing gloves, but I'm also keeping a count of all the things I'm touching. I will wipe them off when leaving.

I take all these precautions because DNA profiling has developed to such an extent that now my opponents can create a profile from a single cell. Aptly named *Touch DNA*, it doesn't matter if I'm wearing gloves. All they need is one cell to destroy my world.

The cell phone's speaker mumbles and I open my eyes. The bright screen shrinks my pupils and tickles deep in my nostrils.

Martha Nelson opens the front door. With her khaki sweater, a brown skirt, and pearl necklace, she looks like anyone's grandmother. I know she reminds me of mine. She's also wearing specs with thick glasses, her hair tied in a bun.

According to Wikipedia, Samuel started the Daily Herald two years after he married Martha. He was quoted as saying that he considers his wife his lucky charm. I'm going to steal his horseshoe and hang it in my place. Hang differently, but hang, nonetheless.

She carries the groceries to the kitchen. Within a few seconds, she heads for the bedroom, a sense of urgency in her pace. Weird. It would have taken at least two minutes to arrange all the groceries in the refrigerator. I put my phone inside my pocket and wait for her.

She comes in. With one eye, I see her through the little opening between the closet doors. She drops her handbag on the bed and disappears inside the bathroom. The sound of running water follows.

Seniors and their overactive bladders.

I smile to myself. Animals can sense danger, but humans, the dominant species in the food chain, cannot. If she owned a dog, even a handbag mutt these rich people are fond of, it would have made its way straight to the closet and barked at the smell of a predator. The outcome wouldn't have been different, however. I would have stomped the mutt, wiped my foot and carried on.

The toilet flushes and Martha comes out. She rummages in the handbag, brings out a cell phone and dials someone.

"I'm so sorry, dear… please don't—I'm sorry… stop worrying. You're going to give yourself a heart attack… I was driving… I know… Ashley is coming? Okay, I'll make her stay for dinner… Love you, too. See you soon." She hangs up.

Ashley is coming? I must make haste. And *see you soon?* People and their complacently greedy fantasies.

I stop snickering, open the closet door and step out.

Naughty, naughty, boy!

3/15/19. 8:30 p.m.

Martha's bag and the cell phone drop at the same time. She places her hands between her sagging big breasts and contorts her wizened face in shock. Why so shocked? Is it the sight of the gun I'm pointing at her? Or that she can't understand what a surgeon in pink running gear is doing inside her closet?

She starts to breathe in, taking in large gulps of air. I know this gesture—her lungs are accumulating enough fuel to emit a scream. Before that happens, I place the top of the gun's muzzle above my mask and tap my philtrum in a shushing gesture. She deflates in defeat.

"I'mma rob your house," I say.

"Please don't hurt me, kid. Take whatever you want. But, please, leave—"

"I ain't your kid. Listen to me, ol' lady." I angle my gun sideways. It's a silly way to hold a weapon, but right now I'm an unsophisticated young hoodlum, not an ingenious serial killer. "You try anything, I'll shove this up your ass and pull the trigger. Got it, bitch?"

She winces when I say that ugly word. It's understandable. People with class never express their emotions by cursing. I don't use profanity either, but I'm playing a role at the moment.

"Pl-Please…"

"I said, you got it?" I shout.

Her shoulders jerk, and she looks at me. Her eyes, magnified by the glasses, fill and threaten to overflow. Then she nods.

"Good. Come with me." I stride past her.

I don't feel her moving. I turn and look.

She's clutching her trembling hands in front of her pressed skirt, and looks down. Eye makeup dissolves in her tears and drops on her glasses. I've seen black tears before.

"I said, come with me."

She shakes her head.

I step closer as she shrinks into herself. I slap her on the side of her head. Her neatly combed hair ruffles and she stumbles sideways, her hands unclasping for balance. Her spectacles hang crookedly for a moment before coming loose and falling at her feet.

Now she waters her cheeks copiously. It's not the pain of the strike, but the humiliation of the physical aggression. I wouldn't be surprised if this is the first time she's ever been hit in her life.

"I need to tie you up. Wanna know why?"

She keeps quiet. When I raise my arm again, she squeezes her eyes shut and turns away.

"I said, do you wanna know why?"

She bites her lower lip and gives a curt nod. Her head and neck have become stiff to accommodate any blow that may come their way.

"I can't search your house if you ain't tied up."

She isn't opening her eyes. The lady is too scared. I'm going to use my soothing voice now.

"Come on, fam. I'm sorry for roughing you up. It's just that I can't control myself when it's time for my fix. Please understand." I give out a twitch just to make the act seem natural. "I promise I ain't gonna hurt you. I'll untie you soon as I get something worth selling."

She opens her eyes and turns my way, but makes no eye contact. That's an improvement. Baby steps.

"Keys and cell phone for starters, granny."

She stoops, retrieves her crocodile skin bag and phone. Holding her hip, she comes back up and hands me the order. I pocket the keys and unlock the phone. No security prompts. Great. I pocket that as well.

"Drop the bag. We ain't gonna be needin' it."

I grab her spongy elbow and guide her to the living room. I tell her to lie on her stomach. She does. A curious thought crosses my mind—to jump as high as I can and land on her back, stomping on her with my full might. I brush the gratifying image away, reminding myself that this is no small animal to play with and I'm on a mission.

I tie her up with a set of zip ties I've brought along. I stuff her mouth with her own handkerchief and gag her. I take the keys out, slide on the reflective Wayfarers, and open the front door.

I drive the Bentley out of the way and go to the garage. While in my car, I pick apart her cell phone and throw it in the glove box. I reverse the car into the driveway and park it in front of the bungalow, the car's tailgate facing the front door.

Martha's pale face shows indignation when she sees me approach. She's been cheated.

I carry her struggling body on my shoulder. She's big, but I guess she's full of air. I lift the door open and throw her inside. Rita looks at Martha in confusion, and then resumes squirming lazily. Has she burned out her energy already, or is she saving it up for some silly plan she's made to escape?

I lock them in and jog back inside, retrieve the phone from the fireplace, end the video call, and walk to Samuel's office. I switch on the PC and it doesn't ask for a password. Samuel must be one of those good millionaires who doesn't keep secrets from his wife. I open the folder for an external drive, and it appears to have a thousand video clips. I remove the hard disk connected to the CPU. The recordings of seven dome and bullet cameras around their bungalow, front gate, and in their garage are now in my hands. It will soon be in the bottom of the Narrows.

I return to the bedroom and steal another cotton kerchief from the closet. I take a transparent, hundred-milliliter bottle from my front pocket. I spray its contents on the cloth until it's damp with the pungent liquid. I start to rub everything I've touched, and wipe my way to the garage door.

I get in the car, remove the green mask and drop it in the bag. From another section, I take a fake beard, set it on my face and check in the mirror. With the Wayfarers and fat blond beard, I don't resemble myself. I put the car in gear and drive out.

I hear sobs. Martha. Then I hear and feel strong kicks on the car's internal panels. Rita. Is this why she's been saving her energy? Does she think she can tear through the metal and jump out?

No. She's trying to get attention. Too bad the avenue is quiet. Rich people's streets are never lively. But Rita will get her attention when we hit the main road.

I stop my car and go to the back, through the space between the front seats. I haven't even exited Martha's neighborhood and I have to deal with this. Why don't people accept death or defeat when it's their time? I know I'd kneel and surrender when my time is up. There is no shame in admitting the logical conclusion of things.

It took two minutes to tame Rita and get back to driving. Anyone who watched the shaking car must have thought a bang was taking place inside. In a way, they'd have been correct. Rita's face didn't bleed—my shoe soles are covered with thick cloths—but the skin where the thunderous stomps landed will turn purple and develop nasty bruises.

No sobs from Martha. Good. I guess she's praying to the Almighty that this is a bad dream and that he will rescue her from it. Just like how Rita might have done before taking the matter into her own legs. Oh, well. You're in devil's territory now. God is nowhere here.

A glimpse of harsh light sweeps inside the car.

I put my hand above my eyes and look in the rearview mirror. A pair of bright lights comes at me. An instant later, a yellow Mustang cuts me off and races away. I swerve right, but a little too far right, and to balance it, I swerve left, my tires screeching on the pavement.

Finally, I wrestle the car back under my control. My heart rate is at a historic high. If I'd been made to crash, everything would have ended before it even started.

For some mysterious reason, I scream and bang my head on the steering wheel, and the car honks. Phosphenes fly around in my vision.

The world would be a better place without drunk drivers and petty criminals.

I look back. Martha is closing her eyes and crying. Rita, being the stuck-up female that she is, stares at me with one eye—the other closed by the swelling—daring me to scare her. I'd drained only her physical strength, but not her mental energy?

Oh, well. Let's see. It's time to teach you a lesson.

*   *   *

Searching and finding a private place in this part of the city was not an easy task, but I found one on Van Brunt Street, Red Hook. It used to be a port village, and had later become a symbol associated with bad things. Al Capone lived somewhere around here. The famous American crack epidemic saw the highest crime waves in the United States, and Red Hook was the neighborhood affected the worst.

Even though it has come a long way since then, evidenced by new schools and housing projects springing up like mushrooms, cops still don't concern themselves with this place. No police cruisers will be doing random drive-bys on this stretch, making it an ideal place to have some fun.

I park the car at the end of the street, near a blue steel railing that overlooks Erie Basin. It's a sheltered harbor used by tugboats and New York water taxis.

As I get out, huge unoccupied brick buildings standing on either side of the road welcome me. I open the rear door.

What am I doing? Something I know I shouldn't be doing.

Martha is cowering at the back, trying to hide her face between Rita's shoulder and the back of my seat. I lean in and grab her hair. I pull her forward and force her face down on the car's rubber mat. I lift my hand and she stays there like an obedient dog.

I pull my gun out and point it at Martha's head. She rears up like she just touched fire and returns to her position. I look at Rita. Her eyes widen.

Where is that defiant look, now?

Martha shakes her head and cries. She's trying to say something, but she can't. Losing the ability to talk and bargain for life must be a hell of its own kind.

Rita looks at Martha, her challenging eyes now softened in sympathy. She raises her eyebrows in commiseration and slumps her shoulders in defeat. She would hug the old lady and coo to her if she could.

I win!

Now I want to play with Martha. The uncontrollable urge, when presented with a sheet of bubble wrap, rises in me. I want to pop one.

I point the gun at her. She jumps and moves to her left. When I point the gun there, she goes right. She tries to hide behind Rita, who protects her new friend by putting her body between Martha and the weapon.

That's... noble? No. It's stupid. Why would you risk your own life to save someone?

When Martha is tired of moving around, her eyelids shut so tight her face is an irregular mess of creases.

A fleeting thought warned me to stop whatever I'm doing now. It's not a garden lizard. It's a human. It's an integral part of my ambition. Stop it!

Too late. I steady myself, take aim and pull the trigger.

Cold water egresses the muzzle and splashes on Martha's face. She opens her eyes to find that it is just a water gun, although an excellent imitation of a Smith & Wesson. I have a real gun with me, but only for emergencies.

"Pew, pew," I say, in a high-pitched voice as I squeeze the trigger two more times.

The water cleans some of the dark liquid from her face. I can't stop giggling while she tries to scream in mortification.

But then she begins to wheeze and her eyeballs roll into her head. She acts as if something has possessed her.

Then she falls, her spine arching one last time, and stays that way.

My face shrinks. I climb in, close the door behind me, and touch her neck. Nothing.

The woman is dead!

Heart attack? Doesn't matter—she's dead and I'm directly to blame.

No use in thinking now. I return to my seat.

What kind of life you had, Martha, I don't know. But what kind of hilarious death you've had, I'm the only one who knows. Well, there is Rita, but not for long. I feel like a god.

I slap the back of my head and promise myself not to pull shenanigans like this again.

Chapter 11

March 16, 2019. 06:12 P.M.

Two minutes after the chilling murder clip ended, Gabriel's phone went on standby. He had begun playing it in Nash's car when they were coming back from Samuel's office. It was a failed attempt to learn about the place, suit, mask or the ice blocks. He didn't gain any new information, but every time he watched the last twitch of the victims' legs, he lost a bit of his belief in humanity.

Gabriel tried to divert his empathic mind.

Why did the ice melt sooner rather than later? Why, even though they stood above the ice, had the victims sweated? And what was that sound, the smooth hum? When he put together these facts, the answer became clear—heaters!

The heaters must have been placed behind the camera, which was around fifteen feet from the blue curtain. They must have been close to the camera, because their noise was loud and sharp. That small space could be heated fast. Was that why the curtain was used? To box in the hot air and melt the ice blocks more quickly? Or was it used to prevent the cops from knowing the actual size of the room? Gabriel guessed Mr. Bunny had both in his mind when he hoisted the thick cloth.

Oh yes, that's what the media had named the murderer after Bones's email reached Tree News, rivals of the Daily Herald. The murderer must have said pretty please and asked them to call him that. Since the name had already achieved notoriety, it was better to refer to him as Mr. Bunny so there would be no confusion between the media, the public, and the PD.

While Gabriel was tolerating the mayor's criminal profiling in City Hall earlier, his team had divided and worked Victor's action plan.

Nash was assigned to tackle Doug Bastian's college and interview Doug's best friend, Pedro. He learned that Doug was supposed to meet his girlfriend the previous night. Nash searched the campus and found the girl. Doug had neither met nor called her. The girl was misty-eyed even before the questioning started, as YouTube reporters had broken the news to her before Nash did.

Since Gabriel was still in the meeting, Nash informed him through a text and went to meet Steve Bastian. The DA was in a peaceful alcohol-induced blackout. Steve's brother, who'd flown in from Arizona that morning, opened the door for Nash. He promised to keep Steve sober for the next day's interview.

Nash met Gabriel in Foley Square. They had a small lunch at Luna Pizza and drove to Samuel's office in Chelsea. The forensics team requested him to stay elsewhere because they had sealed his house.

Questioning Samuel was futile. He'd received an email from ritarayhughes@gmail.com. It was a link to a file-hosting website where the video had been uploaded. He wouldn't have clicked the link if the subject line hadn't read *MARTHA*. Mr. Bunny used the same method to send the video to others, except the subjects read *RITA* and *DOUG*.

Nothing valuable in Samuel's house went missing except a hard disk, Martha's phone, and her set of house keys. Samuel didn't receive any threatening emails or phone calls. Neither did he see any suspicious men lurking around his house.

Ashley Stuart, Samuel's PA, gave them a sheet of paper that listed all the employees the Daily Herald had fired, for a variety of reasons. To summarize the meeting, Gabriel and Nash learned how Samuel had gotten hold of Lolly's bank robbery video and that his PA had found Martha missing. These things helped reconstruct the past, but didn't help them to advance the investigation.

When they were out, Gabriel assigned the task of interviewing these employees to Laura and Mark, Nash's juniors. Nash dropped Gabriel back in the precinct and drove off to Harry's house to check with CSU.

Gabriel went through the papers that Noah had given him in the DA's office earlier. It listed seventy-two convicts who were all scattered over major state and federal pens. Noah's judgment was accurate—Hercules topped the list. Gabriel called the prison warden, who introduced himself as Edward. He made an appointment for Nash to visit Hercules at Attica Correctional Facility.

The only progress they made that day came from David Gustavo. He found what car the killer had used to abduct the victims.

David tracked where Rita last swiped her credit card—a grocery store seven blocks from her home. Since he had access to all the government-run cameras across the city, it was easy for him to search the surroundings of the supermarket. He found Rita's BMW crossing an intersection and going east. No one followed her.

David stayed on her car with the help of many traffic cameras, until she turned right, into her street. That's where the last accessible camera was.

Five minutes later, a red SUV drove from the street. David went further back in the video and found the red SUV, a Chevrolet Suburban, entering the street twenty minutes before Rita's car did. David got the license plate and informed Gabriel.

When Gabriel asked him to trace the Chevrolet in the same way he'd tracked Rita's car, David said he'd already tried but couldn't get a fix on it. The Chevrolet disappeared after it crossed the third block from Rita's house. Mr. Bunny must have known all the routes without CCTV coverage. Even if he'd managed to dodge the cameras just for a few blocks, finding him after that would be impossible, particularly among the Friday night's swarming traffic.

By the time Emma went to Samuel's house that afternoon, Stanley Ming was already there. Stanley was a detective first-grader assigned to the case, from the Forensic Investigations Division. He worked the scene with two other CSU detectives from his bureau.

She left them alone and walked the avenue, canvassing and questioning people. No one even knew that police were in their lane, let alone had seen one of its residents taken. When Emma asked if they remembered anything weird, one of the neighbors said that their Wi-Fi stopped working around the time of Martha's abduction. Gabriel didn't know what to make of it. Neither did Emma. So she moved on.

She found a camera at the end of the street, that belonged to the neighborhood watch. With the help of the locals, she got the previous day's recordings. As Gabriel had instructed, she took note of every car that passed there. A red Suburban had exited the street eighteen minutes after Martha's Bentley entered.

Emma drove down the same street the SUV had turned onto. Nearly half a mile later, she spotted skid marks on the road. She looked around and found a camera covering that section, but it was in a private residence and the house was locked. They'd have to check it when the owner returned.

Gabriel asked Emma to join Nash at Harry's. She said Stanley had almost finished analyzing Martha's house, and they would leave together.

As Gabriel hung up, David stepped into the office.

His face telegraphed excitement. "James Tucker," he said.

"Owner of the plates?"

"Also owner of the car. He's got a record. Guess what for?"

"Homicide?"

Unpaid parking tickets wouldn't have gotten David this happy.

"Right you are. James is a pimp and a jailbird. Last year he killed a nineteen-year-old Lila Morales, his *employee*. He was arrested and charged. Everything went well until one day when the star witness, Abigail Owens, split. Miss Owens had seen James choking Lila, but got amnesia at the last minute. He came out and resumed his merchandising. I've texted you the address."

Gabriel took his phone out and saw the notification. He thanked David and rushed to the captain's room.

* * *

The initial lead, however useless it might become in the future, was always the most important. It was the first break in the case. It meant things would get real and start to snowball.

Gabriel knocked and entered without waiting for an answer.

A familiar woman sat across from Victor. Like earlier that day, her red hair was still parted to its left and tied back. She wore the same work dress—a black suit and black pants. Ashley Stuart turned her head to Gabriel and proffered a formal smile.

"Come in, Gabriel. Sit." Victor pointed to an empty chair beside her.

Gabriel sat.

"I would have called you if you hadn't shown up sooner. Meet Ms. Stuart, Samuel Nelson's PA."

"Hi, Detective Chase. Not exactly nice to meet you again under these circumstances, but here we are."

"We met just hours ago, Captain. When Nash and I went to talk to Mr. Nelson, Ms. Stuart gave us the list of their ex-employees."

"Ah, that's right. Okay, listen." Victor cleared his throat. "She's here to follow and report the case. People trust their news, compared to those nitwits at Tree, who just named the murderer Mr. Bunny. We gotta use the media to our advantage as far as PR is concerned. No offense, Ms. Stuart."

Gabriel looked at Ashley. "I'll let Detective Gustavo know he's free to give out interviews. But be warned, though, he is a butt—"

"No. It should be you," she said.

Gabriel turned to Victor, who didn't offer much help.

"I'm leading this case. I got a lot of things to coordinate. Sorry. I don't have the time," Gabriel said.

"Leading this case is exactly why it should be you. Others won't know what information to disclose and what not to. As per my professional ethics, I should welcome anything, sensitive or not, and use it. But I can't do that in this one. Not if it helps the man responsible gain inside information and evade justice a bit longer."

A bit longer? So she believed Gabriel would catch Mr. Bunny. A glimmer of pride flashed inside him, because investigating serial killers was the toughest project any detective could get.

"I understand, but—"

"I knew Martha." Ashley looked away. "She was close to me. Ten minutes of your breakfast time is all I'm asking for. Please."

He considered. Ashley had a point. There was no telling what other detectives might divulge. And what the hell… he could find ten minutes for anyone desperate enough to say *please*. Another thing—it was personal for her, too, and that, he could relate to. They were on the same boat, sailing together through a cyclonic ocean of emotional turmoil.

"This is my number." He placed his card on the table and pushed it over to her side. "Now if you'll excuse us, we have something important to attend to." He turned to Victor.

Ashley's mouth gaped, but she closed it quickly. She took his card, put it inside her purse, then took her own card and handed it to him.

"Call me if you need anything from me." She got up and walked out the door.

"The DMV—"

"You know you're an asshole, right?" Victor said.

"What?" Gabriel was caught off-guard. "Why?"

"You don't even know you're an asshole. You know what that makes you?"

Gabriel frowned, waiting for the answer.

"An even bigger asshole!"

Gabriel was still confused.

Victor sighed. "Never mind. What's up?"

"You are weird." Gabriel wore a straight face.

"I'm weird? You are so removed from the *good* part of society that you don't even know when you offend people. Ask around the precinct—"

"I don't have time for this." Gabriel went on to explain David's findings. "I need an arrest warrant for one James Tucker."

Chapter 12

March 16, 2019. 08:05 P.M.

They arrested James in his apartment. David waited for Emma in his Corolla as Gabriel walked James inside. When Gabriel saw Emma on her way out, he transferred James's upper arm to a passing uniform.

"Hey, Priyanka, can you please take this gentleman to Room 4? And keep the cuffs on."

The officer ushered their guest into the interrogation room.

Emma waited until James was out of earshot. Then she gave him a quick update on what Stanley had found so far.

The shoe prints in Harry's and Martha's houses were a bunch of oblong dapples. Mr. Bunny had covered the soles of his shoes with some kind of soft material—it would be impossible to identify the make and model. From the width of the tire treads found in their driveways and the distance between the wheels, Stanley concluded that an SUV had been parked there recently. It corroborated their previous suspicion that Mr. Bunny used a Chevy Suburban to abduct Rita and Martha.

Both houses had various clean spots without any dust particles whatsoever. Mr. Bunny had wiped these spots off.

But why? He used gloves—he'd been wearing them when he gave Rita's laptop and phone to Bones.

Gabriel hypothesized that Mr. Bunny did it for the same reason the CSU personnel changed gloves regularly—to avoid contaminating the crime scene with DNA. Mr. Bunny knew about the phenomenon of secondary transfer and had taken precautions against it. That wasn't good.

David and Emma planned to visit Stanley in his office. He was comparing the pink fibers obtained from Martha's closet with what they'd gotten from Harry's couch. When Gabriel asked about Nash, she said he was reporting to Bulldog what Emma had reported to Gabriel. Then she got in David's car and off they went.

* * *

"A bit longer," Ashley had said, and Gabriel had felt proud.

Now a surplus of dread replaced that pride. The dread of failure and the dread of accountability. Did Ashley know what Gabriel was dealing with? Mr. Bunny had been as thorough as he could be.

Who traveled out of the city, to a deserted part of the highway, to send a video clip? Who covered the soles of their shoes and took hard drives? Who researched and located the CCTV cameras throughout the city, and escaped through the grid's blind spots? It was the first time Gabriel had come across a criminal like this—an extremely patient, smart, and fearless criminal.

He stopped feeding negative thoughts to his insidious insecurities and entered Victor's room. He asked Nash to join him in the interview.

* * *

With his blue T-shirt, jeans, and spiked hair, James Tucker looked like a normal twenty-year-old kid. He was just another guy in movie theaters, who rode subways or ate at the opposite table in the local KFC. Murder or ruthlessness wasn't the most powerful weapon in evil's arsenal—it was its ability to blend in.

"Where the hell is my lawyer?" James tried, and failed, to hide his nervousness with bravado.

He flinched when two huge palms touched his shoulders from behind.

Gabriel took his phone out and showed James the video of his Chevrolet, captured at Rita's street corner.

"I want a lawyer," James said.

"What you want is a lot of luck to escape this time," Nash said.

"Uh… what?"

"You've seen the news today?"

"Who didn't? Mr. Bunny is trending like crazy—"

"*Trending?* He murdered the police commissioner's wife and nine other people," Nash spat. "And we saw your car leaving the crime scene."

"What? Are you crazy? I didn't do it. No way you gonna pin that on me," James tried to wipe his forehead, forgetting that his hands were chained to the steel table.

"I believe you. But I'm going to charge you anyway."

"We can't do that, Nash," Gabriel said.

"Is that right?" Nash squeezed James's shoulders. "Tell me, bitch. Can I charge you or not?"

"Yes, sir."

"Why do you think I can do that?"

"Bec—" His dry throat struggled to create sound. "My car was there." He pointed at Gabriel's phone, on the table.

"See, Gabriel. You're wrong. He knows we can charge him."

"I assumed he was stupid."

"He is not stupid." Nash prowled the room and came to sit beside Gabriel.

If the suspect didn't cooperate, Nash would act like an edgy and violent cop. So, he put the table between himself and James.

"Sure, you look like a stupid little shit. But you're not stupid, are you?"

"I... I guess n—"

"Where were you last night, asshole?"

"I was in my pad. Ask those girls who were there when you arrested me. They stayed there last night, too. Can I get some water, please?"

"Then how did your car end up here? Did you loan it to someone?"

"I... yes, but—"

"Give me a name. Fast!" Nash shouted.

Even Gabriel, who was prepared for Nash's tactics, felt his heart skip a beat.

"Abigail Owens! I swear on my mother's life." James's eyes grew moist.

Gabriel gave James a skeptical look. Then he signaled Nash to follow him outside. When they stepped out, Gabriel filled a cup from the water dispenser.

"Abigail was the star witness who recanted her statement against James," he said.

"Oh... I knew he didn't do it." Nash smiled.

"Could you send Mark and Laura to this Abigail's house?"

"Yeah, no problem." Nash dug out his phone and dialed.

Gabriel went inside and sat on his chair. He sipped the water while James looked at the cup, wetting his lips.

"When did you give the car to Abigail?" Gabriel crushed the empty cup and tossed it on the table.

It skittered across the metal and stopped near the edge.

"October 25th, last year." James looked at the unfurling cup.

"How come you remember the correct date?"

Now he looked at Gabriel, and gulped.

"Because that's the date Abigail flipped in court?" Gabriel said. "You bribed her with your car so she would come down with a bad case of amnesia?"

"It was a gift."

Gabriel scoffed. "Do you like strangling teenage girls?"

"What? No... I—"

"People say I shouldn't take things to heart." Gabriel's voice was weak and sad. "But it's hard not to take it personally. Let me ask you this. Have you ever seen a week-old dead body?"

"No."

"Not a pretty sight. Bulging eyes, loosening skin, oozing fat, and maggots eating that goop. But that's not the hard part—surprisingly, you get used to it. You know what the real hard part is?"

James shook his head.

"It's the look on the girl's mother's face. The soul-crushed look when we tell her that her child was killed. Her little princess, the one she thought was going to be a doctor, a governor, or an astronaut, is now just a pile of putrefying flesh that even dogs won't eat." Gabriel clenched his teeth and shook his head at the particular memory. "I've been in homicide for more than ten years, and I've seen hundreds of things like this. Things that animals like you are responsible for. But unlike most detectives, I let these things get to me. If having a heart is called being soft, then I am soft, and I sure as hell ain't gonna apologize for it."

"Okay…"

"Soft means you are prone to injuries. Whenever I see a murder victim, it hurts me bad."

"What's that gotta do with me?"

"You know, James, I got a thing for murderers walking free. I believe they hurt me—in a way, they do—and I hold them accountable for destroying *my* happiness. I really hate them, and I really, really, *really* want to hurt them back." Gabriel stooped toward James and lowered his voice. "And I don't care how I do it." Then he sat back straight. "So trust me when I promise you this. After we close this case, I'm going to come after you. I suggest you leave the state before then."

"But where can I—"

"Not my problem. But don't you dare think you can hide in some rat hole. I got a great nose for scum like you. In fact, I've been called the best nose in the city. If I find out you're still screwing about in Brooklyn, I'll frame you for some rape case and make sure you get sentenced this time. You know what happens to rapists in Sing Sing, don't you?" Gabriel asked.

James was on the verge of having a heart attack.

Gabriel's phone sang, *…father into your hands… I commend my spirit… father into your hands… why have you forsaken me?*

By the time he exited the interview room, the ringing had stopped. It was Emma and he called her back.

"What's up?"

"Fibers from Harry's and Martha's houses matched. Stanley says he needs some time to get us a brand and the model."

"Cameras near Harry's place?"

"Hold on," Emma said, and David came on the line.

"Same as Rita's and Martha's. I was able to track the car for a few blocks, but then I lost it. Not every road has CCTV, right? He's using those roads to disappear."

Nash loomed into Gabriel's peripheral vision. "Okay, gotta go." He stashed his phone in his pocket. "Did they whine?"

"No." Nash gave a knowing smile. "Mark and Laura are new. They haven't learned it yet. They'll go to Abigail's now."

"Thanks. Go home and get some shut-eye. We'll continue tomorrow."

"Sounds like a plan." Nash turned to leave.

"Oh, I almost forgot. You and Emma are flying to Buffalo tomorrow morning to meet a special guy." Gabriel filled him in on his meeting with Noah.

"But why? If Hercules is our killer, why kill so many people? His score is with the DA, right?"

"Haven't you heard about murderers making up serial killers as decoys? They kill five or six random people, and then they kill someone related to them, which has always been the plan. They do this to escape closer inspection by making it seem as if a serial killer did it. Like the Beltway sniper attacks, except they were caught before the plan worked."

"Misdirection?"

"Exactly. I don't believe Hercules is our guy. But I don't wanna discount him now and get surprised in the end. So, it's best to follow up every lead before closing it."

"Hmm, that's an effective tactic. I must make note of it." Nash waited for a beat, and then smiled. "All right, no problem. I'll go."

"Thanks, man. Ask Laura to call me when she finds something." Gabriel fished the inhaler out of his jacket for a quick puff.

"Will do. You get some sleep, too. Your eyes are buried in your face," Nash said.

Gabriel returned to Room 4. "Did you consider my advice?" He pocketed the inhaler.

"Yes, sir," James said.

"Good for you. We're going to check your alibi and this Abigail. If it all pans out, you're free to go."

"Thank you, sir. I'll leave New York first thing tomorrow morning," James's eyes were compassionate and remorseful.

Gabriel shook his head in disgust at the phony emotions, and exited the place.

Room 4 was painted with subservience and oaths from suspects. Room 4 always smelled like cow dung.

* * *

Gabriel opened his office door, dragged himself to his chair and dropped into it. What a day! He couldn't remember the cogs of the police department ever working this fast.

Since that morning, Victor had assembled an efficient team and divided work among them. He even deployed SWAT. CSU finished analyzing the victims' houses. Detectives canvassed the neighborhoods, went through CCTV footage, and interviewed people who were close to the victims. Hell, they even questioned two suspects, one of whom turned out to be a victim.

And it wasn't even twelve hours since Raymond had summoned Gabriel to 1PP.

The whole department was in blitzkrieg mode, but their efforts didn't pay much dividends. Mr. Bunny blocked their aggressive onslaught with his in-depth knowledge of their tactics, creating a shield for himself, which Gabriel believed had been a long time in the making.

Gabriel forced every thought out of his mind and closed his eyes. He needed to give his brain a pause to get the best out of it.

Fifteen minutes later, he heard approaching footsteps. Either by the intervals between the sounds, or the forcefulness of each step, Gabriel knew the footsteps belonged to Victor. And if Victor was coming, then it would be to meet him.

Victor stopped at the doorway just as Gabriel opened his eyes.

"We got the bodies."

Chapter 13

March 16, 2019. 09:13 P.M.

Gabriel received three calls while riding in Victor's Elantra. The first was from Mark and Laura. Well, Laura was the one who'd called, but he was so used to them as a pair that one seemed incomplete without the other.

Someone had stolen the Chevy Suburban from Abigail three months ago. She hadn't reported it because she thought James had taken the vehicle back, and if she had lodged in a complaint with the authorities, he would have made her life miserable.

The second call was Emma to inform him that she and David had reached the location where the bodies had been found. The third was Emma again. She said Raymond had arrived as well and was peering into the Suburban, where the victims were.

After crossing Bensonhurst Park, they got off the well-lit Bay Parkway and took a right into the darker Shore Parkway. Its entrance was uneven, strewn with crushed rocks, most of them sharp. Something pinged off the car's underside, but Victor was too preoccupied to mind about workshop bills.

Once the car crossed the rough sea of stones, it traveled on smooth and unlit road. Scattered grass patches marred Gabriel's side of the road, followed by a guardrail that ran along Lief Ericson Drive. There was another guardrail on the left, acting as a barricade between the road and the steep drop to the Atlantic Ocean.

On a different occasion, this seaside drive would have been one of the most beautiful in the city. Bicyclists and joggers used this path. It also attracted tourists in the daytime, as it covered key landmarks of New York City, including Lady Liberty, the Verrazano-Narrows Bridge, and Forts Hamilton and Wadsworth. Due to the foot traffic, cars were not permitted on this road, but Emma said they had to drive because the spot was far along the path.

Minutes later, blinking blue and red lights heralded the police's presence. A muscled uniform stood guard between two wooden police barriers that blocked the path. His name was Archie and he was from the 122nd. Archie acknowledged the car with a nod and moved one of the barriers.

The Suburban lounged in a grass patch, its bumper facing the guardrail. The right rear door hung open, but its interior wasn't visible as Archie's cruiser flanked it. Emma sat on its trunk lid.

They stepped out of the Elantra. Victor tilted his chin toward Raymond's Ford and then proceeded to the Chevrolet. Gabriel took a deep breath, crossed to the car and climbed in.

With his ramrod posture and fierce eyes absent, Raymond had become a caricature of himself. He sat with his hands on the steering wheel, shoulders slumped. Silent sobs jerked his body.

A beam of light wobbled inside the car. It reflected on the rearview mirror and attacked Gabriel's eyes. He turned and looked through the rear glass.

A white CSU van idled in front of the wooden barriers. Archie verified the credentials and let them through, and the van parked parallel to the Ford. The front door flew open and Detective Stanley Ming hopped out. He wore a pressed white shirt, a navy-blue department-issued jacket, and black pants. He shook out a pill holder, dropped two in his palm and swallowed them dry. Headache?

Two guys wearing similar jackets followed Stanley. They had big suitcases in their hands. Another pair of forensic detectives dropped down from the back, carrying a rolled up yellow and white tarp on their shoulders. They'd erect a tent around the Suburban.

Stanley frowned at something on the ground near his shoes. He followed it with his gaze until it reached the Chevrolet, and then he smiled and shook his head. He called over one of the detectives and spoke to him while pointing at the ground. The detective jogged back to the van, and a minute later he came back with a surveyor's wheel. He placed the wheel on the point where the grass and tarmac met. Then he rolled the device along the path from where Gabriel and Victor had driven into the spot.

The weeping subsided and Raymond cleared his throat. He placed a hand on Gabriel's shoulder. It felt wet and soft, infirm and defeated.

The cameras flashed outside, and the scene became too raw and harshly real—victims photographed in their most vulnerable state.

"Please go home, Ray," said Gabriel. "I promise you, I'll chase him until I either catch him or I can no longer move."

Raymond nodded to the windshield and turned on the ignition.

Gabriel opened the door and stepped down.

He approached Archie, signed the crime scene roster, and asked for an update. A teenage couple biking along the path had stumbled upon the dead bodies and called 911. The first responders from the 68th had cordoned off the

Suburban before Archie arrived. They also helped him with the inevitable rubbernecks. After a while, the small group of curious people left. Then a pair of detectives from the same precinct took the teenagers downtown.

He thanked Archie and located Emma.

Upon seeing Gabriel, she jumped down from the trunk.

"Where's David?" he said.

"Meeting the kids who found the bodies. Then he'll go home." Emma rolled her neck in a slow circle.

"What about you? You seem pretty beat."

The pops from her neck were almost hidden in the sound of waves crashing on the rocks far below the opposite guardrail.

"I stayed back for you and Bulldog."

"You can go now. By the way, tomorrow you're going to Buffalo. There's—"

"Yeah, Nash called." She looked defeated.

"What's up, Em?"

"This place holds some of the most amazing moments of my life. You know this drive is popular among lovers, especially the young ones?"

"I do."

"Well, it was for me, too. Now I can't relate those memories with this place. Whenever I cruised on that road"—Emma pointed toward Leif Ericson Drive, where an Uber came to a halt—"I'd smile at the past. At intimate things. Sweet things. But now I know, whenever I pass here, I'll be reminded of murder and a heap of naked bodies."

That was too much information which Gabriel wasn't prepared to hear. He didn't want to see Rita's dead body. Not yet.

"I'm sorry," he said.

"Me too." She motioned toward the tent. "Your bestie is in there, and goddamn him, I saw him smile once or twice at something funny in this godforsaken place. I'm leaving."

She jumped over the guardrail and got in the Uber. He watched until the taillights disappeared in the distance, engulfed by the city lights. But still, Gabriel hadn't built up the courage to go near the SUV.

The yellow and white tent was up. The zipped-up flaps caved in to the strong winds from the ocean. He wished the air would sweep the tent away, along with the horror inside. But it didn't.

So, he shuffled to it, doing something he hadn't done since he became a detective.

He prayed.

Chapter 14

March 16, 2019. 09:59 P.M.

Stanley Ming was one of the top criminalists in North America and the best in New York State. That was why the FBI preferred that he work the scenes even though they had superior equipment. Raymond suspended him from his regular workload so he could give his undivided attention to the case.

Emma called him Gabriel's *bestie* because they were friends from childhood. It had always been Gabriel, Stanley, Noah, and his brother Casey.

Noah had always hated the Mings. Gabriel suspected that Stanley's better scores in school might be the source of Noah's hatred. But Noah's hate for Stanley had grown a millionfold when Phillip Ming, Stanley's elder brother, became the prime suspect in Casey's murder. Noah and Stanley never spoke to each other from that day forward, regardless of Gabriel's painstaking efforts to mend the old gang.

"Open up, Stan," Gabriel shouted at the zipped door.

He tried to warm his hands by rubbing them against each other, but the oceanic wind getting colder by the minute had nothing to do with the chilliness he felt. When he'd quit alcohol, he'd ridden himself of the anxiety that used to prick him before entering a crime scene involving dead people. But this one didn't have ordinary victims.

The zipper whirred up and flaps unclasped.

Gabriel stepped inside.

Portable LED floodlights beamed white light from all four corners of the tent. He could not hear anyone—he was sinking in water, and everything around him moved in slow motion. Trying to tame his pulsating heart, he inched toward the SUV. A photographer in a Tyvek suit looked up at him from his camera and made way.

Gabriel came to a halt near the open tailgate when he saw exactly what he didn't want to find—four dead people. The rear seats were folded forward, making the cargo space big enough for all of them. Everyone was naked, and they sat with their legs stretched in front of them. There was an uncomfortable stiffness in their postures, like mannequins. Rigor had set in and hadn't passed yet. Petechiae, a cluster of broken blood vessels that resembled blisters, dotted their eyes—a telltale sign of suffocation. Except, Martha didn't have them. How did she die? No way to know that until the autopsy.

Doug sat between the front seats, his huge arms resting beside his broad gym-chiseled chest. His protruding eyes stared down at Harry, who'd fallen on Doug's lap. Rita leaned back in the far right corner of the front seats, and Martha to the left. Rita's face was bluish like the other victims, but only hers had bruises that held her left eyelid shut. When Gabriel played the video the second time, he forced himself to watch Rita's death. Even though she wasn't looking at him now, he felt the open eye accuse him of not having saved her.

She'd cried when he'd landed in the hospital bed after poisoning himself with alcohol. She was there to catch him whenever he slipped. He wouldn't have made it out of the darkest road he'd lost himself in if she hadn't dragged him out by the ear. But where was Gabriel when some madman had abducted her? When he'd thrashed her? When her face contorted, legs kicked, and body convulsed in the unfathomable pain of death?

Gabriel backed out of the tent—he couldn't continue to hold his wet eyes open. He turned and bolted blindly.

When he reached the edge, he kicked the guardrail with his full might. That didn't satisfy him, and he doubled over, closed his fists and bellowed at the massive water. His throat and left knee throbbed, but the steel railing didn't give in to the force and the ocean didn't part in the middle.

He straightened, wiped his face and looked around. Archie stared at him from his post but didn't move. Victor stayed inside the car, avoiding eye contact.

Blood raced throughout his body, stinging in every extremity. It burned with anger, but the air under his eyes and the back of his right hand felt cold. No, he shouldn't cry. Crying made you lose some vital part of the process—a process to hunt down the source of your torment and disembowel it as it kicked and screamed in its own blood. Gabriel shouldn't vent, not yet.

He took three deep breaths.

One day. One day. One... day.

He went back in, trying to avoid the looks his reactions had earned him from the CSU guys. He must see the scene like a professional. He needed to.

The necks and wrists of the victims had similar ligature marks. Brown coagulated blood covered Harry's right forearm, the wound resulting from when his arm had torn away from the bind. No staging or posing. This fact reinforced the idea that Mr. Bunny wasn't a serial killer. Harry's legs drew Gabriel's attention. They were the thinnest pair among the four. They'd atrophied from lack of use, but that hadn't stopped his climb to fame. Years of hard work, all wasted now.

A faint smell of bleach diverted his thoughts and told him why they were naked. Mr. Bunny had removed their clothes and cleaned them with bleach.

"For lack of any better word, I'm going to call it brilliant," said a familiar voice behind Gabriel.

Stanley Ming.

Gabriel turned to face him. A Tyvek suit covered Stanley's body, but his head wasn't in the hood. He was athletic and shorter than Gabriel, and he wore rimless spectacles. His clean-shaven face brought out his charming boyish looks. The only thing off about him was that his eyes behind the lenses were lazy and red, the pupils a little wider than they should be. Gabriel sighed inside.

On account of his surname, most people thought he was Asian before meeting him. But his birth certificate read *Stanley Baptiste, Caucasian*. Mrs. Baptiste, a single mom, had had enough of parenting her adolescent boys and put them up for adoption. An Asian couple who'd adopted them had changed their last name.

"What?" Gabriel said.

"Before we delve into that topic, allow me to say something." Stanley pushed his glasses up on the bridge of his nose. "I understand Rita was close to you. But let's keep our emotions in control, Gabriel."

"What's brilliant, Stanley?" Gabriel said, in a low but menacing tone.

"I'm sorry. I didn't mean to offend." Stanley shrugged. "I'm, of course, talking about the lack of glove prints, vacuumed accelerator and brake pedals, clean gear and indicator sticks, shiny door handles. And do you smell something?"

Gabriel took a moment to digest the deluge of information. It explained Stanley's admiration for the forensic brilliance of Mr. Bunny.

And it brought Gabriel down.

If Stanley admired someone's forensic awareness, then there wouldn't be much they could hope to gather on that front.

Gabriel nodded. "Yeah, bleach?"

"Close. You see, unlike what criminals think, bleach or Lysol do not destroy DNA. They are disinfectants used to kill microorganisms, and DNA is a lot smaller than bacteria and other germs. Nothing is invented yet for the specific purpose of destroying DNA."

"What is it, then? It sure smells like Clorox," Gabriel said.

"Nope. What you smell is sodium hypochlorite, the main ingredient in bleach, which makes it so potent. Normal household bleach contains less than ten percent of this chemical. Even in its purest form, and I think that's what your killer used here, it still may not destroy DNA."

"So, he wasn't sure of the results?"

"Oh, he was sure all right." Stanley smiled. "Even if I manage to swab DNA from a surface where he used sodium hypochlorite, I still cannot draw a profile from it. Not destroyed doesn't mean unscathed."

"Could he have bought it? Or made his own?"

"It's as easy to buy online as it is to synthesize it in homes. That's your job to find where and how. Rest assured"—Stanley pointed back at the cargo space with his thumb—"he bathed them in that stuff, and it has long since evaporated. He also used it on the driver's seat, steering wheel, and other things you generally come in contact with when driving a car. But why? The black light didn't find any fluids. So semen, saliva, sweat, and urine are out of the question. And Bluestar didn't make any latent blood stains luminesce. Then why did he use it?"

"Skin cells," Gabriel said.

"My guess as well."

"Emma said you found a lot of clean spots in Martha's and Harry's houses, too. Did he use the same chemical there?"

"He did. I wouldn't be surprised if the guy was wearing gloves and still cleaned up after himself. That's a paranoid man we are dealing with but also a brilliant man. Let's say I become a god and draw a profile from the damaged DNA, it'll still be useless in court."

"Don't worry about conviction. It won't get that far."

Stanley eyed Gabriel with a fixed smile on his thin lips. "In that case, it'd be a waste of a neat skillset. Anyway, if he could manage this much after his plan went awry, you really can't hope I will find much in the scenes where everything went accordingly."

"What went awry?"

Stanley smiled his hackneyed condescending smile as if his peer's incompetence amused him. He looked down, pointed at the right rear wheel, and walked out of the tent.

Gabriel crouched and cupped his hand on the right side of his face, shielding his eyes from the harsh floodlight.

The tire was flat. The rim had cut through the tire, and its rough, blunt edge peeked out of the shredded rubber, dredging the grass and soil underneath it. Gabriel stood and followed the cleft on the ground. It reached the hard surface of the road and then turned into a prominent white line.

What were the odds of that? If only this had happened twenty-four hours ago in the middle of Friday night traffic.

"See this white line here? One of my guys tracked it to its starting point, with an odometer. He says it goes exactly 453 meters from this place before it disappears. So, what's this mysterious white line? It happens when metal—in this case, the wheel rim—comes in contact with the tarmac. Screechy noises, sparks flying—"

"I know what it is, Stan. Don't talk like that, not today," Gabriel interrupted.

Ever since Gabriel graduated with a degree in Criminal Psychology, Stanley hadn't stop punishing him for it. According to him, it wasn't real science. So he treated Gabriel like an idiot whenever he could. It had become a running joke with him.

"Sorry." Stanley lifted his palms. "Bad timing, I guess."

"You said *exactly*? I don't know how many miles 453 meters are, but the entrance to this road is around one and a half miles away. 453 meters is a far cry from one and a half miles, right?"

"Yup, not even half a mile. He abandoned the car the first chance he got after his tire failed him."

"In other words, when the Suburban entered this road, the tire was fine."

"Yes."

"He wanted to drop them somewhere along here, anyway? He didn't turn onto this path from the main road just because he got a flat?"

"That's correct. You noticed how uneven that turn was? My guess is one of the pointy stones there slashed it." Stanley kicked the mud that the rim had pushed up.

Gabriel walked inside the tent and crouched again. He looked at the rear wheels. Then he craned his neck and looked at the front wheel, frowning.

"Why are these bald?" He waved Stanley in.

"I feared you might miss that. These are worn-out tires, but the car is in good condition like a new car."

"Yeah, but the tires are old."

"Really old. I assume the killer removed the good tires and fixed smoother ones. Worn out treads won't pick up as much soil, vegetation, or other small things that might help us to narrow down his neighborhood, as a new set of tires would."

"But the plan backfired on him. He wasn't able to dump them in the place he had in mind."

"Lucky for us. This is a popular spot for tourists and New Yorkers alike."

"Lucky," Gabriel said, in contempt.

Both stood in silence, thinking of a way to find some useful piece of evidence.

"What about the pink fibers?" Gabriel said.

"Samples from both houses match. I was almost finished with the analysis when I was called down here. But my educated guess? It's a tracksuit. Give me time, and I'll give you a brand."

Again silence.

"You know," Stanley said, "he used a lock-pick to get into Martha's house. I've heard it's a difficult skill to master. He even beat a high-tech security system at their front gate."

"Yeah, Samuel told us. Did the murderer know the pin code?"

"Seems like he did. These things come with internet, you see. Everything's logged in their company's servers. So I called them. They never got an alert that someone was entering a wrong pin code last night. I also went the extra mile and asked them more questions, and got answers that would save you guys some time. Care to hear?"

"Just give it to me."

"No one in their firm has access to their customers' pin codes. If the homeowners forget them, then the company changes it from their HQ, which is in Berlin. But people who work in Berlin don't have access to the pin codes either. They can only help customers change them by sending them an encrypted hyperlink. Final nail, you cannot program the old pin code in if you wish to reset it. Their system won't accept it, they said."

"In other words, there's no lead there. The only possibility is that Mr. Bunny knew the code."

"Yup." Stanley nodded.

"Could he have jumped the system physically?"

"If he tried to tamper with the hardware, the security guys would have known that, too. Either he got lucky with the guess, or he didn't guess it but knew it."

"Anything at all to lift my spirits?"

"I might turn up something useful, eventually. But from initial examinations, all I can say is that he left no shred of physical evidence. We could open the radiator and the AC intake. I'm sure we'll find some speck of dust or soil that came from the place where he took them and killed them. The bad part is that it would have been mixed with all the other dust particles that this intake has drawn in since its last cleaning."

"Shit."

"Shit indeed," Stanley agreed. "Uncle Mills will be here soon. I bet he'll say the same things I've told you, only in ME's language."

The *Uncle Mills* Stanley referred to was Anthony Mills, an old medical examiner.

"I'm sorry," Stanley said, "but I'd be remiss if I didn't say this is the work of an artist. So far in my career, this is the best forensic precaution I've ever encountered. Sometimes even CSU veterans contaminate the scene, but this guy did it like a true lover of forensics."

"Thanks. Just what I wanted to hear." Gabriel couldn't help being sarcastic.

"Well, on the brighter side, whatever he does, he still can't achieve a hundred percent. Perfection is impossible, you see."

"What do you mean?"

Stanley rolled his eyes. "I'm telling you he didn't think of everything."

Gabriel's heart jumped. "Really? How?"

"He thought about almost everything and countered it. But he didn't account for those pointy stones when he made his plans." Stanley motioned at the dark road. "He missed them. Didn't he?"

"Yeah."

"I believe he'll have slipped up like that somewhere else, because his work is tougher than ours. He needs to cut off hundreds of threads that will lead the cops to him, but we need to find only one.”

“Easy to say,” Gabriel muttered.

“What?”

“Never mind.” As a formality, Gabriel said, “How’s your wife?”

“I just wish she’d stop with the Mexican food. It’s not good for my ulcers. But other than that, yeah, we’re doing great.”

“Glad to hear it. I’m leaving now.”

“All right, I’ll text you when I hand the scene over to Uncle Mills. Good night.” Stanley sank onto his haunches to take a closer look at the white line.

“One more thing.”

“Yeah?”

“Are you smoking-up again?”

Stanley’s shoulders stiffened, but he didn’t look up. “No.”

“For the record, I don’t believe you. I’m a detective.” Gabriel waited.

Getting no reply, he shook his head and walked to the Elantra.

Chapter 15

March 17, 2019. 07:15 A.M.

Gabriel slowly opened his eyes and stared at the ceiling. So he was still alive. His heart fluttered like a hummingbird as he slipped out from under the quilt. He entered the shower stall, trying to avoid acknowledging the nightmare echoing on the periphery of his mind. Naked Rita, her blaming eyes, battered face, and stiff body—they all flashed in his mind. He thumped the wall and groaned, willing himself not to cry. He should be robotic.

Before slumbering last night, he wracked his mind trying to figure out why Mr. Bunny did what he did. His tired and depressed brain had spat out a crazy hypothesis. It was an idea that had blinked once and disappeared into his subconsciousness when he was walking with Emma to their first team meeting.

He exited the bathroom and let the ceiling fan and gravity dry him off. He tugged his daily uniform on over damp skin, passively looking at his reflection in a 50-inch Philips UHD TV that hung on the wall opposite the bed. He used it only to play PS4 and watch the Family Guy and South Park DVDs that belonged to Liz.

Gabriel pulled out a wooden dining chair, sat on it, and opened one of the news apps installed on his phone. There wasn't anything from the Daily Herald except a piece about a vigil scheduled to be held in Harry Moore's honor. He called Ashley to check in with her and see if she'd come up with anything new, but she didn't answer. He navigated to other apps.

One headline read, *Mr. Bunny's Victims Found?* with a photo of the Suburban printed under it. In the background, Stanley's CSU van stood in front of Archie as he checked their credentials. The photo had been taken from the other side of the guardrail, and it wasn't clear. Someone from one of the many passing vehicles could have taken it and sold it to the papers.

When he exited that app and selected the next, his mouth parted with a silent exclamation.

This one had Gabriel's photo on top. It was bright and professional compared to the Suburban's picture. Some sneaky reporter had taken it outside Gabriel's precinct when he was waiting for Victor to bring his car around before they went to Shore Parkway. He looked disheveled, as usual, and being in the jacket he'd worn for two days straight didn't help the image.

The caption under it read, *Madman to Catch a Madman?*

* * *

It took him just one minute to get to the office. His apartment was situated on Elmtree Avenue, a cul-de-sac beside his precinct. When Gabriel entered the conference room at 9:54 a.m., everyone who comprised the task force was already there, except Stanley and Anthony the medical examiner. Both stayed late at the scene after Gabriel and Victor left. Stanley had informed him with a text that he planned to open the Suburban's radiator, and he would be more useful in his lab than in the meeting.

Victor covered everything that had happened up to the previous night and collated the data. David said he interviewed Alan and Jane, the teenagers who'd found the bodies and called 911.

They'd gone to Shore Parkway to canoodle, like most local teenagers did. Alan thought it was odd for a car to be on the grass, so he decided to inquire. When David scared them about finding their fingerprints on the car, Alan confessed that he'd opened the back door to have a little privacy, but received a traumatic shock instead. Detectives who took the pair to the 68th got their fingerprints and sent them to Stanley for elimination purposes. David offered the gratuitous opinion that those *spoiled brats* were not murderers.

Victor began when David finished.

"Yesterday I called and requested the reports of the first six murders. The respective detectives who investigated those cases emailed them to me today. I've forwarded them to all of you."

"Shouldn't we concentrate on what's in our hands, now?" Bill asked.

"With the last four victims, we have nothing to move the investigation forward. The car Mr. Bunny used was not

129

his. Only three persons knew the pin code to Samuel's house—him, his wife, and his PA, Ashley. We don't know how he abducted Doug, so we have to talk to the DA to sort it out. Gabriel and David are taking care of that. Rita's phone came back online, and we ran after it twice. They were dead ends."

"I don't understand why we give this much importance to forensics," Bill said. "What are we? CSI?"

Mild laughter circled around the table.

"We don't usually track perps like this, do we? We go after enemies and motives, like revenge. And we get this forensic evidence in the perp's house after we find him."

"The same technique won't work in this case, Bill," Victor said. "There is no conspicuous motive here. Both the DA and our commissioner have a lot of enemies. We're checking them out. Mark and Laura are interviewing disgruntled employees from the Daily Herald." He turned to the pair. "Anything interesting?"

"No," Laura said. "We're halfway through the list, but the people we did meet have alibis."

"Okay. Can you guys finish it today?"

"Sure."

"Then meet Harry's manager, Leroy."

"Okay!" Laura chirped.

"The problem is," Victor said to Bill, "you can't concentrate on one victim. You have a bunch."

"I'm sorry, sir, but I think we should track the SUV. And from what you said, this Ashley woman knew the pin code. What if she shared it? We should also question her."

That was impressive—a uniform standing up to the captain because he believed he was onto something. He'd make a good detective, Gabriel thought. And they could do everything he suggested, but the problem was their guy knew how to escape the scrutiny of CCTV cameras. They wouldn't have any luck tracking the Suburban. As for Ashley, Gabriel didn't think she would disclose something confidential that someone had confided in her. You didn't become second-in-command of a big corporation by leaking secrets. But like Bill said, they should follow those leads.

"All right, Bill," said Gabriel. "You take care of them."

"What!" Victor and Bill said.

"We gotta check them out, anyway. To at least eliminate them from our options."

"You serious?" Bill's face flushed. "But I'm not a detective. And I'm supposed to ride the desk on this one."

"You do that when you're done with this. Laura will give you Abigail's statement. That's the person from whom Mr. Bunny stole the SUV, by the way. Then interview Ashley. In the presence of a detective, of course. We don't wanna lose anything valuable you may get from her to technicalities, right?"

Victor hid his smirk behind his strategically placed hand.

"Yes, Detective Chase," Bill said, proud but still clueless.

A hand hesitantly rose from the back seats.

"Yes?" Gabriel said.

"I'm sorry, but—"

"Sit straight, boss," Victor said. "We can't see you."

Laughter broke out, Nash's laughter louder than the rest.

Mark sat up, red-faced. "I'm sorry, but I'm just asking what's on everyone's mind. Are we dealing with a serial killer?"

Smiles narrowed, and Victor turned to Gabriel for the answer.

"He fits the definition. With the first set of victims, the murder dates are too close to each other. When someone kills in rapid succession, it means he's not well up here." He tapped his temple. "A rabid dog is what he is. We call them *disorganized serial killers*. With all the evidence, or lack of it, we can safely conclude that Mr. Bunny is anything but."

"So… he's not a serial killer?" Mark looked more confused.

"He is, but not in a conventional sense. You saw the video, right? Where he shows the paper at the end like it's some sort of game, completely ignoring the four people hanging behind him? That level of detachment is seen among serials. In fact, most killers believe they have some sort of special bond with their victims."

"Mr. Bunny might have an unique agenda, one that we haven't figured out yet."

Gabriel nodded. "That's why the captain asked you all to go through the six murders and find some pattern. To understand his goal, we gotta understand his actions. Find out why he does what he does and why he chose who he chose. Then we catch Mr. Bunny," Gabriel said.

"Go through all the files and isolate anything you think might help us," Victor said. "Don't just look for something in particular. Keep your minds open and search for everything. Flight manifests, suspects or persons of interest, an odd car, a weird man picking up working girls, anything at all. With what we've learned so far, Mr. Bunny is smart. We gotta be smarter."

"Okay," Bill said, but his face expressed doubt.

He clearly felt guilty for intruding, but couldn't keep his questions inside.

Gabriel nodded to himself. Definitely detective material.

"Come on, Bill," he said. "What's on your mind?"

"You said Mr. Bunny kills people like how a disorganized serial killer would, but he's not one. Why can't it be that he's both crazy enough to kill nonstop and organized enough to escape?"

"Disorganized killers are violent, rude, and have no discipline. They can't keep a job because of their psychological issues. They aren't unknown to juvies and prisons. You with me so far?"

"Yeah," Bill said.

"These guys are mentally unhealthy. They lack the gray matter to plan and abduct four people in a single night and kill them. And they sure as hell don't videotape it and send it to commissioners and DAs. They fly below the radar and choose the homeless, immigrants, prostitutes, or children—people who are easily accessible." Gabriel paused and lifted his eyebrows.

"Yeah, yeah, I'm following you," Bill said.

"They wait in dark alleys, and when they get the chance, they bash someone's head, rape the body if they can. You know, many disorganized killers are also necrophiliacs?"

"Yes, sir, I've read."

"Then they cool off for some time before doing it again. In their temporary blindness of rage or pleasure, they leave an awful lot of evidence. But Mr. Bunny is not like that. He didn't leave any clue for the police to connect the murders, and he didn't cool off, did he?"

"No, he didn't," Bill said.

"In the video, Mr. Bunny walked in only at the last moment. Even then, he didn't pay attention to the hanging bodies. It's as if the victims' deaths don't mean anything to him. And the paper he showed us? Like it's our turn to play?"

"Yeah."

"It tells us that it's not personal. It's more like a game for him. He doesn't cool off, because he wasn't satisfying his blistering urges in the first place. He just murders and murders like a disorganized killer will, but I don't feel emotion playing a role here."

"If there is no sick fun, no revenge, and no money, what else do we have?" Emma said.

Now Gabriel had to share his idea with his team, the crazy hypothesis that had come to him the previous night. The more he thought about it, the more sense it made. But that didn't mean it would make sense to anyone else.

He took a deep breath. "I guess everything he did… it's not for himself, but for us," Gabriel said.

"What?!" She frowned in surprise.

"I don't know about the first six victims, but from the last four, I think I see his goal."

"Which is?"

"He wants to defeat us."

"A cop hater?" David narrowed his eyes as if the idea that someone could hate cops was outrageous to him.

"No. Us as in the whole criminal justice system. The police department is just a part of it. He wants to defeat justice itself." Gabriel floated his theory in a matter-of-fact tone.

Everyone looked at him with inquiring eyes. They needed an explanation, and he'd come prepared.

"Think about it," Gabriel said. "If he hates the cops, what's the point in murdering Martha? Murdering Harry fits that theory—an unsolved murder of a celebrity gives us a bad name. But by murdering Martha, he turned the news and media against himself. And only Rita was related to a cop."

"So, he isn't a cop hater?" David said. "Fine. But why these particular victims if he wants to defeat justice? Or did we overlook the blindfolded body of Lady Justice in the trunk last night?" He smiled and looked around for encouragement. Getting none, he continued. "I'm not speaking ill of the dead, but it's not like these people were the personification of justice."

"The ones he killed were not the intended victims. The people he sent the video to are. Killing these four people will get all the machines that enforce justice running at optimum capacity. For some reason, he wants to defeat us at our best."

"Come again?" David seemed lost.

So did everyone else.

"Stay with me here. He murdered Rita to infuriate the NYPD and make us hop on his tail, throwing everything we've got—freed from other cases, limitless OTs approved, bureaucratic red tapes almost non-existent, quick warrants, swift forensic and medical analysis by the best available resources—we're able to work at our highest potential," Gabriel said.

"Word. Working only one case at a time is refreshing," Laura agreed.

"Next, he murdered the wife of a man who owned the most read and most watched news in New York. As any detective will tell you, the police department's perseverance and the help they get from news networks are the two most important things in catching criminals. Now he's motivated them both. Then there are common people, who, often in the midst of bullshit, give us game-changing tips that have helped us catch criminals more than a thousand times."

"You know we caught our homeboy Son of Sam with the help of a Good Samaritan?" Victor asked.

David said he knew.

"Right. So how do you motivate the public?" Gabriel said. "Kill their least hated and most beloved celebrity, Harry Moore. Now he's got the police, the general public, and the media against him. But he didn't stop there. If he had, then I would have thought he wanted to embarrass the police and give us a bad name. Oh no, he doesn't want to defeat just us, the cops. He wants to defeat the entire judicial system."

"Doug," Emma said.

"That's right. Without courts and prisons, justice can't be enforced. If the team of police, media, and people catch the murderer, it's still useless if you can't convict him. So why not persuade the DA by murdering his son?"

Everyone stared at Gabriel. He raised his hand to deter any comment that might come his way.

"This is not a gut feeling. I've been reading the victimology of these four, which Bill diligently collected yesterday. There is nothing to connect them—different social classes, schools, and colleges. They don't even share a convenience store. The only thing they have in common is that their murders will create the most efficient team of police, media, public, and prosecutors. This is my theory."

"That's outlandish," David said, but the others didn't back him up.

"So is robbing the goddamn FBI and jumping out of a commercial airliner," Nash said. "So is the entire town playing jazz, hoping an ax-wielding maniac will leave for good. Oh, and let's not forget the killer who sent cryptic letters to the cops after murdering innocent teens. Outlandish doesn't mean impossible."

"This killer is a psychopath," Gabriel said. "A really ambitious one. So he's set up the greatest manhunt. A hunt he designed for himself. According to him, if we fail in our best form, he triumphs over the entire system of justice." He looked up at the fan. "And he would be correct to assume that."

A few seconds of silence passed—the silence after a downpour.

"Let's start to work on those files," Victor said. Then he left the room.

David and Bill followed suit.

"All right." Nash got up. "Your car or mine?" he said to Emma.

"Mine. I had to call an Uber last night. I'm not gonna trust you douchebags from other precincts."

"Come on. I'm not like David."

"Whatever. We're still taking my car."

"Call me when you land," Gabriel said.

"Okay," Emma replied. "You remember I found a camera in the street where the Suburban disappeared? The spot with skid marks?"

"I do. The house that had the camera was locked yesterday, wasn't it?"

"That's the one. I'll text you the address. Can you send someone to look into that?"

"Sure."

Gabriel's phone chimed as Emma pocketed hers. He waited until they exited, and then took out his phone. There was a missed call from Ashley. First, he forwarded the address to David. Then he called her back, but she didn't answer.

What are you doing? thought Gabriel.

* * *

"I'm helping you!" Ashley implored, trying to remove the whiskey bottle from Samuel's hand.

He'd been drinking Dalmore 62, one of the costliest whiskeys in the world, and crying rivers since they'd come back from the morgue. Only Samuel could understand what he was going through. A stranger had forced forty-six years of marriage to come to an abrupt and violent end.

"Let me be." He pulled his hand free of her clasp. "If you'd be so kind as to leave me alone. I have a meeting with Tracy."

Tracy White was Samuel's lawyer. But when Ashley had entered Samuel's office ten minutes ago, she'd seen Tracy going out.

"Your meeting with Tracy is over, Sam."

"So is this meeting. Now get the hell out of here." His words slurred and wavered, but not his bloodshot eyes.

It was the first time she'd heard him speak so harshly. Ashley rushed out of the office, wiping at her tears.

She stopped at a water dispenser. As she drank lukewarm water from a cup, she thought about why Samuel would want to meet Tracy. The only thing Tracy was responsible for was Samuel's will.

Drinking the costliest whiskey after seeing his wife dead, and meeting with the family lawyer who'd maintained his will, didn't sit well together in her heart.

"No—" Ashley gasped.

She dropped the cup and ran back to Samuel's office. Just as she reached the doorway, her eyes widened in horror.

Samuel was biting the deadly end of a pistol.

"Sam, no!" She dashed forward.

With the muzzle still in his mouth, he said something. His words garbled, but Ashley understood that he'd said *Sorry, dear.*

His thumb squeezed the trigger.

Blood and bits of reddish pink meat splattered on the painting behind him.

The profound sound of the shot jerked Ashley to a stop. She clapped her hands over her ears, squeezed her eyes shut, and sank into a protective huddle. People rushed inside and stood around her. A pair of gentle arms pulled her back and then onto the floor.

Keeping her eyes clenched shut, she hoped it was all a terrible dream.

Chapter 16

March 17, 2019. 11:48 A.M.

"Thank you, Emily. I'm sorry again for your loss… Goodbye." Gabriel disconnected the call.

Emily, an intern at the Daily Herald, had answered Ashley's phone. Samuel's assistant had passed out, bumped her head on the floor and suffered a concussion. Gabriel postponed feeling anything about the news of Samuel's suicide and made a mental note to visit Ashley in the hospital that evening.

David walked into the office, carrying an opened laptop on his forearm.

"You found the address?" Gabriel said.

"I did. The man who owned the house was in and I got a video clip from him. Look here." David placed the laptop on the table and turned it toward Gabriel.

The screen showed a well-lit street. Twenty seconds later, the Suburban entered the road, moving west to east. A normal citizen driving under the speed limit in a soccer mom car. Except he had two women tied up in the back.

Out of nowhere, a speeding yellow car appeared. It cut the red SUV off and raced away. The Suburban was still wobbling when it exited the frame.

"He crashed?" Gabriel said.

The car they found yesterday was fine, but Gabriel didn't put it beyond Mr. Bunny to have replaced the broken parts before dumping it.

"Um, I don't think so. The skid marks faded along the road, and the curb isn't damaged. Looks like he got the car back under control. There's something interesting here."

"What?"

"The yellow car, a Mustang. It belongs to Ashley."

"Ashley Stuart?" Gabriel's eyebrows rose.

"Uh-huh."

"Wait... you mean she crossed Mr. Bunny's car *after* he abducted Martha?"

"Yes. In other words, *ouch*."

"Shit."

David took a seat across the table and turned the laptop to his side.

"There's more," he said.

"Yeah?"

"Do you remember Alisha Webb and Luis Garcia? The murder victims for which Florida and Pennsylvania convicted the wrong people?"

"What about them?" Gabriel asked.

"I have cellphone tower records from all three recent abduction sites. Alisha's and Luis's numbers popped up in one of the towers," David said. "Their phones have been missing since he killed them, but Friday night they were switched back on. And get this, Alisha called Luis."

"What?" Gabriel narrowed his eyes.

"It's a video call, and it lasted eighteen minutes. The network providers will have voice calls, but not the video calls. The GPS for their phones was enabled. The exact location from where the call was made is Martha's house."

"What!"

"That's what the tower dump records say." David shrugged.

After a minute of thinking, Gabriel said, "I think he used them to spy on Martha. Stanley found pink fibers in the closet in her bedroom where we also found her handbag and spectacles. Mr. Bunny waited in her closet and got her there, right?"

"Yes."

"He hid inside the closet and used these phones to spy on her. I guess he placed one of the phones in the living room to cover the front door."

"Why did he use his other victims' phones? Wouldn't he know we'd find out?" David asked.

"That's exactly why he used them."

"What?"

"Miami and Philadelphia jailed the wrong guys and closed the case. Mr. Bunny doesn't want us to think he's claiming responsibility for murders he didn't commit. Many serial killers do that after they get caught, increasing their numbers to show off."

"I presume you want me to flag the other victims' phones, excluding Rita's?" David asked.

"And Doug's, which is in his house. How long will it take?"

"Five minutes, max."

"Do it on the way." Gabriel stood.

"One more thing. Not sure if this will help." David closed the laptop.

"Yeah?"

"Lacking anything better to do last night, I mapped the Suburban's movement before Mr. Bunny abandoned it at Shore Parkway. I tracked it backward until it disappeared in Arrochar."

"He drove out of Staten Island. So what?"

"This is how we catch a lot of criminals. I thought it's worth a shot."

"This is not *a lot of criminals*," Gabriel said. "I thought you'd have realized that by now."

* * *

Gabriel parked David's Corolla in front of Steve Bastian's house at Tiffany Place, a narrow residential street in Cobble Hill, Brooklyn. True to his word, David marked all the phones in under five minutes. With nothing better to do, he pestered Gabriel with his asshattery.

A big man of around fifty years old opened the door for them. New York's cold weather had reddened his cheeks. He had to be the brother from Arizona.

"I'm Detective Chase, and this is Detective Gustavo. We are—"

"Oh, come on in, Detectives. I'm sorry about yesterday. My brother couldn't…"

He was searching for the right word when Gabriel said, "We understand, Mr. Bastian."

The man squeezed out a smile and led them into the living room.

Steve sat on a couch, pressing his hands against his temples, and a half-empty bottle of Jack Daniel's stood between his feet. He wore a gray T-shirt with *Fordham Law* and *2021* printed on it. Had to be Doug's. Gabriel had yet to understand all the different ways people dealt with losing someone to violent crime.

"Gentlemen," Steve said. He released his head and looked at them with bloodshot eyes.

He didn't offer seats. Gabriel took his cue from David and sat on a chair opposite the couch. He couldn't see Steve's wife anywhere. She might have transferred her ex-husband to his brother's care—she had her own grieving to do.

"Nash visited earlier?" Steve asked.

"He did, sir." Gabriel hadn't realized the DA knew Nash.

"I remember Nash, and I got a conviction for one Bob." Steve addressed the space between David and Gabriel. "The confession he made downtown after he got his teeth kicked up into his gums by Nash didn't help. So we—" He sniffled and rubbed his nose on the sleeve. "Nash and I went to this eight-year-old girl, Jessie, and talked to her. We asked her to tell the truth about her Uncle Bob, who frequently took her for long rides in his car."

Gabriel knew where the story was going.

"This girl was so small, I tell you. She looked like a baby parrot, with her bright green gown. Fragile little baby parrot. You know how hard it was for us to make her touch the anatomical doll in the courtroom? But she did. She trusted us. You know why?"

"No, sir. I don't," Gabriel said.

"When we asked her, she said, 'You're good people.'" He wiped his running nose again on the same place. "Her exact words after the trial—after we booked Bob, the son of a whore, into Rikers. We knew the child had repeated it verbatim from her mother, but it made no difference in what it made us feel. That's the reason I love my job. We lock the bad up and keep the good safe. Now a single man is destroying everything you and I and everyone like us have ever worked for." Steve closed his fists. "It's just impossible, Detective...?"

"Gabriel Chase, sir."

"Detective Chase... the name rings a bell, but I'm sorry. I can't recall from where." Steve managed a smile of brief apology.

"I understand, sir. What's impossible?"

"To win the war between good and bad. It's an infinite game of chess, and people like us are that famous ant on a rubber rope," Steve said. "We will reach our goal, but it will literally take an eternity and then some."

A clock ticked somewhere in the house.

"I'm sorry, Detective. Fire away." Steve took the Jack Daniels, placed the nozzle to his lips and decanted the bottle.

"We talked to Doug's friends. They said that on Friday night he went out with his girlfriend, but she tells us she didn't meet him."

Steve returned the bottle to its resting place. "She broke up with him."

"What? She didn't tell us that. Neither did Doug's friends."

"It makes you feel guilty for breaking up with a boy a week before his murder."

"His friends should have known, right?" Gabriel asked.

"Why do you think he kept it to himself? The boy was afraid of failure. He didn't want his friends to know he was capable of failing, even at something as trivial as that."

"He was trying to be like you, sir," David said. That was a good try at comfort, albeit a cheesy one that made Gabriel cringe inside.

Steve smiled. Even though it was a joyless, empty smile that appeared only on one side of his face, it was a smile, nonetheless.

"Was that why he kept his phone in the house?" Gabriel said. "To avoid Nell?"

"No. Doug was a perfectionist, not petty. He didn't use his phone most of the time. He wasn't addicted to it like ninety-nine percent of the world is."

"Then where was he? We need to know that in order to find out how he was abducted."

"The reason he didn't use his phone very much was simple. He had ambition and he didn't want that small thing to disturb his concentration. Doug wanted to become Mr. Olympia. Where do you think he was Friday night?"

"Gym?" Gabriel said.

Steve nodded and gave him the address. Then he took to the bottle again.

"So, Mr. Bastian, sir? One last question."

"Proceed."

"When we catch the guy who did this to your son, we'll need your help to hurt him back."

Steve smiled humorlessly. "Sure."

"So, can we expect you to be alive and sober when that time comes?" Gabriel asked, and David stiffened beside him.

The DA looked at Gabriel's unblinking eyes. Did he just lose his job?

Steve dropped the bottle and brown liquid oozed onto the white carpet. Then he smiled again. But this time, the smile was full.

It brimmed with venom and a lust for revenge.

Chapter 17

March 17, 2019. 02:31 P.M.

David took the wheel on their way back. They'd agreed that canvassing the gym where Doug had gone that Friday night was a one-man job. David dropped Gabriel at a pizzeria across from the 122nd precinct and drove on to the gym. Gabriel bought two plain slices and a coffee. He crossed Hylan Boulevard and entered the precinct. Once inside his office, he opened the food box.

As he shoved food down his throat, he called Anthony. The ME said he'd completed the autopsies with the help of his colleagues who'd worked graveyard shifts last night, and he would send the reports before evening.

Gabriel hung up and called Stanley. The pink fibers had come from a Puma tracksuit which Mr. Bunny could have bought from any one of a hundred outlets. Forensic geologists had analyzed the soil from the Chevy Suburban's wheels and mud flaps and concluded that they were from suburban New York. They couldn't be more specific than that. Apart from Alan's fingerprints, there wasn't even a partial glove print on the SUV except for microscopic white particles, the vestiges from the evaporated chemical Mr. Bunny had used to destroy DNA.

Stanley said he sent the samples from the radiator and AC intake to a palynologist in Quantico, and it would take time to get the results back. Gabriel muttered a thank you and cut the call.

Bill knocked on the open door and Gabriel waved him in.

"How did the search go?" he said, and Bill filled him in.

Mr. Bunny stole the Suburban from a spot in front of Abigail's apartment which a single camera covered. The superintendent didn't allow Wild Bill to take the video recording, even after he bullied him. He'd later learned the super was an ex-cop who knew that the *obstruction of justice* and *face severe penalties* lines were bullshit. But after seeing the young cop put his head down and walk away, he'd called him back and let him see the footage.

On the night of the theft, around 8:00 p.m., the camera shook like someone took a bat to it. Then the feed went black. The super said the camera was not broken, but he remembered cleaning the camera's lens and discovering that it was splashed with paint. Someone shot it with a paintball gun. With pink pellets.

"Pink?" Gabriel said. "You sure? Not red or something?"

"That's what he said."

Mr. Bunny didn't want the detectives to think that the painted camera was just the work of neighborhood vandals. He'd predicted the police would sniff their way to that particular camera. So, he'd doused it with the color of the clothes he'd use in three months—the color of the fibers he knew the cops would find where he'd abducted people.

Mr. Bunny had countered every move the detectives made even before they made it. Gabriel didn't feel like they were investigating a series of homicides, but more like they were all marionettes that a deranged puppeteer was playing with in his sick theater.

Bill concluded, saying he didn't want to disturb Ashley by interviewing her in the hospital.

"That's all, Detective Chase. I'm going to continue with the file the captain shared this morning. You read it?"

"Not yet. You?"

"Just skimmed the surface. Gore porn is what it is." With that, Bill left.

Gabriel picked up his phone and created a reminder to go to the hospital at eight and visit Ashley. Her loss took precedence over his.

He opened Victor's email and began reading the autopsy reports of the six murders.

The deaths of the first three victims were quick. They never knew what happened to them until they woke up floating in purgatory.

They were the lucky ones.

From the fourth victim onward, the reports did read like *gore porn*. Maimed, burnt, flayed, drilled, sawed, and *sanded?* Gabriel winced. It was the journal of a medieval dungeon master.

The initial victims' tortures were inefficient. The respective MEs concluded that the murderer didn't know where to find certain viscera or how to cut his way to it. But at the sixth victim, it seemed like the pathologists had found merit in Mr. Bunny's work. They mentioned the use of surgical tools and tourniquets, amputations, and precise removal of internal organs without letting the victims pass out from pain or die from exsanguination.

Why did Mr. Bunny become crueler with each murder, but in a controlled setting?

Wait a minute.

Mr. Bunny had been practicing!

Gabriel's muted shiver was trodden on by the ringing phone, area code 585, followed by an unknown number.

"Hello?"

"Nash here. No network coverage in prison, man. They've put up jammers to prevent the inmates from using smuggled cell phones. So I'm calling from a landline."

"You got something?"

"From what Mr. Jones said, Hercules controls the inmates."

"Edward said that?"

"He did. Funny, right? Because he's supposed to be the warden. It seems like Hercules has huge clout inside, and he talks only when he wants to talk. Surprise, surprise, he decided not to talk to us." Nash let out a heavy breath into the speaker. "All in all, it's a waste of time and taxpayers' money, Gabriel."

When Nash hung up, something sparked in Gabriel's brain.

Jammers. Of course!

Didn't Samuel's neighbor complain that their Wi-Fi was down around the time of Martha's abduction? Mr. Bunny must have used a jammer to silence Samuel's home security, and it must have disabled the surrounding Wi-Fi networks. However, it still didn't explain how he knew the code to breach the main gate. Did he own a similar exotic device to do so? Who was this guy?

Disheartened by Mr. Bunny's resourcefulness, Gabriel closed his eyes. He was lost in thought, and then in the nightmares caused by the autopsy reports he'd been reading.

He woke up to the notification sound of his PC. When he unlocked it, he found an email from Anthony Mills waiting in the inbox. Gabriel forwarded it to his team before opening it. He went through the reports in under an hour. When he finished, it was 7:38 p.m.

He clicked on the reminder he'd created and deleted it. He took his keys and helmet and headed out.

* * *

Gabriel placed a bouquet of flowers on the bedside table. The florist outside the hospital assured him that they would make any patient feel better. Ashley lay on her bed, looking out a window. Dried tears peppered the sides of her eyes.

"I'm sorry for your loss. I know you were close to them both."

"Close doesn't cover it." She turned and faced Gabriel.

She spotted the flowers, and smiled. It was an odd first smile that came after hours of crying and depression.

He wanted to tell her everything was going to be all right, but his father hadn't raised a liar.

"I don't know why I'm telling you this, but…" Ashley trailed off.

Gabriel watched her struggle, unable to help.

"Samuel altered his will today."

"He did?" Gabriel asked.

"I get everything related to the Daily Herald, including the news channel. I'm the majority stockholder, with fifty-one percent now. Plus their house."

It was obvious Ashley didn't feel rich. She felt guilty.

"Everything that's not related to the news—and trust me, it's a lot—he gave to orphanages. Sam grew up in one."

"That's generous… wow!" Gabriel had the feeling that she was about to cry, so he quickly added, "Listen. I've talked to the doctor, and she said you can go home. I'll give you a lift."

"Promise me you'll get that psycho." She made no effort to get up.

It was as if only his pledge would give her a reason to move. To live.

He looked her in the eye. "I promise you I will never give up."

* * *

A nurse, *Paul* his name tag said, wheeled Ashley out to the entrance. Paul looked at Gabriel with disapproval when he parked the Kawasaki in front of the wheelchair.

Ashley got on the back seat and guided him to her place in Brighton Beach.

Twenty minutes later, they passed an old black Fiat and she told him to park in front of a high-class apartment building. She got down and stood on the sidewalk, looking like a lost child in a theme park.

Gabriel knew more than he ought to about the gamut of reactions that came after witnessing murder or suicide or accident. It could range from becoming mute, to leading a life filled with pills and weekly psychotherapy sessions.

"This is a good place to live," he said. "What floor you on?"

"Third floor. That one." She pointed at a window that overlooked the street, on the right side of the building.

"Can you see the beach from there?" Gabriel said, trying to sound interested.

"Yes. It gets boring, though. Look, Detective Chase, I'd invite you up. But you don't want to see a miserable drunk."

"Drunk? Maybe. Miserable? No," Gabriel said. "I don't think you can ever be miserable. When I saw you earlier, I thought you were the only person who could look strong in a hospital bed."

Ashley smiled. Gabriel hoped her dry lips didn't split.

"You want to come up for drinks?" she asked.

"It's all right. Next time, I will."

"My head's not feeling good. I really need to get drunk."

"Don't do that." Gabriel hesitated a moment, but continued. "I'm an alcoholic."

"Oh… I'm sorry. I shouldn't have—"

"Nah, you're fine." He waved it off. "The battle I had to wage to defeat the compulsion was tough, but I won. The person who helped me win was Rita Hughes, one of the victims. She was my godmother."

Ashley closed her eyes, sucked her lips in and nodded.

"You told me you didn't know why you were telling me that Samuel altered his will," Gabriel said. "Well, I don't know why I'm telling you this, but… I'm scared."

"Scared?"

"Very much, yes. Scared that I'm going to fall into the bottle again. Scared that I will drown this time. Dying doesn't scare me." Gabriel scoffed. "But dying before I catch Mr. Bunny does. It's the only thing that's keeping me from the bars. Learn something from me, okay?"

"Yes?"

"Don't make liquor a painkiller. That's how alcoholism starts."

"I saw Samuel kill himself!" Ashley's voice broke.

"It's no time to grieve." Gabriel sounded sterner than he would have liked. "I suffer a similar pain, but I know I can't start dealing with it now. It's just not the time, Ms. Stuart. Put it inside a box and shelve it. You can open it only after we catch him."

Ashley stood there without replying, her knuckles white.

"And I need your help to catch him."

"What?"

"I need a person who can use the Daily Herald. Now that you own it, I know you'll do your best to make the man responsible pay."

"M-my help? To catch a *serial killer*?"

"Uh-huh. So please don't drink. I need you. And together, we will bring Mr. Bunny down."

Perhaps he'd said something he shouldn't have, because Ashley grabbed his jacket with both hands and cried into it. Her hair smelled like strawberries.

He had no choice but to awkwardly put his arms around her.

Predators

3/17/19. Post-dinner.

Why did I tell the Tree News to call me *Mr. Bunny*? Do I have some weird fixation with rabbits? Did I own a cute bunny when I was young, and now I'm commemorating him with indelible naughtiness? No. I've always known I should wear a mask when recording my history, but I never thought about the mask itself. You could even say that this is the only part in my plot I planned not to plan. A paradox per se, but you shouldn't plan everything—it's nice to have variables in life. Or just one.

I went to a toy shop last year, willing myself to buy the first mask I laid my eyes on, regardless of the appeals other masks might make. I secretly hoped it would be Mr. Voorhees or Jigsaw. Or even a horse. That would have been adequately creepy. But all I got was a white bunny. How mortifying.

As for the Armani, I wanted to look my best at the only party that has ever meant anything to me. Of course, it's impossible not to anoint a person wearing an expensive suit with the honorific of sir or mister. Sir Bunny sounds awful, like a British superhero's sidekick. So I birthed Mr. Bunny.

It's amusing when you contemplate it. Even if posterity should forget the murders, which I planned for years, they will always remember the mask which I acquired on a whim.

Thinking about plans, I didn't factor in Samuel's weak heart. I'd overestimated its strength. He proved himself an unworthy opponent. A coward. Vengeance should have combusted inside him like coal and compelled the old engine to come after me. After all, I'd snuffed out the flame of his first and last love under my foot like a cigarette butt. I took away his soul and made a husk out of what was once vibrant. Food, liquor, women, cars, or whatever his millions would have bought, couldn't have brought him the tiniest ray of happiness. His only hope of ever again experiencing something that resembled a good feeling would have been revenge. That was the whole point, and the other two seemed to have gotten it. But he shot himself in the head. I learned about his suicide from Tree News, in the same manner the whole country did. It appears that the Daily Herald has a severe rat problem.

Sam couldn't live with the motivation I created for him. By killing himself, he delegated his responsibilities to his assistant, Ashley.

Oh, that isn't the only tidbit I know about Samuel's Titian-haired PA. I know it was her who cut me off with the speeding Mustang, making me jump like a cat and lose control of the Suburban. She lives in Brighton Beach, and I'm driving there to pay her a visit. But then what?

How do criminals decide whether or not to spare someone who has stumbled upon their plot? Does that person remind the criminal of someone they used to know and love? Or perhaps the criminals deduce that sparing a particular individual won't hurt them in the future? A calculated kindness?

I was thirteen when my father took me to Boston to stay with my dying grandmother. As I predicted, I was bored most of the time. So I explored the old Victorian house and its banal environment. This is where I found my destiny that I talked about earlier.

No, *it* found *me*.

There was a vacant lot as big as an Olympic running track behind grandmother's fence, its middle section overflowing with weeds and bushes. Small hills of garbage dotted the embankment on the other side of the lot, and then the ground sloped up to the ugly backs of buildings. A narrow alley parted them in half, leading onto a busy road.

I used to sneak across the backyard and slip between the fences. I went inside the thorny vegetation to look for any living creature. I found them, and as I did back at my home, I entertained myself with them. Though the plants provided me a shady cover, they also silently witnessed these animals' torment.

One day I saw my grandmother's maidservant heading out with a rat trap in her hand, the kind that didn't kill the animal. I blocked her path and told her I wanted to release the rat, giving her my best smile. Curious and bored out-of-town little kid. She ruffled my hair and handed the wooden box over.

I searched the attic and found a transparent plastic box, a set of thick rubber gloves, and pliers. I drilled seven or eight small holes in the box, and then carried it all to my small forest.

I returned home after an hour and dropped the gloves in a bin, hoping no one would see the desperate bite marks on them. I washed the red from the pliers and returned them to their original place. Then I ate dinner and slept peacefully.

Next morning, I acquired warm milk from the kitchen and went to the balcony. Three men stood inside the verdant foliage, invading my land. They wore black jackets, camouflage pants, and military boots. They seemed to be staring at the ground. Were they looking at the box I'd left there the previous night?

I ran down, opened the wire mesh door and walked toward them. As I got closer, I noticed all three of them wore masks: red, blue, and pale green. They looked like demons from a nightmare. Though I tried not to make a sound or be caught in their peripheral vision, the tallest man among them turned in my direction. He wore a pale green mask.

I couldn't see his eyes from this distance, but I sensed that he'd spotted me. I hesitated for a moment, but fear got the best of me. What if they told someone about my four-legged friends? So I kept walking toward the brambles. As I crouched to avoid the last finger-pointing thorn, one of the many that bore witness to all the horrors that happened here, I noticed something on the ground that piqued my interest.

A snake, almost twice as long as I was, lay dead under the tall man's foot, his shoe squashing its neck. Its tube-like body had coiled into two rings, and rested on the side of his leg. As I looked up, my gaze paused at his hip, which was bearing a holster. Um… aren't criminals supposed to conceal their weapons? Like, by not having it in a freaking holster? Puzzled, I peered further up, up until my eyes reached the mask. It was a zombie, and a white plastic straw poked out of the mouth hole.

"What up, junior?" the zombie asked.

The straw moved around as he talked.

"Nothing." I licked my dry lips.

"You did this? Squirrels on sticks? Rat in a box?"

I shrugged.

The zombie bent down, retrieved the box and inspected it.

Sensing movement, the furry rodent woke from its dizziness and scrambled, but to no avail. It had only reddish-brown stumps where the legs used to be. The rat had tried its best to get out—otherwise, there wouldn't have been streaks and streaks of dried blood inside the box.

"Where's the legs?" the zombie asked.

"Don't know. I threw them away. Maybe ants ate them."

"Gimme your hands."

I gave him one, the other holding my G.I. Joe flask to my mouth. His skin was rough like a farmer's. He turned my hand, scanned it before releasing it, then held his hand out in demand. I switched the bottle and gave him my other hand. He examined it like a palm reader. Now I know he really did see my future that day.

"It's a big-ass rat, boy. It must've bitten you. But you got no scratches." He let go of my hand.

"I wore gloves," I said.

"Hm. That's smart. Why these holes, though?"

"A guy on TV said animals have a great sense of smell for blood. I thought I would..." I forgot the word the man had used.

"Lure," the zombie said.

"Yes! Lure! I thought I'd lure some predators."

The zombie nudged the snake's body away and lifted his boot. The snake's neck, if it ever had one, was gooey and flat.

"Seems like you did. But the rat is inside the box. How do you expect—"

"It's time, man," said the blue demon.

The sense of urgency in his tone wasn't lost on my young mind. But the zombie didn't pay any attention to him. He was interested in me. I liked that.

"You wanted to feed the snake, right?"

"No."

"Then why lure?"

"I thought it would be funny. The rat can't escape, and the predator can't eat." Since I couldn't help chuckling at the thought, I covered my mouth and did it.

And the red demon joined me, but there was something different about it. It was a high-pitched giggle. As he cackled like a hyena, I took an instant liking towards him. He was tiny compared to the other two, especially the blue demon standing beside him, who looked like a bodybuilder for whom the world hadn't produced enough steroids.

The zombie looked at me with dead eyes. To everyone's surprise, he removed his mask. The white stick poking out moved up as he pulled the mask over his head, and sprang back into place when he was done.

Out of nowhere, the blue demon pulled a gun, like a cartoon character producing an oversized weapon from hammerspace. He grabbed my shirt to stop me from running away, which I didn't plan on doing. These three men looked like they could catch me even if I had a ten-mile head start.

"You crazy, man?" The blue demon pointed his gun at me and cocked it.

I was scared out of my wits but didn't let it show.

"You remember the ninety-four," said the blue demon, "when that Joshua fool almost caught us? It's because you let someone else see your face."

"Lower your gun," said the man without the mask.

"We have to waste him, man," Blue said. "He's a threat."

The gun's cold metallic nose touched my temple and hovered around my face as Blue argued his point. Thirsty, I took a sip of my milk.

"He won't tell anyone," he said.

I guess the zombie really did believe that, because he didn't bother confirming his statement with me.

"Nah, man. You can't know that."

"As a matter of fact, I do. Look at the way he stands, sipping his goddamn moo-juice while staring into the hollow of your muzzle, into death itself. He ain't afraid or guilty of what he did. He is me. Gifted." Then he traced his holster and removed the strap.

A gun the size of a hatchet gleamed inside it. When he spoke next, his voice changed. It became smooth, but somehow more menacing.

"How about this? I give you two seconds to lower your gun."

The red demon gave out another melodious hyena cackle as the blue demon moved the weapon away from my face.

The zombie took a new candy from his jacket pocket, a lollipop with a yellow wrapper. I stood there, staring at the candy. Was he a stranger? He didn't feel like one, so I took it by the stick.

"What do you say, kiddo?"

"Thank you, zombie?"

He laughed. "No. You say, *I want one more*." He pinched my cheek with his gloved fingers. "And call me Lolly."

I loathed that spicy-salted paradox of a candy. Don't candies mean sweet and pleasant? But though I found that sorry excuse of a confectionery oppressive, I accepted the tasteless zombie's gesture to be cordial.

Boston PD, and then the FBI, interviewed everyone in my grandmother's house. Lolly and his friends killed three people that day and robbed $47,000 from a bank. A bank that was situated on the road that the alley behind the vacant lot led to. The police asked if we'd seen someone lingering behind our house. When asked, I said no.

But I know how he looks.

Lolly was an African-American with a trimmed goatee, a shaved head, and a boxlike face. The most memorable thing was his blue eyes. A pair of light-blue eyes that looked like he'd gone through every war that had been fought in the history of mankind, and attained some great philosophical knowledge about violence.

When I was sixteen, I copied his methods and robbed $98,000 from a bank to fund my ambition. It felt right—he was partially responsible for the said ambition, wasn't he?

Later in my life, I understood why Lolly had showed me his face—one inborn deviant showing respect to another. I suppose I'm the only one in the whole world who knows what Lolly looks like, except his partners in crime. That's less than the number of people who have walked on the surface of the moon. I can't help feeling special.

But the person who came into my plot and almost destroyed it—Ashley—isn't anything like us. I didn't hurt Lolly, but this woman could have hurt me in the worst way possible.

From the timing of it, I've arrived at the assumption that she was speeding right after she found out Martha was missing. But it doesn't change anything. She is still a rash driver. A petty criminal is what she is, and I've always considered them as pervasive and revolting as cockroaches. Before Ashley, I'd had another small-time crook barge into my private party. It's as if I attract them.

I ease the stolen black Fiat to a stop, thirty yards from her apartment. I lower my head and glance at her window. No lights. She would come home late, what with Samuel biting the gun. It appears that it'll be a while. I'll wait.

Should I hurt her? I imagine the carnal offers she'll make to escape the hurt that can come with the application of serrated metal. A lesser man would indulge, but not me.

A motorcycle crosses my car and stops in front of her building, with Ashley on its pillion. They both get down. The rider removes his helmet and his wild hair springs out.

It's Detective Gabriel Chase. That's a shocker! I smile, thinking about the caption *Madman to Catch a Madman*.

And why are they hugging? Is he consoling her? It seems as if I've created a platform on which to grow a beautiful friendship.

Gabriel watches Ashley get inside her house. When she closes the door, he buckles his helmet back on, swings a leg over the motorcycle and drives off.

I open a bag on my passenger's seat. Rusty knife. Check. Mask, cell phones, lock-pick satchel. Check, check, check. I close the bag again.

Before going inside, I'm going to take a little nap and give Ashley some time to fall asleep. Then it'll be easy to invade her house and haunt her dreams forever.

Chapter 18

March 18, 2019. 12:02 A.M.

Gabriel's phone blared and woke him up. He jerked up, his heart pumping gallons of fuel throughout the body. Experience had taught him that midnight calls brought bad news more often than good. He was ready and on his feet as he disentangled his phone from the blanket.

It was David. "Harry's and Martha's phones came online at 11:57. Both of them have their GPS turned on," he said, his voice urgent. "I'm on my way there."

"Where?" Gabriel tucked the Glock into his waistband and lurched down the stairs.

"Brighton 6th Street, Brook—"

Gabriel cut the call because he knew it was Ashley's place. He'd just dropped her there.

He hopped on his motorcycle and jumped down the curb with a wheelie he didn't intend. It peeled out of the street, back tire screeching and splashing dirt in its wake.

Since he was covered only by sweatpants and shirt, the night's cold air drilled into his pores. But he paid no attention to his freezing bones. His mind went back to the last time he saw Ashley. Her strawberry smell.

The wind made his eyes water and drops flew past his temple. Gabriel looked at the speedometer. It hovered on a triple-digit reading. Should he slip, he'd be smeared on the road, but the speed still was not enough. The last time Mr. Bunny switched on the phones in Martha's house, he abducted her in twenty minutes.

Gabriel revved the throttle further. The RPM redlined and the footrest quivered as the beast unleashed the full fury of its 1000cc engine.

* * *

Gabriel arrived at 12:12 a.m. Cruisers weren't there yet, but he could hear the sirens closing in. He dropped the Kawasaki on the street and rushed inside.

Having no time to wait for elevators, he sprinted up to her apartment on the third floor. Her door was locked. He weighed his options, took out his gun and aimed it above the doorknob.

Splinters flew and broken lumps of wood fell with thuds.

Bursting inside, Gabriel ran toward the end of the hallway, to a room on the right, which must overlook the beach. The bedroom.

He found no one inside and his heart sank. The sudden desolation was so deep he almost failed to react when a human form jumped at him.

Almost.

He turned in time to grab the wrist carrying a small kitchen knife—a wrist that was fragile and weak from spending the whole day in the hospital.

He lowered Ashley's arm and kept his finger on his lips. He walked around the apartment and checked all the places where a person could hide.

Once he was sure they were alone, he said, "No one's here."

"Why would there be? What are you doing here? And what was that loud noise?" Nervousness accelerated Ashley's speech.

"I shot down your door." He dabbed at his wet forehead.

"It was a gunshot? I knew it was a gunshot! It stopped me halfway from puking my intestines out."

Gabriel now got a smell of rancid vomit and brandy. After all that speech about alcoholism, she still hadn't listened to him. But he was in no position to judge. He'd done the exact same thing a hundred times.

He called David.

"What's happening?" Ashley said.

He lifted a finger and then spoke into the phone. "I know the units are coming. Just tell me where the phones are… yes, tell me where *exactly*…" He looked at Ashley. "What do you mean you can't narrow further…" He cut the call.

"What?" Ashley asked again. But Gabriel ignored her.

He began sifting through all the items in the bedroom.

When he opened the closet door, he found two phones propped up above the folded clothes.

Between them was a smiling rabbit mask.

* * *

Once the excitement in Ashley's apartment subsided, she went to a tight-lipped colleague's house to get some sleep. Gabriel didn't believe that such a thing called rest was going to be possible for her in the coming weeks.

CSU tested the phones and mask for fingerprints and sweat residues, which was a fool's errand. Even before Stanley confirmed the presence of sodium hypochlorite, both Gabriel and David had recognized the odor. With that in mind, David borrowed the phones from Stanley before he bagged them. He unlocked one with a swipe and found dynamite in it.

The phone's wallpaper was a picture of Mr. Bunny in the same suit, tie, and mask. He'd propped himself on the headboard beside Ashley, who was in a heedless, alcohol-aided sleep, her mouth parting a little. Mr. Bunny had held a footlong rusty knife near her neck and clicked a selfie.

With the flash on.

Chapter 19

March 18, 2019. 07:15 A.M.

CSU had collected the evidence from Ashley's apartment. Gabriel had tempered his expectations, which helped with the disappointment when Stanley called. His information was identical to what he'd told about the Chevy Suburban—not a single piece of evidence.

"No hope from you, then?" Gabriel said into the phone, as he poured milk and cereal into his bowl.

"Unfortunately, no," Stanley replied. "From the fibers we've plucked from Ashley's bedspread, we know your killer prefers expensive suits, but nothing unique."

"Hm. Why doesn't that surprise me?"

"I understand your frustration, but I really can't do anything here. Locard's principle works best when the doer's not aware of it and doesn't take precautions."

"Anyone with a TV could know about Locard these days." Gabriel shoved the first spoonful into his mouth.

"You must know that criminals have been trying to destroy evidence and escape the law from the time forensics convicted and executed the Stratton brothers. But this man, among a few other notable malefactors, has succeeded."

"That won't stop me from getting him." Gabriel gripped the phone tighter.

"Don't you see the big picture, Gabriel? He's aware of that, too. He knows there's a marginal possibility of SWAT guys ramming down his door and barging inside with assault rifles."

"He knows we'll catch him, and he still did it? A bit too elaborate for suicide-by-cop, don't you think?"

"*Marginal possibility*, Gabriel. And I didn't say he's trying to kill himself. I'm saying that when you enter his house and secure his head under your boot and cuff him as blood oozes down his cheek—why, of course there'll be blood, I know you—"

"You bet there'll be a lot of it." Gabriel smiled.

In rare instances, Stanley could express optimism, too.

"But even with blood covering his teeth, he would still smile because he knows he'd already made sure we never get anything to convict him. All he needs is a reasonable doubt, and without a single shred of forensic evidence, he's got a lot more than that."

That was how Gabriel's day had begun. After that, he bathed and put on an unfamiliar suit. Victor picked him up, and they both went to say their final goodbyes to Rita as her coffin descended into the ground. Gabriel couldn't console Raymond, as he himself was fighting an internal battle. Afterward, Victor and Gabriel returned to the precinct, arriving last at the meeting room, just after 10:00 a.m.

"Thank you all for yesterday," Gabriel said. "I really appreciate the sacrifices you guys made on your Sundays."

Everyone stared at him. Did he come off like a two-bit politician? He didn't think so. Maybe it was his clothing.

With his unruly hair and beard, the suit must be an eyesore.

The attendance was full, plus Ashley, who insisted on being there. She said Samuel would've wanted her to be part of the team and help them however she could. She sounded motivated, but with an undertone of fear, which wasn't surprising after what she'd been through the previous night. Both Gabriel and David agreed to keep the information about Mr. Bunny's selfie from the poor woman. It turned out David wasn't a full-time asshole, after all.

The meeting started with Gabriel addressing the latest event of breaking and entering, in Ashley's house this time.

"What's the connection to Ashley?" Victor said.

"I can't place this in Mr. Bunny's pattern. He killed the last four victims to force out the best in us, and Ashley—"

"That's just a supposition," David said.

"I don't have a better one, but I'm all ears, David." Gabriel took his inhaler from the pocket.

No reply.

"She is of no use to him as a victim. He didn't plan this." Gabriel returned the inhaler. "If he did, he could have taken Ashley the same night he got them all. It must be for something else."

Victor assigned Mark and Laura to canvas Ashley's locale, and they moved on to the next priority.

The ME's office had an update, and Anthony took the stage as its representative. He was the oldest and the shortest in the room, even smaller than petite Laura, but not at all weak. Although his face showed sixty-five plus years of age, his sinewy body looked like an iron statue.

"We've completed autopsies on all four, and I've sent the reports to Gabriel. He assured me he forwarded it to you all. Learned anything interesting?"

"Yes, sir," Bill said. "Harry has a pair of small burn marks about three millimeters in circumference on the back of his neck. You commented that it's possible that they came from a stun gun. Rita has them, too. Her face, shoulders, and the left side of her torso were bruised. No imprints on her skin to find what Mr. Bunny used to beat her up with. And all the victims died of asphyxiation, except Martha."

"You train them good down here at the Island, Victor." Anthony turned to Bill again. "What's your name again?"

"William." He touched the rim of his cap. "Everyone calls me Bill."

Gabriel thought Bill resembled a young Nash—arrogant and self-righteous, but also curious and hardworking. He wasn't required to read the autopsy reports, but he did. Witnessing his dedication, Gabriel decided that he'd tell him to take the exams for detective when the case was over, and write him a recommendation letter.

"And, Bill?" Anthony said. "Do you know what the cause of death for Martha is?"

"Sudden cardiac arrest."

"A heart attack?" Mark said.

"No. People use these terms interchangeably," Anthony replied, "and that's wrong. Irregular circulation causes heart attacks, and an irregular nerve impulse called arrhythmia causes cardiac death. A block in any one of the arteries in the heart stops oxygen-rich blood from reaching the muscles inside, causing that specific part to die—heart attack. Cardiac arrest is when the whole organ stops functioning. The brain sends erratic electrical signals to the heart, forcing it to malfunction. It will either pump faster or slower than its usual rate, and the heart will fail. The blood can't be pumped to the brain, resulting in cerebral anoxia. Then the loss of consciousness, followed by death."

"So, it is more like a brain suicide?" Bill smirked.

Maybe Gabriel should hold on to that recommendation letter until the young blood learned compassion, which was one of the most important character traits a detective should have. Which most didn't, anyways. Mockery shouldn't be a coping mechanism.

"What causes it?" Mark said.

"Long-term stress, sleep disorders, drugs, unhealthy diet, strong emotions."

"Fear?" Bill said.

"We can never be sure, but that's my theory, too. Martha died somewhere between 9:00 p.m. and 11:00 p.m. I found enough traces of nitroglycerine in her to make an educated guess that she was no stranger to heart problems. Sudden cardiac death is more common among people who have heart problems than people who don't." Anthony turned a page. "The others died between midnight and 2:00 a.m."

Mark and Laura said that Harry's manager, Leroy, had dropped him at his house at 10:30 p.m. David found the last camera that recorded the Suburban after Mr. Bunny got Harry. It read 10:49 p.m. Martha was dead by then. Serial killers didn't take pleasure in hanging dead bodies unless they were the kind who played with dead bodies. But seeing that Mr. Bunny dumped his victims as soon as he killed them, it was safe to say that he couldn't care less about the corpses. He hanged Martha's body for the sole purpose of inducing shock and rage in the late Samuel's mind. This new information went along just fine with Gabriel's *supposition.*

"In the other victim, Doug Bastian," Anthony continued, "I found an abundance of gamma-hydroxybutyric acid, aka GHB. This is similar to a date rape drug."

"Can we track it to the manufacturer?" Bill said.

"They are mostly homemade. It's easily derived from any medication that has sodium oxybate as its main ingredient, which is a lot of pills."

"Oh." Bill's shoulders dropped.

"It's been mixed with whey, a milk-based protein drink. The GHB's dosage, while not lethal, is a lot more than the amount necessary to render the subject unconscious. We can safely assume your guy's knowledge of pharmaceuticals is limited."

Everyone listened to the old doctor with solemn faces.

"I've swabbed Doug's nasal cavity and found an interesting chemical."

"Ammonium carbonate," Bill said. "But why didn't he use it on the others?"

"There was no need. Ammonium carbonate is an active compound in smelling salts. Your killer used it to wake Doug up. Rita didn't need it because he didn't drug her. Harry was sitting on a wheelchair, and Martha was already dead when he hanged her." Finished, Anthony took a step back.

Their team had made a new discovery with Steve Bastian's help. The previous day, David spent his entire afternoon with the videos he'd collected from Doug's gym, Hardcore. He had gone home from Ashley's apartment, given up a good chunk of his sleep, and turned them into sensible playbacks.

David left his chair and told Bill to kill the lights. Victor switched on the projector after the room darkened, and passed the remote to David.

The first video showed the recording of a CCTV camera inside the gym. It covered the main door and a good part of a narrow corridor that led to the workout floor. A yellow timer on the bottom right corner read 9:33 p.m. when a man in a pink tracksuit entered the gym. Rough beard, reflective Wayfarers, and a black baseball cap obscured the remaining part of his face that his gloved hand couldn't hide. He moved with confidence and opened a door on his left along the corridor.

David said it was a locker room and didn't have cameras.

Mr. Bunny came out after a minute, not even casting a glance in the camera's direction. Gabriel could see a hairnet at the back of Mr. Bunny's head as he left.

David pressed a button on the clicker and a different video was projected onto the board. The footage was from a camera across the street, and a neon sign above the gym's entrance blinked *Hardcore*. When Doug came out, it read 21:47. Disoriented and confused, his demeanor was that of a person coming out of a bar, not a gym. He turned right, away from the camera, and went out of its focus.

Then the Suburban rolled into the frame from the left and followed him.

The next camera was on Doug's side of the street. He staggered in the camera's direction. Five stumbling steps later, Doug stopped and put his left hand on the wall of a building. He held his chest with his other hand and bent forward like he was on the verge of puking.

The Suburban slowed and halted beside Doug. He looked into the window and listened to Mr. Bunny. Then he nodded, opened the door and got in. The car moved toward the camera and drove off under it. The time read 21:49 when the video ended.

Doug was the strongest among the victims. He could have killed Mr. Bunny with one hand, yet it took minimal time and almost no physical contact to incapacitate him.

"See something interesting?" David said.

Everyone looked lost. Gabriel was just as much in the dark.

"You guys will never get into Computer Crimes." David rewound the video to the point where Doug got into the cab.

He paused it when the car was nearest to the camera, and zoomed in on the driver's side.

The dark interior hid Mr. Bunny's face, but his gloved hands were visible. He drove with the universal ten and two hand position on the wheel. However, what was non-universal about it was that he held the steering wheel with only eight fingers, with the two middle ones saluting the windshield. It wasn't meant for the person driving in front of him, but for the camera—to the police and the FBI.

"You gotta be..." Nash said.

"So, Doug finishes his workout," Anthony said, as the lights came back on. "His body screams for some liquid to get rehydrated, and Doug drinks his post-workout shake. His thirsty body absorbs it, ignorant that the protein drink has a little something extra in it. Doug's heart rate increases. He gets lightheaded, which scares him."

"And a Good Samaritan comes along and offers a ride to the nearest ER," Victor said.

Chapter 20

March 18, 2019. 11:03 A.M.

After the meeting was over, Emma, Nash, and David assembled in Gabriel's office. Ashley got an urgent call from Samuel's lawyer, and left.

"Why target Ashley?" Emma asked.

"We found out that she nearly made him crash," said David. "Remember the skid marks you wanted us to look at?"

"Yeah, Gabe told me. But seriously? Mr. Bunny kills someone for cutting him off?"

"It's more complicated than that," Gabriel said. "Martha and Rita were in that car. If he'd crashed, he would have lost the game before it even began. That thought scared him. He wanted revenge, but he couldn't kill Ashley because she's become Samuel's replacement. Now she's one of the important pieces in his game. So he settled for just scaring her."

"That's enough psychology for today," David said. "Let's do actual police work. How are we going to take it from here? A little brainstorming session wouldn't hurt."

"Guys?" Emma said. "Sorry if I sound stupid, but why aren't we following the ice blocks? I mean, you can't make them in your refrigerator, right?"

"Fishermen buy them all the time," Nash said. "If you got a van equipped with a freezer, you can bring them here, even from Mexico. Mr. Bunny is too careful about leaving even something as small as lint and skin cells, Emma. I'm sorry, but you really are being stupid expecting him to leave evidence on those big ice blocks."

Emma gave Nash two birds as she stretched her arms above her head and grunted.

Gabriel thought about David's question. They could ask Vice's help to track the GHB. Although they might have a list of all the sellers, they couldn't know every buyer. And the dealers wouldn't remember someone who'd bought it from them just once, as Mr. Bunny would have done. He wouldn't allow some drug dealer to learn his face by meeting him twice.

What else could they do? David could review the footage from the gym for an entire year, but he could not do anything with what they had—a man in a pink tracksuit with no face. But David also had the membership records, and he could crosscheck it with the videos to identify any strangers who weren't regulars.

Since they had no other clues to steer the investigation toward a specific goal, they decided to go on with those angles—GHB and Hardcore.

Gabriel asked Nash and Emma to meet with Vice, and David to work on the videos. Everyone moved out and left him to his thoughts.

* * *

Investigating the first six murders was proving to be as tough as the last four—no physical, biological or electronic evidence, no eyewitnesses, and no CCTV. The only difference between them was that Mr. Bunny videotaped the last four. It was like what Stanley had said—there was no shred of evidence.

Then the answer hit Gabriel like a thunderbolt.

Why the hell were they searching for evidence exactly where Mr. Bunny had pointed them to? Stanley, Victor, and Gabriel—they all agreed that Mr. Bunny must have slipped at least once. Murdering that many people without a single misstep was impossible. But like Mayor Roth feared, a smart criminal like Mr. Bunny would know where he had slipped, and he obviously wouldn't have included it in the list.

How could Gabriel find that victim? An idea popped into his head, but it would be a herculean task and he'd need help to execute it. Since he had assigned the detectives to other work, he dialed Bill's extension.

He was in Gabriel's office in less than twenty seconds.

"So, Bill, you and I, we're going to do a little research."

"Are we going out?" Bill asked, beaming.

"No. We're going to look at all the unsolved murders in the United States in 2018," Gabriel said.

Bill scoffed and began to say something, but stopped when Gabriel raised his hand.

"I know it's huge. That's why we're going to apply some filters. We'll concentrate on murders involving torture. We search New York, and if we can't find anything, we fan out to other states, prioritizing the ones on the East Coast. The later the murder, the more defined and precise the torture will be. We shouldn't have that many torture murders in our country. So, you think you can do that?"

"I think it's a waste of time. It's too much work for little to no gain," Bill said.

Gabriel always appreciated an outspoken man.

"We haven't found any leads in those six victims, and I'm beginning to think there won't be any. So, I want to try a new approach. I know it's a jump in a completely different and dark direction, but that's all we've got," Gabriel said.

Bill didn't seem thrilled.

"You know, Bill, I understand you hate going after false leads. We all do. But know this—most of a detective's work is to wade through ninety-nine percent of the bullshit to get to that one percent of necessary information which solves the case. A good detective is someone who can spot the bullshit and save time by avoiding it, and I saw you as a natural. But I get it. You're not interested. That's all right. Go send Officer Priyanka in. I hope she isn't as whiney as you are."

That did the trick.

Bill apologized and assured Gabriel that he didn't need *Priya*. He needed *William*. Then he strutted back to his desk, chest inflated.

Chapter 21

March 18, 2019. 02:03 P.M.

A notification from one of the news apps lit Gabriel's phone and he touched it. The headline read *Candlelight Vigil for Our Comedian*. The picture showed a little boy holding a phone up, and on its screen was a photo of a burning candle.

As Gabriel read the article, he received an email from David.

It was a video clip from the gym, dated two days before Mr. Bunny abducted Doug. It showed Doug walking down the corridor and entering the locker room. Mr. Bunny, with the same apparel and gestures, followed him in, but he came out before Doug did. So that was how he knew Doug's locker number and in which shaker he should mix the GHB.

Gabriel made a call to David and learned that Mr. Bunny used the same Chevy Suburban on that day, too. David tracked it with traffic cams until it disappeared in Arrochar, Staten Island.

Gabriel cut the call and resumed going through the detective notes he'd been reading before the news notification. The records were about the murder of a street worker named Miranda. Someone strangled her with a length of plastic wire, after sexually assaulting her. It wasn't Mr. Bunny. But Gabriel got only these types of results when he entered *torture* as a keyword in the search.

Ten minutes later, Nash called with an update.

The vice unit in the Narcotics Bureau had stacks and stacks of information about drugs like GHB. Dealers sold them in night clubs, which was one of the primary domains of Vice. They processed Victor's request and sent Nash a list of known assholes who sold GHB. But first, Nash said, they were heading out to eat lunch. Gabriel disconnected the call and looked at the display—2:34 p.m. It was indeed time to refuel.

There wasn't anything from Bill yet. What was he doing?

He called the pizzeria opposite and ordered two plain slices and a cold coffee before continuing to read the report.

Miranda was murdered in November. According to the list Mr. Bunny had sent them, by November his torture skills had developed to such an extent that Shirō Ishii would have praised him if he was still alive. Strangulation seemed too tame for him by that time.

Up until the last weeks of September, Mr. Bunny's murders were simple. If Gabriel searched before that month, then he would get many unsolved cases.

But the tortures began in October, and it was March now. There wouldn't be many torture murders in the entire country within this period. That murder would be easy to spot, unless the victim was still a missing person and Mr. Bunny had hidden the body. Unlikely. He didn't hide bodies. He discarded them.

Gabriel began his search, and since he didn't find any unsolved torture murder in New York except Miranda, he spread out.

When his phone rang again, he cut the call and headed for the precinct's entrance.

The regular kid delivered his order at the front desk and Gabriel paid the regular tip. On his way back, Gabriel went straight to Bill's table on the first floor. It was empty. Was he eating lunch as well?

He questioned the officer sitting next to Bill's chair, and she informed him that she hadn't seen Bill for almost three hours. Perhaps Bill wasn't detective material and Gabriel had been stupid in assuming his dedication to the job.

"You know where he is?"

"Lieutenant Lamb's office," Priyanka said, in a tone that suggested the scenario was all too frequent and she was tired of telling people about Bill's whereabouts.

But why did Bill go there?

Gabriel jogged up to his floor, placed the lunch on his table, and went to Peter's office.

Inside, Bill was stooping over a PC and Peter sat beside him, watching the monitor. His thoughts weighed down on top of his nose's bridge and blanketed his gold-rimmed spectacles. He had fastened a blue pillow to the chair to support his back. As he hunched, his spine arced in an abnormal way.

Gabriel knocked on the door. Bill looked up and gave a thin smile, then continued his work. But Peter smiled wide and got up, hands supporting his knees.

"Gabriel! Come on in, son."

Gabriel sat across from them and scrutinized Bill. What was he doing here?

Reading Gabriel, Peter said, "I knew Billy long before he became a cop. He was kind enough to keep me in the loop of one of the greatest murder investigations of our time—my kind of party, for which you guys forgot to send me the invite."

Gabriel didn't feel a pang of guilt, even though it was his idea to keep Peter out of it. The old man did more than his bit in helping people. Now he was just days away from retirement. He didn't need this headache. When Peter slowly lowered himself into his chair, after flocculating the blue pillow and balancing the center of his mass away from his lumbar to avoid any strain on it, it made Gabriel's decision more justifiable.

Gabriel looked above Peter's head, at a framed cutting of a newspaper article that read *Lone Masked Man Kills One and Robs $98,000!*

"The one that got away," Peter said.

"We all have those," Gabriel said. "This case may or may not involve Lolly. But Mr. Lamb, my dad sure didn't frame any of the clippings about him."

"Boy, know this. Josh was affected more than any of us. I have my share of unsolved ones, but I didn't leave the force for them. Your father did. That's how obsessed he is."

Gabriel pointed at the wall. "That's the one Lolly robbed alone."

"You believe Lolly did it? Damn. I guess Josh and I are the only ones left who don't think it was him."

"What's so special about it? It wasn't Lolly's first robbery, or his greatest." Gabriel shifted to a more comfortable position.

He didn't mind supporting Peter by allowing him to indulge in reminiscences.

"If he did it, then it wasn't even his bloodiest. His gang murdered forty-nine people that we know of, and he earned himself a cozy seat on the FBI's top ten. But this was the one that dragged me in."

"This wasn't your case, was it? You were investigating Casey's murder, and when this robbery happened you wanted to investigate it, too, because you believed they were linked."

"True... true. No murder has ever gotten to me like Casey's did. Who in their right mind would murder an autistic boy? The boy already had a fight on his hands just to live, and someone murders him."

"He was battling, but he was happy. He was always fun to be with. Noah and I supervised him most of the time, but he didn't really need a lot of care."

"As far as I'm concerned, it's a murder of a child."

"It is." Gabriel shifted in his seat. "Can we not talk about Casey, Mr. Lamb? Please?"

"I'm sorry, boy. I forgot you guys were close. Anyway, six weeks after the murder, this robbery happens. Two violent crimes in two months, at a calm neighborhood in Staten Island? Shit doesn't happen like that. The same person could very possibly be the culprit."

"I understand why you'd think that way."

"I came to know about a drug fiend who'd slashed Casey with a knife. He'd absconded two nights before his murder. I wanted to bring this local hood in for questioning, but Josh didn't put much stock in the possibility. It's like my ideas weren't important to him."

"You suspected Phillip Ming."

"With good reason." Peter's voice went up a notch. "He was the only criminal in that neighborhood. He had a record for breaking into liquor stores, robbing people with dummy guns, among others—incidents that point to a budding maggot."

"That's true. Phillip was a violent drug addict. Hell, he even bullied me."

"He did?" Peter asked.

"Twice a week."

"That sucks. But he disappeared before you grew up big enough to whoop his ass?"

Gabriel laughed. "That's correct, Mr. Lamb."

"I don't think you'll ever get a chance. Anyway, that twat blows Casey's head off and disappears. Six weeks later, he comes back, kills a cashier, and robs one hundred thousand dollars from a local bank. This was the theory I applied in my investigations."

"I'm sorry my dad behaved the way he did, Mr. Lamb, but I don't believe Phillip Ming is capable of robbing a bank," Gabriel said.

"Uh-huh. Why is that?"

"Drug addicts can't plan and execute a bank robbery that's sophisticated enough to be mistaken for the work of the most elusive bank robber in the United States. It's just beyond their cognitive abilities."

"You're correct. But I truly believe Phillip murdered that Casey boy. I still search all the federal and state criminal records once a month to see if he's made an appearance."

"You do?"

Old people were stubborn.

"Yes. Not just our state records, but also our neighbors. No luck so far."

"You're incredible, Mr. Lamb." Gabriel shook his head.

"A man's gotta do what a man's gotta do. Casey's murder aside, I no longer believe Phillip robbed that bank. Josh said the same things you just said—like how he's not smart enough to pull that off—and convinced me. The apple really doesn't fall far from the tree." Peter nodded to himself. "He also threw in some complicated bullshit about ballistics to prove me wrong, but when he explained, he didn't take a slow and understanding approach like you did. He is smart, and a straight shooter, but he's also an arrogant prick."

Gabriel laughed. "You watch the Daily Herald last Friday night? Lolly is back."

"Yes, and we ain't inviting you to that party, boy." Peter smiled, showing his gold canine.

"I don't want in, Mr. Lamb, thank you. Lolly belongs to you guys. You talked to my dad about it?"

"Sure did. Josh and I are going to Detroit this Friday."

"But that's when you retire!"

"Technically, yes. But there is no law preventing two old men from having a retirement project."

"Why Detroit?"

"We believe Lolly was born there." Peter was getting more enthusiastic by each second.

"I always suspected you guys killed him and fed the body to the dogs."

"Wish we'd had the chance." Peter looked at Gabriel with a stare that turned from happy puppy to thoughtful, before finally settling on cold. "We're not going to bring him in when we catch him. Fingers crossed."

Gabriel didn't reply. He didn't want to have philosophical discussions about law and penal codes. Peter was an old school cop, and those guys tended to care more about an eye-for-an-eye and a-life-for-a-life justice. What good was law if all it ever did was put a criminal in a prison where he enjoyed life and got fat on the working man's taxes?

Would Gabriel act any different if he came face to face with Mr. Bunny? Would the court of law provide an answer to the tears he'd shed for Rita? Tears only his pillow and quilt could attest to? Almost everything was subject to the law, but not a mother's love. Nor the retribution for her death.

"I vowed at Casey's grave to catch his murderer." Peter looked down at his thinned palm lines, the lifeline eroded to the point of invisibility. "I fear I'm going to fail."

Gabriel couldn't think of a way to further the conversation without making hollow reassurances. Harsh truth—some cases you died without solving, just like how some criminals took their secrets to their graves.

"I've heard Phillip's brother is now a top criminalist?" Peter said.

"Yes, sir."

"That's nice. At least one brother turned out good." Peter clapped. "So, what's your take on this new serial killer?"

"We're not sure if Mr. Bunny is actually a serial killer."

Peter smiled at Gabriel. "Yeah, I agree. The pattern, if there is one, is dynamic. You know something, Gabriel? I'm not good at intimidating people the way I used to, but this"—he tapped his temple twice with a forefinger—"didn't become blunt. On the contrary, it's sharper than ever. You and that cue ball captain of ours should have used me."

"Sorry, sir."

Peter smiled, a little too wide this time. "It's all right. I know you're trying to do good by me, son."

An awkward silence followed, which Gabriel abruptly filled.

"So, Bill, mind telling me what you doing there?"

"Wading through the bullshit, Detective Chase."

Gabriel lifted his eyebrows, dropped the edges of his lips and nodded, feigning wonderment. Bill had been waiting for Gabriel to ask him just that so he could reply with a touché. Trying to appear smart before a reporting authority was a good sign. A lot of work would go into earning that admiration.

"Great. If you find something, you know where I'll be." Gabriel got up.

He almost reached the door when he heard, "How do you filter Hispanics out in the search, Dad?"

Dad?

Gabriel stopped and turned. His eyebrows met in confusion.

Peter was moving the mouse and looking into the monitor, but addressed Gabriel.

"My ex-wife remarried twice. But Billy Boy never lost touch with his real dad."

That was a surprise. Now Gabriel knew why Bill was the way he was. Smart and hardworking, with a touch of rebelliousness.

Chapter 22

March 18, 2019. 03:29 P.M.

To actualize the idea he had conceived before meeting Bill and Peter, Gabriel extended his computer search. It now included the homicide databases of New York's neighboring states. While he worked, he emptied the carton of stale pizza and coffee that had become cold.

An hour into the search, he opened the case file of AJ—real name, age, and nationality unknown. He was murdered on December 9, 2018, and found the next day in the parking lot of a Home Depot in Donston, a town in Providence, Rhode Island.

An unfortunate early morning walker who had discovered AJ's remains reportedly said, "I thought someone had dumped their Halloween decorations."

Gabriel could see why anyone would think that. The bloody head rested on the torso which it had previously been a part of, and the limbs scattered around it. It was surreal and disturbing.

Forensic odontology didn't turn up a match. Neither did the Automated Fingerprint Identification System or the Missing Person File, nor did the Immigration Violator File or the Foreign Fugitive File in the National Crime Information Center. Hence the investigating detectives concluded that AJ was an illegal, and they added him to the mass of unidentified bodies documented in NamUs. Tattoos on his skin inferred that he might be a member of a gang based in El Salvador, which operated out of Los Angeles but also had a strong foothold in Rhode Island, Connecticut, and the rest of New England.

From their confidential informant, the detectives learned that AJ lived with his associates in a small house that also doubled as a drug den. He wasn't a criminal in his country, so there would be no record of him in the FFF. He wasn't arrested in the United States, so there were no photographs of him in the system.

Well, now there were.

The first picture showed a torso without a head and limbs. The next showed, for classification purposes only, a head. His hair had been cut off, along with the scalp. It had no eyelids, ears, nose or skin, making it just a red skull with big eyes. The last picture had all the limbs arranged in columns.

A forensic pathologist put AJ's age around fifteen. The autopsy report said that the flaying and amputations were clean and done while the victim was still alive. The cause of death was *vagal inhibition triggered by extensive injuries to the body*. In layman's term, it was shock caused by pure pain.

The ME also noted that the murderer employed professional tools, and he could very well be a surgeon. Gabriel didn't think Mr. Bunny was one of those angels-of-death type killers. He wasn't related to the medical profession. Anthony said the dosage of GHB administered was a lot more than necessary. A doctor would know the correct dosage, wouldn't he? And what about the initial victims? Their tortures weren't as neat as the ones that came later. If Mr. Bunny were a surgeon, then there wouldn't be a notable difference in his proficiency.

The Providence PD wrote down AJ's murder as gang-related. Perhaps they thought that the thugs had imported the techniques they used to scare their rivals in their own countries. Yet the cruelty perpetrated on AJ's body was unheard of among the gangs of Rhode Island. How the detectives had concluded this and closed the case, notwithstanding the dismemberment being too clean for any doped-up thug, local or foreign, was beyond Gabriel.

The other results from his search, with *torture* as their keyword, were strangulations, slashings, drownings. No result turned out a case where the torture was procedural and exact like in AJ's case. After each paragraph Gabriel finished reading, he became more confident that AJ was Mr. Bunny's victim. One he didn't mention in the list.

That meant he'd slipped up here!

In what way, Gabriel didn't know, but he'd slipped.

Gabriel called the PPD and requested the operator to transfer the call to Detective McDuffie from the Organized Crime Bureau. That was who'd investigated AJ's murder. Gabriel used his inhaler when the call was on hold.

"Detective Chase? As in Gabriel Chase?" McDuffie didn't try to hide his surprise.

"Yes." Gabriel hated the fame he'd started experiencing from the previous day.

"I saw you on the front page. I don't think you look like a madman, but my partner thinks the ass-wipes pissed right on the target this time." McDuffie laughed, and then coughed, which sounded like he might have some serious health issues. "Differences of opinion aside, we sure had a wicked laugh last night at our watering hole."

"Glad to be of service."

Gabriel closed his eyes. He needed to concentrate to understand McDuffie's heavy accent.

"Come on. Don't be like that. We all hate the news, but we can use a good laugh once in a while." McDuffie cleared his throat and his voice became serious. "So, what can I do you for?"

"I wanted to talk to you about a murder investigation you handled. The victim was a male Hispanic in his teens, street name *AJ*. Do you remember him?"

"Gimme a sec."

Gabriel heard the usual background racket of the police station—laughter followed by a racist remark, telephone ringing, radio beeps, and transmissions.

"Vic was murdered two weeks before Christmas?" McDuffie said.

"That's the one. Reports in ViCAP are not detailed. Could you help me out here?"

"Why? Is it related to the case you're working on?"

"Yes."

"No, it is not. It's the work of the Thirteenth Posse, rivals of the gang that AJ worked for."

Gabriel didn't think that. Mr. Bunny killed people whose deaths wouldn't be investigated thoroughly.

"No arrests? Not even a single person of interest?"

"Nope."

"That sounds—" Gabriel stopped himself before saying *irresponsible*.

Then he asked for any CCTV footage from where they'd found AJ's remains. McDuffie said they didn't collect any, and the case wasn't their priority.

"I'm sorry, Chase, I don't know why you're so worked up over AJ. Helping rapists and child molesters. Bloody punk had it coming, if you ask me. Even if his murder isn't a gangland thing, I wouldn't be surprised if an angry father, brother, or a boyfriend butchered him. Good riddance—"

"Whoa, whoa! What're you talking about?"

"He sold a rainbow of drugs. No problem for me. But his specialty was roofies and goop."

"Date rape drugs?"

"GHB, yes. That's what my CI told me."

Christmas mornings hadn't made Gabriel as happy as he was now. His team had many dead ends—all of them intentional false leads Mr. Bunny had created to disappoint them. But Gabriel *knew* this one was real, and a minor charge of euphoria went off inside his brain, refreshing him.

Gabriel got McDuffie's number, thanked him, and hung up. He slowed down and thought about it. What were the odds of someone who could've been murdered by Mr. Bunny having sold drugs that Mr. Bunny had used to incapacitate Doug, another one of his victims?

Gabriel was sure that AJ was the one who'd supplied Mr. Bunny with GHB. And he had paid the price for it.

Chapter 23

March 18, 2019. 06:48 P.M.

Gabriel felt refreshed in spite of spending the entire day inside the confines of his office. For a change, he didn't feel stymied in the investigation. Now the marionettes had a good grip on the strings. It was just a matter of time before they yanked hard and pulled the deranged puppeteer down, made him crash onto the stage and exposed him to the world.

In his ecstatic mood, he dialed Stanley and let him in on the latest developments. Stanley received most of the news with *mmms*, and when Gabriel finished he agreed that it did sound hopeful and wished Gabriel luck on his *hunt*.

Nash and Emma spent a better part of their evening at the Home Depot's parking lot in Federal Way, Donston, where the morning walker had found AJ's body. They had to go in person to find the cameras, which were not connected to the police servers. When they finished collecting every recording they could, Emma cc'd Gabriel and sent them to David. Then they started their three-hour drive back home.

In addition to these videos, David searched the feeds from traffic cameras, speed monitoring systems, and so forth. He also compiled a list of dashboard cameras of the PPD's patrol cars that were found to be in the area of AJ's dumpsite at the time—all of which he got access to by a special request Raymond made to the PPD's chief of detectives.

Videos spanned from December 9th—the day AJ died, according to the autopsy—to December 10th, the day his disassembled body was found. David was a miracle worker when it came to analyzing videos, but still, it would have been hectic for one man to watch them all. So, Gabriel pulled Mark and Laura out from their current task of canvassing the surroundings of Ashley's apartment and interviewing the Daily Herald's ex-employees, and asked them to help David with the videos.

Bill would have been made to assist David too, but Gabriel didn't know where he was. He wasn't answering his phone, either. But he knew Peter and Bill were working the case, and Gabriel wasn't going to question Peter's ways. He was, after all, one of his mentors. Gabriel just wished that the father-son duo came back with something solid to build around his growing excitement.

* * *

Bill did call him a while later.

"Bill here, sir. We got some new info."

No apology for going out on his own. Why did almost every good detective have some kind of problem with authority?

Gabriel said, "Yeah, tell me," when he remembered that he, too, was once a big name in insubordination at school, university, and for a short period, the precinct.

"We found someone who *might* have been murdered by Mr. Bunny? One he didn't mention in his list."

"Uh-huh." Gabriel expected to hear AJ's name.

"Her name is Kenosha Hansen…"

Gabriel felt his poker face being replaced by confusion.

"…and Mr. Bunny might have used a silver Range Rover to dump her body."

Gabriel's mind paused. He didn't know who Kenosha Hansen was. He didn't even remember seeing her name in his searches. So he asked Bill to elaborate.

Bill refused, catching Gabriel off guard. Bill said he would give the information when he got back to the precinct, and he'd called just to check in. Gabriel demanded that *William* spill what he knew, in a harsh tone, but then Peter came on the line.

"Gabriel, this is a case breaker. We intend to give the information in person. Say, one hour?"

Gabriel wasn't sure if he had the audacity to order Peter. Not that the detective lieutenant would oblige anyway.

Gabriel muttered, "Yes, sir," and cut the call.

He realized what was happening.

Peter must have coerced Bill to call Gabriel with an update. However, the only purpose of this *update* would be to get Gabriel all hot and bothered but leave him hanging. Much like sex without climax. It was a payback for Victor and Gabriel leaving him out of the investigation. And all that crap about *trying to do good by me, son* was a façade to hide the particular kind of grudge only old people held on to. Gabriel cursed himself for not using Peter before.

He massaged the sides of his head and the back of his neck. Then he positioned his fingers on the keyboard.

* * *

Ten minutes later, Gabriel located Kenosha's file in the same cloud archives where he'd found AJ's—a federal software he'd grown used to by now, as he'd spent the better part of his day navigating it.

Kenosha Hansen was another Miranda whose violent death society had long since forgotten. The twenty-one-year-old girl was murdered on December 23, 2018, and her roasted body was dumped at a dock in Perth Amboy, New Jersey.

Gabriel opened the crime scene photographs.

The perp didn't set her on fire, but instead tied her up with chains and burnt her methodically. The detectives found several empty canisters of blowtorches in her apartment. Fourth-degree burns had destroyed Kenosha's body. Most of her flesh melted to the bone, and the areas that weren't melted—places where the fat and muscle were too thick for the fire to burn through to the bones—were blanketed by pustules and charred flesh.

It was the most painful death Gabriel had ever come across in his career, let alone among Mr. Bunny's victims, if she was indeed one.

One of Kenosha's Johns hadn't thought up this type of diabolism—there was no sexual element here. It was thought up by the man who clinically tested and studied the effects torture had on body and mind.

Gabriel's heartbeat raised the second time that day. It was Mr. Bunny's work. He knew it.

A person called Fred D'Cruz had been indicted for her murder and put in jail. He was a nineteen-year-old kid who supported his mother by delivering for DoorDash. In spite of him protesting his innocence, the detectives arrested and charged him. The cops didn't believe his story and closed the case, making no effort to check whether it was true or not. If they had, then Mr. Bunny's first mistake would have been documented and a lot of time would've been saved for their team. But Gabriel couldn't blame them—it did seem like an open-and-shut case.

With his years of experience, Peter must have taught Bill to search for cases in which a person was indicted and awaiting trial. The indictment didn't mean conviction, true, but it also didn't mean unsolved. It was in a gray area called *cleared by arrest*, in a pending status. That was why it didn't pop up in Gabriel's search results.

He read the case details, and then the court transcripts.

Half an hour later, Gabriel already believed Fred was innocent. He closed his eyes and took a breath that he thought was the deepest he'd ever taken in his life. He held it in for five seconds and then let it out.

He got the feeling he usually got when he outsmarted criminals who were actually smart—exhilaration.

* * *

"Fred says he broke into a silver Range Rover," Bill said. "Then he helped himself to Kenosha's phone and its battery, both of which were on the backseat."

"He isn't a regular thief," Peter said. "No priors. He says he did it to buy some booze and food for that night. So, he sells her phone at a pawn shop. The owner switched the phone on and was later shocked to have a couple of detectives knock on his door. He gave up the boy, and you said you know the rest of the story."

Gabriel knew about the not very air-tight indictment and an eventual grant of bail after Fred's mother provided an alibi for him. But it wasn't just her word that had saved him. At the time of Kenosha's death, Fred was at home, talking to his girlfriend and begging her to take him back. When his pleading hadn't changed anything between them, he went to the bar.

Sharon Goldberg was a fresh law graduate who probably wanted to prove her mettle in the law community. So, when the court appointed her to defend Fred, she apparently saw her chance to shine, and gave it everything she had. Sharon contacted Fred's network provider and requested his phone's activity, its location during Kenosha's time of death, and the call recordings between Fred and his girlfriend. She made the last request so that she could prove it was really Fred who was at his home when Kenosha was being tortured in her apartment.

That, in combination with his mother's testimony, had saved Fred from a horrible fate.

The judge revised the bail bond amount, which had been set at the rate of three supercars at the beginning due to the severity of the case, and granted it for a pittance. Even the judge didn't find it plausible that Fred, who wept to his girlfriend to take him back, could have the heart of a murderer who'd burned a person alive and dissolved her body.

Gabriel thanked Fred's girlfriend in his mind. If she hadn't broken up with him when she had, Fred wouldn't have gotten shit-faced that night and stolen Kenosha's phone, learning about Mr. Bunny's car in the process. Mr. Bunny didn't count on his vehicle being identified, and that was where he'd slipped up.

Since Mr. Bunny murdered AJ before Kenosha, chances were that he used the same car. Gabriel's team could use this new information to filter videos near the dump sites of all the people Mr. Bunny had killed, starting with AJ.

Twenty minutes later, Serj Tankian sang from Gabriel's phone. The display read *Douche King*.

"Yes?" Gabriel answered.

"Wanna know who owns the Range Rover?" David's voice said.

Chapter 24

March 19, 2019. 04:37 A.M.

Adding to the sixty-one miles Gabriel had ridden on it that night, the Kawasaki's digital odometer had breezed past ten thousand miles. His back and buttocks felt numb, triceps and palms ached.

He tossed and turned, trying various positions to bring the sleep his weary brain and body needed. But he couldn't stop concentrating and let the mind wander outside the restraint of his consciousness. The information he possessed now had the potential to wrap it all up.

The silver car—a Range Rover Evoque—belonged to Helen Ruiz, a stockbroker from a mid-level Wall Street firm. Gabriel called her phone, and Helen said her drug addict son, Cody Ruiz, had borrowed the car a few months back and never returned it. Since Cody didn't answer his phone, Gabriel decided to pay him a visit, riding his motorcycle to Hunts Point, Bronx, where Mrs. Ruiz said Cody stayed.

Gabriel met Cody outside a tenement. The building was gang tagged and rundown. It didn't surprise Gabriel to learn that Cody had sold the Range Rover—it would have been surprising if he hadn't. Cody had placed ads on many websites, and a week later he received a call from a guy whose name he'd forgotten. Not that it mattered.

The guy was a *businessman type, with a beard and cool glasses*, who paid cash and didn't argue over the price. Cody *got no time* to check the DMV to see if the buyer had transferred the papers or returned the plates, even though the idiot had let Mr. Bunny drive with them.

Gabriel verified Cody's alibi for Friday night, and rode straight back home.

David didn't come along to the Bronx. Gabriel told him to track the Range Rover, and he found two points where it was last spotted.

On the day of Kenosha's murder, David had followed the car from the dock in Perth Amboy, New Jersey, where her body was found. Mr. Bunny entered Staten Island through Oldbridge Crossing and disappeared right after he cut into Heartland Village. No camera recorded the car after that. At least, none that David had access to.

As Gabriel suspected, Mr. Bunny had used the same car for AJ, too.

On December 10th, at 1:14 a.m., the Range Rover was recorded leaving Home Depot's parking lot, in Donston. At 1:20 a.m., it climbed Providence Beltway, which later merged into I-95, going southwest. A few tollbooth cameras recorded the Range Rover, and from the direction of the route it took, David was able to conclude where the car traveled to.

Mr. Bunny was coming to New York City.

Could it be his home?

He entered Staten Island at 6:32 a.m., from the north via Bayonne Bridge. David had followed it until Elm Park, but he couldn't track it after that. Gabriel had asked David to check the six victims' dump sites for the Range Rover and call him if he found anything. The phone hadn't rung since then.

Gabriel's desiccated eyeballs brushed against his eyelids. His throat and the edges of his lips were dry, too. He got up, switched on the lights, and visited the kitchen. After drenching his face, neck, and the back of his head with cold water, he cupped his hands underneath the faucet and filled his stomach. Fresh and relaxed, he returned to the living room and picked up the inhaler from the table. His thoughts left the apartment as he paced around the eight-by-ten-foot rug.

Two times Mr. Bunny had driven into Staten Island and disappeared. Two times could be a coincidence. But that Sunday morning, when Gabriel and David were about to go to Steve's house, David said he'd backtracked the Suburban the night it was found with four dead people in it. It disappeared in Arrochar, just a few minutes after it crossed Fort Wadsworth. Before that, it disappeared in the same place after Mr. Bunny visited Hardcore to find Doug's locker.

Four times Mr. Bunny had disappeared into Staten Island. It couldn't be a coincidence.

Did Mr. Bunny live on The Rock? Maybe he had a safe house that he crawled back into after murdering? If so, could that be where he'd hung four people and videotaped it? Would Gabriel find damning evidence there?

He needed to find that place.

But how? All he had were the three neighborhoods where Mr. Bunny's car was last spotted. He paced faster as his mind shifted into higher gears.

Then the frenetic pacing came to an abrupt halt.

Gabriel stepped over to the pinboard fixed on a wall above his work-cum-dining table. It had a detailed map of Staten Island. He put a thumb pin on Arrochar—point east. Then he took two more and marked the others. Heartland Village—point west, and Elm Park—point north. Three points on three different sides of Staten Island.

The quietest of five boroughs possibly housed one of the craziest psychopaths in the United States.

Gabriel needed another point to have a square, a perimeter to work with.

He measured the distances between the pins with the map application on his phone. The routes it showed didn't look straight enough, so he changed it from driving to walking. The distances from Elm Park to Arrochar and Heartland Village were around four miles. With them as the reference, he created a fourth point in the south. The phantom point hovered on Oakwood where Staten Island met the Atlantic Ocean. He put a pin on that—point south.

Now the distance between all the points was four miles, give or take a few hundred meters.

He opened the top drawer, rummaged inside without looking, and grasped a green Staedtler marker. He connected all the pins with lines that could be called straight if not scrutinized closely.

When he connected the last dot, he stepped back and looked at the result. It was neither a square nor a rectangle, but something in-between, and Mr. Bunny had disappeared into this perimeter. He might have lived his entire life here, not unlike Gabriel. All he had to do now was to find Mr. Bunny's burrow.

A few problems prevented Gabriel from doing it, two topping the list.

First problem: there was no way anyone could be sure this wasn't one of Mr. Bunny's ploys to mock the police—to direct them after false leads and waste precious resources and even more precious time.

But if it was a ploy, then why didn't he mention Kenosha and AJ in his list? That was the surest way of making sure the detectives would follow them. He couldn't have predicted the cops would find Kenosha and AJ among so many unsolved murders and link them to him. So, it might be an actual lead.

Second problem: it was a large area. Gabriel's middle school mathematics told him that it must be around sixteen square miles. His team couldn't knock on every door within this area. Even if the murderer opened the door, they had no way to identify him. Gabriel had to do something to decrease the search area. Maybe ask Raymond to get them a specialist in forensic geography, from the FBI. Gabriel had no idea what he planned to do after he reduced the area to the smallest possible size. But that thought was bound to bring negativity, so he paid no heed to it.

He opened the camera app and aimed its lens at the board. The flash whitened the map and made it shinier.

His phone vibrated as he selected the last contact to send the picture to. He saved the photo and the selected recipients in the drafts folder and opened his inbox.

An email from Noah waited for him. Odd, at this late an hour. The subject read *NOAH*. Inside the email was a single attachment with the name *Catalyst.mp4*.

A sick premonition released a thousand butterflies inside Gabriel's stomach.

Oh, God. Please, no!

.357 Magnum

3/19/19. Middle of the night/early morning.

The cops, on top of being vituperated for having been purblind to my iniquities all this time, would be crucified when the news about the murder of an assistant district attorney hits the media. When the commissioners, DAs, and ADAs—the protectors and enforcers of law—are affected by crime, people will finally understand how flimsy justice is.

Poor Gabriel, though. I've already killed one person close to him. And now this is another massive hit for him. Just like how it was for Ashley. But what can I do? It isn't personal. I never wanted to make any of my pursuers become blinded with rage and lose focus. That's why I didn't torture the last four. It's philanthropy of sorts, with the knowledge I have in that area.

Anyway, I pull my mask down and stride up to the chair on which my current victim is sitting. I touch his chin and lift it up.

Noah Smith's face stares at me, his eyes red, big, and full of fear. His nostrils are flaring in and out like he's having trouble breathing. The gag is tight, pushing his tongue and the soft muscles bearing it up inside his throat, blocking the airway, probably threatening him with the sense of choking.

I glide my hand up to his cheek and then down to the chin. It's wet and slippery. Tears and snot have escaped, unabsorbed by the sodden gag as they cascaded down.

I release his chin. "Hold still," I say, superfluously.

Of course he will hold still—he's tied to the chair.

I cross to the camera on a table that I placed parallel to the chair. It's in position, the lens focusing on its target. I switch it on, return, and stand in front of him. I pull a Colt Python from my pricey suit. When I point the four-inch-long barrel's end at his forehead, he drops his face.

I transfer the Colt to my left hand. I struggle to lift his face, as his skin is greasy and he's manically trying to thwart the inevitable. This time, I make the face stay where I want it to stay with a tight, backhanded slap across the right cheek. If he drops his head again, I'm going to whack him with the gun.

But he isn't trying to escape the bullet by not facing the gun this time.

I take aim with both hands. The Python has a strong recoil and I don't want to get a cramp.

As he bawls, his lips quiver and eyelids squeeze shut, and tears flow like rivers between them. Pathetic.

I brace myself, shoulders and arms ready to act as shock absorbers.

Then I pull the trigger.

Chapter 25

March 19, 2019. 09:46 A.M.

Gabriel was inconsolable. Words from his team members, meant to make him feel better, felt empty. Done was done. Joshua Chase was there. So was Victor and the whole team. But Raymond wasn't. He had a loss of his own to deal with.

Peter Lamb sat in the chair across the table, his face red. Gabriel couldn't talk. Some people lost their ability to vocalize pain after experiencing something traumatic, and he feared it was happening to him. Gabriel buried his face in the crook of his elbow which was on the table.

The *Catalyst* ran for eight seconds—the longest seconds of Gabriel's life.

Noah was bound to a chair, with a gag in his mouth and despair in his eyes. The same masked bastard stood in front of him with a large revolver in his hand. Without warning, he casually lifted the gun and shot Noah in his left eye.

Bloody mist sprayed out of Noah's head. Hair, bone, skin, and brain matter all ejected in lumps and whumped down. His head whiplashed from such a violent force that it might have broken his neck. Before the video went blank, Gabriel heard the eerie sound of Noah's blood trickling onto the floor.

Everyone in Gabriel's team had seen the video. The assistant district attorney had a lot of enemies—it came with the territory. But it wasn't Noah's work that had killed him. It was his friendship with Gabriel. Mr. Bunny had made it personal again, but this time to *motivate* the leading detective. Guilt made a guest appearance at the internal show that grief and anger had orchestrated.

He felt a hand on his shoulder. "It's all right, son," his father's voice said.

"We'll find him, boy," said Peter. "Don't worry."

Gabriel shook Joshua's hand away as he sat upright.

He looked at Peter. "You n-never solved the murder of one S-S-Smith, and you're telling me we'll f-f-find the murderer of another? What happens if I follow the same route and fail like you?" Then he turned to his father, unable to control the words he knew he would forever regret speaking. "And you? You w-w-were outsmarted by a robber who kills and loots at his w-will? What do you have to show for your t-twenty-five years' ef-effort?"

Joshua turned away.

"Don't you dare talk to your father like that, you little runt!" Peter got up from the chair so fast he didn't even hold his hips.

He looked angrier than Gabriel felt. Bill touched Peter's shoulder, but Peter moved away like it had just touched fire.

"Don't," he said to Bill, and then looked down at Gabriel. "What do you think we do when we lie down at night? Sleep? We are at an age where the angry promises we've made to the dead are becoming silent, shameful apologies. Still, we go on without hope, without anything. But what we never did out of the helplessness and frustration our jobs cause, and what we'll never do, is get mad at someone who loves us."

Gabriel stared at Peter, trying to match his menace. But in the end, he gave up and put his head down. He was wrong to yell at them.

"I'm sorry," Gabriel muttered to his shoes.

When he got no acknowledgment, he looked up. Joshua wasn't there. Neither was Peter.

Now guilt took a solid place in the orchestra.

Gabriel wished he had something to do. He wanted to go to his friend's house and do what he did best, but the Major Case Squad and the FBI had taken it over. Gabriel's team could access it only when they were through with the house. Even Stanley wasn't permitted onto the scene, because the FBI had flown in specialists from Quantico. Killing a public prosecutor created that much heat, though that's exactly what the murderer wanted. As a professional courtesy, the FBI said Noah's body wasn't in his house and Mr. Bunny didn't kill him there. He'd taken Noah someplace else, probably where he took Rita and the other three. Gabriel needed to find the place.

He took his phone, opened the drafts folder and sent the email he'd composed last night—an image he had drawn on the map of Staten Island. Phones chimed all around.

Gabriel told them his presumption about Mr. Bunny living in this area, and all the work his team had done over the last forty-eight hours came down to this. If they were to find any camera within this border that recorded either the Chevy Suburban or the Range Rover, it would shorten their search.

"A-a-apart from this, y-you make and d-divide your own assignments. I can't think or d-do anything," Gabriel said to no one in particular. "Report to Nash."

The office emptied. A silent buzz echoed in Gabriel's head as he made a difficult choice.

He called Stanley to fix an appointment for drinks later that evening.

Stanley suggested they go to a deli. "There's no such thing as a cured addict."

But he gave up the persuasion when Gabriel insisted with harsher words. He couldn't drink alone; that was dangerous. And Stanley was the only friend he had now, wasn't he?

* * *

Gabriel wasn't sleeping, but he kept his eyes closed to the world and tried to drift away from reality. He was in that gray area where he didn't hear things around him, but his consciousness didn't quite let go of him. It was always in the corner, meddling, reminding him that he was merely fooling himself that he was sleeping, attempting to escape the fresh pain.

Only when Emma and the others came back and shook him up did he know it was already evening.

The team found cameras in many houses within the perimeter, and their owners let them take a look at the playbacks. If they spotted the cars that matched the colors, the model was never the same, and vice versa. Meaning, no cameras ever recorded the red and silver SUVs inside the area. Now they had nothing else to use to narrow down the search.

This neighborhood was a sophisticated choice for Mr. Bunny. Not all the lanes or avenues had cameras installed in them. If one found these roads and used only them, he could go round and around the place without being recorded even once.

Mr. Bunny's knowledgeable shield which blocked the detectives from discovering his identity was not just powerful, but also had different layers. Mr. Bunny didn't think his vanguard defense would fail him, but he didn't take the liberty of being arrogant. Hence, he avoided all the cameras in this sixteen square mile area. It was the second layer of defense that protected him after Gabriel had wedged his way through the first. Gabriel wasn't sure if he could do it again.

Who had the knowledge of this area? Half a million people did. But who among them had the forensic know-how? About LCN DNA? About trace evidence or tower dump records? With TV and the internet, anything was possible these days.

What other way did Gabriel have to find the place?

He asked his team to listen to 911 calls made from the neighborhoods within the perimeter, for the last year. They should concentrate on complaints concerning screams, reports that were investigated and closed when nothing fishy had turned up.

Next, he told them to skim through all the criminal cases registered in those neighborhoods in the last three decades, prioritizing cases pertaining to arson or cruelty toward animals—typical behaviors of budding psychopathic killers. Gabriel was grasping at straws, but what else could he do?

The members of his team went to their desks, with faces reflecting what he felt inside—hopelessness.

Chapter 26

March 19, 2019. 08:52 P.M.

Gabriel gripped his umpteenth glass of vodka. He couldn't—wouldn't—think about what he was doing. He just wanted the peace and numbness alcohol brought. But it brought along with it a sense of shame and defeat. Still, who cared? Just that night. Just that one miserable night.

"Where is your brother?" Gabriel said.

"What?" Stanley put down the milk.

"I'm serious."

Stanley's eyebrows dropped, lips slowly shrunk. Now, he knew there was no punchline.

"Where is this coming from? Are you—"

"Just answer me."

"I don't know."

"Well, I don't believe you." Gabriel knocked back the drink. He didn't even know what he was saying, let alone if he meant it. He rode shotgun while his inebriated brain took him for a ride. Anyway, he'd already talked bad to the people he loved and made lasting sour memories. What was one more?

"Phillip robbed eighteen dollars with a dummy gun. Why would I lie, Gabe? Are you listening to yourself? Jackass!"

"Was that all?" Gabriel stared at Stanley. "He slashed Casey."

Stanley closed his eyes, the vivid memories undoubtedly flashing behind his eyelids.

* * *

Noah and Casey Smith, Gabriel, and Stanley were fooling around in a pool in Mr. Smith's backyard. They were all fifteen or sixteen. Phillip Ming was older, at twenty-one. He arrived in his usual style, his motion jerky, his manner erratic and mercurial, like he was faster than all of them, and he was ready to do something with that speed. Something bad.

Phillip slapped Stanley and asked him for money. When he said no, Phillip started pushing them all around. He hit Casey in the head, and Casey's eyes welled up. Gabriel was so angry his fingers shook. Enough was enough. He didn't mind getting beat up, but he was not going to let anyone hit his dear friend. A special friend that he should always care for—that's what Rita had told him to do. He stiffened his lips, balled up his fists, and went at Phillip.

After a few seconds and two popped-off buttons, Gabriel wound up face down on the ground. He'd forgotten that Phillip was a foot taller and a lot stronger than him.

With his knee pressing on Gabriel's back, Phillip came closer to his head, his long hair touching Gabriel's cheek.

He whispered, "Stay down."

Casey and Noah had Phillip's build, but neither helped. They weren't disloyal, but scared of this piece of shit, who, unlike his younger brother, exploited the lovely family that had adopted him. Not only did the Mings try to make

Phillip go to school again after he was released from juvenile, they even took him to the best of rehabs. But Phillip never let go of the drugs or lousy friendships.

Phillip wasn't just hurting his parents, but also Stanley's chance of becoming a doctor or a lawyer. What if they gave Stanley back to the Child Protective Services? Gabriel was old enough to understand if CPS took Stanley away, then it'd be for good, and Phillip was old enough to understand that foster parents weren't always the best. He wasn't behaving well because he got addicted to something some dirty guy scratching his butt crack made in his basement.

Gabriel tapped into the growing hysteria inside his head. Without thinking any further, he swung his head back as fast as he could. He felt the back of his head contact something sharp.

Phillip's knee relented.

Gabriel got up, rubbing the back of his head with one hand while patting down the mud from his wet swimming shorts with the other. Phillip held his mouth and stared at Gabriel, his eyes a lighter shade of the liquid peeking between his fingers. Calling Gabriel a nasty name, he took out a switchblade from his jeans.

Gabriel was ready—the responsibility to save his friends fell on his shoulders.

But to everyone's surprise, Casey screamed something indistinct and sprinted at Phillip. It disturbed Gabriel to watch Casey whenever he got angry, so he and Noah had always avoided that scenario. Since Casey had autism, his body movements were wayward and alarming if something pissed him off.

Casey slapped Phillip square in the face and grabbed the blade. He tried to wrestle it free, but Phillip pulled it back. Casey fell, holding his hand and screaming in pain. The cut was deep, and the sight of blood made everyone panic, including Phillip, who high-tailed it out of there.

A few nights after the incident, two explosions from Noah's house woke everyone in the street. Shotgun blasts.

Detective Lamb surmised that it was Phillip who'd killed Casey because he'd embarrassed him. Back then, when the city was battling the worst drug epidemic, addicts functioned just like that. They were known for explosive violence.

Gabriel's best friend was buried, and weeks later Mr. Smith vacated the house. He would become an alcoholic and abandon his family printing business.

Gabriel felt responsible for Casey's death. If it weren't for him, Casey wouldn't have jumped in and attacked Phillip. How Gabriel wished he could go back in time and handle it without anger.

* * *

"Let's say Phillip is as evil as you think, why the hell should I hide him? Where would I even keep him? I'm married, for God's sake!"

"You riied to me," Gabriel said.

The conversation hopped onto a different topic, just like how drunken ones tend to.

"What?" Stanley asked.

"Lied… lied to me." Gabriel shook his head in an attempt to sharpen his concentration. "You lied to me the other day. You said you quit the weed. But you haven't. Have you?"

Stanley looked down. "Yeah, I didn't quit. I don't want to. It's not like it's destroying me, like booze is destroying you."

"A lie is a lie. You're a pothead, and I'm an alcoholic!" Gabriel screamed the last word.

Stanley grabbed Gabriel's elbow and tried to get him up, but Gabriel pulled away.

"Leave me alone!"

Stanley shook his head and walked out.

Gabriel squeezed his eyelids, focused through its gap and read the time on his phone—9:37 p.m.

"Bartender!" Gabriel was vaguely aware that he'd just shouted. "Keep it coming."

"You've had enough, man."

"I'll tell you when I…" Gabriel paused to think.

He'd forgotten what he wanted to say.

"Come on, man. You should leave. Give me your keys. I'll hail you a cab. You're too drunk."

Gabriel pulled his shield and banged it on the table. "I said keep it coming. Got a problem with that?"

The barman looked at the shield, and then at Gabriel. "No, man. Just take it down a notch, will you?"

* * *

Gabriel staggered out to the parking lot twenty minutes later. Taking his keys out, he stumbled to his motorcycle. Bare trees lined the narrow curb, their pointy branches stretching up toward the sky. Were they trying to get saved from this rotten world? No, more likely pull heaven down and corrupt it too.

Gabriel missed his footing and tumbled, but regained his balance in time to stop himself from falling over. He laughed to himself. The old boozehound had got him pretty good.

By the time he realized he shouldn't even be thinking about riding, he was already on his motorcycle. How did that happen? Hmm. Now that he was, maybe he should rev the throttle to the fullest speed and see if fate wanted him alive or dead. It sure seemed like it hated his guts and wanted to take his body and mind apart. So why not help fate achieve its goal, and at the same time help himself achieve peace forever, with a little bit of help from his Kawasaki?

He slid the kickstand back, but his knee buckled and he fell sideways, his vehicle still under his crotch. Not having the courage to face another day, he closed his eyes, wishing he would never wake up.

* * *

"…is five-O, man. You nuts or something?"

"Maybe. You gonna help with the wheels, or what?"

Gabriel felt two pairs of hands locking onto his wrists. His thighs slipped from the seat, and they dragged him through the wet lot.

Skinny fingers frisked the inside of his jacket.

"Put the Glock down, fool! You ain't got no need for that."

"Stop bitching. The drunk pig don't deserve it, a'ight?"

"What the?! Why you taking that for? It may be his asthma medicine or something?"

"And you think I care about this, why? Man, the popos are here. Scram!"

Gabriel heard the faint sound of his motorcycle racing away. He laughed at the trees as warm tears flowed down his nose.

"You are a d-d-disgusting coward, Gabriel."

Chapter 27

March 20, 2019. 12:32 P.M.

"Isn't this the same bed they had me on?" Ashley said.

"Yes." Gabriel's voice was raspy.

His throat had swollen and he had trouble swallowing.

A police cruiser found Gabriel in the bar's parking lot around 2:00 a.m. Nine-one-one received a call from a worried bartender, to whom Gabriel owed the biggest apology and thanks. The officers didn't find any ID on Gabriel, but they recognized him from the papers and brought him to the ER. The doctor told them that their friend was just drunk and cold, nothing serious. They had understood enough not to call Gabriel's captain, so they found out who his partner was and called Emma.

Nash was with Emma when they visited him earlier that morning. After giving him an ear-full of obscenities, Emma had promised that his secret was safe with her and she wouldn't tell anyone about the shit he'd pulled last night, except Ashley, who'd called Emma the previous night. When Emma said she wasn't able to reach Gabriel either, Ashley had sounded worried.

Gabriel had given Nash the key to his apartment and password to his MacBook. An anti-theft app in the laptop could track his stolen iPhone. He hoped the pricks didn't use the gun or the shield.

Two hours later, Nash and Emma re-entered the ward.

Nash held Gabriel's keyholder in one hand, and flattened his tousled hair with the other.

"Man, was that sweet!"

The keyholder had a toy—a plastic doll of Stewie Griffin from Family Guy. Liz had bought it for him when they were together. Nash tossed it to Gabriel, who didn't even try to catch it. It landed on the comforter, which covered him up to his chest.

With narrow eyes, Emma stared at Gabriel without blinking as she took his gun, shield, phone, wallet, and inhaler out of a paper bag and arranged them on a table beside his bed. Then she headed out.

"Emma?" Gabriel called after her.

She answered by flipping him off, without turning.

Ashley tried to hide her smile by looking down. "I'll go talk to her."

When Ashley went out, Nash said, "So you wanna know what our pals at the FBI found?"

Gabriel nodded.

"Cameras in Noah's house? Mr. Bunny stole their hard disk."

"But how did he gain entry *into* the house in the first place? Noah knew the risk his work brought."

Noah had been paranoid about home invasions even before he became an assistant district attorney. No one could enter his house without entering a pin code at the front door. Ever since Casey's murder, he was high on home security.

"There was no sign of foul play. Our killer used the pin code. He must've known it somehow, like with Samuel's house."

"How! How the hell is he—" Gabriel tensed.

Razor blades cut inside his throat.

Nash didn't answer the question. Instead, he carried a half-empty jug from the coffee table and gave it to Gabriel, who emptied it in seconds.

"One more thing," Nash said.

"Yeah?"

Nash came close, and Gabriel became confused. Then he smacked Gabriel upside the head.

"Dude!" Gabriel held his ringing head. "What the—"

"I don't know." Nash shrugged. "Stanley told me to smack you in the head and call you an effing dildo. But we're friends, and I know your aversion to the F-word, so I made you a discount by not calling you an effing dildo." Nash lifted his palms. "He said you'd understand."

Gabriel owed another apology to Stanley.

Shit. For seven years, he hadn't touched a drop. Seven proud years, and one night he grieved the loss of his childhood friend and bam, he was hurting his friends, threatening kind bartenders, getting robbed, and ending up in a hospital. And hadn't he contemplated suicide at some point?

"It's nothing. Never mind," Gabriel said.

"You know something? We've been ordered off the case."

"Come on, Nash. It's not TV. The FBI doesn't have authority over us."

"I didn't say FBI, smartass. Our own brothers-in-blue did."

"What?"

"The Major Case Squad kicked us out. They persuaded the commissioner to sacrifice our team."

"Why? Raymond wouldn't do that!"

"Not Mr. Hughes. Our new commissioner."

"The mayor fired Raymond?"

"No. He forced Mr. Hughes to take a long leave. The mayor will reinstate our old commissioner when this case is over. At least, that's what his secretary told me. Now Mr. Hughes's deputy is in charge, and he's asked us to leave the party. Politics. The media is watching us like hawks, and the higher-ups need to look good. So, replacing the commissioner and suspending the old team will make it seem like they're making some radical changes, that they're making progress of some kind."

Gabriel wanted to punch someone.

"The FBI sent us a written request to give them what we've found so far. Should I send them?"

Gabriel massaged his throat but didn't answer.

"Got it. By the way, you're free to leave whenever you want. So stop lying on your—"

Gabriel put up his hand.

He frowned and angled his head to the left. "What's that sound?"

"What sound?"

"Hmmmmm." Gabriel imitated the whirr.

"Heaters, you drunk fool! You were out in the cold last night. The doctors had to turn up the heaters to full blast to defrost your ancient ass."

Heaters!

Gabriel threw the comforter back and piled off the bed. Blurry eyes, the gift that comes the morning after a night of binge drinking, spun his body, and the right side of his lower back throbbed. Besides his kidneys and liver, he'd also abused his brain.

But it forgave him and threw him a new method to track Mr. Bunny. In their team meeting earlier, Nash had said Mr. Bunny was too careful about leaving evidence as small as lint and skin cells. So Gabriel just had to follow something smaller than cells: electrons.

Chapter 28

March 20, 2019. 01:14 P.M.

ZEUS Corp was a utility company that provided electricity to New York and a few other east coast states. Gabriel searched the web and found that out of the three branch offices ZEUS operated in Staten Island, the one that controlled the area was the one he was interested in.

Gabriel heaved himself up and got his helmet and keys. He'd almost puked when he rode to the precinct from the hospital, so the thought of riding again repulsed him. He didn't want to risk vomiting inside his helmet and crashing.

He hurried down to Emma's desk. She refused to tag along at first, but he grabbed her wrist and pulled her up. Then he dragged her out back to the parking lot, trying hard not to be disheartened by the expletives she spat at him. When they were out, Gabriel begged her to be his *driver* because he was too sick to operate a vehicle. She wore the helmet and rode the Kawasaki while Gabriel rode pillion.

ZEUS's office was in Eltingville, a five-mile ride from the 122nd. With light afternoon traffic and lucky green lights most of the way, Emma flipped the kickstand out in ZEUS's parking lot in under eight minutes. The company inhabited a two-story concrete structure with a single door, and it had a tidy veranda.

An old receptionist greeted them. His stitched-in name tag read *Mort*. After a brief stay in the lounge, a woman in her late forties, with frameless eyeglasses, met them. She introduced herself as Lily, the logistics manager, and eyed Gabriel. Lily said she had been working with ZEUS for almost a decade, and with the Eltingville branch for a month shy of three years. She asked them to follow her to her office on the second floor.

It was modest, not unlike Gabriel's. A table sat in the middle, and a vase holding fresh roses was placed on top of it, beside an HP monitor. The only chair in the room was behind the table. Lily probably wasn't used to having visitors.

"You look familiar," Lily said to Gabriel. "Have we met before?"

"No, ma'am, I don't believe we have."

"No. I've definitely seen you somewhere."

Gabriel braced himself for the *madman* comment.

She stood there, biting her fingernail. "I have it right here... some famous actor..." Then she burst out laughing.

Gabriel released a breath of relief and smiled.

"Seriously, Detective? Cut your hair and have a shave. You'll look hot."

"Will do, as soon as I get my paycheck."

Lily nodded and walked toward the door. "I'll go get the chairs."

"Let me help you." Emma followed her out.

While Gabriel waited, he took a closer look at the flowers. They seemed odd. The petals were synthetic and the stem was plastic. He'd fooled himself thinking they were authentic. He hoped their search didn't end like this.

After everyone sat—Gabriel and Emma in a pair of folding steel chairs—they stated the purpose of their visit.

"Oh, now I get it!" Then Lily hunched and lowered her voice. "I really know you. Is this about Mr. Bunny?"

"Yes, ma'am," Gabriel replied.

"They called you a madman. Aren't you going to sue?"

"No, ma'am, it's beneath the dignity of my office," Gabriel said, in a dry tone. "So, could you help us out?"

Lily said that Harry was one of her favorite comedians. He made her laugh and think at the same time. She'd participated in the candlelight march held for him. She promised she'd do anything in her power to help them find Mr. Bunny.

"Where should I start?" Lily typed on her keyboard, her glasses reflecting the monitor's bright screen when it woke from its slumber.

"We aren't sure." Gabriel scratched the back of his head. "Do heaters consume a lot of electricity?"

"That depends. You have heaters that use one and a half kilowatts per hour, and then you have some industrial types that can consume as much as seven kilowatts per hour."

"Say, if a person used four or more one-and-a-half-kilowatt heaters, the power consumption would be the same as having used one industrial-sized one, right?"

"Yes. And if he used them for domestic purposes, then his electricity bill would have given him a heart attack."

"Let's hope he didn't go that easily." Gabriel gave her a contrived smile. "Okay. I have an area spanning over sixteen square miles, and it has many neighborhoods. I need the power consumption record of every single domicile and facility within this place for the last three months. I could give you the vertices of that area or show it to you on the map."

"I can get the records of neighborhoods falling under the control of my office." Lily smiled apologetically. "But I'm afraid I'm not allowed to do the same for other neighborhoods."

"We detectives can only catch criminals with the help of people like you. I'm sure that even if you have no control over the other neighborhoods, you can still access their records. Time is of the essence, and if we go through official channels we may miss Harry's murderer."

Lily thought, biting the insides of her cheek, and Gabriel knew he'd gotten to her.

"All right, fine. Show me the map."

Gabriel opened the photo and handed the phone across the table. Lily took it and started working.

Emma got up, signaled Gabriel out, and walked to the door.

"Excuse us for a minute," Gabriel said, and got only a half-hearted *uh-huh* as a reply.

Lily was already lost in her work.

"I called you here to ask about your idea, and then find holes in it. Like how we do."

"Try me."

"Are you going to use power consumption records to find the place where Mr. Bunny hanged them?"

"That's the plan, yes."

"Because you believe he used heaters to melt the ice?"

"Yes."

"What if he used gas heaters or one of those LPG things that can be buried in backyards?"

"You heard of *don't shit where you eat?*"

"Yeah. So?"

"Mr. Bunny doesn't live where he killed them. If he doesn't live there, then he couldn't keep a continuous eye, which gas heaters would require—"

"You lost me." Emma crossed her arms.

"We know Mr. Bunny had a bad experience with Fred, the phone thief?"

"Yeah, yeah."

"So, Mr. Bunny is wary of small-time thieves."

"What's the connection? Are you intentionally screwing with my brain?" Emma sounded frustrated.

"No, stay with me. When you install gas heaters, you gotta do it at least a few days before you start using them. You need to fix conduits, like a chimney or flue, to vent the emissions."

"That's correct."

"Some street dweller sees four heaters getting unloaded and installed in a place that's locked almost every day of the month. What does he do?"

"He'll try to steal them himself, or kick up the information to other maggots."

"And Mr. Bunny has four stolen heaters on his hands."

"What if he's already installed them?"

"Even then, the same problem occurs. Locks never keep burglars out. Mr. Bunny is smart. He doesn't kill people where he lives; he has a separate place for it. We haven't come across anything that points us toward the idea of an accomplice. Since he can't watch the place by himself, and since he doesn't have anyone to keep an eye on it, the paranoia of theft is a real problem for him. More so after the incident with Fred."

"Yeah. Now I follow."

"There are other problems with gas heaters, too; the most problematic one is smoke. Natural gas and propane themselves are smokeless, but not the dust and other debris that gets collected in the burner. All it takes is one concerned neighbor, and Mr. Bunny has got fire department trucks with sirens blaring on his street, and big firemen axing down his door."

"You've got a point there. Electric heaters don't emit smoke. But still, burglars would try to steal them, right?"

"He must've fixed them the evening he abducted the four. It takes ten minutes to install one heater, an hour at best to install them all. Why go through all the hassle of gas heaters when the alternative provides him safety and comfort?"

"Wait a minute. How do you know he used four or five heaters? Why not one?"

"You've seen how fast the ice melted, right? That always bothered me. So, I began a Google search as soon as I returned to the precinct from the hospital. I found that, according to some law of thermodynamics, you can't melt the ice blocks that fast with one small heater, not in our cold NYC weather. You need one large heater or several smaller ones. Assuming Mr. Bunny works alone, it'll be a chore to move around a heavy heater. So he must have opted for the smaller ones."

Emma's eyes beamed. "You win."

When they returned to Lily's table, Gabriel was measurably happier. Whenever they get a *you win* in their game, it meant that they'd solved the case. Or were about to.

Gabriel said, "How we—"

"Westerleigh, New Springville, Todt Hill, and Castleton Corners." Lily didn't look up from her screen.

"Huh?" Emma looked at Gabriel as if he knew what Lily meant.

"These are the neighborhoods that have a lot of housing units within the area you've given me, and I've already downloaded their data. In just under a minute, I'll cover the rest."

Sixty long seconds later, Lily beckoned Gabriel over. He circled the table and saw an Excel spreadsheet opened on her monitor.

"It's done. I've scanned the entire demographics and downloaded the data in this sheet. We've got about fifty thousand entries."

"Fifty thousand?" Emma asked in disbelief.

"Fifty thousand is good, Em. There are more than one hundred and seventy-two thousand houses on Staten Island. What we got is a lot less." Gabriel turned to Lily. "Could you filter only the entities that used little or no power at all in January and February?"

Lily did. Gabriel couldn't see if the fifty thousand had shrunk into two thousand or two hundred—the screen showed only until row number 31.

"Let's say he used one-and-a-half-kilowatt heaters, and he used four of them for an hour. That gives us—"

"Six kilowatts, duh." Lily smiled.

"From this result, could you filter places that used only six kilowatts or a little over that in March?"

Gabriel looked at the screen in anticipation as Lily maneuvered the spreadsheet with the mastery only veteran office workers possessed.

"Done." She banged the return key. "You have twenty-two units that used six kilowatts more this month than the last two months."

Gabriel pointed at one column in the spreadsheet that didn't make sense.

"What are these numbers?"

"They're the ID numbers assigned to our company's meter boxes fixed to houses and facilities. Give me a moment and I'll convert those numbers into names and addresses."

Gabriel watched her bring up a different program that had ZEUS's thunderbolt logo on the top right corner. It must be their software. She copied the column of the meter box numbers and pasted it into a box in the software. After that, Gabriel lost track of what she did.

"All right, I'm done. Take a look." Lily moved a little to her left.

When Gabriel read what was on the screen, almost all the cells in his hungover brain were mystified. *It can't be. It just can't be.*

The first entry read *Smith Press.*

"Can I see the detailed record for *Smith Press* this month?" Gabriel heard himself say.

Lily showed Gabriel the record. The power consumption was nonexistent throughout the month, except the fifteenth and sixteenth—the period Mr. Bunny had killed Rita and three other people.

"May I have a copy of this list?"

Ten seconds later, Gabriel passed the warm papers to Emma. He thanked Lily and shook her hand with both of his. He promised her that Harry's murderer would soon go to prison, and she'd played a crucial part in it. Lily blushed.

Gabriel stopped halfway to the door. He turned and walked back, feeling embarrassed.

"I'm sorry to—"

"No, it's fine. Tell me what you need."

"Record for the same address. The date is December 9th, last year."

Gabriel waited, listening to the rhythm of keystrokes he'd grown familiar with in the last hour.

"Yeah, there was some activity, but not like what we've got with the heaters. Maybe just lights or fans?"

Maybe. Or maybe power saws.

AJ's skinless head and the heap of his body parts flashed in front of Gabriel's mind.

Chapter 29

March 20, 2019. 02:49 P.M.

No one wanted to buy the Smiths' house after Casey's murder became a thing with the media. Mr. Smith closed the printing press in their basement, sold all the big machinery that churned out millions of books, and relocated to Tribeca. He found oblivion in whiskey, turning a blind eye to business, home, and family alike.

A few years later, realtors began showing interest in the house, as it was located on Edinboro Road, Lighthouse Hill, where the property values went only one way: up. But Mr. Smith had changed his mind by then and never tried to sell it again.

When Gabriel questioned Noah about it, he replied that his old man had grown attached to the place. Sometimes Mr. Smith visited the house at the exact time Casey had been shot, hoping to see his ghost. However, Noah stopped his father from visiting, and vegetation, decay, and time slowly consumed the old house.

The same house in front of which Emma eased the Kawasaki to a stop. Huge wrought iron gates and tall peripheral walls hid it pretty well from the street.

Gabriel stepped down and crossed to the gates. When he pushed them open, they parted without a noise. One would expect the hinges to be bonded with rust and make a teeth-shattering scrape when used after all these years of abandonment.

As they strode up to the desolate house, Gabriel felt movement on his right. Drapes moved on the window of a building parallel to the Smiths'. That house belonged to an elderly neighbor who Gabriel's gang used to pester when they were children. Gabriel smiled and continued walking.

He climbed a short series of creaking steps and traversed a dirty porch that ended at the front door. A big lock secured it. Gabriel went around the left side of the house and reached the back door. It was locked as well, and he couldn't find any windows to break in. He needed something to jimmy it open.

Wait. Lily had said *Smith Press*, hadn't she?

Gabriel headed to the right side of the house.

A medium-sized Mitsubishi truck—a Fuso, they'd learn on closer inspection—was parked in front of a metal railing that flanked a small section of the wall. From his old memories, Gabriel knew the railing guarded a steep drop of stairs that led to the basement where Smith Press had operated.

"Is… is that a refrigerator truck?" Emma asked.

"Yes. It seems like Nash was right. Mr. Bunny must have used it to transport the ice."

"Holy shit, Gabe. This is it! You found the place."

"*We* did."

Gabriel made his way to the railing, stepping over long wooden planks on the ground. He descended the flight of concrete stairs; they used to feel like a lot of steps back in the day, but now felt like a lot less.

When he reached the bottom, a door halted him, and a lock bigger than the ones he'd found above protected it. But it didn't dishearten Gabriel, because this lock was something they had all encountered when they were kids. They used to sneak into the press, explore the metallic beasts, and play with big sheets of paper, which was one of their favorite activities back then. From playing cards to monopoly, any indoor games they chose for the day, they had used this place to play it. Gabriel remembered Mr. Smith's warnings about the dire consequences they'd all face if they snuck into the press and messed with his work.

Gabriel turned back and saw Emma standing at the top of the stairs, with her arms akimbo.

"Locked too, huh?" she said.

"Not for long." Gabriel passed his partner.

When back on the ground, he crouch-walked and examined the lower side of the house's wall for a small dark hole. It was a secret mark on a plank, inside which they used to hide a spare key. Noah had stolen it from his father and hid it here, and only their little gang was privy to its location.

And there it was!

Gabriel bent low and pulled the plank aside, revealing a dark space about the size of an apple. Inside, a bronze key glinted, announcing its presence.

Should he wear gloves before touching it? What did he risk contaminating? Fingerprints? DNA? *Yeah, right.* He took the key with his bare hand.

It felt wrong that he and Emma were making progress without informing the team. Well, Stanley was angry with him, and the new commissioner had ordered Nash and David out, so it wasn't really his fault.

He tossed the hefty key to Emma and asked her to open the door and take a look inside. Then he dialed Bill and pressed the phone to his ear. With his elbows propped on the railing, he watched Emma and relaxed.

A sudden palpable change in the atmosphere sharpened his senses. The flow of wind he'd been feeling on his back was disrupted and felt different. His body stiffened and the hair on the back of his neck and forearms stood up.

Danger!

The cocking of a gun pierced the silence.

From all his years in the service, Gabriel knew the cocking sound didn't come from a small handgun like the Glock 19 he had holstered against his hip, but from a bigger and uglier one—a gun that could make a bloody lotus of the unfortunate head it was pointing at.

Gabriel hoped Emma would turn and see his face. But the hope waned when she turned the key in the lock.

"Oh my God, this door is heavy. And it smells like strays had an orgy..." The basement swallowed Emma's voice as she walked inside.

Every man for himself.

Gabriel slid his hand toward his hip.

"You gotta death wish, do you?"

Gabriel stopped his movement. "Who are you? I'm a cop."

"Cop?" The voice sounded indecisive. "Turn around very, very slowly. That's right. Easy does it."

When Gabriel completed the rotation, he faced the weapon. He was correct about the gun. It was a long, double-barreled shotgun. However, the muzzle lowered to reveal a face with a hundred grooves. A familiar face.

"Gabriel? Is that you, tiger?"

"Mr. Edison." Gabriel placed a hand on his chest. "You scared the bejesus out of me."

"Sorry about that. I thought someone was breaking in." Mr. Edison un-cocked the hammer. "How you doing, sport? It's been years since I've seen you."

Mr. Edison wore boxers, a tank shirt, and a maroon robe over it. He was bald at the top, and white hair puffed at the sides like a clown. He had to be around eighty now.

"I'm good. How about you and Mrs. Edison?"

"Living, boy, just living. Diane passed away last year. God rest her soul."

"Oh, I didn't know. I'm sorry to hear that, Mr. Edison."

"Yeah, well, thank you. Joshua attended the funeral." Mr. Edison motioned to his house, behind him. "How about a cup of coffee? Rum, perhaps?"

"I'm on duty, Mr. Edison, but thank you." Gabriel's stomach gurgled. "So, how's the neighborhood?"

Gabriel asked that question to fish for any information that might contribute something vital to the investigation, but he regretted asking it a minute later. Mr. Edison talked at length about everything that had happened in the neighborhood during the last decade. As a compliment, he even threw in some racist remarks about several Sri Lankan families who'd moved into the community.

"I'd love to catch up, but my partner needs me down there."

"Yeah, about that. What you doing here?"

"Police business, Mr. Edison."

"It's about damn time you lot—"

Rapid tromping on the stair interrupted him.

"Gabe, you gotta come take a look at this!" Then Emma looked at Mr. Edison, and eventually his gun.

Her found-a-new-toy-to-play-with puppy eyes changed into the getting-real-tired-of-your-bullshit mom eyes.

"The last time I checked," Emma said to Mr. Edison, "open carry is still illegal inside the city."

"So is trespassing, young lady."

"What was that, sir? Let me see your permit." She stood there as if she really contemplated kicking a pensioner's ass.

"Let me see your warrant." Mr. Edison matched the venom in her tone.

"He's got it, Em. Let's go see what got you stoked."

Emma glared at the old Republican, then rolled her eyes before she turned and led the way for Gabriel. When down on the landing, she shoved the door in. If Gabriel wasn't mistaken, she did it with some effort. Why? She was strong.

He pushed the door, and it weighed a ton. Once inside, he pushed it nearly closed, leaving only a half-foot gap between the door and its frame. It was dark, so he switched the flashlight app on his phone and took a closer look at the other side of the door. It was insulated with soundproofing rubber, acoustic caulk, door gasket, automatic door bottom, the whole set up. Mr. Bunny had spent a big penny to stop the noises of the outside world from blaring in. Or more likely, to prevent the wails of the hell inside from seeping out.

"Gabe. Leave that. The real interesting thing is here." Emma's voice came from the shadowy part of the basement behind him and echoed in the big vacant space.

Gabriel's phone beeped, notifying low battery—the thieves hadn't charged it. Gabriel switched off the flashlight.

Through the little opening in the entrance, a long beam of light streamed inside. There was something near the left side wall. It was rectangular, as tall as Gabriel, seven-feet wide and three-feet deep. A shiny red cloth covered it.

"What's that over at the wall?" he said.

"I don't know."

Gabriel edged toward it, his hand on the butt of his pistol. Just in case someone was hiding in it. Though they'd had to open the lock to enter the basement, Gabriel wouldn't put anything past Mr. Bunny. For all he knew, it could be a secret passage.

But when he yanked the cloth down, he found a mountain of books—paperbacks about how serial killers were caught, about chemistry, lock picking, forensic biology and all its sub-disciplines, ballistics, police procedural fiction and non-fiction, criminal syndicates of the world, a few about torture and interrogation, stealth and hand-to-hand combat…

The titles went on and on.

"Gabriel Chase! Are you gonna come here, or what?"

"Coming."

It was best to obey her when she addressed him with his full name. He squinted at her silhouette and headed toward it. As he neared Emma, the door opened fully, lighting up the whole place.

"This is a crime scene, Mr. Edison. Please…"

Then he registered something and looked back at Emma. Or more accurately, toward what she was pointing at—a motorized wheelchair.

"Crime scene?" Mr. Edison said. "I knew it!"

"Give me a moment, Mr. Edison." Gabriel turned to Emma. "I'll deal with him. In the meanwhile, do a spiral around the wheelchair."

First the truck, now the wheelchair. Minute by minute, evidence was piling up to prove that this was where the murders had taken place. If Gabriel had reserved any doubt about it, then the seven electric heaters sitting along the right side wall, behind Emma and the wheelchair, cleared it for him.

"How do you know it's a crime scene?" Gabriel asked Mr. Edison.

"Those Ming boys were up to no good. Always trouble. He sneaks into the basement sometimes, thinking no one can see him."

"Phillip Ming?" Gabriel said.

"No. The smaller one."

"Stanley?" Gabriel frowned.

"Yeah. Him."

"When did he come here last?"

"Last Valentine's Day. I remember because that was the first one I spent without Diane. I went to the terrace with a bottle of rum. The sky was starless, as if God had had enough of our shit and gone away. He took his heavens with him and let us rot in our own filth, smog, and light pollution. Scripture says—"

"Could we please stay on topic?"

"Yeah, sorry about that. February 14th, the last time I saw Stanley."

"How did he come?"

"What do you mean how? Walking, of course. He still lives on the next street. Don't you remember?" Mr. Edison shifted the gun to his right hand.

"You ever see a red or a silver vehicle here? An SUV?"

"Can't say that I have. Might have heard them, though. After I went to bed, that is. Doctor's orders. Dinner at nine and snoring at ten."

"At what time did Stanley usually come?"

"Seven or eight. Leaves before ten. If he stayed after that, I wouldn't know."

"I'd like to take you up on that offer of coffee if you don't mind, Mr. Edison."

"Really? That's great."

"And some eggs and toast. Also, a sandwich if that isn't too much trouble."

It had been more than thirty-six hours since he'd eaten anything.

"I hope you have cheese."

"No trouble, Gabriel. Nice to have company." Mr. Edison's face brightened.

"Wait outside and I'll join you in a minute."

Gabriel headed for the heaters and inspected them. They were medium-sized, with rollers under them. The truck parked above was big enough to transport the heaters and the ice blocks in a single trip. The wooden planks must have helped to get them all down here.

"What you got there?" Gabriel joined Emma, who was crouching near the wheelchair.

"Nothing. Just junkie stuff."

"What junkie stuff?"

She got up and showed Gabriel a small zip-lock evidence bag.

"I know we have to use paper bags for this kind of evidence, to let it breathe and prevent mold, but I have to make do with what I've…"

Emma continued to talk, but Gabriel's mind dissociated. He couldn't hear much because the object inside the zip-lock sealed the deal.

It was the butt of a marijuana cigarette.

"…I'm not trained to collect joint butts. I may screw it up. We need professionals. Call your bestie and—"

"Give me a minute." Gabriel closed his eyes and his mind became as quiet as the room. Now he knew what he had to do—devise a perfect trap to catch the animal, else it would disappear forever.

He didn't know how long he'd kept his eyes closed, but when he opened them, the basement seemed to radiate with brightness.

He looked at his partner. "You know what, Em? You're right. Let's call my *bestie*."

Chapter 30

March 20, 2019. 04:27 P.M.

Gabriel ate a hearty lunch while Emma drank water. He thanked Mr. Edison, and they both left the house, heading for the Kawasaki.

Before knocking on Mr. Edison's door to cash in on his offer of hospitality, Gabriel had made a few calls.

First, he called Bill and instructed him to go to Stanley's building and wait outside. Once Stanley's CSU van left from there, he needed to go inside the office and meet the secretary. When Bill finished his work there, he was to come out and wait for a special delivery from David.

Then Gabriel called Nash and asked him to follow Stanley's forensic van. Just in case.

The last call was the toughest.

"Do you want to leave your wife for a change?"

"What?" David said.

"I'm talking about leaving your laptop and doing a different kind of work."

"What's that?"

"One that involves a strong backbone." Gabriel explained the assignment amid rude protests.

Finally, he got him to accept.

"One more thing."

"What?" David barked.

"I need a state-of-the-art tracking device." Gabriel told him the specs.

"That's high-tech. It'll take time."

"You got an hour."

David hung up.

Now Gabriel and Emma listened to the wind and stood in mutual boredom.

"What's up with the books?" Emma propped herself on the motorcycle. "A *nerd* played us?"

"Don't underestimate the power of a lone person who's spent a lot of time with books."

"I disagree. What are you gonna say? Someone reads a bunch of books and becomes a huge shit?"

"With unshakable determination, yes. You heard about a guy named Wang Enlin?"

She stared at him, aping the look of a bored teenager.

"This guy, Mr. Enlin, was a Chinese farmer who lived a hand-to-mouth life. A chemical factory polluted his village and its pond, destroying their livelihoods."

"So what? Wang fought them and rescued the village?" Emma smirked and shook her head.

"I'm getting there. See, Mr. Enlin can't fight the factory owners with just a few of his tough friends. Their enemy, the corporation, has a private army at their disposal. He knows he has to fight it legally, but he's dirt poor. So, he goes to a bookshop, gives the owner his corn in exchange for sitting there and taking notes about the law, from the books. Over the course of sixteen years, he teaches himself everything there is to learn about the Chinese legal system."

Emma's indifferent smile vanished.

"After that, he sues the corporation. You know, those types tend to fight with everything they've got. And remember, the lawyers on their side have gone to the best law schools and were paid handsomely to argue their case. But this one poor person, an elementary school dropout, defeated them all, one by one, and won the case."

"Bullshit!"

"No bullshit. Leonardo da Vinci, HP Lovecraft, William Blake, Malcolm X, the Wright brothers—they were all self-taught. The moral of the story is never underestimate someone who is willing to educate themselves. With enough motivation and persistence, anyone can become an expert in anything. With Mr. Enlin, it was to defeat corporate evils, to fight injustice. With Mr. Bunny, it's to gain enough knowledge to defeat cops and the law. Autodidacts have changed the world a lot more than aristocrats—”

Emma whistled and pointed her chin behind his back. He turned and saw the forensic van driving their way. Emma rose from the motorcycle and hooked her thumbs in her belt loops.

The van halted beside them, and moments later Stanley and a new guy Gabriel had never seen before got out. Stanley was dressed in his usual sharp clothing, but his face looked like he’d tried to swallow a rock and it got stuck in his throat.

Emma collected the fresh face and walked him in, but Gabriel placed a hand on Stanley’s shoulder, stopping him.

“Brings back memories, huh?” Gabriel said.

“What do you mean?”

“Nothing.” Gabriel gave him a rictus grin.

Stanley squirmed away from his touch and regarded Gabriel with disdain. Then he followed Emma.

Once he was out of sight, a nondescript car entered the street and stopped five houses down. Its headlamps blinked twice.

Gabriel went back in and descended the stairs. He leaned on the doorframe and folded his arms. The new guy clicked pictures of the heaters, and Stanley dusted the wheelchair, his face a kaleidoscope of fraught emotions.

At last, Gabriel’s phone rang. Everyone glanced in his direction and then resumed their work, but Emma continued to look at him. He answered the call. It was Bill, and he gave him the confirmation Gabriel had been waiting to hear.

He disconnected and nodded to Emma.

She moved close to Stanley. “You are under arrest, Mr. Ming. Anything you say…”

She read him his rights as he glared at Gabriel. Then she cuffed him and took him to Nash’s car.

Chapter 31

March 20, 2019. 06:34 P.M.

David entered Gabriel's office and slumped into the chair opposite him. His clothes were fresh, but Gabriel doubted if it was the first set he'd worn that day. David's face expressed pain, meaning he had done what Gabriel had asked of him.

"Well?"

"I've delivered the sample to Bill."

"You were covert?" Gabriel breathed from the inhaler.

"Why do you think my ass feels numb? But still, I couldn't do it, not by myself. It's not as easy as in the movies, so I had to call my pals from my precinct."

"I owe you one, David. You want me to owe you another one?"

"Shoot."

"I'll give you a phone number, and I want a record of its history for the last year."

"Thank God. Finally, my type of work."

Gabriel texted him the number. "You get going and start working on it."

* * *

"Why are you guys checking people at the entrance? The clumsy officer took five minutes to clear me! What is this? An airport?" Ashley sat where David had been sitting an hour ago.

"I'm sorry for that," Gabriel said. "You should've called me. Victor's tightening the security because we suspect the information about Mr. Bunny's arrest might have leaked. He's killed a lot of people. Some of them were gangsters. We don't want an angry relative or a gang member busting in with a gun, seeking revenge."

"But he's going to go to prison forever. Why kill him and ease his suffering?" Ashley's beady eyes focused in vengeance.

"Gangsters aren't as rational as you are. Apparently, not as bloodthirsty either."

Ashley laughed. "So tell me, why am I here, Gabriel?"

"I've just sent you a photo. Have you seen it?"

It was Stanley's photo. He was in orange prison garb, his hands shackled in front of him. Nash and Bill held his elbows on either side, looking grimly satisfied and competent.

"I did. How did you get him?"

Gabriel told her about the heaters and the wheelchair, about Mr. Edison's testimony and the butt of the joint. Also, Stanley knew his way around the cameras inside Gabriel's perimeter—he had lived in that neighborhood ever since the Mings adopted him. Stanley's hands were tested positive for trace metal detection, too. Their team was waiting for the gunshot residue results to come in anytime now.

"These tests come out positive only if we test the perp's hands within forty-eight hours after he held a weapon. Noah was shot around 3:00 a.m. yesterday."

"But isn't Mr. Bunny well-read in forensics? Why didn't Stanley clean up after himself like he always does? And wasn't he wearing gloves when he shot…"

"He might've smeared it on when he was removing the gloves," Gabriel said.

"Oh… you asked him how he got them on his hands?"

"He says he went to a shooting range to practice."

"Why?"

"He claims he's scared of something happening to his close friends or family. Mr. Bunny's MO is to hurt people who are important to police investigations by killing someone related to them. Stanley is right to be afraid because he is the greatest forensic scientist we've ever had."

"But you don't believe him?"

"It's bullshit, because he is Mr. Bunny."

"All right. Getting down to business. Why'd you call me here? How do you want me to run the story?"

And Gabriel told her how.

Rio

3/20/19. Middle of the night.

It took me twenty-four hours to leave New York City, the United States, and my life behind. A nameless man, who'd also gotten me an authentic Mexican passport, stole one of the several rafts marooned on the bank of the Rio Grande and helped me sneak across. We drove to Chihuahua, and from there I flew to Mexico City, and then to Rio de Janeiro.

I ate some native dish they call Moqueca for dinner. A hint of garlic and coriander still lingered on my taste buds. Annie, an elementary school teacher I'm engaged to, had cooked it. I met Annie a year back, in Mexico City. I've cajoled her to relocate to Rio, telling her that only childhood education can reduce crime in these parts of their country, and she'd do a great job at that.

I love Rio. Not just because it has Annie, but it also gave me the most villainous of its children, Juan. A smuggler and a slumlord, Juan has murdered over ninety people in his twenty-eight years of life. Annie and I are living in a favela controlled by his gang. Juan is loyal, trustworthy, and ferocious like a pit bull. I've used him a few times in the past. The RF jammer and the Colt Python came from him, and his contact helped me cross the border.

I ate Annie's food, and we made love. Now she's sleeping naked beside me, her tanned thigh resting on my stomach. I'm so tired from all the driving, sneaking, and fleeing, my eyes close without my consent. I'll sleep anytime now, but before that, I want to catch up with what's happening back home.

I slip from the bed, go to Annie's workbench, switch on her desktop and type in the Daily Herald's web address.

And then I died on the inside. Or at least I felt like it. *Felt*, I tell you. Um… I don't exactly remember what happened to my body when I saw the top news on the Daily Herald's website, but let me describe it the best I can picture it. The photons from the monitor entered my pupils, got converted into electrochemical impulses and transferred to my sleep-deprived brain, which woke up with a jolt of indignation. It fired sets of electrical and chemical signals of its own to many synapses in different areas of my body. To the eyelids, which opened as wide as they could. To the heart, instructing it to beat at its fastest rate. To the stomach, making it fluttery. And to the spine, causing me to recoil.

It all happened in a matter of microseconds, and it happened because the headline read *Rabbit is Caught!*

The news was published on March 20, 2019, at 10:50 p.m. Factoring in the difference between time zones, I calculate that the Daily Herald uploaded it online just five minutes ago.

I continue to read the rant, which reports that a forensic scientist working for the NYPD, Stanley Ming, has been indicted on a series of murders that shocked the United States last week. There is a photo. Some King Kong and an NYPD officer posed with Stanley Ming. Ashley herself has written the article. She lambasts, "narcissistic … over-confident of his skills … worthless …

hot-air … overreaching … run-of-the-mill little imbecile …"

Imbecile? *Little* imbecile. Incompetent rectal worms. You're imbeciles. You got the wrong guy. My mind screams and my ears become hot. Could it be anger that I'm feeling now? Symptoms say it is. The first time ever, and I'm not a fan.

This isn't what I've envisioned for my future. This case was supposed to be the greatest unsolved mystery of all time. My toil is supposed to disprove justice.

It's time to right the wrong. And fast.

Very well, Ashley. I allowed you to live before because you were an essential part of the hunt. But I can't do that now since there won't be a hunt anymore.

Chapter 32

March 22, 2019. 07:13 P.M.

Ashley shifted her weight on Samuel's chair and regarded the art on the back wall. The painting, which had been splattered with blood and bits of brain, and pierced by a bullet, had been restored as much as possible. The evidence that Ashley's mentor had escaped his worldly torment had been scrubbed away, and the resultant hole and white patches on the canvas had been redone.

After staring at it for some time, she turned her back to it and laid her head on her forearm.

Smiling Martha didn't make Ashley feel good. She understood guilt was a meaningless pain her brain inflicted upon her. She didn't know how God worked, but she knew the brain worked in mysterious ways.

It told her she was wrong to be sitting there, ruling the kingdom that Samuel had built from the ground up. How could she cope with the fact that she was the only person who'd substantially gained from the psycho's atrocities?

She'd gained Samuel's decision-making position. But his power, shares, and millions came with his responsibilities. Could she be him? Could she be a clutch player like him, making critical decisions when it counted most? He'd known all the tactics necessary to build the Daily Herald into one of the top news networks in the country. Did she know when to take a risk and when to retreat?

Wasn't it more likely that she was going to screw things up and become a princess who didn't know how to rule and lost power to enemy kingdoms?

She faced it squarely and realized she didn't fear the Daily Herald's rivals as much as she'd imagined she would. Then what was making her depressed?

Was it the charity that Samuel had made minutes before drawing his last breath? Or was it her fear of the overwhelming duties that went with the charity? Could she handle it?

But wait.

Samuel had decided to make her the new head, hadn't he? He could have given his ultimate position of power to other senior employees—and Ashley knew he had several viable options—but he hadn't. His decisions were always wise, and the predicted consequences of those decisions accurate. He wasn't some old man who'd lost his mind to age and stress. He'd even personally taken it upon himself to acquire the footage of the notorious Lolly, hadn't he? Just days before his death? He wasn't senile at that time, so having made her the head wouldn't be a bad decision. Would it?

Funny how the human mind rationalized things and tried to escape the suffering which it had created in the first place, trying to free itself from the incarceration it had put itself in.

Mysterious ways.

But the pain was constant. So, the guilt of sitting in his chair and the obligations it demanded from her wasn't the primary issue.

The real problem was the grieving process.

That day haunted her, the playback of Samuel killing himself looped relentlessly in her mind. His sad eyes looking at her, his mouth muttering, *"Sorry, dear."*

And then, *bang.*

Blood, brains, nightmares, and therapies cascaded into her life. A person didn't slide through something like that. But she had managed to successfully shut it out over the last few days. How had she done that, and why was it returning now?

Gabriel. That was why.

In the days following Samuel's death, having an inflexible purpose hadn't given her space to grieve. She'd needed to believe that she would somehow hurt the psycho, that she would play an essential part in his capture. As soon as Gabriel had said it, she'd boxed in all her emotions and shelved it, focusing her energy to help the police.

But now that Gabriel's team had arrested the psycho, there wasn't anything she could do to avenge Samuel. Nothing but an angry article she'd written. Some revenge. She sat up and tried to take a deep breath, feeling stifled.

Stifled.

Samuel had given her an important role but had denied her a chance to prove what she could do with it. Gabriel had given her hope when he'd said he needed her to be able to catch the psycho, but then he didn't ask her for any help. By not using her, he denied her a chance at retribution. These two denials, which she couldn't do anything about now, were destroying her peace.

You assholes.

She looked down at the wet marks on the sleeve of her sky-blue shirt. They were like the inkblots her shrink had showed her.

She wiped the tears and mucus off her face and got up. She opened her office door, which had gone unanswered quite a few times that day. As she left, she didn't make eye contact with anyone, though she felt many stares on her.

The elevator carried her down to the parking lot, and the Mustang beeped twice when she pressed the key fob.

She got in, dropped the handbag on the passenger seat, and dug her phone out of it. Twenty-three messages, fourteen calls, and thirty emails waited for her. She swiped all the notifications away and promised herself that from tomorrow, she'd excel at work and keep Samuel's business on top. She wouldn't screen calls, avoid meetings or people. No more procrastination.

Just not today.

Then, something on the phone's screen made her frown.

The battery was at ninety-five percent!

No, no. It should be at one hundred. Ashley had made sure of it the last time she put her phone inside the bag. It wasn't even on vibration mode. She'd turned off notifications. So why had it drained to ninety-five?

All those calls and emails must have used that significant five percent. No one knew like she did, the importance of keeping the cell phone battery fully charged. If only she'd had enough juice to call the cops the day Martha was abducted.

Anxiety hijacked her emotions and a sweat drop emerged from her forehead. She held her breath and hooked the new charger cable to her phone. The battery meter changed shape—ninety-five and charging.

She relaxed and her hands stopped trembling. As she laid her head back on the headrest, a single teardrop rolled down her right cheek. Breathe. In. Out. In. Out.

Mysterious ways.

Once she collected herself, she tapped on her playlist. She drove the car out of the basement and entered 9th Avenue. Twenty seconds later, she was stuck in a jam at an intersection where she had to make a right on West 17th.

Ashley had argued with Samuel once that INRIX had made an error when they'd ranked NYC as the third worst city in the world for traffic congestion. It should have been the first. He'd let out a giant belly laugh—oh, how bad Ashley missed that Santa Claus laughter—and promised her that he would get her a driverless car when Waymo opened for business.

It had not been funny to Ashley. The volume of rage induced by the jams on Lincoln and Holland tunnels, FDR Drive, or even George Washington Bridge paled in comparison with what these small-street jams could induce; the traffic here didn't have uniformity. The double-parked delivery trucks, yellow cabs, the honking idiots, the selfish motorcyclists, and bicyclists who shoehorned between angry drivers worsened Ashley's anxiety.

Fourteen horrible minutes later, she entered West Street, massaging her right calf. The traffic thinned, which relaxed her a little and allowed her to take in the beauty of the Hudson River, which ran on her right. It marked the border between NYC and Jersey City. Calmed now, she felt like rolling down the windows and breathing in the cold river air.

Just as she took her hand from the wheel to switch off the AC, she felt something cold at the nape of her neck. Cold and metallic. Round with a hollow center. She froze.

"You don't want your brain decorating the windshield, do you?" a smooth voice drawled behind her.

Ashley's eyes widened.

"I'd answer if I were you."

She had to swallow twice before she could speak. "No… no, I don't."

"Then listen to my instructions. First, change the music to something melodious. These devilish songs hurt my ears."

Ashley turned off Iron Maiden's *The Trooper*.

"Good girl. Now take the Brooklyn-Battery Tunnel."

Mustering enough courage while her heart tried to explode was hard, but Ashley somehow did it and looked in the rearview mirror.

A white rabbit mask looked back at her with its vacant blue eyes.

Chapter 33

March 22, 2019. 08:19 P.M.

The psycho had disconnected Ashley's phone from the charger cable, removed its battery and dropped the pieces in the footwell.

He instructed her to take a left. When she did, the light from her headlamps reflected on a street nameplate that had *Edinboro Road* painted on it. Now she knew where he was taking her—to Smith Press. That's where Gabriel said the psycho tortured the victims to their deaths. She'd left it out of her article because Gabriel told her that Mr. Smith had already gone through a lot of suffering, and it would hurt him to see the house mentioned in the news again.

As she neared the place, she hoped that some forensic people were still there. Did they carry guns? It sounded stupid. Why would they carry weapons? Harsh, cold reality wasn't a late-night cop drama. She was doomed, and the worst part was that they caught the wrong guy.

The front gate hung open. Had the psycho checked the place out before coming to pick her up? He must have—the psycho thought of everything. Her hope of finding someone inside vanished.

"Don't park it up front. Go through the lawn and park it near the railing."

She parked the car between two dark houses. The one on her left was dark, spooky, and abandoned. The one on her right was also dark and spooky, but not abandoned.

"We're both going to get down at the same time." The psycho opened his door and planted one foot on the ground. "Get down, now."

They walked past the iron railing. He crouched and did something with the wall. Then he rose and marched her to a descending set of stairs. The air thickened as he hustled her down the steps. Once they reached a door, he gave her a key.

"Open it."

She did, and they entered a dark room. Ashley heard the latch close behind her and the sound of switches being flipped. Fluorescent bulbs above illuminated the basement. The first thing she noticed was the size of the room. It was huge. The next was a lonely wheelchair against the opposite wall.

"I wanted to dismantle that thing and throw it in a dump, but I never found the time." He circled around her and stood in front. "Been busy the last few days."

Too mortified to look at the mask, Ashley looked down at the floor.

"*Imbecile*, huh, sweetie?"

Nothing from Ashley.

"So, did Samuel cry? I don't know, if you ask me, killing one's self is the stupidest thing. Ever see an animal do it?"

Ashley's mind flooded with that horrible memory. The blood splattering on the painting as if it had been shot from a paintball gun, and a feeble sound of water splashed on a sheet of paper. Her eyes welled up.

The psycho closed in on her, put the gun's muzzle under her chin and lifted it up.

"Awww, don't cry, sweetie. I just meant that Samuel lacked the intelligence of even the stupidest of animals."

Ashley clenched her jaws and dug her nails into her palms.

"Good riddance is what I say. Now that Samuel is gone, you are free to enjoy his wealth. You don't have to stick around the old fart to dig gold anymore."

People said anger was a sin. They said it because it made you stupid and got you in trouble. And so it was with Ashley when she grabbed the gun he held under her chin.

And the gun came loose!

She was as surprised as the psycho was. He lifted his hands, put his head down, and took a step back. He surrendered.

"Listen to me, please," the psycho said. "I have this condition, you see. I never—"

Ashley screamed from the bottom of her heart, squeezed her eyes shut, and pulled the trigger. Behind her closed eyelids, she saw Samuel. She saw Martha. The primal rage made her shoot not once or twice—she squeezed the little trigger a hundred times, shouting like a pissed-off sailor.

When the last ounce of her energy drained, she opened her eyes. And her heart dropped.

The psycho was still standing, chuckling.

"Wow. You really did it. And fast. You have no drama in you, do you?"

She looked at the gun. Water dripped from its muzzle. She felt like she was going to faint and die of heartache.

He slipped his hand inside the wet suit and pulled out a bigger gun. A revolver. With his thumb, he pushed its cylinder out and showed her the bullets.

"Now this is the real deal. Hollow points. What you have in your hand is… well, let's just say it's not entirely harmless." With one quick motion, he clicked the cylinder back into place. "After all, it killed your dear Martha."

Ashley didn't understand what he meant by that.

"Sit."

After a moment of hesitation, Ashley sank onto the floor. She had no options now. To avoid looking at his legs, she turned her head. She spotted something peculiar near the wall. A large, shiny red cloth was draped over something big like a container.

"That's my small book collection from before." He waited.

Did the psycho want a reply?

When Ashley didn't offer any, he continued. "I buy e-books these days."

No response.

"Reading your diatribe, I thought you'd have something to say to me, a lot to talk about. But now, other than trying to kill me and bellowing that I have coitus with my mother, you don't want to interact in any way?" he said, with amusement in his tone.

Ashley shrank in her place.

"It's quite all right. You'll find, shortly, that talking to me is irresistible. I like to talk to people while I operate on them. And in time, they all talk. Most of it will be a ballad of unintelligible lament, but it could be considered an improvement, don't you think?" He nudged her head with his knee. "Within no time, you'll offer me your non-existent udder, bland lady parts, or fellatio in exchange for a faster death."

Ashley closed her eyes, tightened her jaw, and vicious bile surged in her esophagus. She wanted to charge at him with her sharp nails. Just rip the evil son of a bitch to shreds. He could kill her before any of that happened, but he had no right to talk to her like this. She decided she was going to jump him. One scratch, a little drop of blood drawn before she died could be considered a victory.

"Time's up. Turn around, lie on your stomach, and keep—"

BANG!

Ashley looked up in time to see his gun flung aside before landing with a *clank*. He rubbed his right hand. A second later, he tilted his head, ever so slightly, like a dog listening to a strange sound for the first time. Then he dropped his head in a peculiar motion. Ashley's ten-year-old cousin did the same whenever his mom called for him to come inside when it was dark, which meant only one thing—no more playing.

Ashley crawled on all fours to the revolver. She didn't know what had happened, but it was her chance to kill the psycho. She heard his shoe grate on the floor and risked a glance back. He wasn't going for the gun or coming for her. What he was doing confused Ashley and slowed her down.

He knelt down, threading his fingers behind his head.

BANG! BANG! BANG!

The psycho fell forward. He rolled on the floor, holding his stomach and left thigh while also trying to touch his back. It looked weird that he did all this without making a sound.

Ashley caught movement out of the corner of her eyes. She turned and saw the red cloth pushed up. A man the size of a quarterback emerged from within; his vest read *SWAT*.

He had spiked blond hair and blond eyebrows. Well, not *brows*—he had only one. The right side of his face was burned, and the scar tissue had hindered the hair growth above that eye. But to Ashley, he looked like the most beautiful thing she'd ever seen in her life.

The SWAT guy didn't show any urgency in his pace, casually swinging a machine gun as he walked. Without any reason whatsoever, he sprinted and kicked the psycho square on his mask. The plastic shattered and some of its pieces skittered along the floor. The SWAT guy hunched, looked at the wriggling man on the floor.

"Stay down, sir!"

But the psycho was staying down even before the kick.

The SWAT guy retrieved the revolver from the floor and pocketed it.

"You okay, Ashley?" He gave her a hand.

That surprised her. How did he know her name? She took his assistance and heaved herself up.

He strode to the door and opened it. Ashley had never been happier to hear sirens in her entire life.

Gabriel stood at the door. He wore a brown jacket, jeans, and a white shirt. Did he own anything other than that? She must talk to him later and ask if he needed some money for new clothes.

Gabriel smiled and walked past her, acknowledged the SWAT guy with a shoulder pat, and went to the psycho. He turned him over and pulled him to his feet.

"Do you know who I am?" The psycho panted.

"No, I don't know who you are. But then again, I never did. Did I, Noah?" Gabriel pulled off the mask, along with the cloth underneath it.

Ashley's heart stopped beating for a second.

It *was* Noah!

Wasn't he dead? She wanted to pinch herself.

Noah sported a busted lip and a nose that was leaking blood and starting to swell. Without them, he would look like a model or an actor. An angel, even.

Noah dropped his gaze. "How?" A tear escaped his eye.

"I know it'll kill you not knowing."

Gabriel put handcuffs on Noah, who cried rivers, like he was the saddest person on Earth. He screamed, *"How,"* a hundred times, each time louder than the last. He screamed until his voice lost all power, and the only thing that came out were painful gasps. He was still mouthing, "*How,*" as Detective Nash dragged him outside. All this time, Gabriel never lost eye contact with Noah, smirking with ice-cold deliberation as the psycho squalled in agony.

"So, miss, how are you?" the SWAT guy said. "Do you need any help?"

"She's high-class, Liam," said Gabriel. "She doesn't date fuglys."

Ashley's mouth gaped.

Liam retorted, "Well, a beauty like Elizabeth dated a drunk hobo; I'd say anything is possible."

Ashley winced. Wasn't Gabriel a recovering addict?

Both men stared at each other, and Ashley felt her stomach churn at the prospect of two burly men fighting in her presence. Then they burst out laughing, and Ashley rolled her eyes and sighed. Samuel used to say that men offended one another with their shortcomings so they could come to terms with them. But Martha had a different opinion. She said men were pigs, and Ashley was leaning toward that explanation.

"Give me your phone," she said.

He took it from his side pocket and handed it over. She fed her number into his contact list as Liam drooled, his gratified blush overlapping his rugged, manly looks.

"Fugly here is my most trusted man," Gabriel said. "You were never in danger."

"But I was." Liam showed mock worry on his face. "I had to spend my time with that crazy old man. And his gun is meaner than mine. No offense. Mr. Edison did make some fine meals, but also some really vulgar and racist jokes."

Ashley narrowed her eyes and looked at Liam with a poker face. Really? *He* was complaining about offending jokes?

"He's a good man," Gabriel said.

"That he is. He even wanted to come and help me when I started gearing up after you called."

"Excuse me?" Ashley got both their attention but addressed Liam. "You shot him with that…" She pointed at the assault rifle he held by his side.

"M4 carbine. It's air-cooled, and it has the best—"

"Yes, yes, very interesting. You can tell me all about your toy at tomorrow's dinner. But for now, tell me why the psycho isn't bleeding? You shot him like… I don't know, three or four times?"

"Let me explain." Liam went near the door, crouched down and retrieved an object from under it.

He came back and showed it to Ashley. It looked like a pea-sized ball.

"Rubber bullets," Liam said, when Ashley couldn't guess what it was.

"But why?"

"Gabriel said we needed Mr. Bunny alive."

"No. I mean why did you shoot him only four times?"

"What?" they both said.

"You should've emptied the clip. Then grabbed the barrel and thrashed the psycho black and blue with the stock."

They laughed at the joke. But Ashley didn't, because she hadn't made one.

Chapter 34

March 22, 2019. 10:49 P.M.

Ashley, Peter, and the whole team sat around the conference table, except Victor and Nash. Victor had agreed to do Gabriel's paperwork, and Nash was booking an important lowlife who had a pivotal role to play in the denouement—George, Don's partner, who raped and killed Loretta.

Gabriel hadn't shared his idea with the team, because the Major Case Squad had taken the investigation from them. They could have landed in a lot of trouble if the new commissioner found out that the suspended team was working behind his back. By not sharing, Gabriel ensured that he alone would take full responsibility, while the others could claim plausible deniability.

Even Emma sat beside him with a questioning expression. *Funny, she didn't get it.* She'd been with him when the plan was in the making. He'd even told her that they were possibly framing Stanley and to take it easy on him when, and after, cuffing him.

"Well, are we entitled to know the how?" Peter said, when Nash finally came in and joined them.

Of course they were!

Gabriel began by stating that he'd almost believed Stanley was the murderer when Mr. Edison told him about Stanley's frequent visits to the basement. But when Emma found the butt of the marijuana cigarette, Gabriel knew Stanley wasn't Mr. Bunny. The wheelchair, books, and heaters proved the crime happened at Smith Press, but didn't help to identify the sadist. But the joint made a direct connection to Stanley. Being one of the smartest criminalists in the United States, he wouldn't have left biological evidence like that lying around, not if he was the murderer. Stanley was scared when Gabriel called him to the Smiths' because he knew they would find his joints there.

But Gabriel couldn't eliminate Stanley, not without solid proof that he was innocent.

When Gabriel had closed his eyes for a long time back in the basement, he'd teleported to another world, the world every detective on the planet loved—the world of flowcharts. He'd drawn one in his mind to simplify the results.

Now, in front of his team, Gabriel left his chair and drew the same flowchart on the whiteboard. He wrote the heading *Bill's finding*, and drew two lines under it. Two possibilities.

Possibility A: If Stanley was Mr. Bunny, then Gabriel needed to be sure of that. So he sent Bill to crosscheck Stanley's attendance at his office with the murder dates. If he wasn't present on those dates, Gabriel didn't want to lose him, so he put Nash on Stanley's tail.

Possibility B: What if Stanley was in his office? But the real question was, if Stanley wasn't the murderer, which Gabriel believed was the case, then who was?

Apart from Stanley, five other people knew how to get into the basement without breaking the lock. This included Gabriel and Mr. Smith, too. Gabriel drew a line under Possibility B that produced five more subdivisions, and wrote a name under each. Gabriel knew he hadn't done it, unless he was a murderous somnambulist or an undiagnosed schizophrenic, so he crossed his name out.

Mr. Smith didn't know the location of the hidden key, but he might have held on to his own key and gotten access to the basement. The problem with this possibility was that Mr. Smith was a delusional old man with one kidney. He'd have had to have carried an IV pole along when he abducted people. Gabriel crossed Mr. Smith's name out.

Only three names remained. Phillip—option three. Noah and Casey—options four and five. Gabriel included Phillip because Stanley might have told him about the key.

Both Casey and Noah were dead, making Phillip the lucky winner. But that was where Gabriel struggled.

According to Peter, Phillip Ming was never registered with ViCAP, CODIS, or NCIC. New York had only his juvenile record. Peter said he'd also searched the registries of New York's neighbors, and they didn't have anything on him.

Where did Phillip go?

He ran away after slashing Casey, and that was the last time anyone had ever seen him. Gabriel knew Phillip's type. He'd dealt with them from the days he cruised the streets in uniform. They were the regulars with drug or alcohol problems. This class of criminals lacked the mind to conceive mega plans that required discipline, commitment, and education. From experience, Gabriel knew Phillip couldn't be Mr. Bunny.

But he didn't pay attention to his gut feeling and eliminate Phillip. There was a slim chance that he might have bid goodbye to drugs, got his act together, and prepared himself to become a legend among lowlifes. Neither plausible nor impossible. Gabriel drew a line under option three and left it open.

Now he had options four and five, the Smith brothers. Casey had been dead a long time.

Or was he? All these years, Gabriel never had a reason to ask this question, but now he did.

He knew the old case report by heart, and the holes in it began to show. Casey's head had been blown apart with a shotgun. Twice. Peter thought that the unnecessary second shot had come from hatred. But what if it had come from the necessity to destroy the head? Since Casey was missing everything north of his neck, the laceration on his left palm was the only thing they'd used to ID him. An autopsy wasn't performed because Mr. Smith declined it since the cause of death was obvious, and he didn't want anyone to cut up his boy. The investigating officer couldn't make the coroner do it without Mr. Smith's permission.

Gabriel needed proof that it was indeed Casey who'd been shot. Hence, he sent David to exhume Casey's remains, without a warrant, and take a DNA sample. They could compare it with Noah's.

If it wasn't Casey in the coffin, did it prove his guilt? It seemed far-fetched. Did Casey plan his own death? Did he cheat everyone with a disability he never had? No. Gabriel had played with Casey from the time they were in kindergarten. He took care of him and even fed him from time to time. When Gabriel went out with Liz, Casey didn't even know the difference between a boy and a girl. How could he plan a life of criminality for two decades to come? Gabriel crossed Casey's name out.

But one of the Smith brothers was dead. In the video playback he'd received, Mr. Bunny shot Noah. What if it was Casey? If Casey didn't die in the home invasion, then he would have required special care to live all these years. Who could provide it? Who could gain from it all? These questions dissolved down to one nominee.

Noah.

Because Casey and Noah were identical twins, they shared the same appearance. Noah could fake his death after committing a series of murders, the last victim being himself, and then disappear. No one would suspect a dead man.

This was the second theory that made sense.

Phillip and Noah were Gabriel's two options when he'd opened his eyes back in the basement. Then he'd assigned work to his team and went to eat at Mr. Edison's.

They all knew what had happened next. Bill called and confirmed that Stanley was in his office during the dates of the murders. Considering his two options, Gabriel still needed to arrest Stanley.

* * *

After they had brought Stanley to the precinct, Gabriel went down to the holding cells and shared his theory with him.

"What now?"

"I don't know," Gabriel lied.

He had an agenda—that was the reason he'd arrested him in the first place—but he wanted Stanley to arrive at it in his own way.

"Neither of them like you."

"That's correct. Noah always hated me. So did my brother. Noah, because I was better than he was in school. Phillip hated me because I was an overachiever." Stanley shook his head. "He thought our parents, both real and foster, favored me and hated him."

"That wasn't true. They let him stay and tried to educate him, even tried to get him off the drugs."

"He didn't understand it, though. He had it fixed in his mind that everyone looked down on him because he'd gone to juvenile. Maybe Phillip turned into Mr. Bunny to get back at a world that was unkind to him?"

Gabriel wasn't surprised to hear it. Scientists didn't genuflect in temples, but before hard logic.

"Maybe Phillip did it, but it doesn't sit well with me. If it is Noah… I don't know, Stan. I've prevented myself from thinking about that."

"I couldn't see Noah doing it. He had everything. Looks, education, a great job. And he's filthy rich. But if it is Phillip, then these murders would be his lifetime achievement."

"It would be," Gabriel agreed.

"Tell me how I can help?"

"I've got a way to trap him."

"How?"

"Ashley."

"Mr. Bunny doesn't much like her."

"And if Mr. Bunny is either Noah or Phillip, then he doesn't much like you, either. We could combine these two factors and cook up a trap."

Stanley's face betrayed bafflement.

"We could try running a fake news story that we caught Mr. Bunny," Gabriel said. "I'm going to ask Ashley to write a demeaning article about him."

"Okay. I can see him getting mad at her."

"In his eyes, we'd be heinously wrong in giving the title *Mr. Bunny*, in your own words, his *lifetime achievement*, to Stanley Ming—someone Phillip and Noah, who are both suspected of being Mr. Bunny, hate with an equal passion. The world would be wrong to celebrate Mr. Bunny's apprehension."

"And Ashley would be wrong to write about it."

Gabriel nodded.

"But what if he doesn't come? Or what if he decides to come a week later?"

"I thought about that. He'll want to prove us wrong as soon as he can. According to him, the police are stupid. So he'll fear we'll say it's a copycat if he comes out after a week and murders someone. But we can't say it's a copycat if he makes his move, say tomorrow. I mean, copycats need time to learn. Anyway, that's what I'd be thinking if I was Mr. Bunny." Gabriel frowned. "Stop smiling, asshole. Criminal Psychology is real science. Goddamn it!"

"No, it's not." Stanley laughed. "Anyway, if he doesn't show up, well… I don't know. I guess that's all we could do from our end, criminal psychology or not."

"Ugh…"

"What do you want me to do now?" Stanley asked.

"Pose for a photo with Nash and Bill?"

* * *

Gabriel returned to his office and met Ashley. When she left, Bill called him with the DNA results. Gabriel was not shocked when Bill said that the DNA didn't match

Noah's. However, Bill still managed to shock him. The initial results matched Stanley's DNA. Every forensic scientist's profile was stored in the database for elimination purposes.

But Stanley was alive and well in the holding cell. Who was in the coffin, then? Gabriel didn't need to wait for three days to learn that even though the DNA matched Stanley's, it would not be a one hundred percent match.

It was Phillip Ming who had been dead all along. He crossed out option three in the flowchart, which left only option four—Noah.

The option made sense. Noah could have used his power as an assistant district attorney to get details about the number of CCTVs installed throughout the city. With that, he found the Mustang's plate, and then Ashley's address. When the news about Samuel's suicide was broadcasted, Noah must have gone through Samuel's legal documents and found that Ashley was going to become the new head of the Daily Herald, so he spared her.

While Gabriel was convincing himself that Noah was Mr. Bunny, David sent him an email. It was the record of Noah's phone activity for the last year.

On the dates of the murders, Noah's phone never left New York City. Mr. Bunny was too smart to take it with him when he'd been touring the country killing people. Though the phone was in his home, he never answered a single call on the murder dates. They all went to voicemail.

Gabriel was so sure of Noah's guilt that he ran to the precinct's toilet and threw up. It meant Noah had kept Casey, his twin brother, with special needs, hidden away from the world so he could use him as a scapegoat. Noah had let his father drink himself to a slow death every day. Mr. Smith's body rotted away, and his family business died. Noah watched all this happen without batting an eye. He was a demon wearing human skin.

"I thought... no... I'd *hoped* it would be Casey's body in the coffin. I couldn't imagine him penned like a pig for more than fifteen years, only to be slaughtered in the end. I'd hoped it was Noah who was killed in the video. I couldn't imagine him being the purest form of evil." Gabriel waited for the questions.

"I get that you and Mr. Ming made a plan to trap Mr. Bunny," said Bill. "But you knew it had to be either Phillip or Noah before consulting with Mr. Ming?"

"I did."

"You also said you didn't believe Phillip was capable of this type of crime, even before knowing that he was dead. So you pretty much knew it was Noah? Otherwise, you wouldn't have asked Detective Gustavo for Noah's phone records, right?"

"Yes."

"You did these predictions while you stood there with your eyes closed. Are you some kind of wizard?"

Gabriel had to laugh. His whole team did.

"No, Bill. You don't have to be a wizard to go where logic takes you."

"But how, with so much speed and accuracy?" He wasn't letting go.

"It's much like a sharpshooter or a professional soccer player taking a shot in a different direction, on account of wind speed, spin, and the distance of travel. Even if they take a shot aiming at a place that's off-target, it will still make an accurate hit."

"Yeah. I've seen those in soccer matches," Bill said. "Read about those kinds of snipers, too."

"It's a sixth sense developed over the years, from living and breathing the game. You'll get it in any field if you love what you do and spend time thinking and dreaming about it." Gabriel looked resigned. "But…"

"But what, Detective Chase?" Bill said.

"In this profession," Peter said, "being a homicide detective, that sixth sense means you get a depressing view of the human condition a little faster than others do. A little faster than you'd like."

"Wizard?" David said. "I'm sorry, but I think we caught the killer by coincidence, because the case was given to Gabriel. I mean, we wouldn't have known who else knew about the location of the hidden key, right?"

"Wrong, boy," Peter said. "Noah lost his sick game as soon as Gabriel discovered his slaughterhouse." Peter pointed at Nash. "You there. Tell me what you would've done after finding the place?"

"I send the joint for testing. The DNA result points at Stanley. I bring him in, but I know he ain't Mr. Bunny—he's got an alibi. He was in his office at the time of the murders. I interview him and ask him who else knows about the place where the murders happened. He tells me about the four kids who knew how to sneak into the basement without breaking in."

"That's correct," Peter said to David. "You see, after finding the four, it's just a matter of elimination. And any good detective would have found the place. No personal knowledge required." Peter turned to Gabriel. "Well done, Gabriel. You've outdone yourself and made us all proud." He propped himself straight in the chair, supporting his back.

When he started to clap, so did everyone else.

When the claps died out, Ashley cleared her throat. Gabriel looked at her and nodded. He owed her answers as well.

"I understand you used me to run the story," Ashley said. "I was the bait. But why didn't you tell me?"

"If I had, then you would've been self-conscious and wouldn't have been natural. If Noah knew it was a setup, he would have killed you and bailed."

"That's fair; I can't act," Ashley admitted. "How did you know where Noah took me?"

"We have David to thank for that."

"We do?" Ashley glanced at David.

His Adam's apple bobbed as he swallowed.

"He borrowed a thin GPS device from his old pals in Computer Crimes. All we had to do was take out your phone's battery, remove the case underneath it and stick the device there. It doesn't just siphon power from the battery, but it also has its own storage system to stay alive even if the phone's battery is taken out. We knew Noah was fond of removing batteries after he abducts people, so we predicted that's what he'd do after he took you. And when he did that, the GPS device sent us an alert that the battery had been removed, and it was running on its own power."

"When did you bug my phone?"

"Remember the checking at our front desk?" David said.

Ashley did. She also remembered the ninety-five percent battery power that made her sweat in her car.

"You must know something else, too," David said and explained that the red SUV she almost crashed into the night Martha had been abducted was driven by Noah.

Ashley listened to David, her hand on her chest. When he finished, she turned slowly and gave Gabriel a flat stare.

"I-I'm sorry. I was sure Noah would take you to the press," Gabriel said. "That's why I stationed Liam in Mr. Edison's house as soon as you published the inflammatory article. But I needed the security that the bug provided because I couldn't take any chances. I'm really sorry, Ashley. Noah hated you for jeopardizing his plan when you cut him off with the Mustang. Why else would he break into your house and scare you? I couldn't think of anyone perfect enough to get a response from him. You were the key player. We wouldn't have caught Mr. Bunny without you. It was wrong—"

She thrust back her chair and marched toward him. He braced himself for what was coming. Perhaps his beard would cushion most of the force.

But to his surprise, she hugged him like she was relieved of something. Each had their own demons. And again, her hair smelled like strawberries.

"I helped to catch him?" she whispered, still hugging him.

"Without you, he would be somewhere halfway around the world, sipping coconut water. Not down there in the holding cell."

Ashley let go and looked at Gabriel with tearful eyes.

"Excuse me." She took her bags and headed out.

"You're lucky it wasn't me." Emma kicked a chair in Gabriel's direction.

"That I was." He caught the rolling chair and seated himself in it.

"Two things bother me, Gabriel," said Nash.

"Go on."

"First, why didn't Noah clean the basement?"

"Noah believed we wouldn't find his place. If we did, then he knew he'd have lost his game, and his conceited mind won't allow him to believe that. He meant to dump them, anyway. He cleaned Harry's wheelchair with his favorite chemical. But in the end, he didn't dispose of them."

"That's complicated, Detective Chase," said Bill.

"Psychopaths always are. Why he didn't clean the basement doesn't matter. It's not like we can use that to convict him." Gabriel turned to Nash. "Second thing that's bothering you?"

"Why was a man the size of a mountain—I think Jerry was his name—eating and playing with my daughter at my house the whole day? Now all she wants is to become someone who can carry assault rifles and wear cool gear." He gave a sour face.

"I was sure Noah would target Ashley, but I wouldn't underestimate his ability to surprise us. So I put SWAT guys in the houses of everyone from our team. Emma's girlfriend was teaching yoga to another mountain of a man.

My dad was playing chess with another SWAT guy. Stanley's and David's houses had one SWAT guy each. The captain's, too."

"And Liam agreed to this?" Nash said. "Where did he get the authorization to dispatch that much manpower for two full days?"

"Where did you guys get the authorization to continue the investigation even after the case was taken from us?"

"We didn't. We trusted you and wanted to help."

"There. Like I am to you guys, Liam is to his team. And he's also my friend, to whom I owe a lot now."

"What's next?" Bill said. "After all our hard work, we still can't prove Noah is Mr. Bunny."

"We don't need to." Gabriel winked at Nash, who gave a knowing smile.

"What?" Bill's gaze ping-ponged between them.

"I didn't know who Mr. Bunny was, but I'd always known what I was going to do to him the day I caught him. I made a promise to my late mother."

"What promise?"

"That I'd obliterate him. That I would make him wish he was never born."

Gabriel explained the end he had planned for Noah.

"Needless to say, this doesn't leave this room."

The team agreed in unison, and Bill seemed even happier than the others.

Peter said, "All right, wrap it up. Let's go punish Mr. Bunny the way he deserves."

Chapter 35

March 22, 2019. 10:45 P.M.

George was an armed robber, murderer, and a rapist. He was also Don Miller's neo-Nazi partner whom Don had given up after Gabriel arrested him at the Chinese restaurant.

"So, George, you've spent a lot of time inside, haven't you?"

"I want my lawyer."

"Sure, sure. Do you want me to call the same cross-eyed hick whatshisname who defended you the last time? He got you a five-year stretch, didn't he?"

George said nothing.

"One of my assistants argued against your lawyer and defeated him."

"Y-your assistants?"

"Yeah. I'm sorry for not having introduced myself. My name is Steve Bastian. I'm the DA."

George's breath became shallow.

"We picked up Don last Friday. Needless to say, he's rolled. Otherwise, you wouldn't be here. He confessed to all the murders, armed robberies, and rapes you committed together."

George's eyes looked like they might pop out of their sockets.

"Since he accepted his part in Loretta's murder and saved resources for the court and the State, we made him a sweet deal. We sent him to one of the prisons where your gang still exists. I mean, he's never coming out, but still, he's living happily."

"Good for him."

"He also gave us the phone."

"He gave you the phone? What phone?" George said, faster than he'd intended.

"He did, and we saw the rape video. You are a sick, fat, son of a whore, aren't you?"

George's look said it all. He wasn't embarrassed. He was terrified. The cops had caught him with damning evidence.

"And the audio quality is the best. I could still hear the poor woman begging for mercy and crying in pain. I mean, that was before she passed out," Steve said between his teeth. "But that didn't stop you, did it?"

George looked down. "We got carried away… I'm—"

"Shut up." Steve banged the steel table.

When he'd calmed, he said, "Your face is clear in the video. You know what kind of an impression it'll make on the jurors. And that video is only the tip of the iceberg."

"Tip of what?" George scrunched his brows.

Steve puffed his cheeks and blew the air out. "It means that is not the only evidence we have against you. There's a lot, including Don's testimony. Do you know how powerful State-turned witnesses are? From what we have, we can jail you for the rest of your life."

"I'm not a coward. You know, I *made* Don. If that snitch don't fear the slammer, why should I?"

"Yeah, I thought so, too. But I'm sending you to one of those prisons in California your Mara Salvatrucha buddies control."

"No, no, no, no, Mr. DA. MS-13 ain't our buddies. They're our enemies—"

"That was sarcasm, dumbshit. I'm telling you, I'm going to put you in a place where you'll be sodomized every single—"

George's face expressed confusion again.

Steve let out another exasperated breath. "Where you will be raped every night. Sounds good?"

George's new expression said it didn't. He was a big strong oaf, but three men could overpower him and hold his head down in a prison where he would have no brothers to protect him. He knew that—his bald forehead dotted with sweat said as much.

Steve told George he would give him a better deal than he'd given Don—fame among his kind. George became interested, and Steve explained the deal. George was going down for life, one way or another. He could either go to trial for Loretta's murder.

Or he could go down as Mr. Bunny.

If he chose the trial, Steve would prosecute him before the jury, and he would request the judge to send George over to San Quentin because of his gang affiliation. If he chose to become Mr. Bunny, he could join his brothers inside the prison of his choice.

"I'll be Mr. Bunny?" George said. "The guy who's giving the cops a run for their money?" He was more curious than scared.

Disgusting repeat offenders. Steve hated them.

"Yes. Make up your mind soon, fatty."

George said he'd lived more than half his life in prisons, and he was one of those *breeds* who would be happy inside rather than out. The deal was a no-brainer because he would now be famous among his brothers until he died. What more did a man need in his life?

George signed the papers, posed for a few photos, and became Mr. Bunny.

* * *

Noah sat in the same interrogation room George had been sitting in half an hour ago.

Gabriel had asked Peter to conduct the interview. It was Peter's last working day, and since Casey's murder had been solved, he could retire in peace. Peter never gave up on Casey's investigation, for over seventeen years. It was the right thing to do.

Gabriel didn't join the interview because he didn't trust his temper. Beating Noah to death wasn't outside the realm of possibility. So, he resigned himself to watching the interview from the other side of the mirrored glass.

"This is Detective Lieutenant Peter Lamb. Today is March 22, 2019. Time is 11:27 p.m. I'm interviewing Noah Smith, in the presence of District Attorney Steve Bastian. The suspect has waived his right to counsel. Is that correct, Mr. Smith?"

"That is correct, Detective Lamb," Noah said to the camera, smiling.

His broken nose had been fixed, and his mouth and nose looked reddish. Soon, they would turn purple. He was still dressed in his black Armani suit, shirt, and pants. His red tie and shoelaces were confiscated—a procedure to prevent any individual from taking the easy way out.

Steve said, "We are charging you with one count of possession of a controlled substance—in this case, heroin—with an intent to distribute. For that, we are booking you under title 21 of U.S. Code section 841..."

Noah's smile disappeared as his groomed eyebrows met.

"Two counts of kidnapping. Victims are Casey Smith and Ashley Stuart. For these offenses, we are booking you under title 18 of U.S. Code section 1201. Two counts of murder. Victims are Phillip Ming and Casey Smith. For these offenses, we are booking you under title 18 of U.S. Code section 1111."

The heroin came from Nash's old buddies in the Gang Squad. Gabriel had talked Mr. Bastian into charging Noah with these crimes. That would be the punishment which would destroy Noah. Jailing him as Mr. Bunny wouldn't affect him. So Noah was booked as a drug dealer who'd used Casey and Phillip to fake his own death.

Noah would consider drugs and drug-related murders beneath him. Training all these years only to be tagged with crimes that were so commonplace and mundane, should hurt him. If Noah felt even ten percent of the agony Gabriel suffered when he saw Rita's body, then it would be enough to break Noah to his core.

Noah's expressions said it all. It changed from amusement to confusion, then a hint of hopelessness… but wait, then back again to amusement?

"Well… as for the heroin, the job I had as an assistant district attorney was just a cover. I started dealing when I was young. Really young. I got a taste for it, and I wanted to become the greatest dealer ever. I sat down and planned the entire thing when I just started to grow pubes. As per my plan, I killed Phillip and made everyone believe it was Casey. I kept Casey alive to fake my own death in the event of police suspecting me. They started doing just that, and I killed Casey, disguising myself as Mr. Bunny everyone was so hyped about. I did that so no one would look at me twice." Noah paused and wet his busted upper lip.

Gabriel's mouth gaped. At the same time, Noah looked at the mirror, showed his perfect row of teeth and winked. The bastard knew what Gabriel was playing at. And it felt like Noah's statement was layered, and mixed with truth.

"So, Mr. Bastian," Noah said. "I believe you have a deal for me in that little suitcase of yours? Bypassing trial, I presume? I would sign it on one condition."

"We have testimonies from Ashley and from countless police officers. There is no way we would lose the case if it went to trial. You're in no position to bargain for anything—"

"I could give you Casey's body."

"What?"

"My elder twin. I thought Gabriel might need the body. The retard was always a weight on my back, and it's high-time I dropped the garbage to his lover. I also want to know how Gabe caught me. That's going to be a part of the deal."

Peter and Steve looked at Noah with as much disgust as human eyes could summon. Peter got up, opened the door and met Gabriel.

"Do the deal, Mr. Lamb. Tell him how we caught him. No problem. It's a small price." Gabriel's jaws were so tight he worried they would implode. "Ask him where he kept Casey all these years. And warn him, if he ever calls me by my first name again, I will crush his eyeballs with my thumbs."

Peter nodded and went back.

He conveyed Gabriel's warning, then said, "We can negotiate. But before that, tell us where you held Casey?"

Noah laughed. "First, tell me how you all found out it was me."

As Peter told him, Noah's face showed no emotion.

"Where did you keep Casey all these years?" Peter said.

"Long Branch."

"That can't be. Casey was…" Peter stopped and struggled.

"A retard?" Noah looked at the mirror again and smiled.

"How could he live there? Was he taken care of?"

"You aren't brilliant as your reputation suggests, are you? I told you I wanted him to die in my place, *as me*. If he was in a care center with his bunch, and if someone who'd nursed him learned from the news that an assistant district attorney was dead and they saw my photo, wouldn't they call and say that the dead person was Casey and not some ADA?"

"Then how?"

"What do you mean *how*? You think people with intellectual disabilities can't live alone? You're an old, partial fossil." Noah feigned being offended. "You want to know how? Years of patience, that's how. People with that thing, autism, love routine. They lose their calm if their routine gets disrupted. I taught him a new routine after I rented out an apartment and hid him there."

"Where did you get that kind of money?"

"I robbed $98,000 when I was sixteen, and an incompetent policeman investigated that case."

Nothing Noah had said surprised Gabriel, but Peter looked taken back.

"So Casey lived by himself?" Peter said, when he could talk again.

"He did. First few months were a real pain. A lot of torn belts and stomach kicks later, he learned to live alone. I taught him to cook, to do dishes and laundry, the entire household chores. It's much like teaching your dog to bring you a cold one or a TV remote. He got used to that routine and lived with it ever since."

Gabriel couldn't even begin to imagine how hard it must have been for Casey. Poachers and human traffickers had never brought out the anger he felt now. Who would show this much indifference to a special child? Casey was older than Gabriel, but in his mind he was just a four-year-old kid.

Peter said, "Socially—"

"No. I never allowed Casey to touch the front door. He knew that got him the most dangerous of punishments—darkness. I would switch off the lights for an hour, and he would look so white when I switched them back on. The minute he touched the doorknob, his world became dark. He was smart, because he never got that punishment since we were teenagers. That small apartment was his world, and the locked front door and the freedom beyond it was his forbidden fruit. And he knew I was always watching over that world, like a god. But instead of omniscience, I used cameras."

"You, sick mother—" Peter slid his hand to his holster.

Was he putting on a show? It didn't seem like that to Gabriel. Maybe he should get in there and help Peter, who was actually pulling his gun out.

"Hey, hey!" Noah feigned anger and fear. "I'm not all bad. I got him cartoons, a fridge full of ice creams, and chicken breasts when I made my weekly runs there to refurbish supplies. I'm the best brother. He hugged and told me I'm the best every time I opened his front door. In fact, he said the same the last time I visited there." Noah smirked and winked at Peter. "Before I tied him to a chair that is."

Peter balanced his hands on the arms of the chair and pushed himself up. Gabriel wanted Peter to shoot. Not a headshot. Perhaps knees and elbows. In that order. Then a headshot, after getting enough of the beautiful sound and the sight of blood art on the floor.

No. Then Peter would go to jail. Just when Gabriel came out of his mesmerizing anger and decided to go out to stop Peter, Steve got up and held Peter back.

"No, Lamb."

"What do you mean, no?" Peter spat at the DA.

"I mean, death is too kind a punishment. He deserves the worst kind of hell. The kind he'd get in a place where we're sending him now." Steve turned and looked at Noah. "He's doing it with a smirk on his face, but he's really begging you to kill him. Can't you see that? To escape that hell. Are you going to help him?"

Peter thought for a long time, staring at Noah's smiling face. Then he put the gun back in its holster. When the tension in the room came down, Peter smiled.

"We can stop screwing about now. Let's go back to the topic."

"Sure. I took good care of Casey, called him on Skype every night, and that was the favorite part of his day. He loved me. I didn't even lock him in chains…"

Peter's cool disappeared again.

"…not because I loved him, but because it would madden him. He tended to hurt himself when he was mad. Also, he needed his sunlight to maintain skin color, so I didn't put him in chains—"

"Address in Long Branch?" Steve said.

At least he had control over his emotions, which Peter was about to lose for the second time. Which Gabriel had already lost, the mirrored glass separating his feelings and the possibility of Noah acquiring the look of a runover zombie.

"If you want Casey's address, I want to make a deal."

"What do you want?" Steve said.

"Attica. General population."

Steve stared at Noah for a few seconds, before he broke out laughing.

"All this drama for that hellhole? That's where I was going to send you anyway!"

Gabriel memorized the address as Noah iterated it. Steve opened his suitcase and took out the agreement. He pushed the papers and a pen toward Noah's side of the table. The nib rolled on the paper above the metal, making a smooth grating noise. Once Noah signed the deal, he threw the pen to his side. It bounced twice and spewed dots of ink on the floor before rotating on its clip and coming to a halt.

"I'm sorry, Steve, it slipped. My hand is swollen, as you can see. I got shot. That Visconti was a gift from your late son, right?"

Steve looked at the pen and closed his fists. Then he relaxed and retrieved the pen.

"Terrible. Just terrible, I tell you, what happened to Doug. I hope they find the responsible party soon." Noah looked at Steve with empathy.

"And I hope when he goes to prison"—Steve gave a cold smile—"his clumsy hands drop soap in showers more often than they drop invaluable pens."

One hundred years inside, without the possibility of parole, was a long haul, even for heavy hitters. But Noah didn't seem to be bothered at all.

Which unnerved Gabriel.

Hellraiser

3/23/19. Afternoon.

I'm lying on a workout bench, mild sunlight without any warmth, shining on my face. The hybridized smells of pee, sweat, and cigarette smoke are assaulting my nostrils. Sounds of inmates lifting weights and talking about their daring conquests and sexual fantasies, followed by long moans or laughter hurt my ears.

I'm the only white guy in this part of the exercise yard, which belongs to the Mexicans. The whites are lounging on another set of benches diagonal to our *turf.*

Hercules is sitting beside me, looking at the guard towers. Is he planning an escape? Or is he looking at the sky, challenging the Almighty to a dust-up for the life he'd given him? Whatever he's looking for, he can't get it.

Hercules, though he's not a Mexican, is the leader of the Mexican gang that I'm now with. He was born Terry Carvalho, in Los Angeles, to an immigrant couple who were from Magé, Brazil. He escaped the LAPD at the age of fourteen, after he murdered his partner over a drug deal, and he never looked back from the moment he set foot in New York.

He joined a gang. Dealt drugs. Moved drugs. Killed for drugs. Then killed more for drugs. Built an empire. Controlled some shitty housing projects in a shittier part of the city. Loud rep. A lot louder than he needed it to be. Then the bust. RICO. Frozen funds. Lost said empire. Jailed for life. Same music, same lyrics, but a different dancer with different dance moves.

His wife, Rosa Carvalho, and his two daughters aren't out there on the streets, because I'd taken care of them for the past two years.

I met Hercules on the other side of the glass partition twenty-five months ago. Through the corded telephone receiver, I introduced myself and proposed a deal—he should be a part of my back-up plan, as he is the most respected/feared man in this prison, and he agreed, for a price. I paid double, providing financial freedom for his family. Whenever Rosa visited him, she talked to him about how kind and generous I was. So, he is super submissive and grateful to me.

He set up a meeting outside and introduced me to Juan, whose sister is married to Hercules. It was another part of the same back-up plan. At first, I asked Hercules to get me in touch with people in Mexico City, where Annie Jones worked. But he didn't have the amount of clout I expected him to have there. The only person he knew, who was the controller of a ruthless gang, was Juan, and he lived in Rio. So, I brainwashed Annie and shifted her from Mexico City to Rio. Then I met Juan.

He asked one favor, and that was also for Rosa. He said the DEA wasn't making it easier for him to transfer money to his sister, and that's why she was on the brink of poverty. He called her to Rio, but she wouldn't return to the favelas again. I told him not to worry, and I would take care of it. And I have.

Hercules turns his head toward the whites. "Here they are, Mr. Smith."

Is he expecting me to acknowledge his sharp eyes? I yawn and half-close my eyes. The thought of the future is starting to drain my energy.

I know who *they* are. It means Juan came through and my back-up plan is in motion. It also means I have to start worrying about my travel plans. I did that twice this week, and my body still vibrates from all the driving.

A man clad in a black uniform and dark green aviators blocks my un-warmed sunshine. I take a closer look at the correctional officer. He's a double-chinned, fat hippo who seems to get breathless just by standing.

"Been working out lately?" I say.

A wave of laughter rises around me.

Fatso takes a step closer to me, removing the nightstick from his belt. Hercules gets up to his full height and stands between us. Another guy in uniform, whom I've missed, as he was standing behind Fatso, gets close to Hercules. He's short but young, his biceps threatening to rip apart the seams of his sleeves.

I sigh and get up.

"The warden wants to see you," Biceps says.

"I know." Then to Hercules, I say, "Wish him luck."

The three of us walk past the white gang, who glower at me as if I've betrayed them by being with different-skinned animals. In particular, two huge men sitting in the middle of the crowd scowl at me. One, with four teeth missing, has funny tattoos on his cheeks and ugly bruises on the side of his head. The other is the center of attraction in the whole prison now. I know him. George aka Mr. Bunny.

With his access card, Fatso rubs a small black box fitted beside the gate. The default red LED light in the sensor turns green for a moment, followed by a beep. The steel mesh gate closes behind us as we walk on a long ten-foot-wide tiled path.

Then we come across another obstacle. A solid steel door without any see-through glass. Another beep sounds. Once inside, the cacophony of inmates shouting and playing stops hurting my brain.

We take a left and come face to face with Fatso's arch enemy—stairs.

Four flights of stairs lead to a landing on the third story. Fatso is alive, but only barely. He knocks on a door that has a nickel name plaque with black borders. It reads *Edward V. Jones*, and under it, *Chief Warden*. Do people use middle initials on door plates? I never did. That feels weird. Southerners.

Mr. Jones opens the door. He is a six-foot stocky man with a barrel chest. An American flag lapel pin adorns his black suit. He tells the guards to wait outside. They offer to shackle me before leaving, but Mr. Jones dismisses them, closes the door, and ushers me in. He has worse things to worry about than his life.

I walk around his desk and sit in his chair. It feels good on my back and makes it straight. Prison transport vehicles aren't exactly known for their comfort.

Mr. Jones looks at me with pleading eyes. Perhaps he's owned this chair for a long time, and the possibility of losing it destroys him. Power is so important to men. Too bad it won't be his in the next few days.

"Please sit, Eddy," I say.

He chooses to stand. "I told you where my daughter lived when I thought you were prosecuting criminals." He points his finger at me, his wet lips quivering. "When I thought you were on our side."

"That you did, Eddy."

"Please let her go. She's getting married this week."

"She can't without a groom."

"What did you do to Lance?" he asks, his glare intensifying like this is going to be the final straw.

"You've never seen this Lance's picture, have you?"

"How do you know that?"

"I'm Lance, the law professor from Boston, whom your daughter is madly in love with. I was extra careful in avoiding photos."

"You rotten, unholy…" His eyes aren't as intense as before.

"Let's talk about why I'm here."

He grabs a shiny flask from the table and drinks a strong-smelling liquid.

When he is ready, he says, "I received a video twenty minutes ago. My little girl—" He looks away.

Not a very authoritative image is projected when the warden of the most dangerous prison in New York has water brimming in his eyes.

"My baby had no clothes on her. She was tied upside down, and a huge guy in a ski mask... ran a machete across her back and said something in Spanish—"

"Portuguese."

"My daughter is begging me to let you go."

"That guy in the mask is Juan. He is unpredictable and hyper-violent, Eddy."

"Why can't I force the information out of you?" he says, in a tone that neither convinces me nor him that his statement is a viable option.

"The minute you wrap a wet towel around my face, or copper wires around my testes, I'll clam up. Or to stop the pain, I'd send you on a wild goose chase. By the time you realize that... well, let's just say, what you consider torture is nothing compared to what those Brazilian gangs can do."

He clenches his hands and grits his teeth. "If anything happens to my baby—"

"If this meeting is about measuring ego sizes, then by the end of tomorrow's evening you'll know who's got it big. I believe that's the time limit Juan has given you." I get up and walk to the door.

"What do you want me to do?" he says, when I touch the doorknob.

"My acquaintances will stage a riot at 7:00 p.m. Nothing fancy, and no life will be lost." I walk back to my chair. "I'll wait near gate three when it starts, and you're going to open it and escort me outside to safety. I expect a change of clothes, two thousand dollars, and a car."

"You'll suffer. I'll find you and—"

"Come here, Eddy."

He looks puzzled, but shuffles to me. I get up and slap him on his ear with my left hand. It's not a good hit, but that's all I could manage since my dominant hand is powerless. Anyway, physical hurt isn't the point.

"You think you know what suffering means? I'm practically a genius in that field. You don't know who you're talking to. Else…" I look at the ceiling, my ears becoming hot. "Gabriel, you cheating dog."

Mr. Jones covers his ear and stares at me with tears of indignation and sadness brimming in his eyes. "7:00 p.m. it is."

* * *

"Mr. Smith." Hercules stands up when I reach the workout bench.

"We are on schedule." I take a sip from Mr. Jones's flask.

"Everything went well with the warden?"

"It did."

"Good to know."

"I'm going to meet Juan when I get out. I need his help to finish this whole thing off, for my finale."

The alcohol feels warm in my throat. Inmates around look at the flask, salivating. But not Hercules.

"He'll help with anything, Mr. Smith. Big machine guns, hit squads…"

Hit squad? Yes, I can order a hit squad and kill Gabriel's cartload of monkeys if I want to.

"…bombs, poisons, anything."

"I know he's resourceful. And for you, Terry, I'll wire Rosa a hundred when I'm out of here. That'll be enough to get her and the kids going for this lifetime."

"Thank you, sir. I owe you a lot."

"You do, and it's time you pay me back." I pass the flask to a man near me.

He smiles like I'd given him redemption. He's like Doug—a bodybuilder, but brown. A skull tattoo covers his face, teeth drawn above and below his lips. Infantile gangster. What kind of a witness in the world would ever forget seeing something like that? Was he even trying to get away after committing a crime? What a dunce!

"What do you mean?" Hercules asks.

"Start the circus by stabbing George." I point at the white gang.

"But George is Mr. Bunny, and he belongs to you-know-who."

"I don't care." I massage my right hand.

It's starting to hurt.

"But Mr. Smith, if we kill him, then a full-blown war will start. Hundreds will die."

"Don't care, again." I move my head front and back, then from side to side.

It makes me feel good, but only temporarily. The pain from the bruises on my face has spread around. It feels like a hundred pins are stuck deep in my head.

"That's wrong, Mr. Smith. Did George disrespect you? I'll talk to his leader and make him apologize, sir. Tell me what he did?"

"He's stolen the only thing that ever meant anything to me."

"I can get it back—"

"You can't, Terry. It's lost forever. Kill him."

He is starting to get on my nerves.

"We all came to a truce, and it's finally peace."

"Is it? Then I won't leave. Like you said, we are all chummy here. Let's hold hands and sing Kumbaya. Too bad for your Rosa, though. I guess she'll be evicted next month. She'd be forced to live in a car with two girls who are almost teenagers. Next thing you know, all three will be turning tricks for food and utilities—"

"Shut up!" Hercules moves near me.

Sounds around us abate. The skull guy holds the flask I'd just given him, as a weapon. Ungrateful termite. This is why no one cares if these vermin die. Common criminals.

"Tell me, what's wrong in my prediction?" I say.

Hercules's face is close to mine. So close that he'd slip and kiss me if the speed of the Earth's spin increased by just another mile.

"Tell me, Terry."

Hercules can't, so he backs off.

"You owe me. I created Mr. Bunny, and now I want him dead. If you don't agree, then I'll stay here. Is that what you want?"

"No."

"No, what, you decrepit pile of shit?"

"No, Mr. Smith." He bit down rage.

"Attaboy." I lie back on the workout bench.

I need to get some rest before I begin my two-thousand-mile journey.

Chapter 36

March 23, 2019. 09:56 P.M.

Emma was lying on her bed, watching Netflix with Kate, her girlfriend of five years.

Their dog, Beast, whined from under the bed. He'd previously witnessed the murder of a family member and he was a nervous wreck. So, he hid there whenever he got the chance.

"What's wrong, baby?" Kate slipped down.

She eased the puppy out and carried it to the bed.

Emma looked at the big eyes of the dog. It had been Gabe's case, and he had remembered Emma wanted a pet for Kate. He had called and asked if they wanted to adopt Beast. They did.

Beast cried and wriggled in Kate's arms.

"What do you think he wants?" she said.

"His dad. We all want something that we can't have."

Someone knocked on the door. They weren't expecting anyone, and they had long since stopped ordering food online. Who could it be?

Emma dragged herself out of bed and walked to the door.

When she yanked it open, her face went white. A man was standing in her corridor.

With a submachine gun in his hand.

* * *

David was enjoying the silence, because his wife had left to go on a short run.

He took his phone and opened a hidden folder. From a list of videos, he played the one named *3SumInJail.*

Thinking about jail, David thought about Noah. He was spending his first night in prison, and David hoped the toughened criminals passed around the new fish. Finally, some dangerous guys could match Noah's evil and put him in his place.

The sound and sight of women making out on his phone's screen excited him. Just as he got up to go to the bathroom, his front door began shaking. Startled, he turned off the video and ran to answer his door, which was almost knocked off of its hinges.

David froze when he saw a man with a machine gun standing behind his wife.

"It's too dark outside to let your wife go for a run alone, David."

* * *

"Slow down, monkey. You're gonna choke!" Nash said to his six-year-old daughter.

"Jerry said I should eat a lot so that one day I'll be big like him. Then I can be SWAT." Peyton took another mouthful of broccoli, and curled her face up at the taste.

What was up with all this SWAT stuff? Couldn't she forget it already? Like the time she wanted to become a cow doctor, flight driver, or the president?

Nash looked at his wife, Dorian, who made a face and smiled.

"Daddy will take you out now," Nash said, "and buy you an ice cream."

He went around the table and lifted Peyton. He lugged her away to the door while she hit his back, yelling that she hadn't washed her hands and they weren't clean.

"Learn to live with it, monkey. After all, you're gonna become a politician."

He opened the front door, Peyton still on his shoulder. He stopped dead in his tracks when he saw a guy with an assault rifle climbing the steps to his house.

* * *

Gabriel decided he was going to play video games the whole night. Last weekend was the worst in his life. He wanted this one to balance it out. What was life without a bit of fun here and there? And that night, he was going to be entertained.

The previous day, he found Casey in Long Branch and buried him. He didn't inform Mr. Smith. Gabriel couldn't imagine the sadness the old man would feel if he knew what one of his sons had done to the other. Gabriel didn't order a service because no one knew Casey—he'd been dead for a long time. So it was just Gabriel, Raymond, and Stanley who had said goodbyes to Casey.

Gabriel retrieved his vibrating phone from the table. He'd received a picture message from Emma. It was a group selfie—Emma and Kate on both sides, and Beast in the middle.

She messaged, *Thnx 4 the pup.*

He replied, *No problem.*

He exited Emma's chat and opened Liz's.

Gabriel had sent her a meme that evening, which he thought was funny. It was a screenshot from Twitter. A teenage girl had tweeted, *Wake up people. Don't use solar power. We will overuse the sun and exhaust it pretty soon. Then we will have to live in the dark and cold nights forever.* A different picture under it showed a cartoon character flying with a jet pack, and a caption that said, *Time to leave Earth.*

Two blue ticks denoted that Liz had seen the message. Did she smile? Or did she delete it before the image loaded? Gabriel couldn't know because she never replied to his texts. God, he was pathetic. But what could he do? She was irreplaceable.

Gabriel looked at the time—8:11 p.m. Time for some binge gaming.

He locked the phone and retrieved his PS4 controller from the floor. That was the third one in the last twelve months. Those things tended to be too fragile for sudden bursts of anger. He crushed the plastic sometimes when an opponent just didn't give him an opportunity to score. Gabriel wasn't a bad sport, but when he was losing continuously it drove him nuts.

He selected *Call of Duty: WWII*. After a massive dilemma about which online mode to choose, either Domination or Hardpoint, he finally chose Domination. The server waited for the players to log on.

Twenty seconds later, the countdown ended and all hell broke loose. Bullets flew, grenades exploded, and the players made mincemeat of their opponents' team. Gabriel rushed to Point C, the nearest from his location, gunning down two guys who'd jumped out of nowhere. He secured the point and scored for his team, but was killed a second later by a guy wielding a sniper rifle. Disgusting snipers! Gabriel hated them.

Just as he respawned and searched for the sneaky dog that had sniped him, his phone rang.

It was Victor.

"Yes, Captain," Gabriel said, holding the phone between his ear and shoulder while his hands smashed the buttons.

As Victor was explaining the reason for his call, Gabriel was killed with another headshot. He tightened his grip on the device, and moments later he cleared the way for the fourth controller.

But it had nothing to do with the cowardly sniper.

* * *

"You can ask me."

"Ask what?" Ashley tried to hide behind her wine glass.

"About my face," Liam said.

Was she that obvious? She looked away from him. The restaurant was romantic, its food delicious, and the service was kind. The background music, Chinese pipa, was good for her nerves.

"I spent four years in the navy and three years with the Marine Corps, touring many parts of the world where conflict is a way of life. You can't kill and hurt a lot of evil without losing a part of yourself. Some lose their arms or legs, or like me, faces. We're the lucky ones. Some lost themselves to PTSD. When the pills they're taking don't cure their psychological pain, they swallow a bullet and cure it themselves. I lost some good friends to that." Liam crossed himself.

Ashley's mind dissociated the moment he'd said *swallow a bullet*. Images of Samuel's head bursting flashed in front of her mind. She tried to keep them at bay with open eyes. When that didn't work, she squeezed them shut, hoping the forced blackness would consume the vivid playback.

But it didn't work either.

Ashley's heartbeat rose as anxiety took control of her. She needed a diversion, like her therapist said. She pressed the unlock button on her phone. The time was 8:17 p.m., and the charge was 98 percent. Ninety-eight? Why? David had removed the bug, hadn't he? Then why ninety-eight?

OCD kicked in and her fingers began trembling.

Calm… calm…

But her heart refused to follow orders. She was sitting with a person who had toured through hell and lived to tell the tale about it, but she couldn't survive one night without the visuals of graphic death violating her mind. She couldn't even cope if her phone battery wasn't always at one hundred percent charge. She had to go to her car to charge it. Give in to the obsession. It was better than fighting it. Did her right eye just spit out a teardrop? Shit! She was making a scene.

Breathing was hard, and her mind became so distorted she had to make a hard effort to keep her concentration together. Any day now, she would scream and run into the road, ripping her hair out.

She felt sandpaper brushing against her skin. She looked up at Liam's hand holding hers.

"I wish I could tell you that I'll always be with you," Liam said. "That I will protect you and let nothing ever happen to you. But I can't. You know why?"

Ashley didn't know why, but *please keep talking*. She appreciated the distraction.

"Because you ain't a snowflake. You're a badass. When Noah abducted you, you knew how dangerous he was. He's killed so many people, torturing them first. He's even killed guys who were gangsters and bodybuilders. What chance did you, Ashley, the skinny news reporter, have up against that dangerous hellhound? You knew all the odds were stacked against you, yet you went for his gun. For that, you should be proud."

Ashley did feel proud. Her heartbeat decelerated and her mind sorted itself back out.

"And not only did you get Noah's gun, but you also screamed like a maniac and pulled the trigger. My old squad captain used to say, *'The purest fear will bring out the purest personality.'* At that time, in that basement, your personality was that of a tigress. No, wait. Screw tigress.

Your personality was that of my grandma's. That crazy old hag scares even me." Liam winced and bit the tip of his tongue. "I'm sorry. I don't… I don't mean you look old or ugly. In fact, you're—"

"I know what you meant." To her surprise, Ashley smiled.

Liam let out a heavy breath. "The point is, whatever depression or OCD or any of those things that are bothering you, I know you won't let it win. When push comes to shove, the Ashley I saw in that basement will reappear and curb-stomp your problems. You were a badass down there, and you're a badass in here." He poked in the middle of his chest. "Real grit. Nothing can kill you."

Ashley felt like a different person. Like the strongest person alive. Liam was right. She'd team up with the shrink, take the pills, and curb-stomp her problems, whatever that meant.

"Thank you," she said. "I feel a lot better now."

"Most welcome."

She observed his face. The left half was boyish, charming, and innocent, while his right half was burned, suffered, and leathery. But the lips on both sides ticked up. Well, the right ticked up as high as it could.

They both returned to their dinner. When they emptied their plates, Liam ordered dessert, a mango sundae.

"I can assure you." He sucked the cold treat from the spoon. "We all need a backup every now and then. God knows I do. And there's no shame in that. So, when you need a backup, *especially* when it's a psychological thing you need help with, you have my number. And I'll be there"—he snapped his fingers—"like that."

The panic attack had stopped and Ashley felt stronger already. This time, she moved her hand toward his and held it. His phone vibrated and spoiled the moment. The display said it was an incoming call from DH.

"Your friend," Liam said.

Ashley looked at him with confusion. Who would call him from the Daily Herald?

"Yeah, Gabriel," he said into his phone.

She gave him the sleepy eyes when she understood the abbreviation. *Drunk Hobo.*

Liam's face was blank as he listened to Gabriel. "All right, I'll deploy the guys." He hung up.

"What's wrong?"

"Bunny boy escaped."

While Ashley's eyes widened in horror, Liam seemed unbothered by the news. He scrolled down his contacts and selected the one that said *Jerry.* He held the phone to his ear and continued scooping up the dessert.

"I think I'll have one more sundae."

Catharsis

3/25/19. Late evening.

I'm sitting cross-legged in front of my laptop, at a shack I own in El Paso. Having grown up in colder parts of the country, the Texan heat is unwelcoming. It's covered my naked upper body with a thin coat of sweat, adding a disgusting sheen to it, even though a pedestal fan in the corner is facing me and circulating sultry air at its full speed. Sometimes a random piece from the many cobwebs hanging on the fan's frame unclasps and shoots out and sticks to me.

The breeze from the fan does not deter the persevering skeeters from trying to purchase a foothold on my sticky skin. All of this combines with the maddening screeches of a million amorous crickets and urges me to escape this hostile asylum, but I'm a fugitive now, and I know I can't.

I chose this neighborhood because of its proximity to the most famous border in the world. My initial plan was that if I were charged with everything I've ever done, I would have confessed and made a deal with someone authorized to put me in Attica with the general population. Then I would have broken out, reached this place, and escaped into Mexico and then to Brazil, like I did last Tuesday.

I would have lived a peaceful life there as Mr. Bunny. That might have released a lot of endorphins in my brain—I've never used them my whole life, and they're all stocked up there somewhere. If they were all released at the same time, like a wild flood, it might have been enough to break through whatever blockage is stopping the endorphins from traveling to a different part in my brain where they can be processed and make me feel good. If that happened, maybe I'd have at last experienced happiness. I'll never know now.

Forty-eight hours ago, I stepped out of Attica with Mr. Jones, and we walked to the car he got for me—a brown truck of the kind hillbillies drive. He cast a nervous glance at the light beams dancing behind him from inside the prison complex. The warlike commotion was loud, with a mixture of sirens, shouting, and gunshots piercing the night sky. Goddamn rubber bullets. I caressed my swollen right hand. Misreading the gesture, he held out my two thousand dollars. I made him wait, changed the prison wear in front of him, and then accepted the wad.

I warned him that my friends would search the truck for a tracking device, and if they found one his daughter would be returned to him bit by bit, and every piece would be carved while she was still alive. Mr. Jones didn't budge. Either he was confident that he'd hid it pretty well, or he hadn't hidden anything at all. I believed it was the latter.

Before leaving, I told him not to alert the authorities for an hour.

My first stop was Irving, a small town in New York, on the bank of Lake Erie. I drove to a place I've been renting there. It's another part of my backup plan that I didn't use before because I wasn't a fugitive back then, but just a dead guy.

I parked the truck on an empty street, in front of a lonely house. I walked to the porch and lifted a flowerpot that had no plant in it. I dug in with my hand and sifted through the mud. When I felt the key, I gripped it and dropped the pot. It fell and shattered, the damp earth scattered at my feet.

I unlocked and entered the house that had no furniture, and walked upstairs to a bedroom that had no bed. I took a sledgehammer I'd kept in the empty closet and went to work on a particular spot on a wall—a secret space. After five minutes of tearing it down, which would definitely affect my deposit for the worse, I retrieved a single duffel bag from within.

I sat and opened the bag. It had a few changes of clothes, twenty grand, a prepaid cell phone, a SIG Sauer P320, two full magazines, and a thing that cost me a lot, which was also hard to obtain—an original driver's license from the DMV, but under a different name and address. Forged ones have ceased working. All the cop who is pulling you over needs to do is enter the license number in his phone, and bam! He finds it's counterfeit. Next thing you know, he drags you out and presses your face against the hot hood of your car. So, you have to meet the right people, and by serving the state as one of its prosecutors for all these years, I've come in contact with more than a few. For a ridiculously high price, they can get you an original license through their inside connections.

I took the cell phone, dialed Rio and told Juan to get Annie on a flight to New York, back to her daddy. I also instructed him to meet me at my hideout in El Paso, and when coming he should bring me a laptop with an internet connection. I hung up, removed the battery and threw the phone into the hole in the wall.

I changed into jeans and a white T-shirt, took the key for a Benz S-Class sedan I'd stashed in the garage, and didn't bother to lock the house as I hit the road again.

The second stop I made was at a cybercafé in Indianapolis. I used the new ID to rent a cubicle, then searched and found the breaking news.

A prison riot in Attica Correctional Facility ended with one dead and one escaped convict. A metal shiv crafted from what they believe to be a flask was used as a weapon. Edward Jones was suspended, and an investigation had been initiated. I skimmed through the details, and there it was—George had been shanked fourteen times and bled to death. There was a huge section devoted to George and his achievements as Mr. Bunny, but only a small part covered the escape of Noah Smith, a former assistant district attorney who had become a drug dealer and was convicted for two counts of murder and possession of pounds of heroin.

I clenched my teeth and closed my eyes.

There, there, it all ends soon.

Two minutes later, I wiped my eyes and logged on to my offshore bank's website. I had created this account in the Cayman Islands for two possibilities. If I was *dead*, I needed to transact money without arousing any suspicion. Or to transact after I had been arrested and escaped prison, because money in the US would be frozen once I was put in prison. Now this was useless to me. So I transferred $250,000 to Rosa Carvalho. Enjoy the extra, honey. Then I transferred $300,000 to another account, to my protégé.

Missouri and Oklahoma were my next two stops, both times to refill gas and unload my digested highway noshes.

Sunday had officially ended, and El Paso was still nine hours away when I crossed Red River and entered

Burkburnett, a town that bore the *Welcome to Texas* billboard. It's funny to think I'd end up here. My first plan had Texas in it, and it seems natural that my last part did, too. This was where I'd sent Phillip after he cut Casey.

I had paid Phillip to slash Casey anywhere below his head so the cops would have an identity mark when they found the body without a head. It was serendipitous that the lackwit had jumped in to *save* us, making the whole act seem more legitimate. With another hundred, I made Phillip cut his long hair short and then his own hand where he had cut Casey. I knew if the next of kin made a positive ID, the cops wouldn't bother with fingerprints or DNA identification. Persuading my father not to give permission for the autopsy and cut up his already hurt child was yet another stroke of my genius. Phillip being as tall and big as Casey was another lucky chance. If not Phillip, I simply would have gotten someone else who resembled Casey's physique. It was never a problem.

After calculating the time it took to cover the distance, I had told Phillip to make a trip to Dallas and then come back home. He must have loved the journey, because I gave him enough money to buy drugs to keep him high the entire time. He came to my house to collect the last installment of the deal like I'd asked him to.

I told him to wear Casey's clothes. As he did so in his drug-infused stupor, I shot him in the face with a shotgun I'd bought illegally in Vermont. I hid the gun. I hid Casey. For a long time, I acted like I was an angry person and hid my true self. I hid a lot in my life. Not anymore.

A glimmer of Monday's dawn bounced on the rearview mirror and shone in my eyes. It's beautiful to watch the sun rising at your back. It was as if all your attempts to run away from the light had failed and it finally caught up with you. It alleviated my turmoil and anxiety, and a luculent idea presented itself—an idea of how this was going to end. The thought gladdened me. A perfect ending.

I reached the abandoned shack on Cassidy Road, El Paso. I thought Juan would be waiting for me on the porch with a beer, but he wasn't. So I waited for him since he is an integral part of my final move. The last laugh is what it's all about now.

When he arrived after 6:00 p.m., he thanked me a thousand times for giving his sister a new start. I told him the specs of what his last job would be for me, and it shocked even him. He tried to persuade me to reconsider since I had a chance now. I could start fresh, like his sister. But I said there is no other way. He hung his head and went to the porch, saying he'd be ready when I called him.

Life is crazy. Random. I've tried to control that randomness as much as I can, but today I don't want to.

You may think I wrote this to kill time until Juan arrived, or that lack of sleep made me behave out of character, but the truth is… I want at least one person to know about me. The real me. And only you are worthy of it. So, I started writing my story ten hours ago, and I'm still typing away, working on the final chapter, which I've named "Catharsis". It's fitting, don't you think, as I am releasing strong emotions.

Emotions. You made me understand what sadness is. I cried for the first time in my life when you caught me. I now know what anger is and what being wronged feels like. You destroyed something I've lived for. I'd never have thought it would take losing my life's work to activate something in my brain that made me understand sadness and anger. I had a similar plan to be happy.

Anyway, I'm not a skilled writer, so forgive me if I've made any errors. As you read my letter, I want you to see what I saw and feel what I felt. I want you to be me. That's also why I'm delineating every single thing, from the little to the big, that happened in my life which I believe relates to this drama. I even wrote what I was doing or thinking or imagining at certain times. Or perhaps I just want to experience my odyssey again, relive this intellectually sublime part of my life by recollecting things and writing them down to their minutest details.

I spent a few hours in prison. Not what you had in mind, is it? But for me, that's a lot of time to think.

I could say I wouldn't have been caught if it wasn't for that thief, Fred. But it's my mistake and I should own it. I should have thought about creatures like Fred when I started this. If Fred hadn't stolen Kenosha's cell phone, I would have included AJ and Kenosha in the list, and still you would have caught me. I should have thought about the heaters and cops using power consumption records. But I didn't. You did. That makes you better than me. The only thing I'm great at is crime, and you defeated me in that. I respect you for it.

The punishment you've given me is the cruelest. It was your idea to destroy Mr. Bunny by giving that name to a fat racist. You robbed my one, my only, and my greatest creation. Since then, I haven't slept. There is this thing wrapped around my mind, squeezing it, not letting me relax or sleep or simply just *be*. Sometimes this thing crushes my heart so much that it flares up into my throat, tickles deep inside my nostrils, and my eyes feel hot, and tears roll down in gallons. This is sadness, isn't it? You are the first person to make me feel the way I do now. Broken. Utterly destroyed. You've understood me enough to know what would hurt me. If friends are people who understand each other, then what are you to me? My second real connection in this world.

Since you've made me feel emotions, and you've proved that you are better than I am, I'm going to give you two things. Parting gifts.

The first gift is the link I've attached at the end of this email. It's a crime article. The perpetrator of that crime is an American, and he lives in the United States. Even though he's a serial killer, he is not like me. Remember my protégé I talked about a few paragraphs earlier? That's him.

When I met him, he'd already killed thirty people and he'd taken that many trophies. His murders were sadistic. His inherent cruelty far surpasses my academic one. So naturally, I adopted him and taught him everything I know—my genes aren't going to be my legacy, but my knowledge is. And ever since, he's been butchering more people than his average rate. The best part? No one even knows he exists!

I can tell you who he is, but that won't certify as a gift, will it? There will be no fun in it. Maybe a week of celebration? No, you love this work, don't you? If solving murders is important enough for you to leave your marriage, then fighting serial killers like us is the best you can get out of your weary life. And you love it like you loved alcohol, your hamartia. A moth and fire. You and I both know that one day you'll cease to exist because of your job. It will make you bite the gun. I hope that by giving you this gift, the information about another killer, I'll play a vital role in your death.

If you fail in this case, which I hope you do, remember I found him all by myself. It's a hard thing to do without your badge. And we would be equal in points if you fail. Maybe that's also why I'm not giving you his name. I want to settle the score, no pun intended.

Unable to find him, you'll grab the bottle again, the pistol a week later. Even after knowing how it'll end for you, you still can't keep away, can you?

So be fast. I know you have a burdensome workload, but do the dead really need your attention more than the people who don't yet know they will die tomorrow? By the hands of a serial killer who scares *even me*?

And the second gift is an attachment. It's a video. And yes, it contains murder.

So long, Gabe.

Yours truly,

Noah Smith

Chapter 37

March 25, 2019. 10:18 P.M.

Gabriel finished reading the long letter—a short memoir, really—that he'd received from Noah. A lot made sense. Like how Martha and Phillip had died, how Rita had gotten her bruises, how Noah had broken into Samuel's house, and how he'd escaped prison. He dated all the chapters, and they correlated with everything that had happened up to this point.

More than all, Gabriel understood why Noah, his *best friend*, had murdered seventeen people, including George and Samuel.

Noah had been ill. Though he would have never accepted it, he was sick psychologically. Killing animals because he liked doing it? Noah believed he was indifferent toward his victims, but he was tempted to *play* with Martha for fun? Why would he even use a water gun in the first place? He claimed he was never angry, but when Ashley stumbled upon his plot, he banged his head on the steering wheel? And later, he went to scare her.

Noah felt emotions, all right—he just didn't understand them due to his condition.

Noah also had a god complex. Using the highfaluting narrative and ruminations in his letter, for which Gabriel often had to refer to the dictionary, any criminal profiler would agree with Gabriel that Noah thought highly of himself.

One didn't need to be a psychologist to know his many derisive remarks signified a deep-seated contempt for women. Noah's mother had left him when he was young, just as Gabriel's had. Maybe that was what had made him hold women in disdain. But again, because of his condition he wouldn't have understood what he felt.

The most important exhibit was that Noah had chosen crime when the coin said police. He'd always wanted to be evil, a criminal legend, but he couldn't accept that he was just another sicko. He lied to himself, thinking he was working toward proving something to the world. It was a delusion that had spanned two decades, and it was pathetic. He had lived a dog's life, with no hint of joy.

Gabriel called Victor and informed him about Cassidy Road, El Paso as soon as he read that line. Victor said he would call the local sheriff and request them to go check it out.

Noah's email grabbed his attention. Part of his brain told him to go home, switch his PS4 on and shoot strangers in the virtual ruination of the Second World War. Another part wanted to open the *gifts* that Gabriel knew wouldn't be based on a spirit of generosity or goodwill toward mankind. It had to be the same part of his brain that prevented him from calling a halt to the alcohol once he started drinking. A part that made him too weak to resist temptation.

He downloaded *Second Gift.mp4* and hit play.

The video showed Noah squatting close up to the camera, in a room lit by a sodium vapor bulb. The bruises on his face had turned purple. He was bare-chested, bare-footed, and wore jeans that had crease marks stretching from his crotch to the knees. The kind someone got if they were sitting for a long time. He'd said he hadn't stopped the car more than was strictly necessary, hadn't he?

Noah then walked backward and the camera shook. Was it handheld?

Juan?

As Noah's body shrunk into the center, the ceiling, along with the entire room, became visible. A white noose hung from the ceiling, and a tall stool, the kind used to paint houses, was placed under the loop.

Oh-uh.

Noah pulled himself up on the stool. He did it with some effort, as if he was obese, which he wasn't. Once up and standing, he had to bend his neck sideways to accommodate his head between his shoulders and the ceiling. Then he wore the noose around his neck like a garland and secured it tight.

He looked at the camera, tears cascading down his neck.

"Can't stand losing, Gabe." He sniffled. "Let's try hanging."

Then he jumped!

Gabriel cringed when he heard the bone give out a wet breaking sound. The fall was long enough to break his neck and kill him in an instant. No twitching of the body, no last-minute clawing at the rope. Then the video went blank.

What were the odds of suicide? After Victor informed him that Noah had escaped from prison, Gabriel called Liam, who in turn dispatched his friends to the team members' houses, with weapons. But that didn't kill Noah. Roadblocks that almost always gunned down fugitives hadn't killed him either. Noah had escaped all these traps to die in his own way, to get his last laugh.

Juan, the ever faithful, did his last job. He named the video clip, attached it to the letter, and emailed everything to Gabriel.

Gabriel thought about forwarding the video to his team, but decided against it. Emailing murder was something Mr. Bunny would do, not him. Noah had challenged the entire concept of justice by hurting people, police, news, and prosecutors. And Gabriel's team, along with help from Ashley, Steve, and Lily, the logistics manager at ZEUS, had defeated him.

Gabriel eyed the first *gift*. It was a hyperlink that didn't end in the usual *.com* or *.gov*, but in *.kr*.

No! Gabriel was better than this. He was not going to bite.

It's not your job.

He would go home, take a bath, and order a big pizza. Maybe play video games. God knew that a certain overambitious sniper needed to be taught a lesson or two about messing with Gabriel.

And it's not your job.

He got up, switched off the lights and left the office. He sauntered toward his home, whistling. As he exited the precinct, he thought about whether or not he should quit being a detective and perhaps join a corporate security firm. Many of his buddies worked in that line and made good bucks. Maybe he should shave his beard, cut his hair neat, and start dating again. Live like a decent man.

Instead of enjoying the retired life peacefully, like Gabriel had thought, Peter had tagged along with Joshua and planned a trip to Detroit to catch Lolly. Gabriel didn't want to fight bad guys that long. Enough with this martyr shit.

And it's not your goddamn job to go on a wild goose chase after some other supposed serial killer. Or any serial killers, for that matter.

He wasn't even going to think about it.

Epilogue

Gabriel tried to divert his mind, but he couldn't. His new PS4 controller worked like a charm, helping him gain points in the game. He even got that sniper more times than he got Gabriel. Lessons taught. Now what?

Gabriel was never entirely focused. A part of his mind repeated something in a loop, whispering to him like a tireless ghost.

…killed thirty people… butchering more people than his average rate… people who don't yet know they will die tomorrow…

Gabriel couldn't deny it anymore. He had been trying to for the last hour, and failed.

Like a dutiful robot, he walked to his laptop and opened the email. The mouse pointer changed into a white hand as soon as it hovered over the blue hyperlink. After frowning at the screen for a long time, he cursed himself and pressed the button.

A different tab opened and took him to a website called Korean Sun. Everything was in Korean, but the ever-mighty Google asked if it should translate it for him.

Yes, please!

Seconds later, the website loaded in the only language most Americans knew.

The title read *Horror in Yongsan District. A Local Restaurant Owner Found Murdered in His Home.*

Gabriel read the news article. Google didn't translate certain words, making the information murky, but when he finished reading, he had enough keywords to search the news by himself. He found a few pages where the story was written in English.

It took Gabriel an hour and a half to get acquainted with the case. Victor called once, in the middle of his read. He sounded excited, and Gabriel remembered he hadn't told the captain about Noah's last video. So he acted surprised when Victor said that the deputies had found Noah's body with his neck snapped. Noah was sitting on a chair, dressed in a nice suit, pants, a tie, and a rabbit mask. Noah had left out that part in his letter. To surprise Gabriel?

Gabriel put the phone on silent and resumed his online reading.

Byung-Chul Woo was a fifty-two-year-old man from Hangangno neighborhood, Yongsan district. He lived alone in his house, above his seafood restaurant. The chef had helped Mr. Woo close shop, as usual, and went home. When he came back the next morning, the restaurant was not open, which was unusual. So, he went upstairs and found the door to Mr. Woo's house ajar. He went in.

Mr. Woo was on the bed. His arms and legs were sawn clean through. They had been sawn lengthways, so no limbs were amputated.

On his arms, the cuts started between the ring and middle fingers, then ran up through the forearms, elbows, and ended a few inches below the shoulders.

Same with the legs. They were cut through the middle, starting from the feet, and traveled up through the knees and thighs. The sawing didn't stop at the hips. They traveled further up his abdominal cavity, rib cage, and ended below the collarbone.

The final partition was in the midsection. It started from the crotch and ended at the top of his sternum, spilling out the remaining innards.

The Seoul Metropolitan Police Agency investigated Mr. Woo's murder, but made no arrests.

Han, a senior inspector in charge, told the press that their preliminary investigation pointed toward a Caucasian male. That didn't narrow down the results, but Noah had cut the work short. He had said this new killer was an American who lived in the United States, hadn't he?

Gabriel took Han's number from the SMPA's website and stored it on his phone. He wanted to see the pictures of the crime scene—at least the dead body—to get the feeling of it. The photo in the newspaper was blurred, but Gabriel knew websites devoted to these kinds of things.

Twenty minutes after dosing himself with gore that shocked even a veteran detective like him, he found the pictures.

The bedroom walls were splattered with brownish-red patterns. Mr. Woo was in the center of the bed, and his intact head was placed in the middle. It seemed like he had eight limbs instead of four, and they were all sprawled out around his vertically propped-up body. The tips of the arms and legs, if connected, would form a circular pattern.

He looked like a red octopus that had fallen from the top of a tall building and landed straight on a pile of guts and goo.

The hair on the back of Gabriel's neck stood. This killer indeed far exceeded Noah in terms of cruelty. Gabriel picked up his phone and unlocked it but didn't do anything else. He was thinking. No. Not thinking, more like fighting a battle inside. A battle he eventually lost, and his thumb found its way to the *dial* button in the phone.

"Hope you rot in hell for this, too, Noah," he muttered.

The phone was answered on its eighth ring.

"Good afternoon. I'm Detective Gabriel Chase from the NYPD. Am I speaking with Senior Inspector Han?"

List of characters

Gabriel Chase – homicide detective, 122nd Precinct

Mr. Bunny – the antagonist

Joshua Chase – Gabriel's dad

Emma Stein – Gabriel's partner

Victor Ivansky – Gabriel's captain

Raymond Hughes – NYPD's commissioner

Rita Hughes – Raymond's wife, Gabriel's godmother. One of Mr. Bunny's victims

Harry Gallant, Martha Nelson, Doug Bastian – other victims of Mr. Bunny

Samuel Nelson – the chairman of The Daily Herald, Martha's husband

Steve Bastian – District Attorney, NYC, and Doug's dad

Nash Parker, David Gustavo, Bill, Mark, and Laura – Gabriel's team

Léonie Böhm, aka Cherry – Mr. Bunny's third victim

Taylor Roth – the mayor

Bones – the drug addict Mr. Bunny uses to send the video from the commissioner's office

Carlos – the uniformed cop who helps them at the security room in the commissioner's office

Martin Brown and Tony Freeman – people who were wrongly convicted for Mr. Bunny's crimes

Alisha Webb and Luis Garcia – Mr. Bunny's victims

Elizabeth (Liz) – Gabriel's ex wife

Noah Smith – Gabriel's childhood friend, Assistant District Attorney

Casey – Gabriel's childhood friend, a murder victim, Noah's brother

Ashley Stuart – Samuel Nelson's PA

Lolly – the most wanted bank robber in the US. Joshua's archenemy

James Tucker – a pimp whose car Mr. Bunny steals and kidnaps people with

Lila Morales – James' victim

Abigail Owens– star witness in James' trial

Archie – the cop who maintains the crime scene and the dump site

Stanley Ming – top criminalist in NYC, working with the NYPD

Anthony Mills – medical examiner

Peter Lamb – old detective with the highest clearance rate in the NYPD

Bill – an unformed officer included in the team. Peter's son

Lily – a manager in Zeus Corp

Acknowledgments

Madeline Harris, you are the first person who read my words, gave me confidence, and encouraged me to go on. This book simply wouldn't have been a reality without you.

I also want to thank Becca Taylor who is sort of a cool big sister to me. Whenever I had doubts, she was there to answer me.

Then there is Tara Neilson who lives in a remote part of Alaskan wilderness. She is the kindest person anyone could ever meet.

I want to give a shout-out to my three beta readers: Ellen Whitfield, Farhaanah Fawmie, and Ben Cotterill from Scotland. Your time and input have made the manuscript a lot better.

Many thanks should also go to my editor, Ashley Conner. And finally, to Erik Empson, my mentor in the publishing world.

If you enjoyed this book, please let others know by leaving a quick review on Amazon. Also, if you spot anything untoward in the paperback, get in touch. We strive for the best quality and appreciate reader feedback.

editor@thebookfolks.com

www.thebookfolks.com

More fiction by Nathan Senthil

If you enjoyed *The Immoralist*, you'll be pleased to hear that there are two more in the series.

When Detective Chase determines to pursue Mr. Bunny's tip-off that another serial killer is at large, he is met with disinterest from the authorities. Suddenly falling seriously out of favour with the FBI and suspended from his position, he endeavors to hunt him down alone. He is looking for a homicidal maniac who is cannibalizing his victims. But one who has learnt from the best how to evade the police. Chase will have to find a crack in his armor.

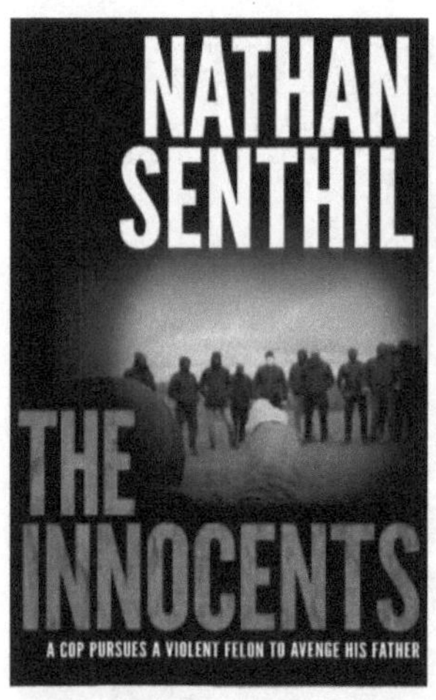

The father of Detective Gabriel Chase, Joshua, has become obsessed with tracking down violent bank robber, Lolly. Now Gabriel must pick up the pursuit. But will he get to him before others, hell-bent on revenge? And if he does, just what is in store for the hard-nosed cop?

Other titles of interest

If you enjoy books about serial killers, you're in luck.
We've got several! Check out the following selection, or
visit *www.thebookfolks.com* for more titles.

IMPURITY by Ray Clark

Someone is out for revenge. A grotto worker is murdered
in the lead up to Christmas. He won't be the first. Can DI
Gardener stop the killer, or is he saving his biggest gift till
last?

Available on Kindle and in paperback.

ONE STEP AHEAD by Denver Murphy

He spent his life fighting crime. Now he has a taste for it himself. His first attack is a stab in the dark. Next time, he'll kill.

Knowing how the police work, ex-detective Jeffrey Brandt will stay one step ahead of their investigation. He will even taunt those trying to establish his identity and catch him. One woman, DCI Stella Johnson, is responsible for finding him. Has she got what it takes?

Available on Kindle and in paperback.

SHE by Pete Brassett

With a serial killer on their hands, Scottish detective Munro and rookie sergeant West must act fast to trace a woman placed at a crime scene. Yet discovering her true identity, let alone finding her, proves difficult. Soon they realize the crime is far graver than either of them could have imagined.

Available on Kindle and in paperback.